# BILLY JOHNSON AND HIS DUCK ARE EXPLORERS

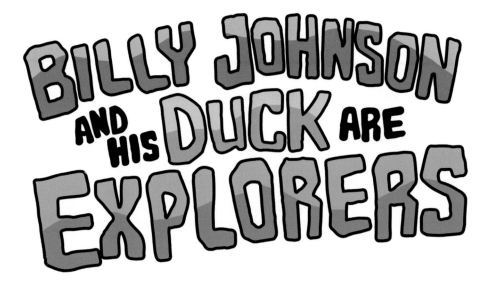

by Mathew New

CAPSTONE EDITIONS
a capstone imprint

JOHNSON, BILLY
GATE
A13
DEPARTURE
4:00 PM
TRACKING
BOARDING ZONE
D
JOHNSON, BILLY
SEAT
23B
ECON

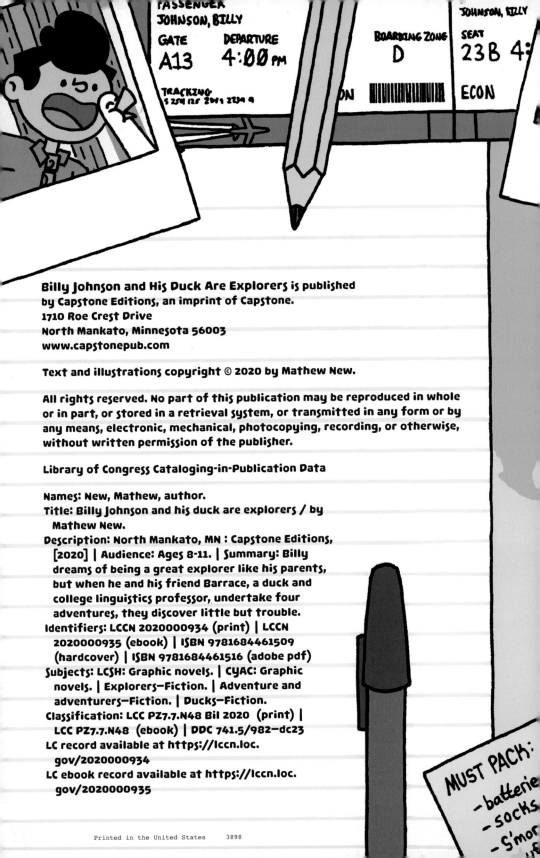

Billy Johnson and His Duck Are Explorers is published by Capstone Editions, an imprint of Capstone.
1710 Roe Crest Drive
North Mankato, Minnesota 56003
www.capstonepub.com



Library of Congress Cataloging-in-Publication Data

Names: New, Mathew, author.
Title: Billy Johnson and his duck are explorers / by Mathew New.
Description: North Mankato, MN : Capstone Editions, [2020] | Audience: Ages 8-11. | Summary: Billy dreams of being a great explorer like his parents, but when he and his friend Barrace, a duck and college linguistics professor, undertake four adventures, they discover little but trouble.
Identifiers: LCCN 2020000934 (print) | LCCN 2020000935 (ebook) | ISBN 9781684461509 (hardcover) | ISBN 9781684461516 (adobe pdf)
Subjects: LCSH: Graphic novels. | CYAC: Graphic novels. | Explorers—Fiction. | Adventure and adventurers—Fiction. | Ducks—Fiction.
Classification: LCC PZ7.7.N48 Bil 2020 (print) | LCC PZ7.7.N48 (ebook) | DDC 741.5/982—dc23
LC record available at https://lccn.loc.gov/2020000934
LC ebook record available at https://lccn.loc.gov/2020000935

MUST PACK:
-socks

Printed in the United States 3898

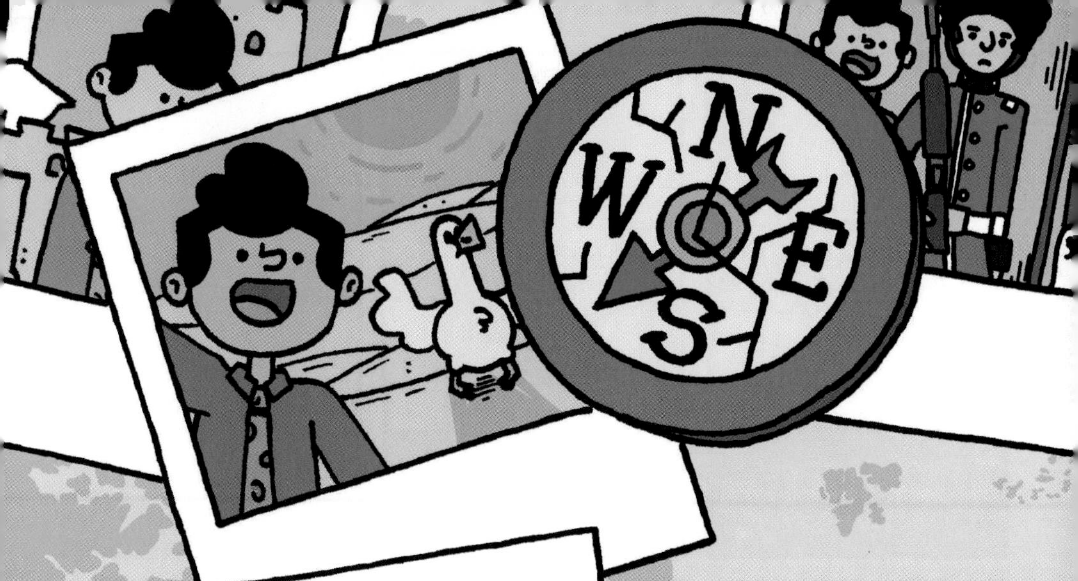
N
W
E
S

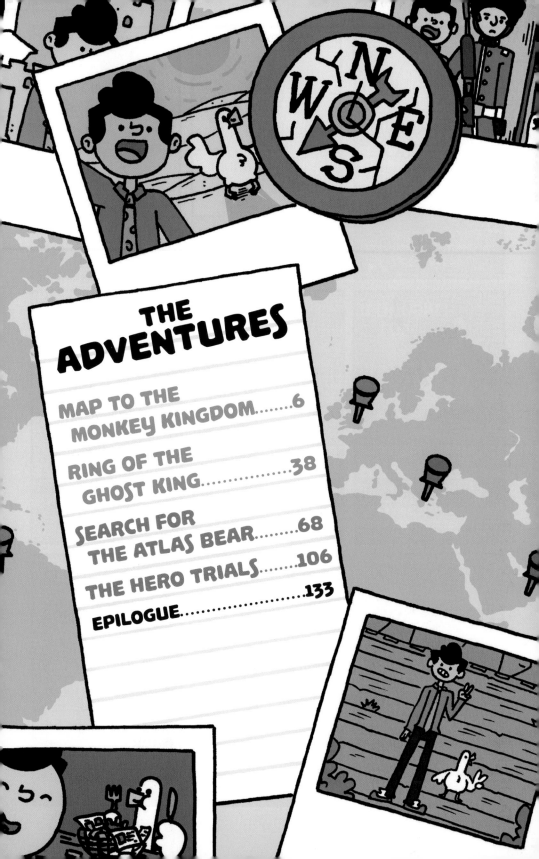

# THE ADVENTURES



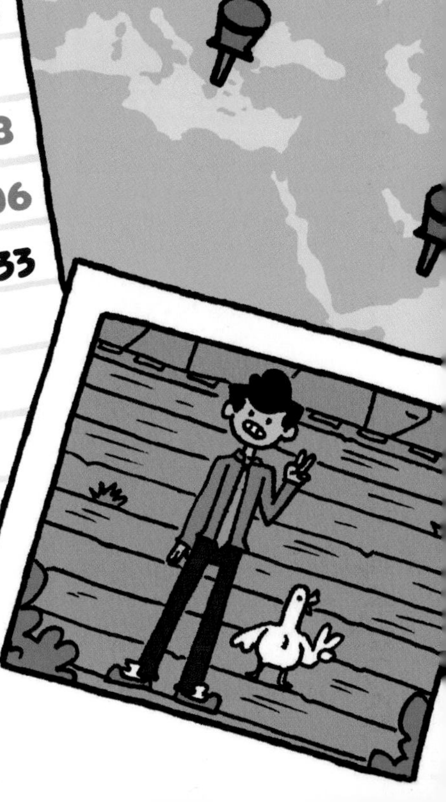

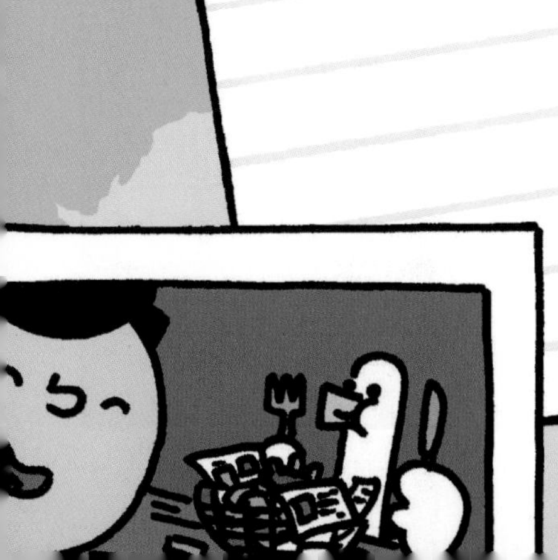

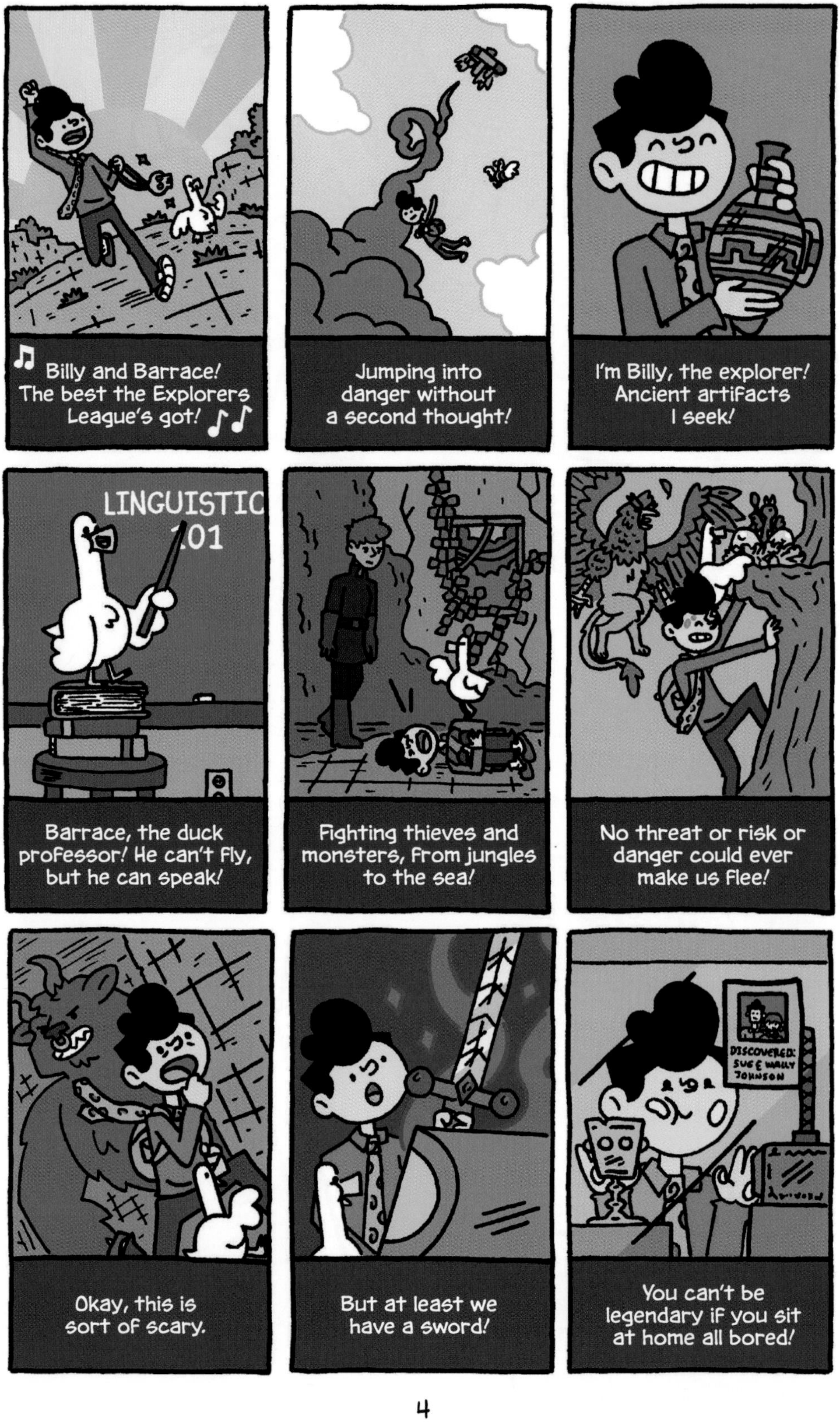
Billy and Barrace! The best the Explorers League's got!
Jumping into danger without a second thought!
I'm Billy, the explorer! Ancient artifacts I seek!
LINGUISTIC 101
Barrace, the duck professor! He can't fly, but he can speak!
Fighting thieves and monsters, from jungles to the sea!
No threat or risk or danger could ever make us flee!
Okay, this is sort of scary.
But at least we have a sword!
DISCOVERED: SUE & WALLY JOHNSON
You can't be legendary if you sit at home all bored!

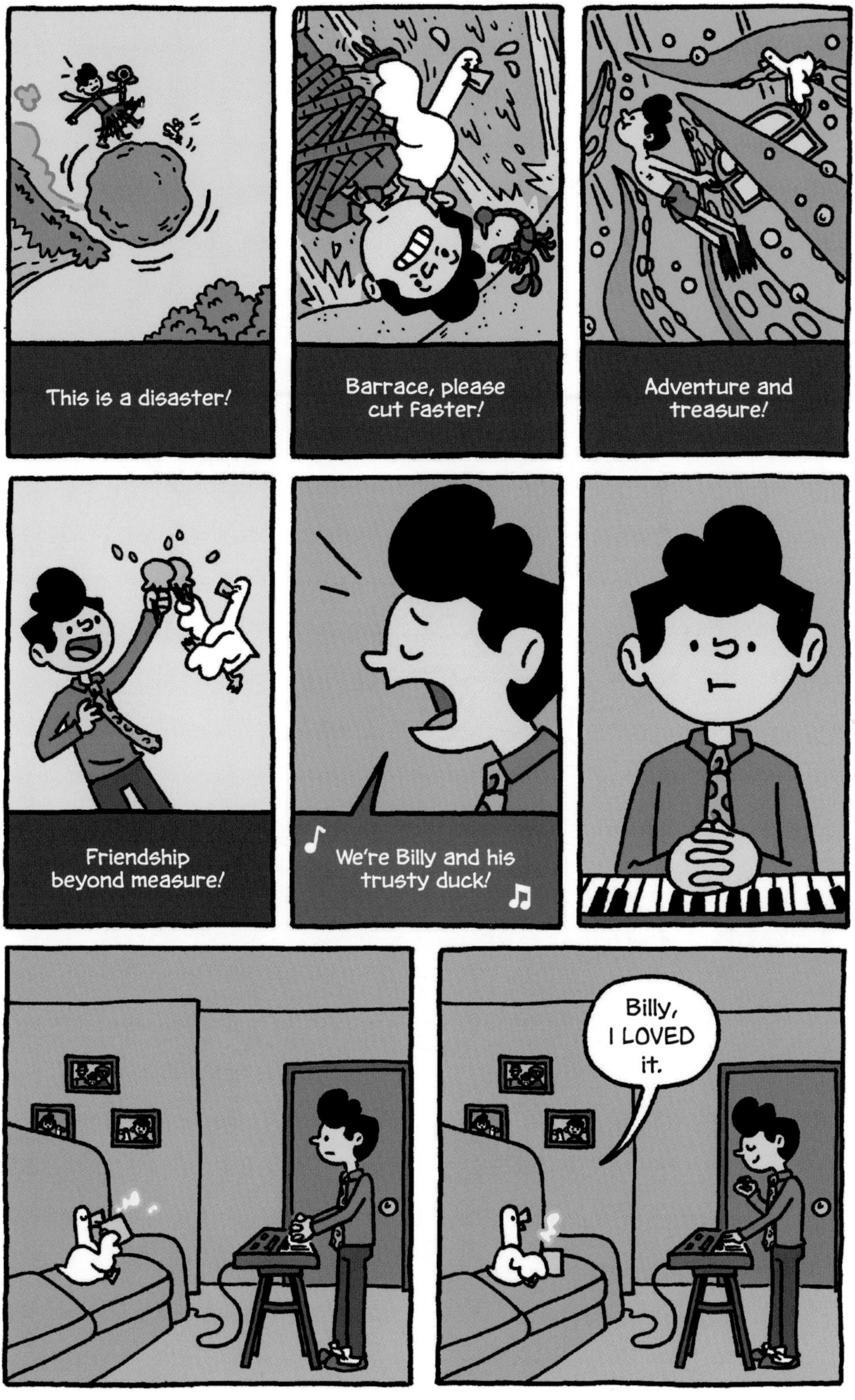
This is a disaster!
Barrace, please cut faster!
Adventure and treasure!
Friendship beyond measure!
We're Billy and his trusty duck!
Billy, I LOVED it.

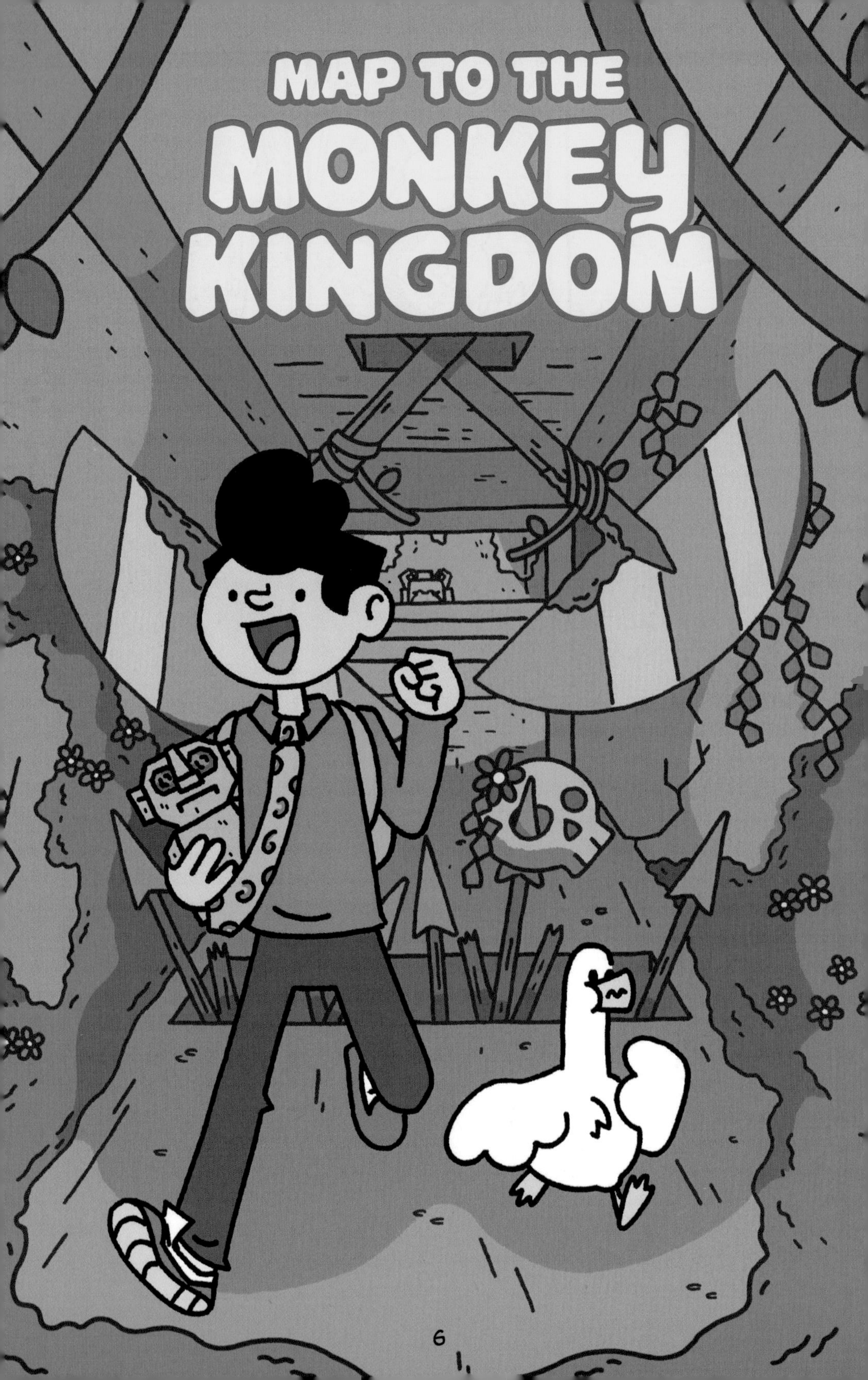
MAP TO THE
MONKEY
KINGDOM

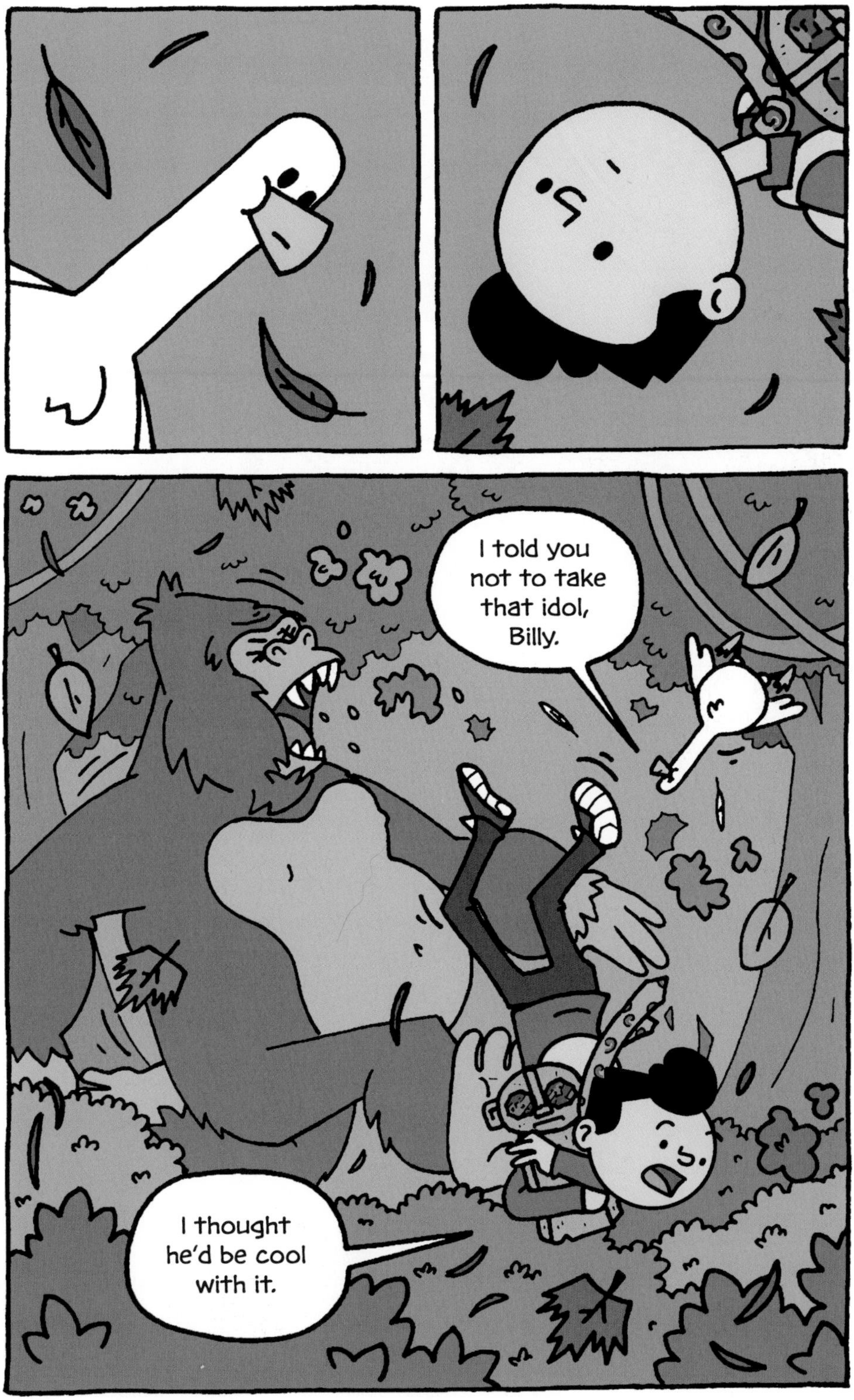
I told you not to take that idol, Billy.
I thought he'd be cool with it.

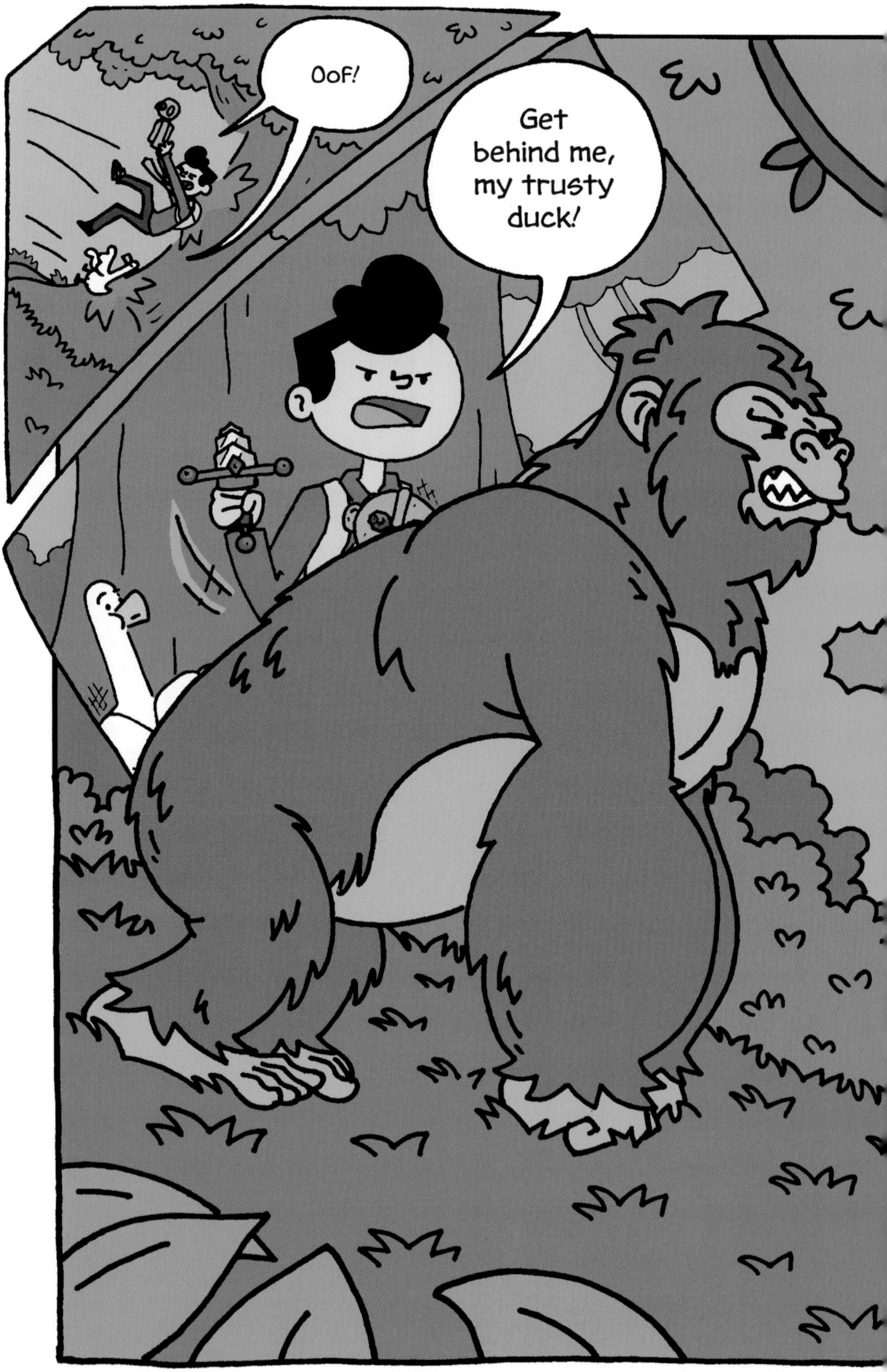
Oof!
Get behind me, my trusty duck!

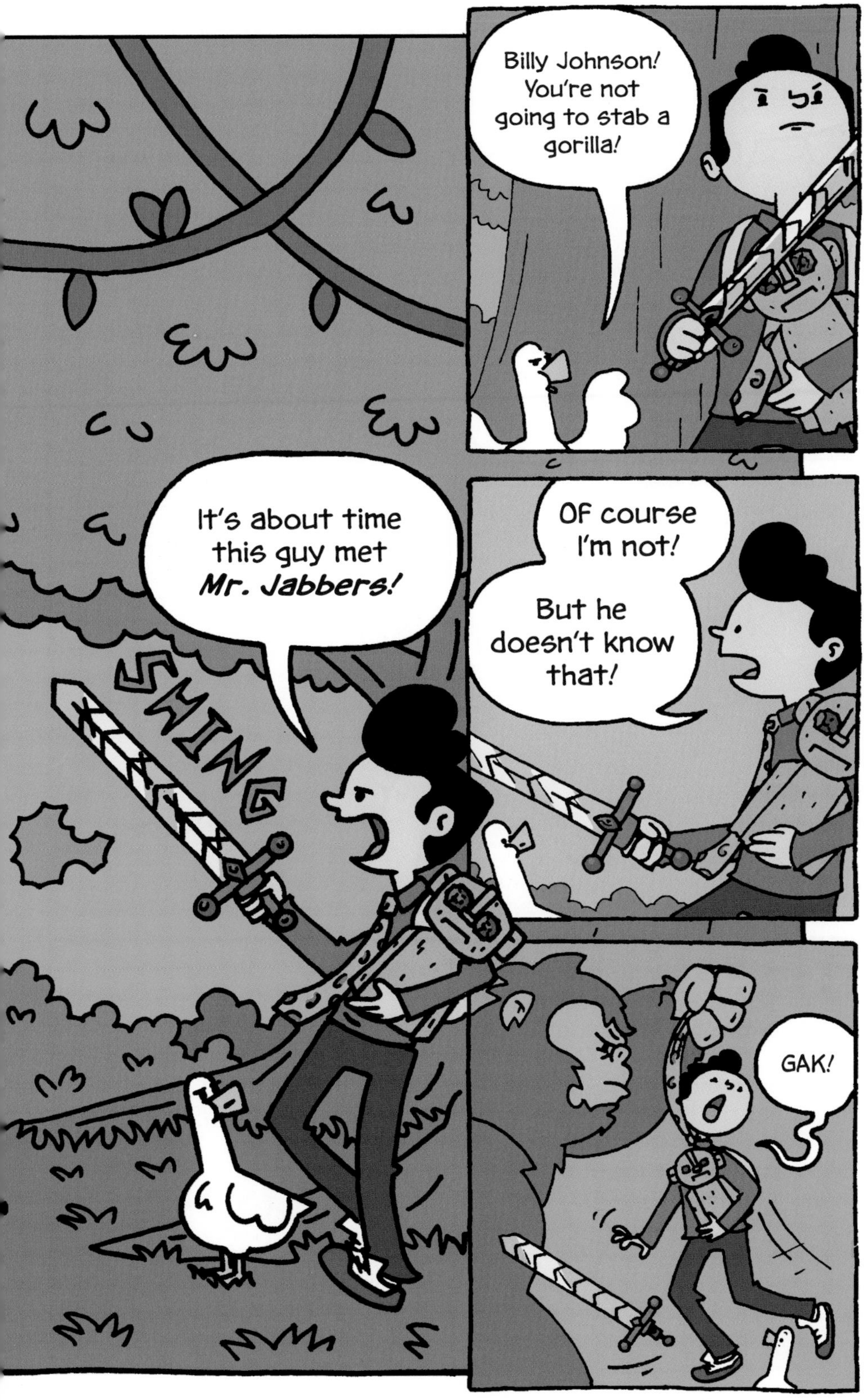

Billy Johnson! You're not going to stab a gorilla!
It's about time this guy met *Mr. Jabbers!*
SHING
Of course I'm not!
But he doesn't know that!
GAK!

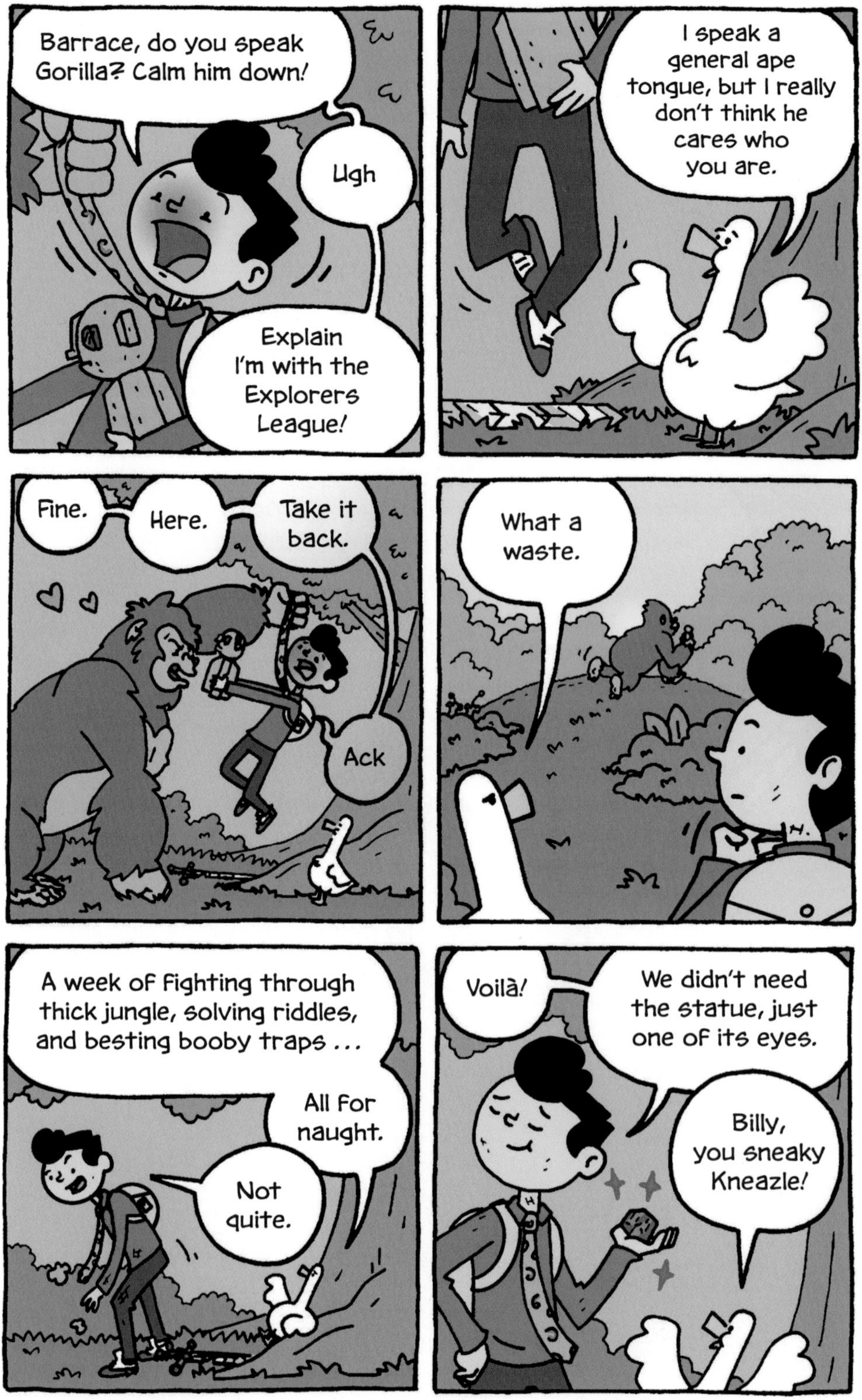
Barrace, do you speak Gorilla? Calm him down!
Ugh
Explain I'm with the Explorers League!
I speak a general ape tongue, but I really don't think he cares who you are.
Fine.
Here.
Take it back.
Ack
What a waste.
A week of fighting through thick jungle, solving riddles, and besting booby traps . . .
All for naught.
Not quite.
Voilà!
We didn't need the statue, just one of its eyes.
Billy, you sneaky Kneazle!

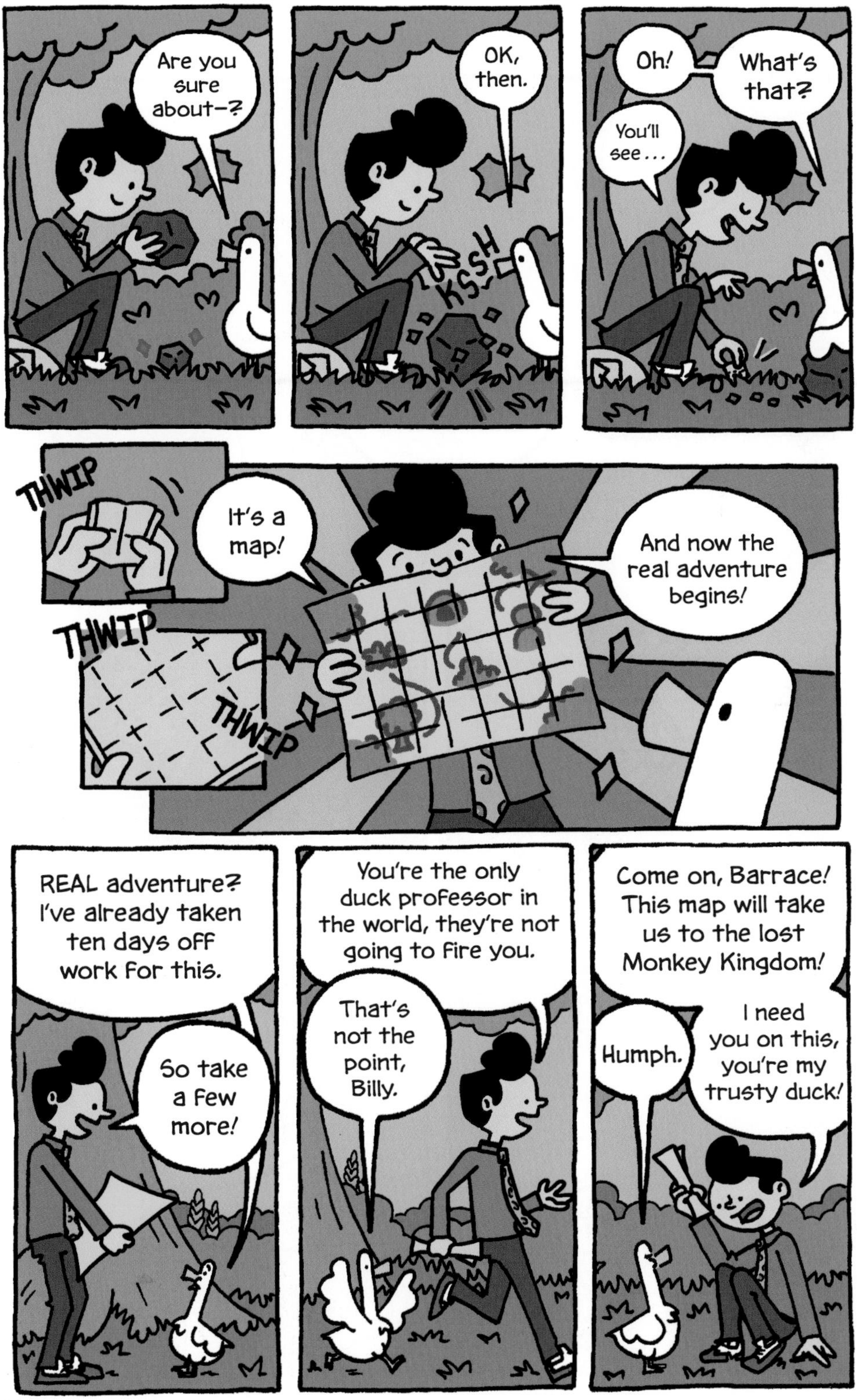
Are you sure about–?
OK, then.
KSSH
Oh!
What's that?
You'll see...
THWIP
THWIP
THWIP
It's a map!
And now the real adventure begins!
REAL adventure? I've already taken ten days off work for this.
So take a few more!
You're the only duck professor in the world, they're not going to fire you.
That's not the point, Billy.
Come on, Barrace! This map will take us to the lost Monkey Kingdom!
Humph.
I need you on this, you're my trusty duck!

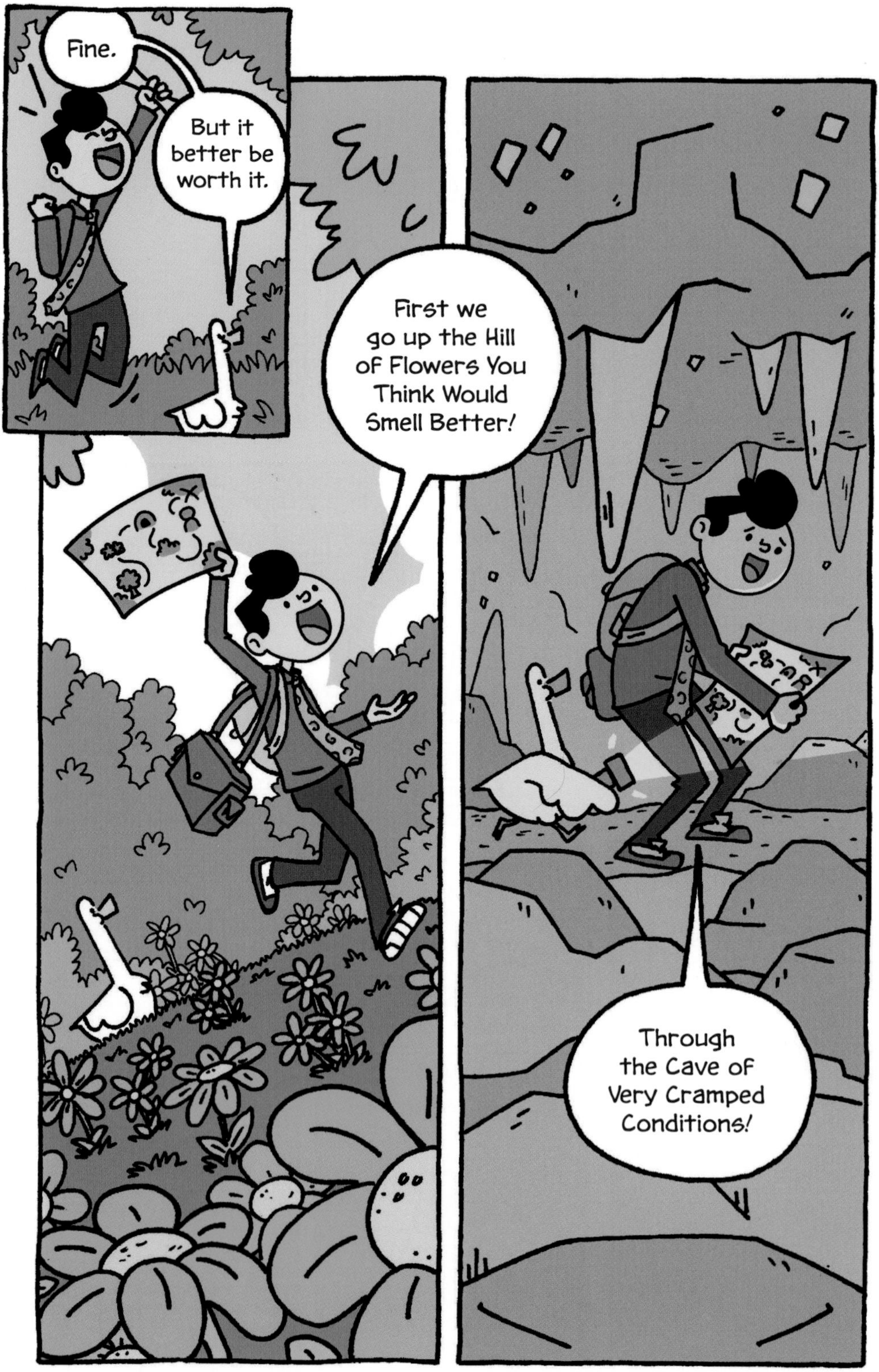
Fine.
But it better be worth it.
First we go up the Hill of Flowers You Think Would Smell Better!
Through the Cave of Very Cramped Conditions!

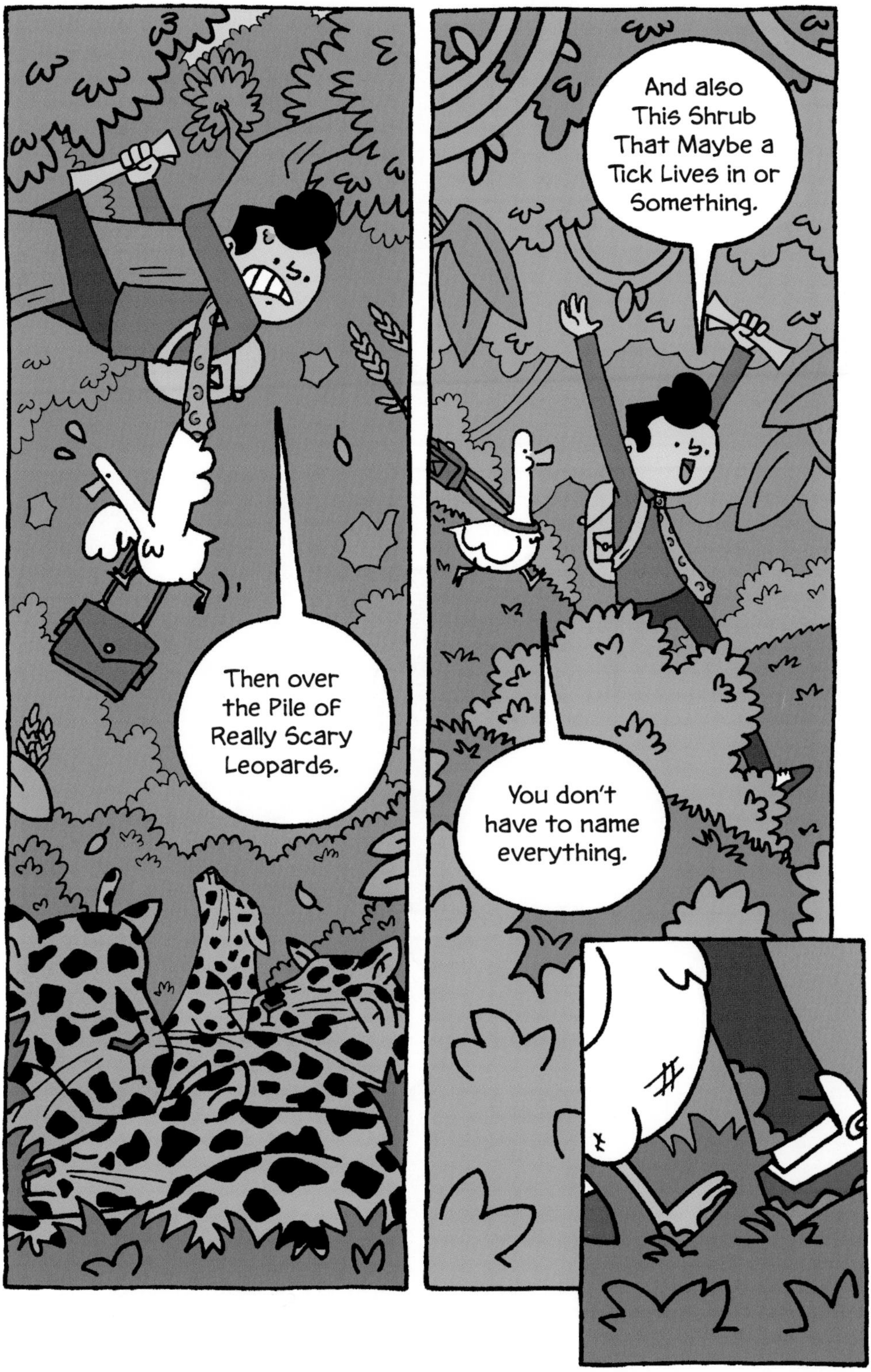
Then over the Pile of Really Scary Leopards.
And also This Shrub That Maybe a Tick Lives in or Something.
You don't have to name everything.

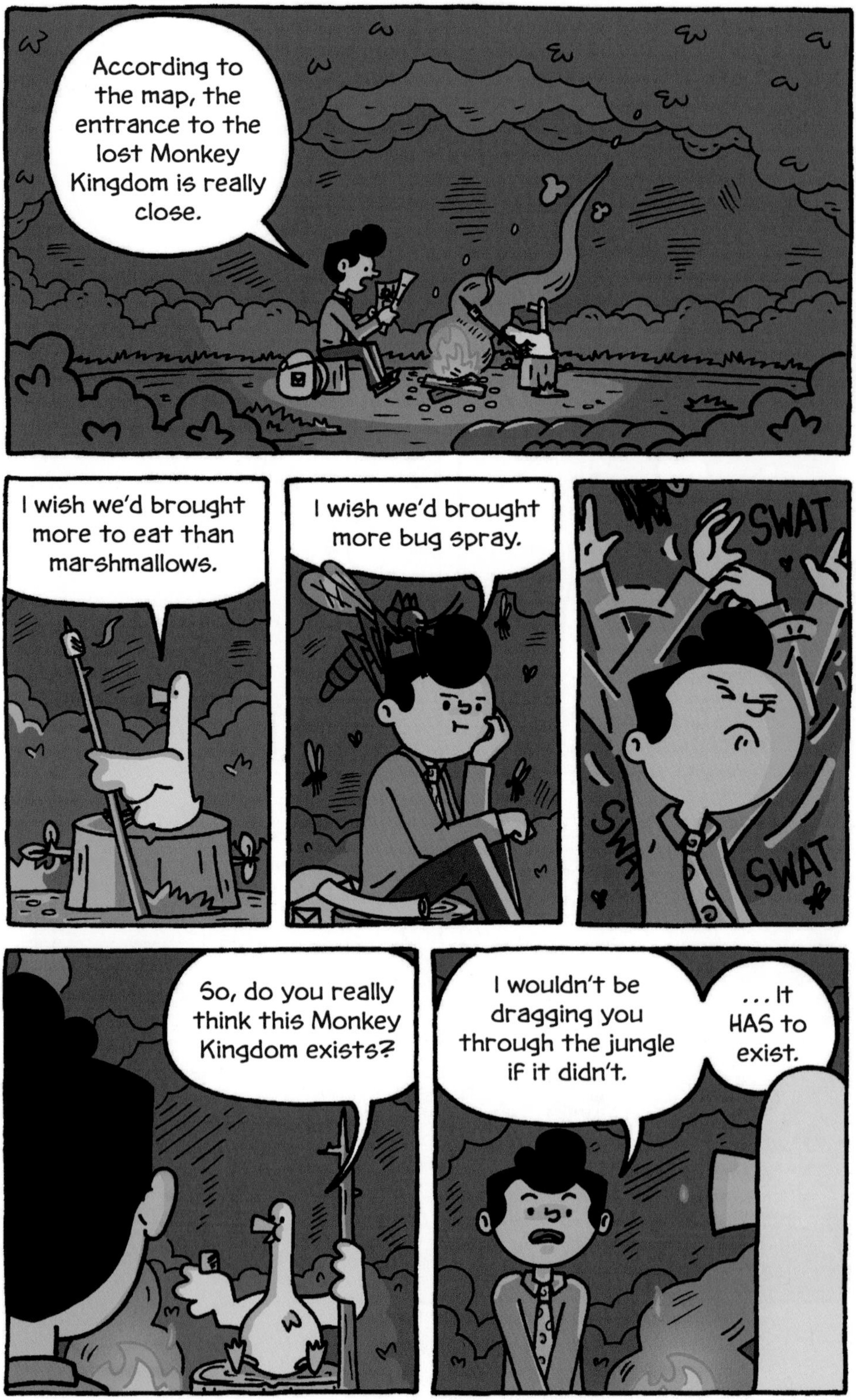
According to the map, the entrance to the lost Monkey Kingdom is really close.
I wish we'd brought more to eat than marshmallows.
I wish we'd brought more bug spray.
SWAT
SWAT
SWAT
So, do you really think this Monkey Kingdom exists?
I wouldn't be dragging you through the jungle if it didn't.
. . . It HAS to exist.

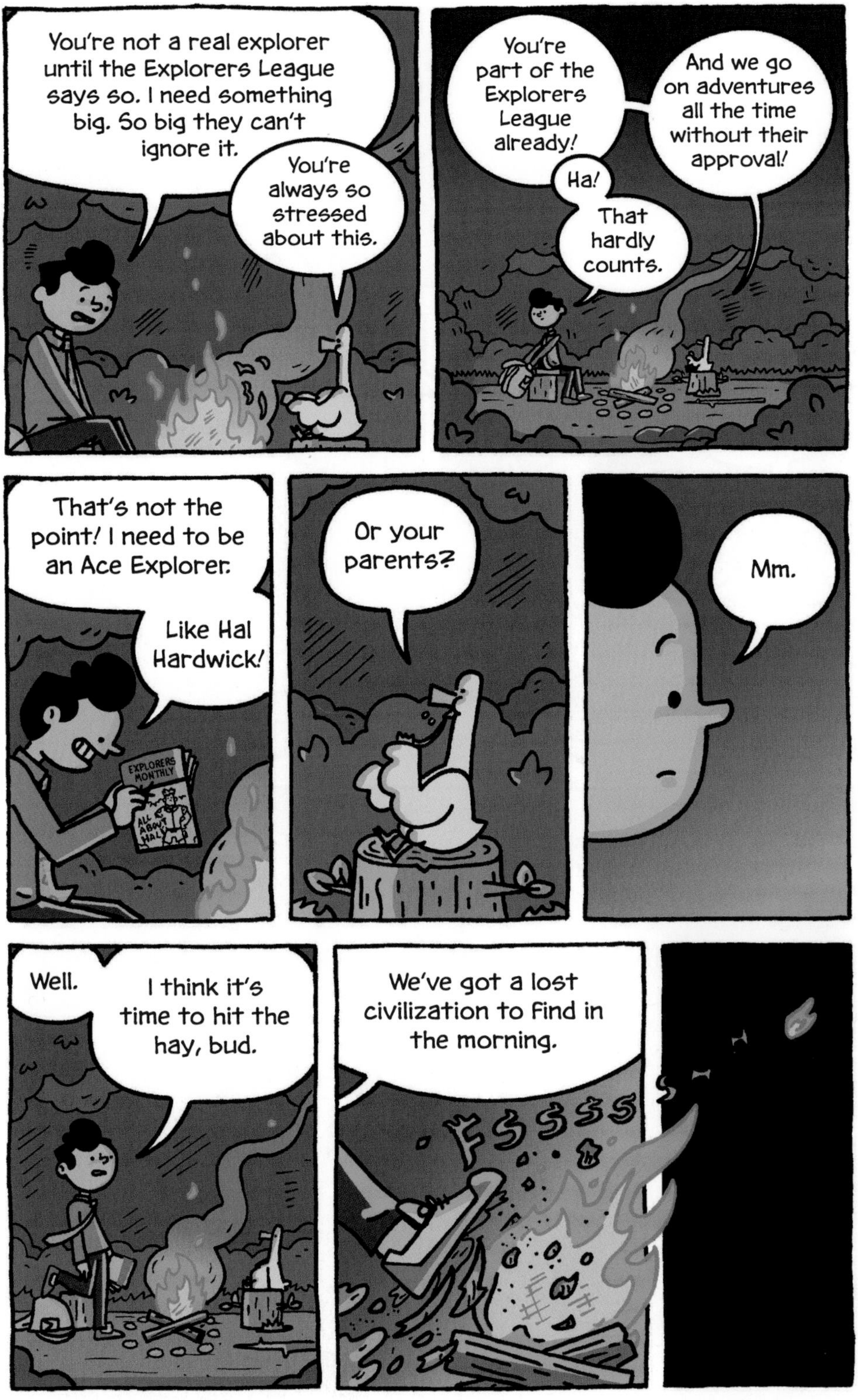
You're not a real explorer until the Explorers League says so. I need something big. So big they can't ignore it.
You're always so stressed about this.
You're part of the Explorers League already!
And we go on adventures all the time without their approval!
Ha!
That hardly counts.
That's not the point! I need to be an Ace Explorer.
Like Hal Hardwick!
EXPLORERS MONTHLY
ALL ABOUT HAL
Or your parents?
Mm.
Well.
I think it's time to hit the hay, bud.
We've got a lost civilization to find in the morning.
FSSSSS

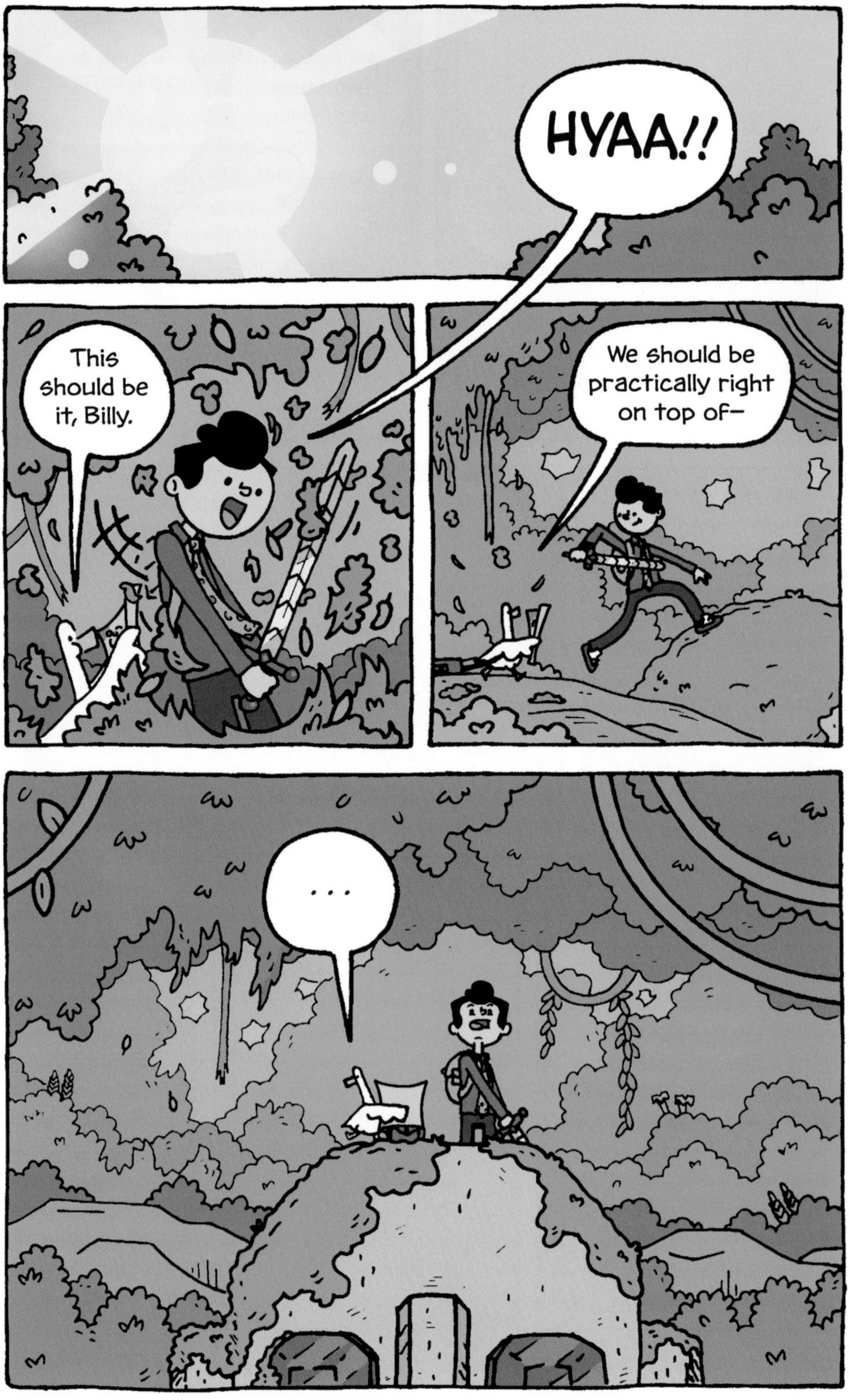
HYAA!!
This should be it, Billy.
We should be practically right on top of–
. . .

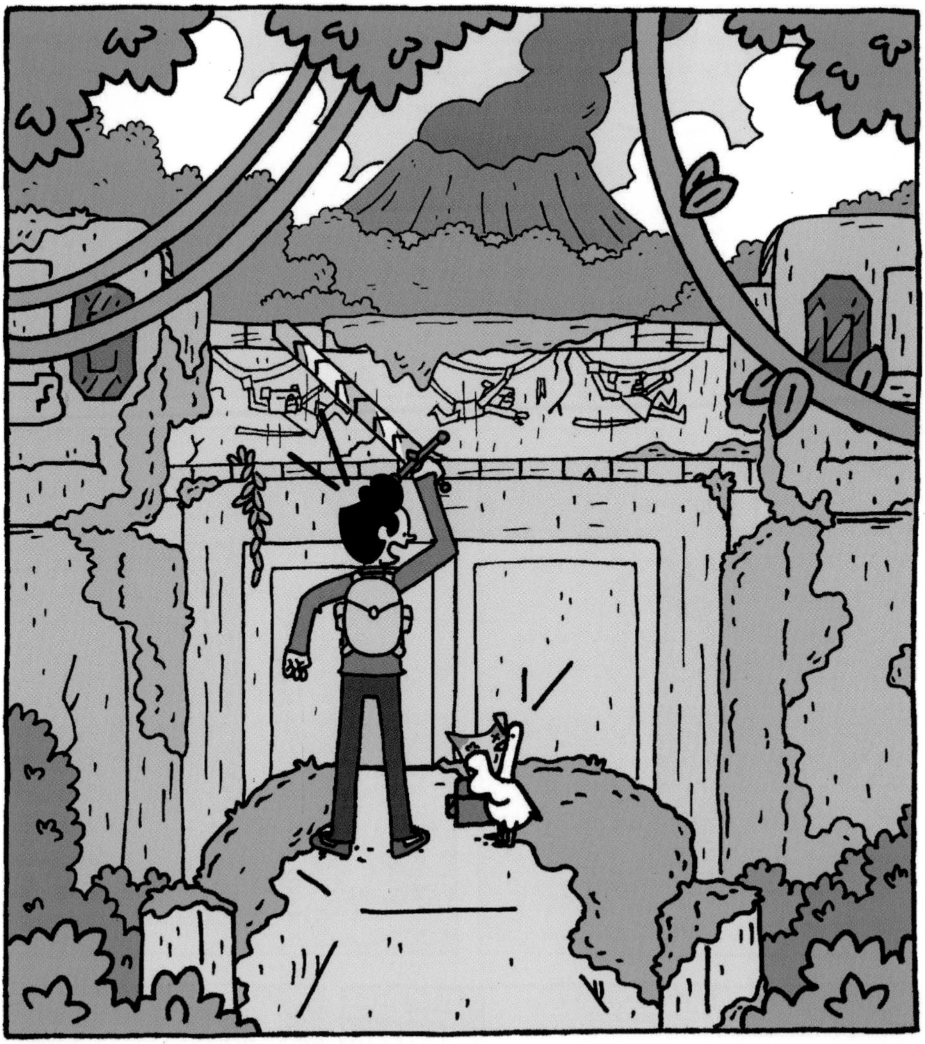

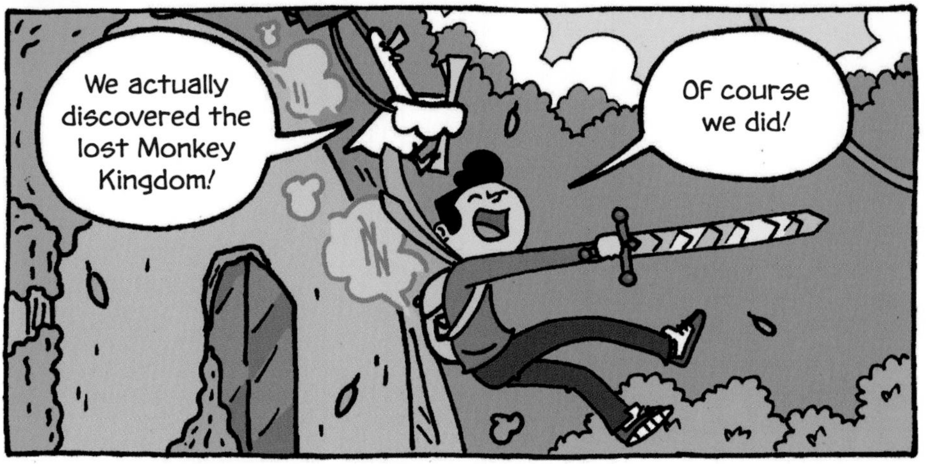
We actually discovered the lost Monkey Kingdom!
Of course we did!

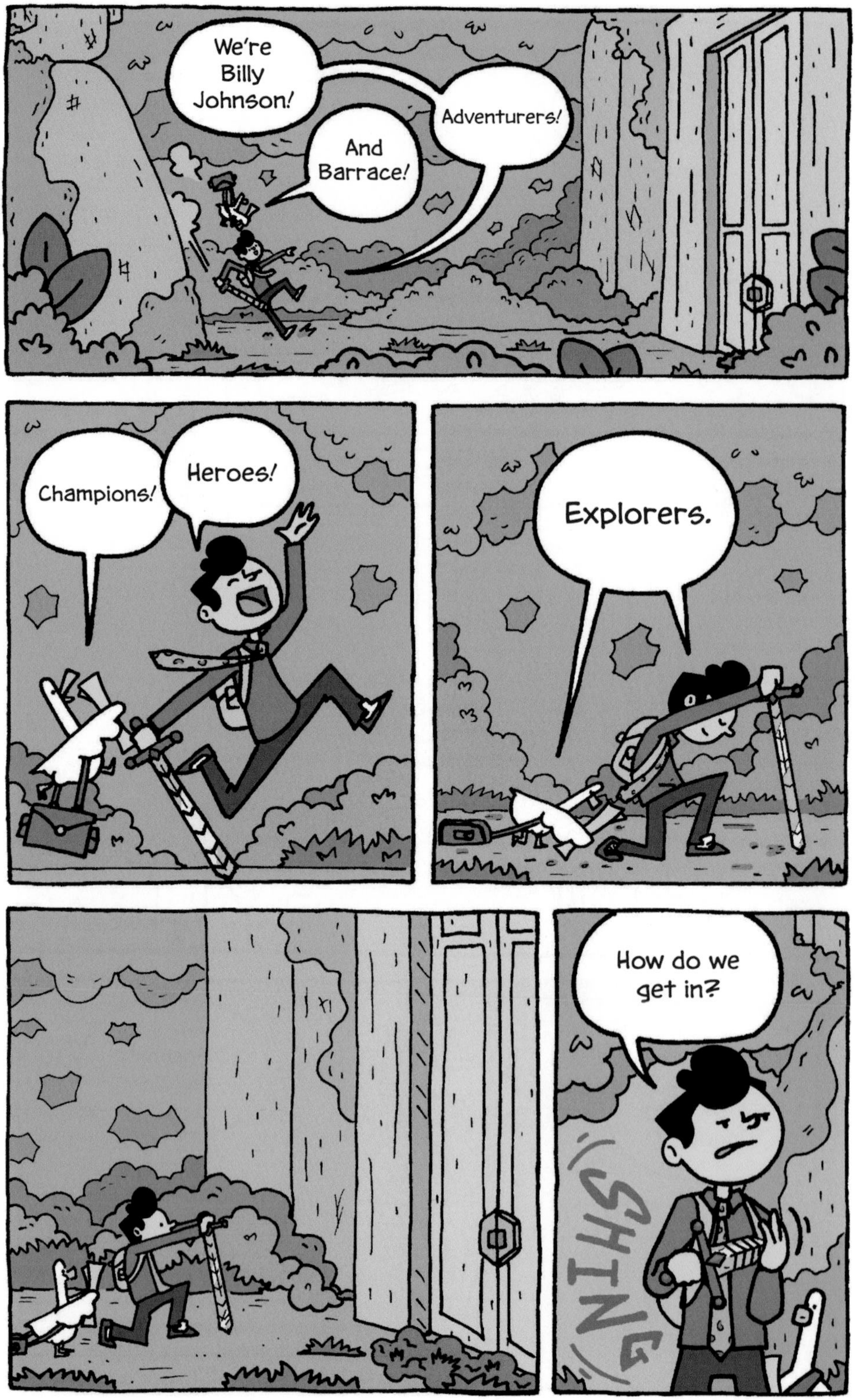
We're Billy Johnson!
And Barrace!
Adventurers!
Champions!
Heroes!
Explorers.
How do we get in?
SHING

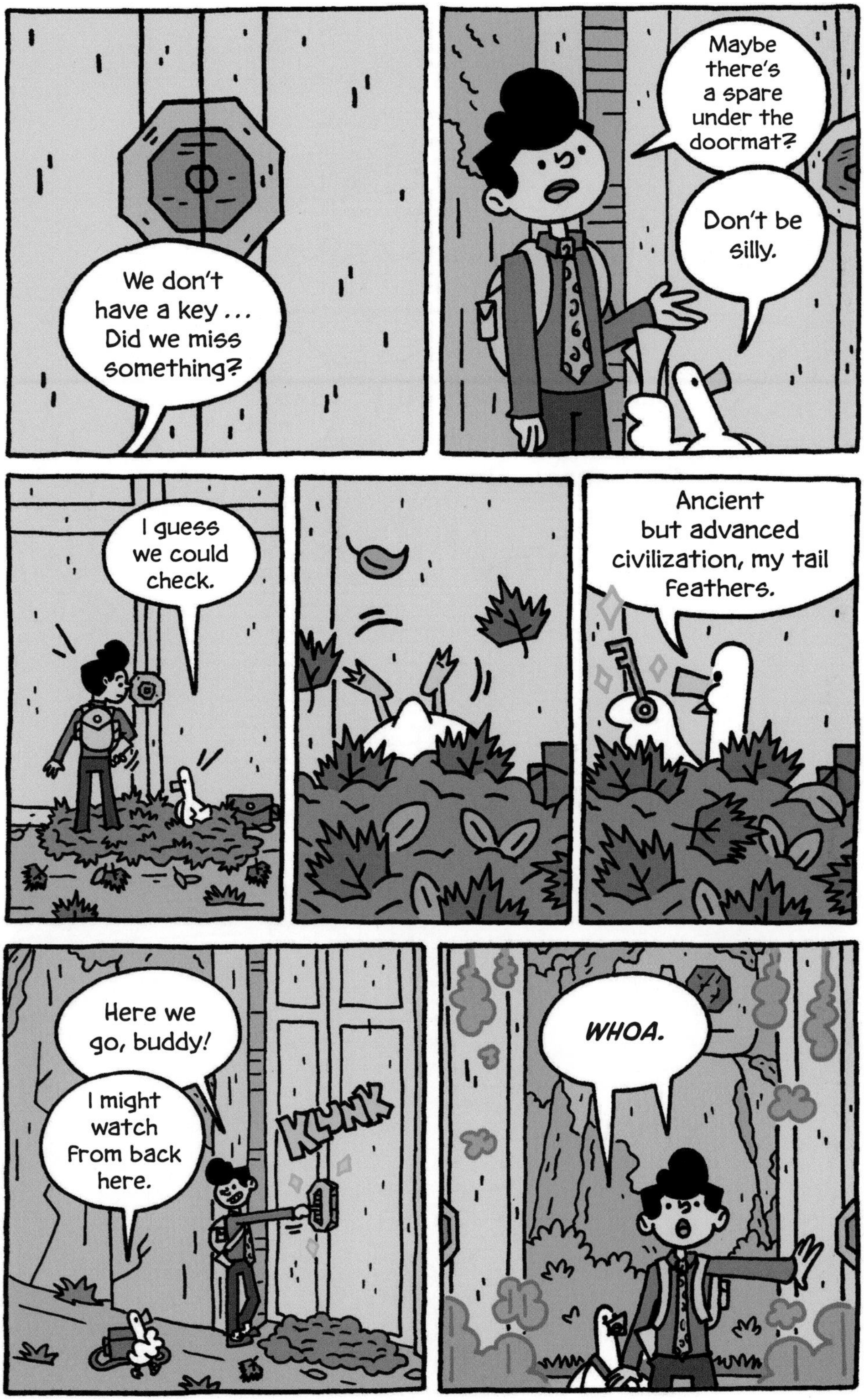

We don't have a key . . . Did we miss something?
Maybe there's a spare under the doormat?
Don't be silly.
I guess we could check.
Ancient but advanced civilization, my tail feathers.
Here we go, buddy!
I might watch from back here.
KLUNK
WHOA.

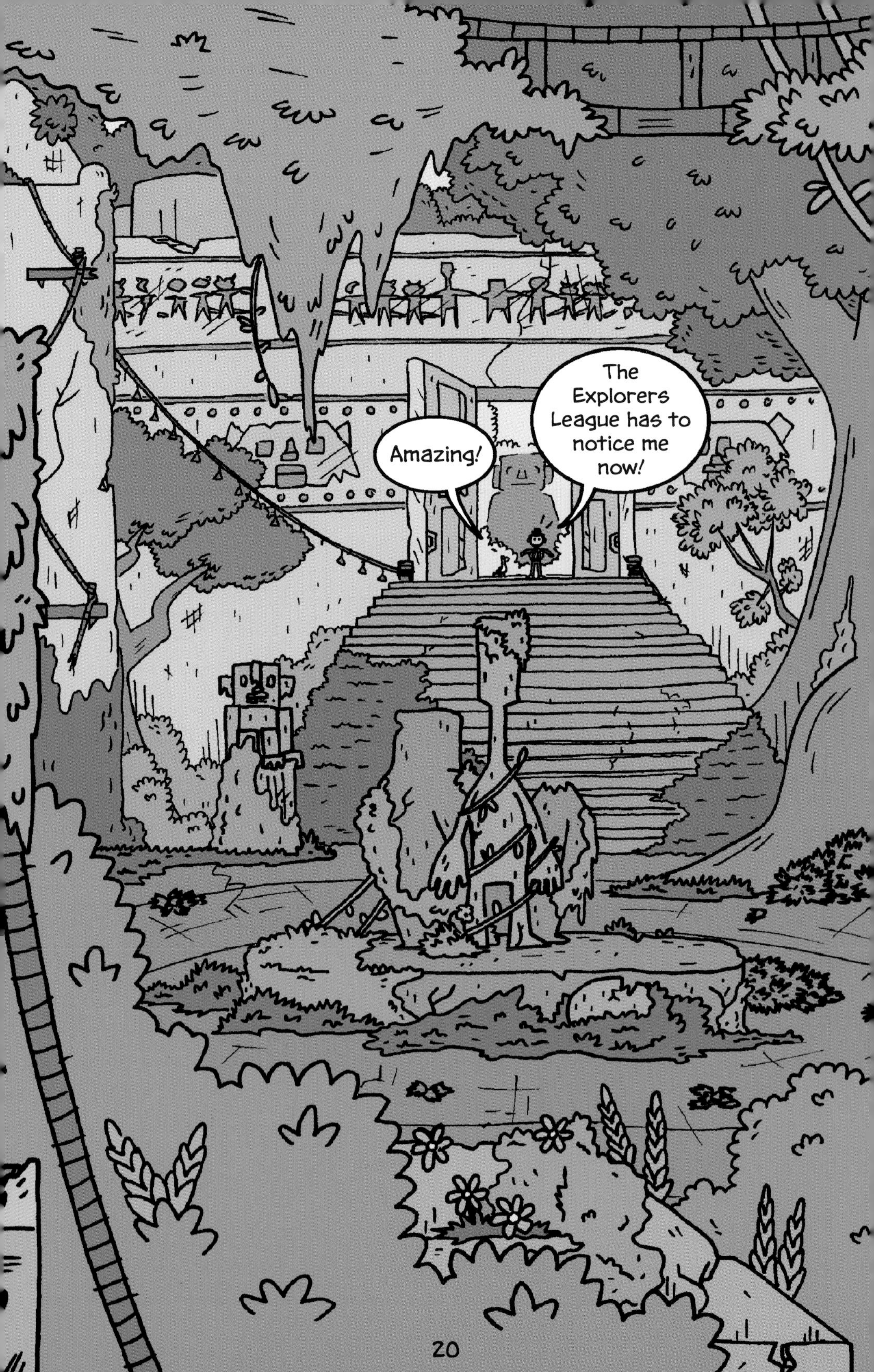
Amazing!
The Explorers League has to notice me now!

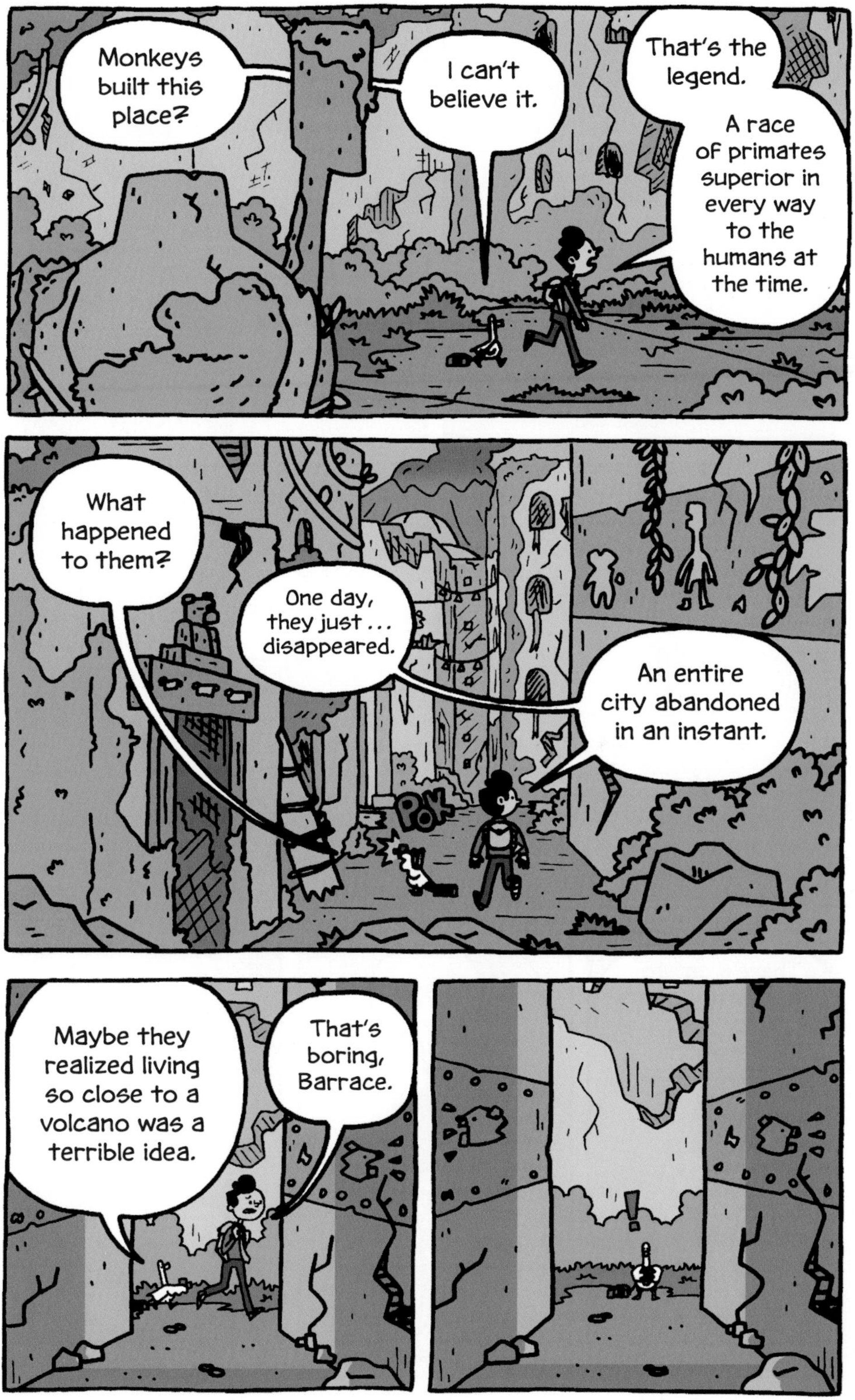
Monkeys built this place?
I can't believe it.
That's the legend.
A race of primates superior in every way to the humans at the time.
What happened to them?
One day, they just . . . disappeared.
An entire city abandoned in an instant.
POK
Maybe they realized living so close to a volcano was a terrible idea.
That's boring, Barrace.
!

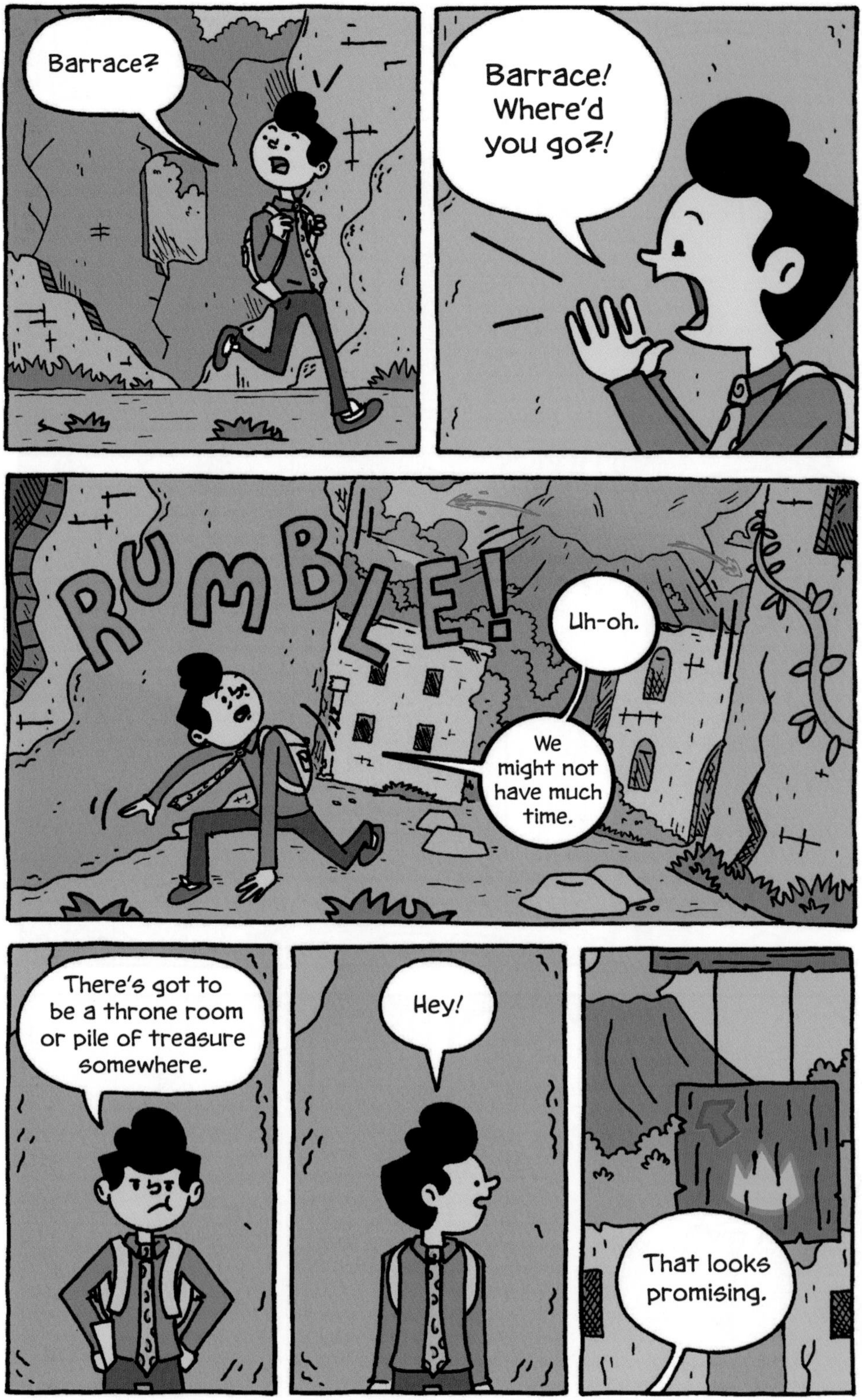
Barrace?
Barrace! Where'd you go?!
RUMBLE!
Uh-oh.
We might not have much time.
There's got to be a throne room or pile of treasure somewhere.
Hey!
That looks promising.

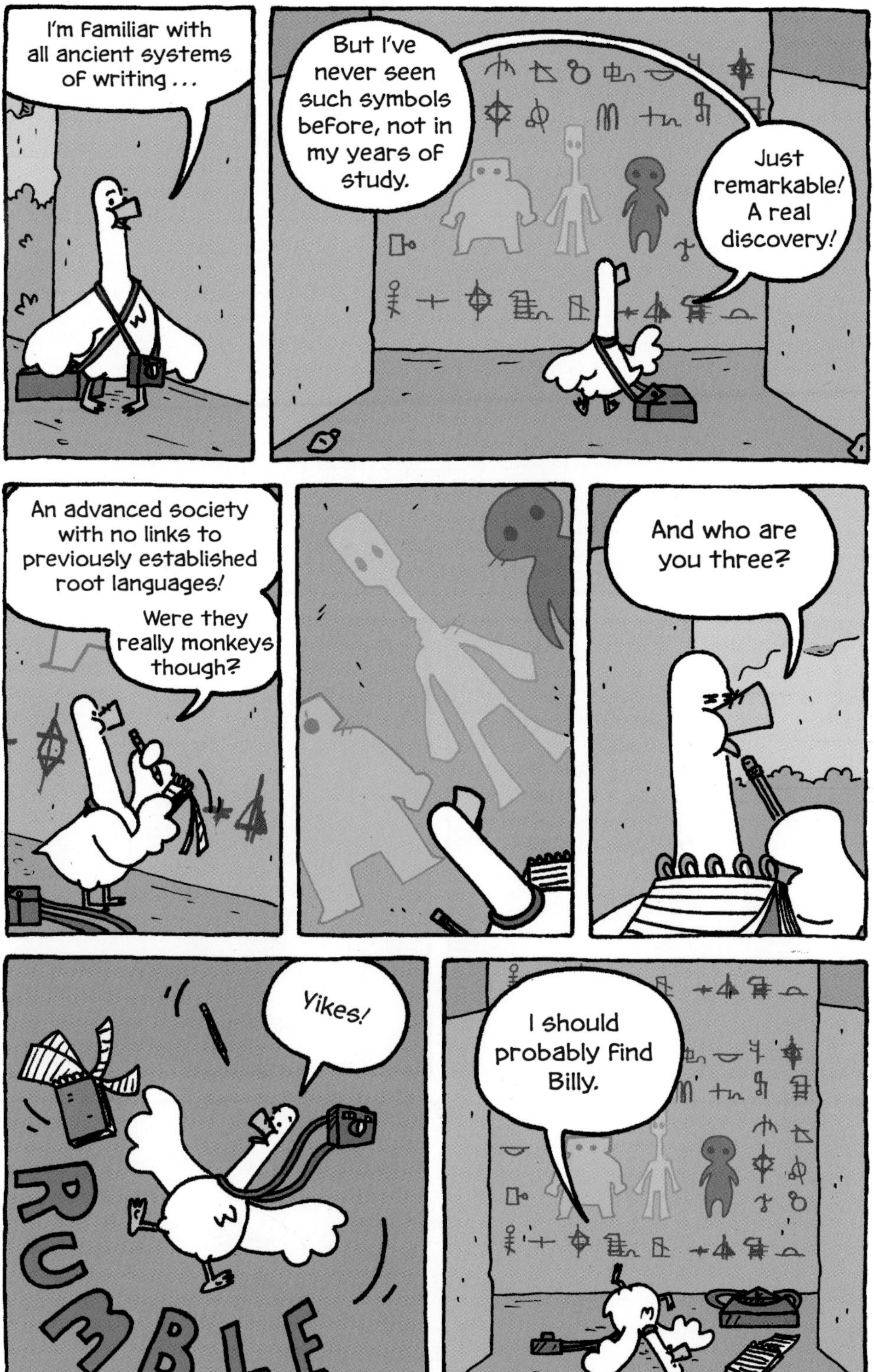
I'm familiar with all ancient systems of writing . . .
But I've never seen such symbols before, not in my years of study.
Just remarkable! A real discovery!
An advanced society with no links to previously established root languages!
Were they really monkeys though?
And who are you three?
Yikes!
RUMBLE
I should probably find Billy.

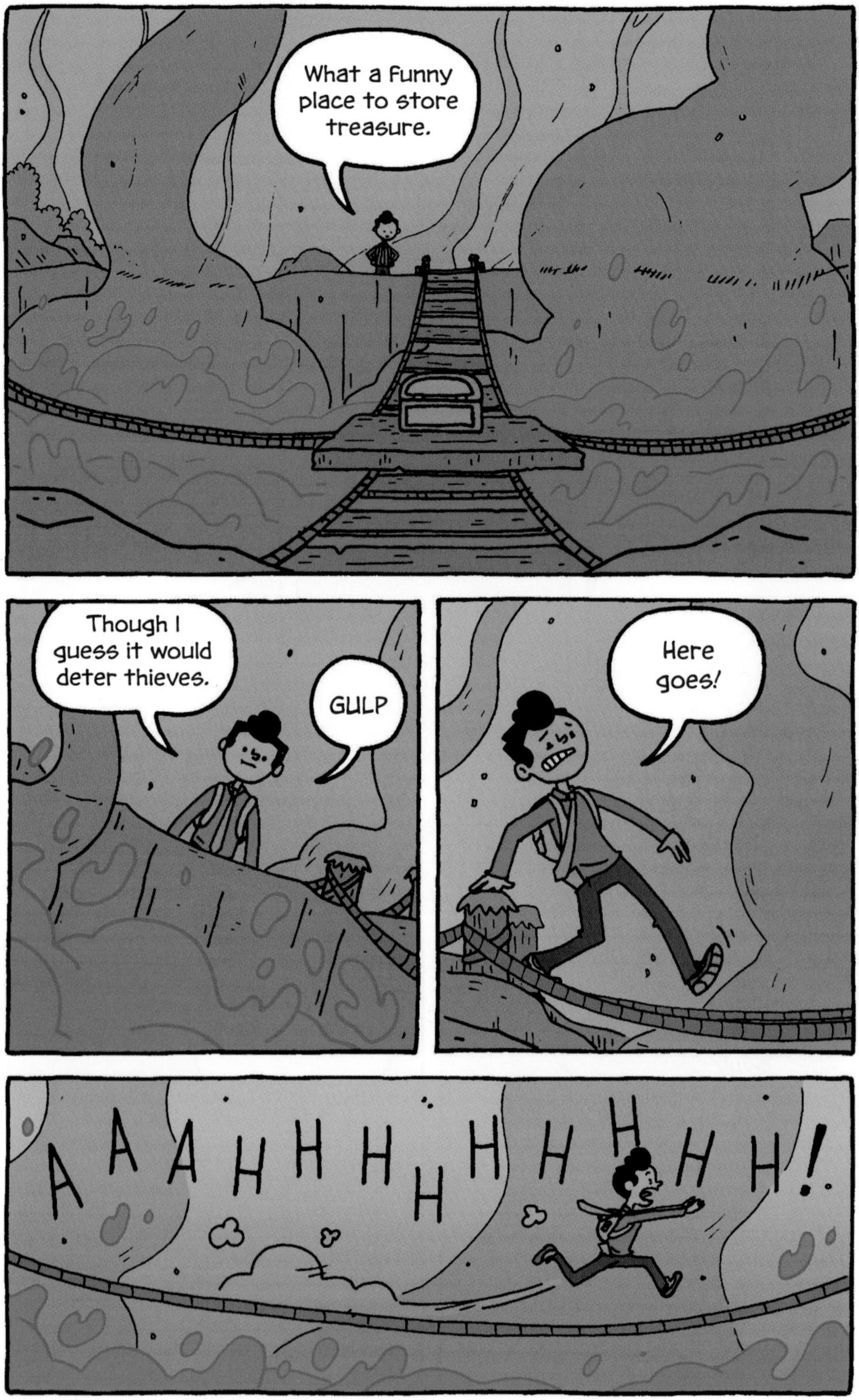
What a funny place to store treasure.
Though I guess it would deter thieves.
GULP
Here goes!
AAAHHHHHHHHH!

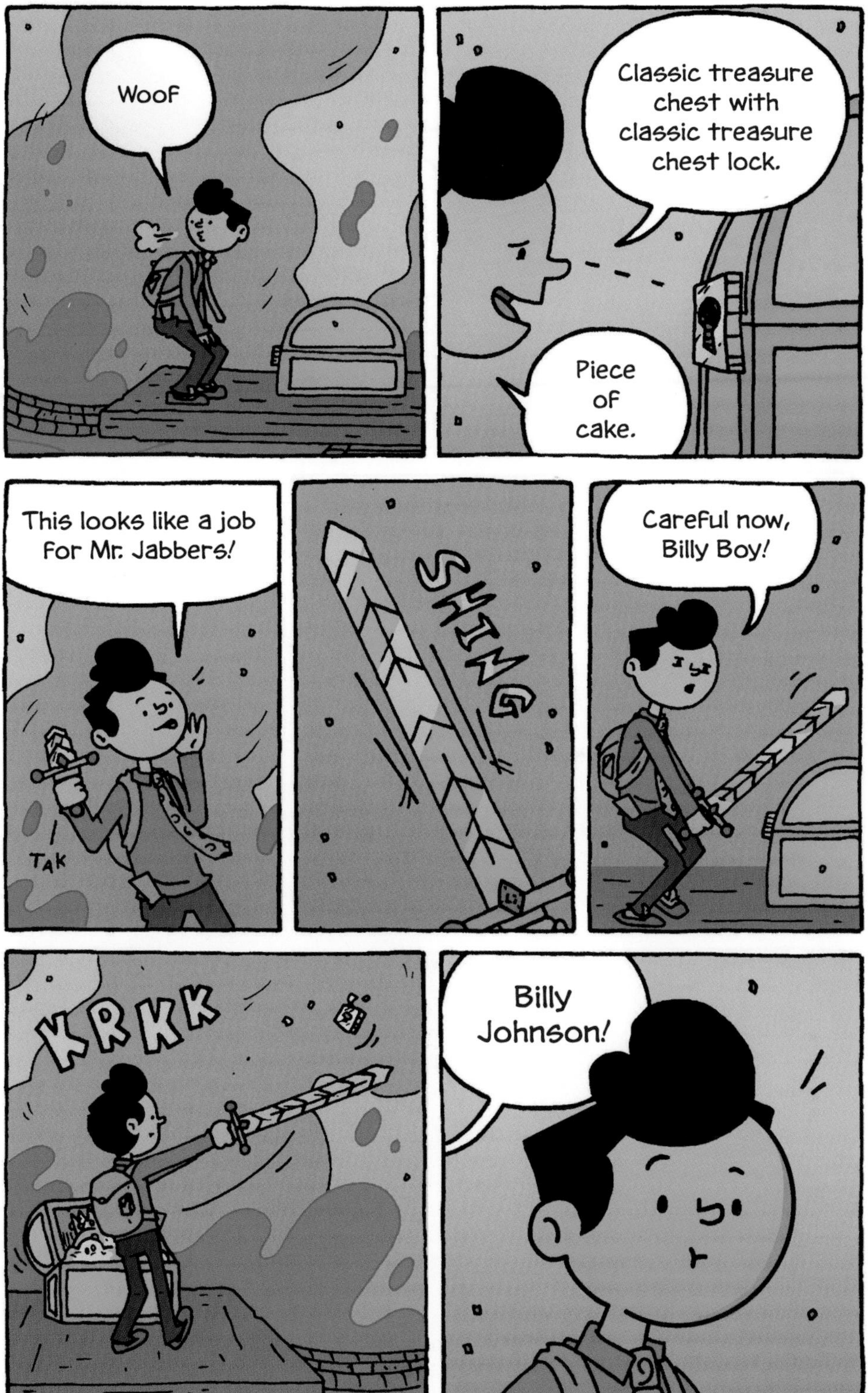
Woof
Classic treasure chest with classic treasure chest lock.
Piece of cake.
This looks like a job for Mr. Jabbers!
TAK
SHING
Careful now, Billy Boy!
KRKK
Billy Johnson!

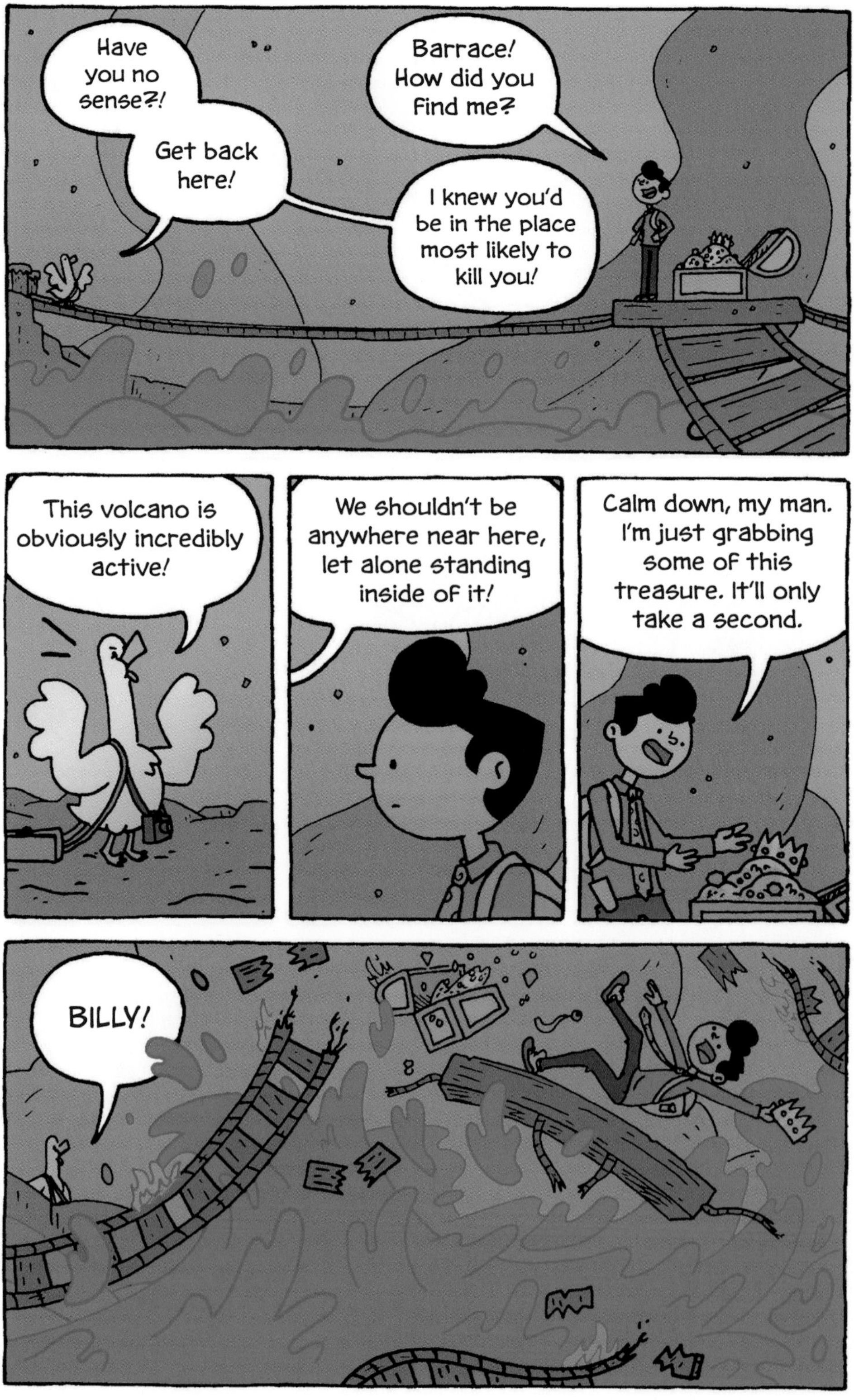
Have you no sense?!
Get back here!
Barrace! How did you find me?
I knew you'd be in the place most likely to kill you!
This volcano is obviously incredibly active!
We shouldn't be anywhere near here, let alone standing inside of it!
Calm down, my man. I'm just grabbing some of this treasure. It'll only take a second.
BILLY!

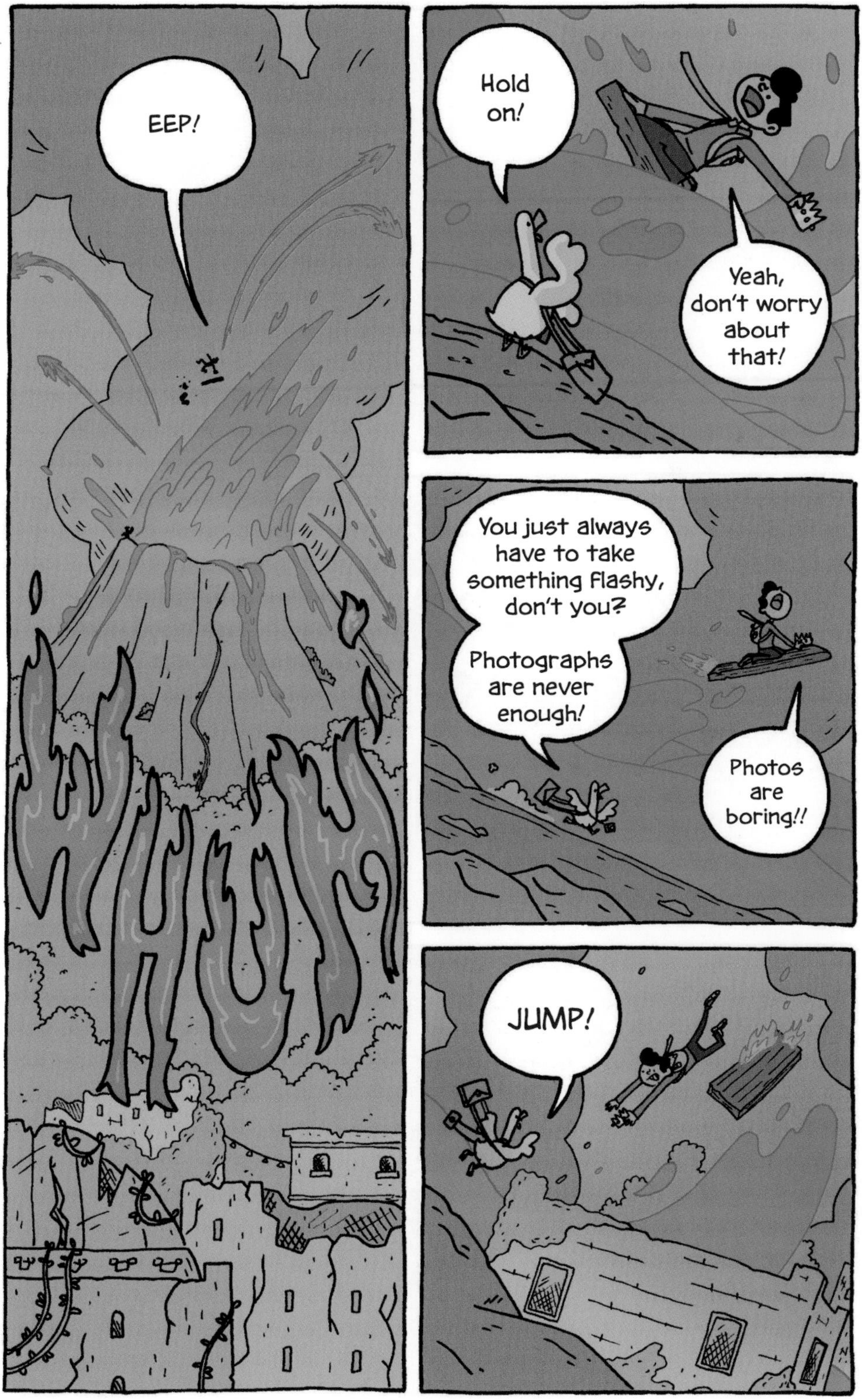
EEP!
Hold on!
Yeah, don't worry about that!
You just always have to take something flashy, don't you?
Photographs are never enough!
Photos are boring!!
JUMP!

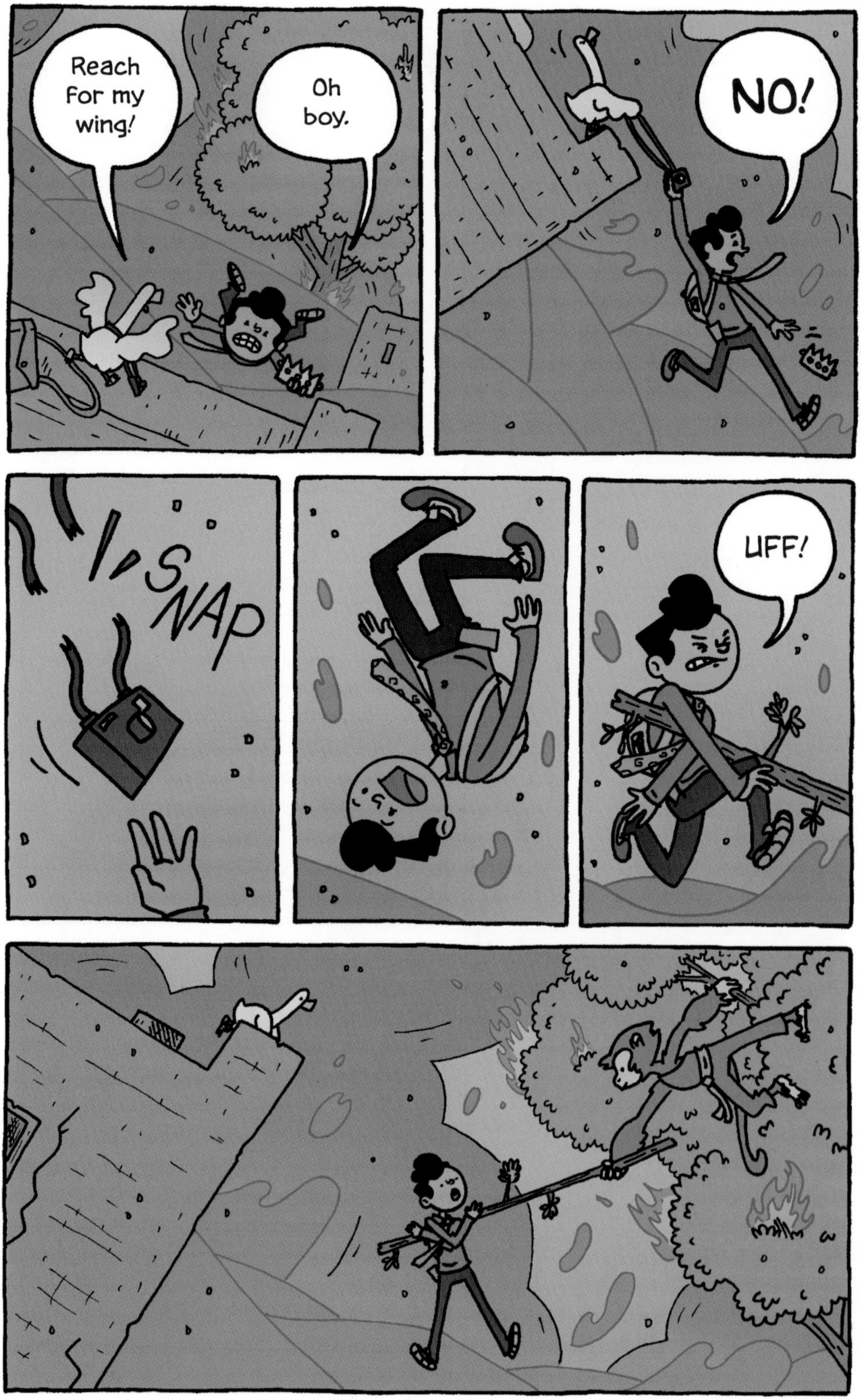
Reach for my wing!
Oh boy.
NO!
SNAP
UFF!

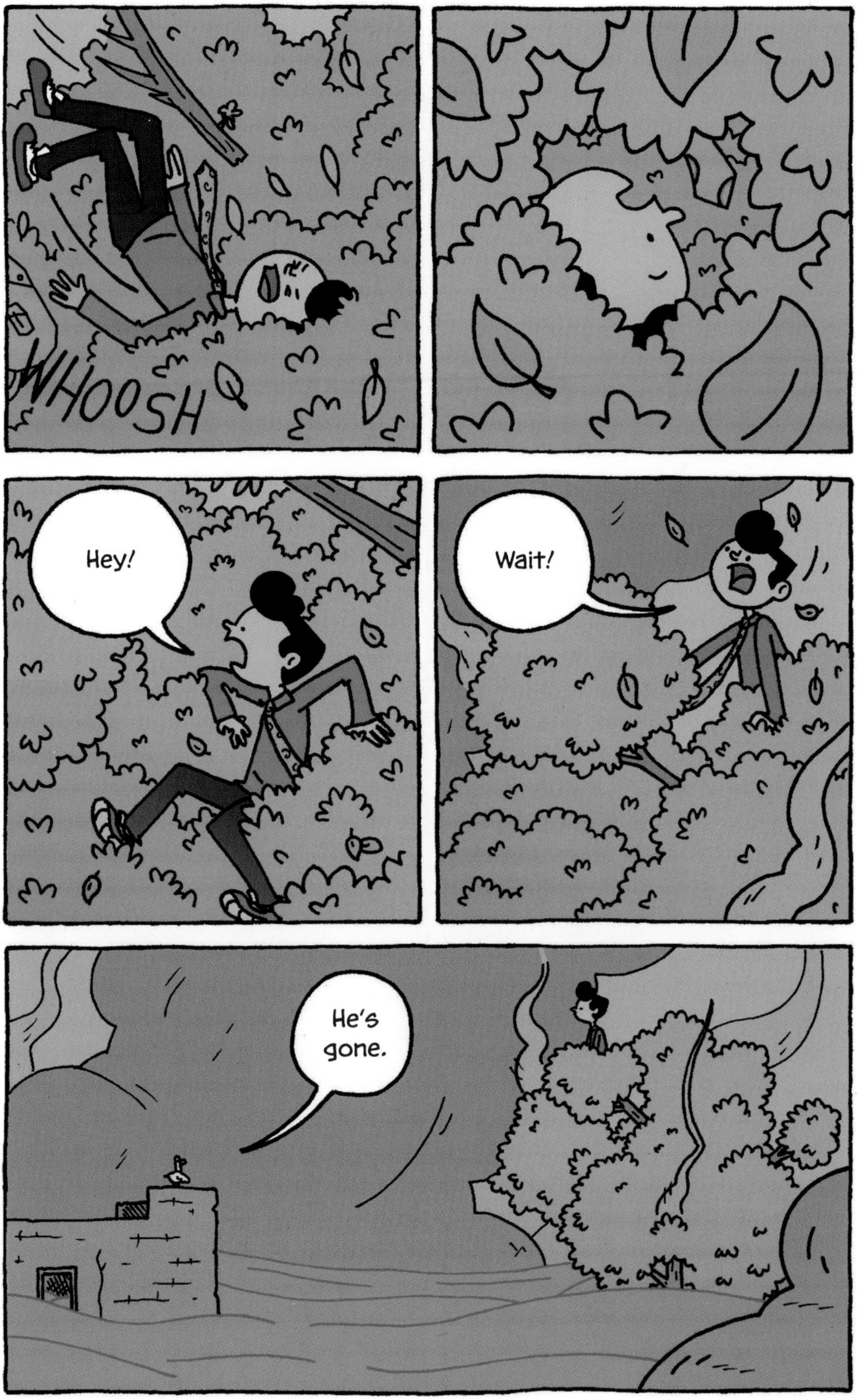
WHOOSH
Hey!
Wait!
He's gone.

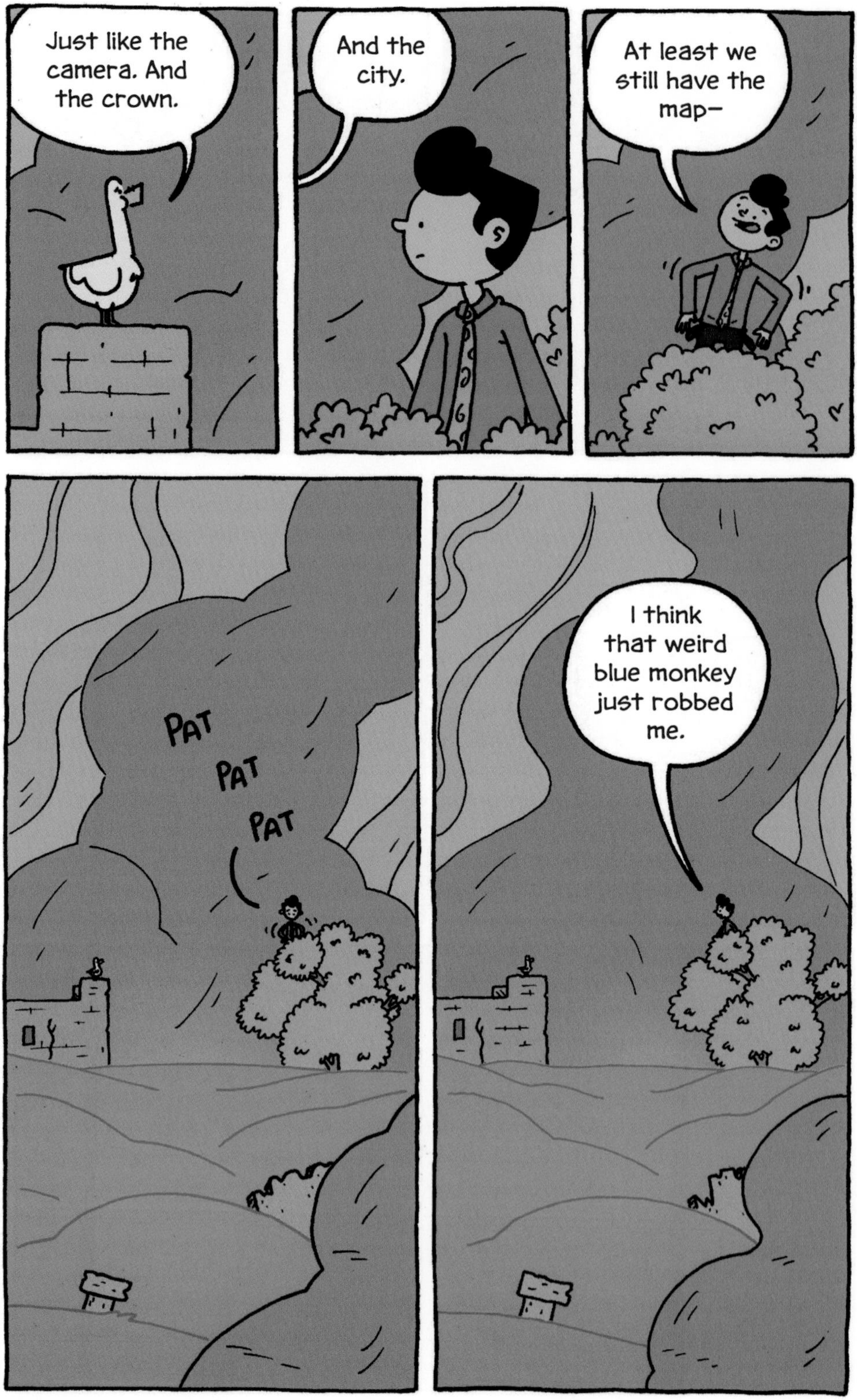
Just like the camera. And the crown.
And the city.
At least we still have the map–
PAT
PAT
PAT
I think that weird blue monkey just robbed me.

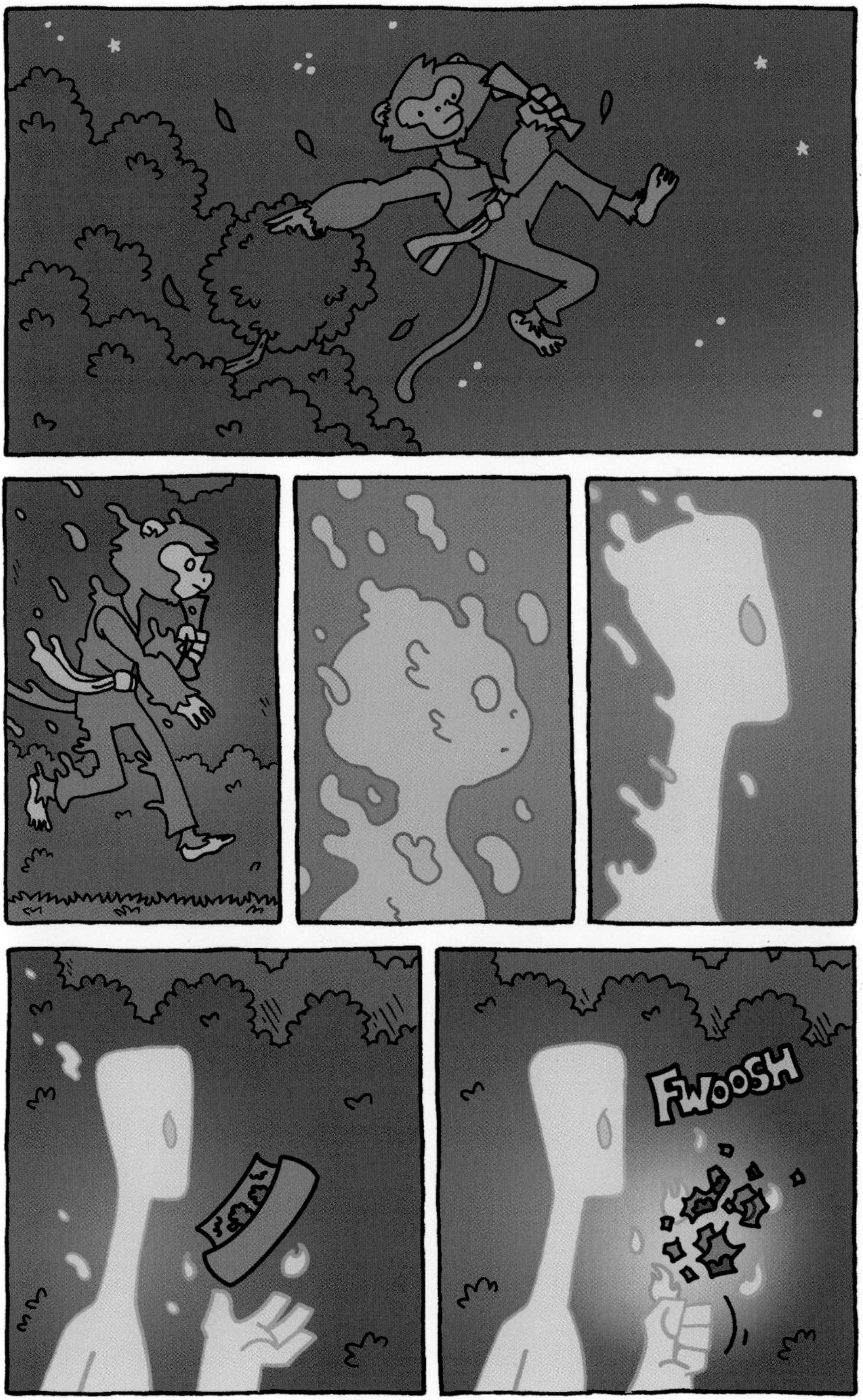
FWOOSH

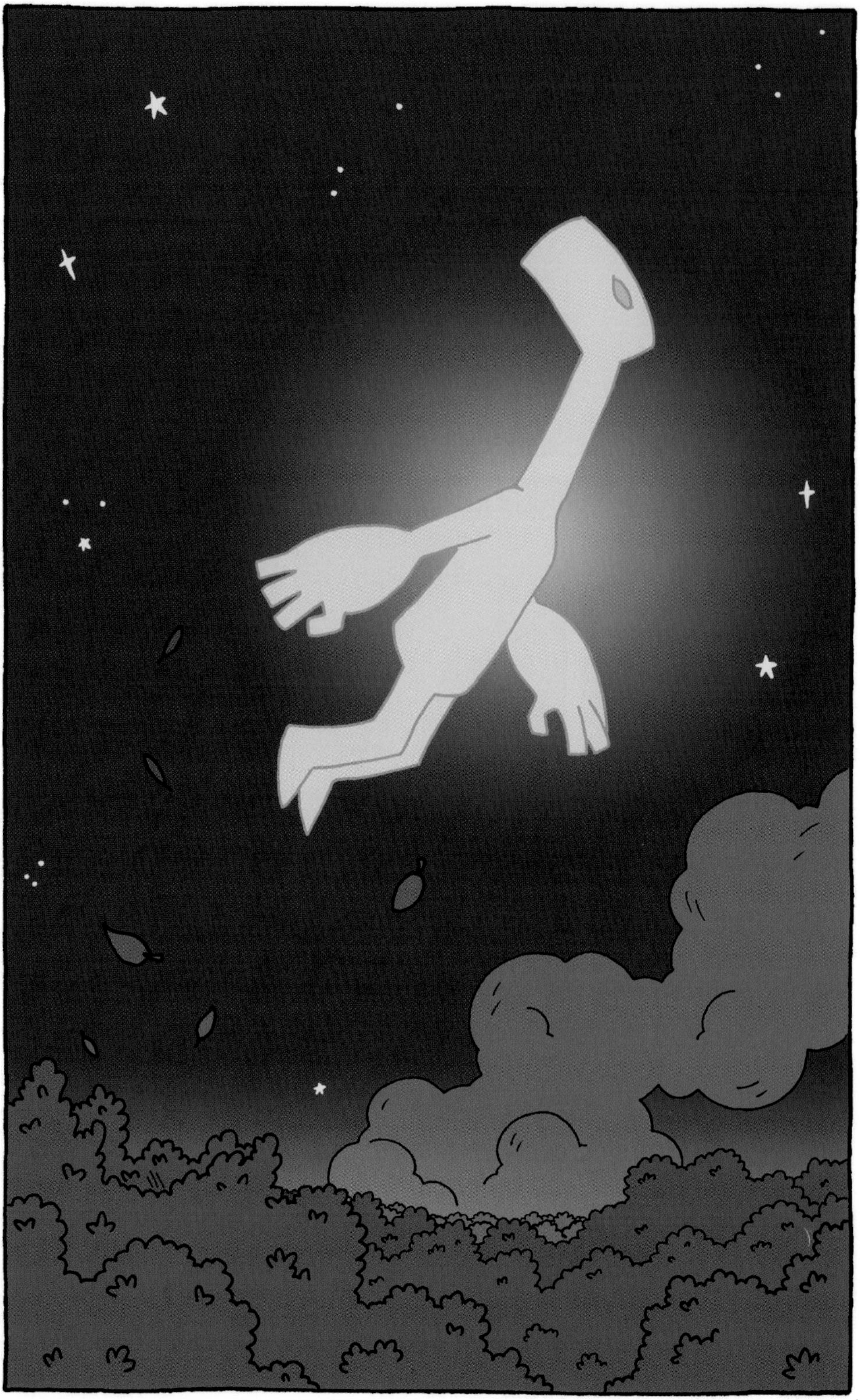

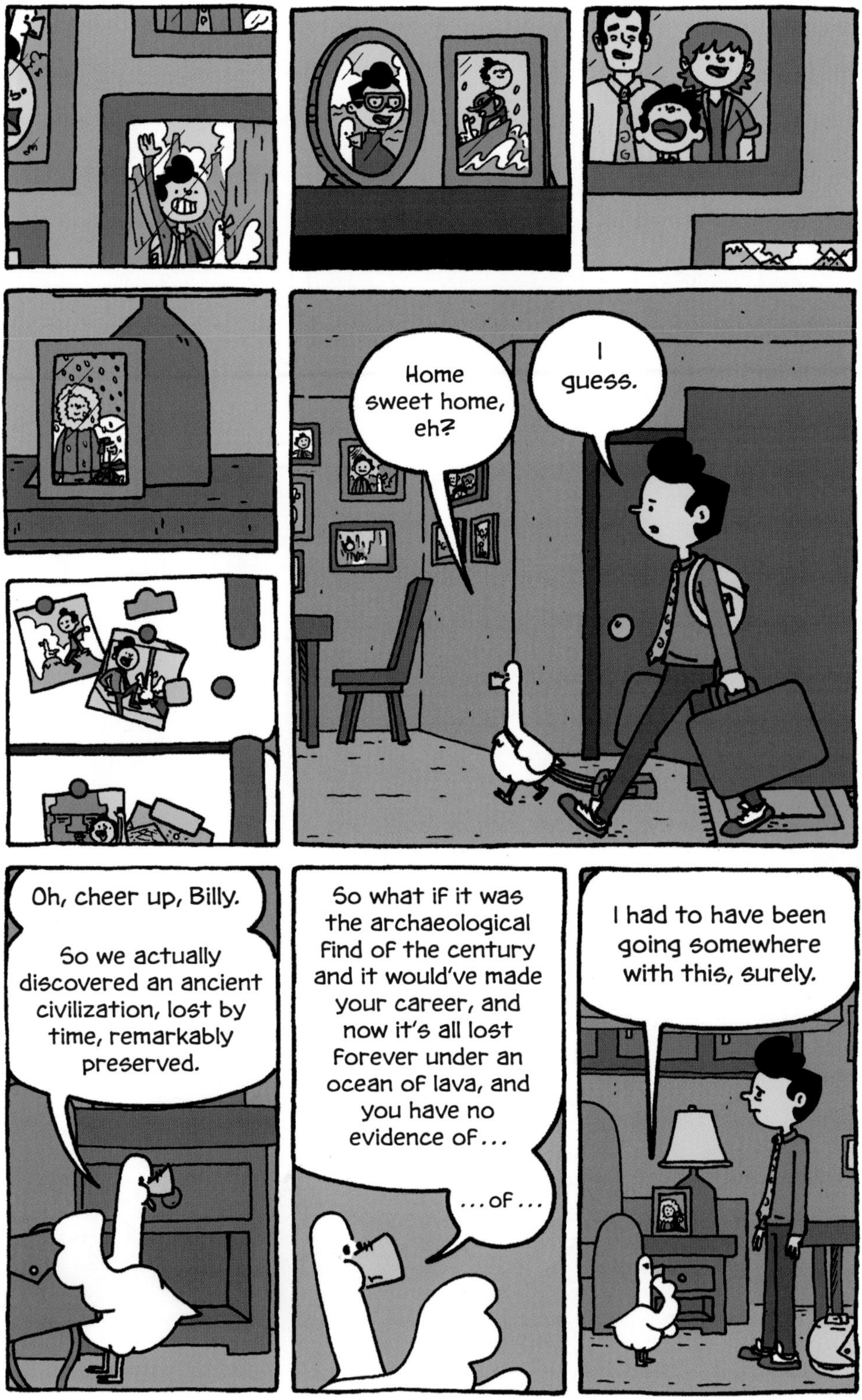
Home sweet home, eh?
I guess.
Oh, cheer up, Billy.
So we actually discovered an ancient civilization, lost by time, remarkably preserved.
So what if it was the archaeological find of the century and it would've made your career, and now it's all lost forever under an ocean of lava, and you have no evidence of...
...of...
I had to have been going somewhere with this, surely.

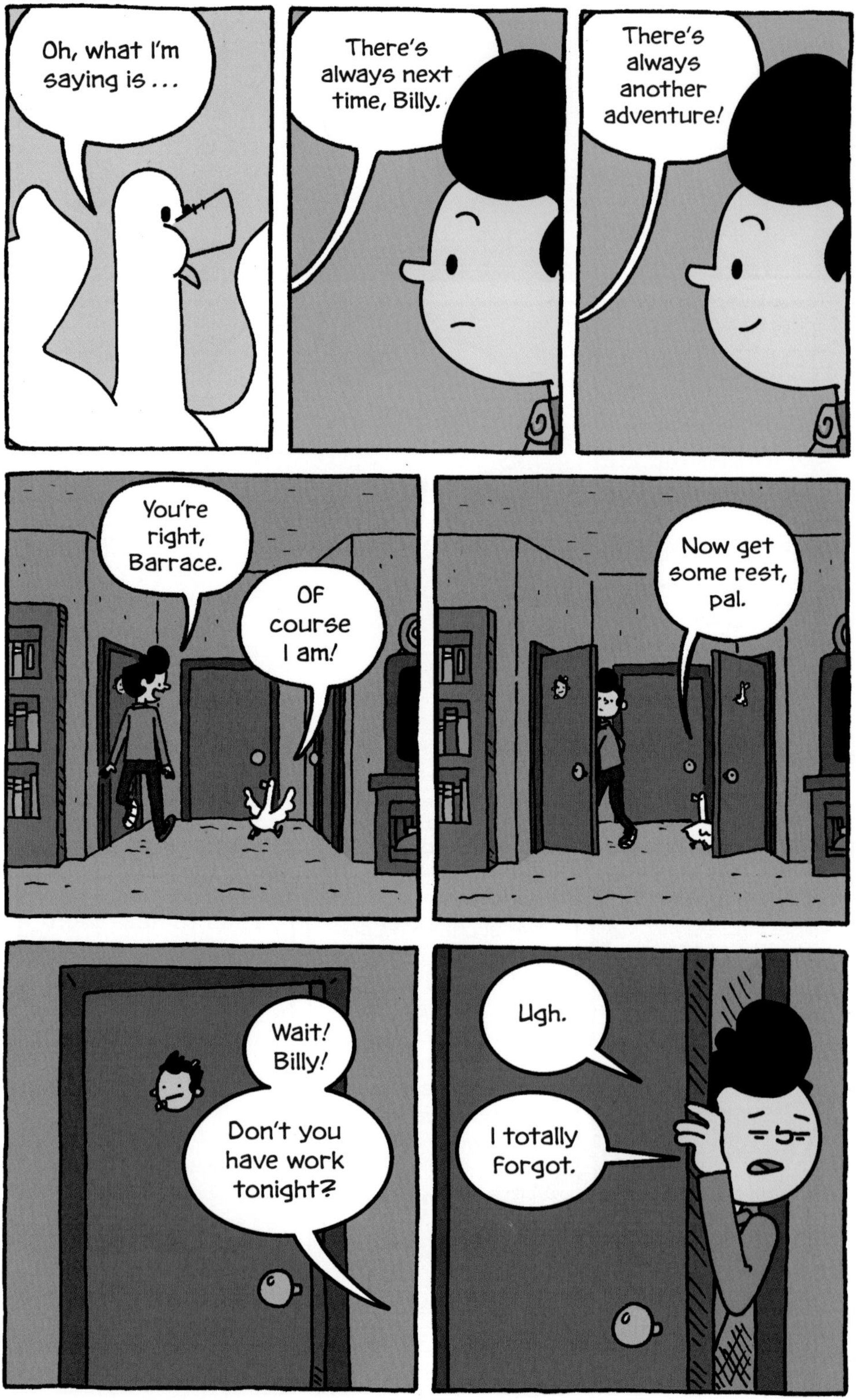

Oh, what I'm saying is . . .
There's always next time, Billy.
There's always another adventure!
You're right, Barrace.
Of course I am!
Now get some rest, pal.
Wait! Billy!
Don't you have work tonight?
Ugh.
I totally forgot.

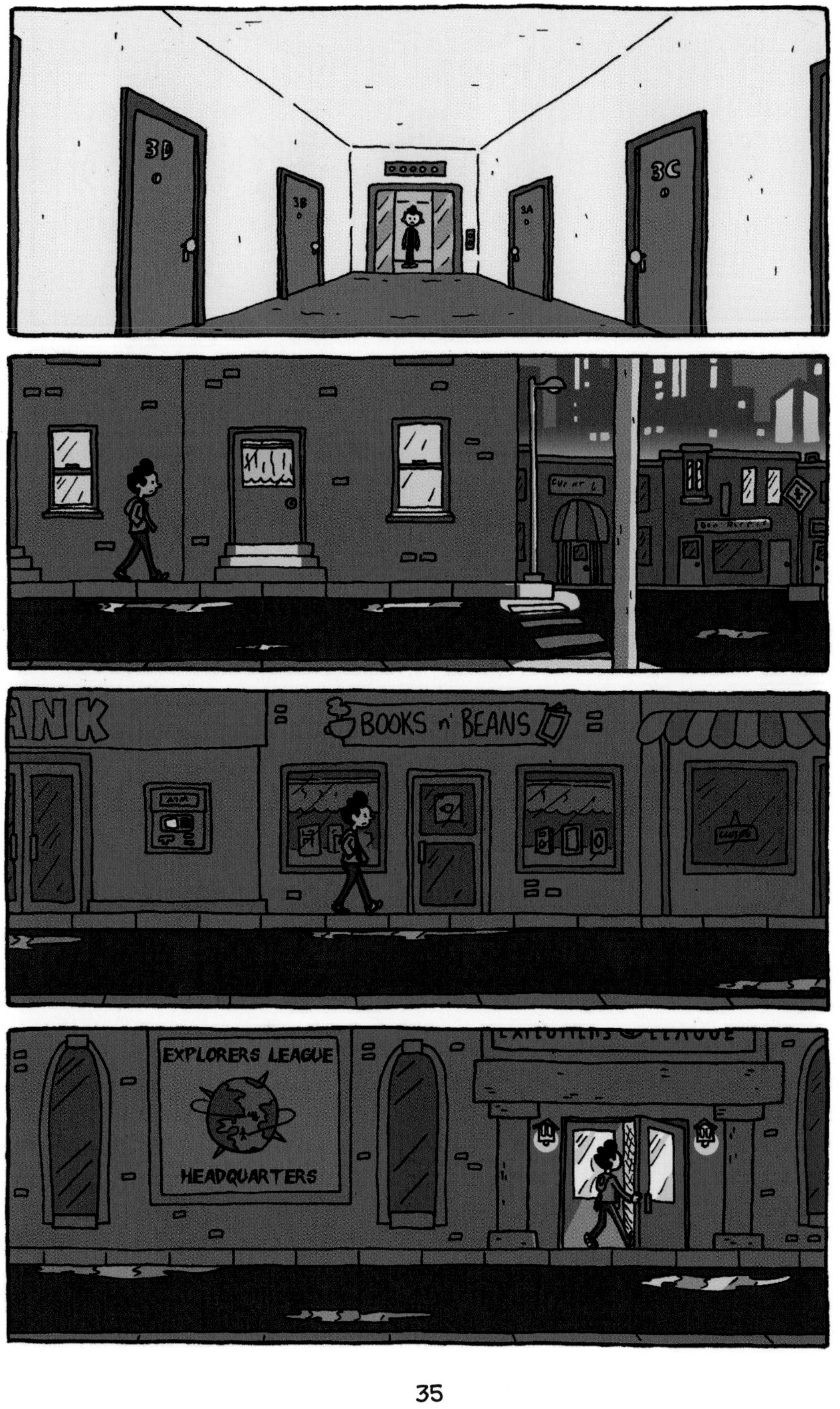
3D
3C
ANK
BOOKS n' BEANS
ATM
EXPLORERS LEAGUE
HEADQUARTERS

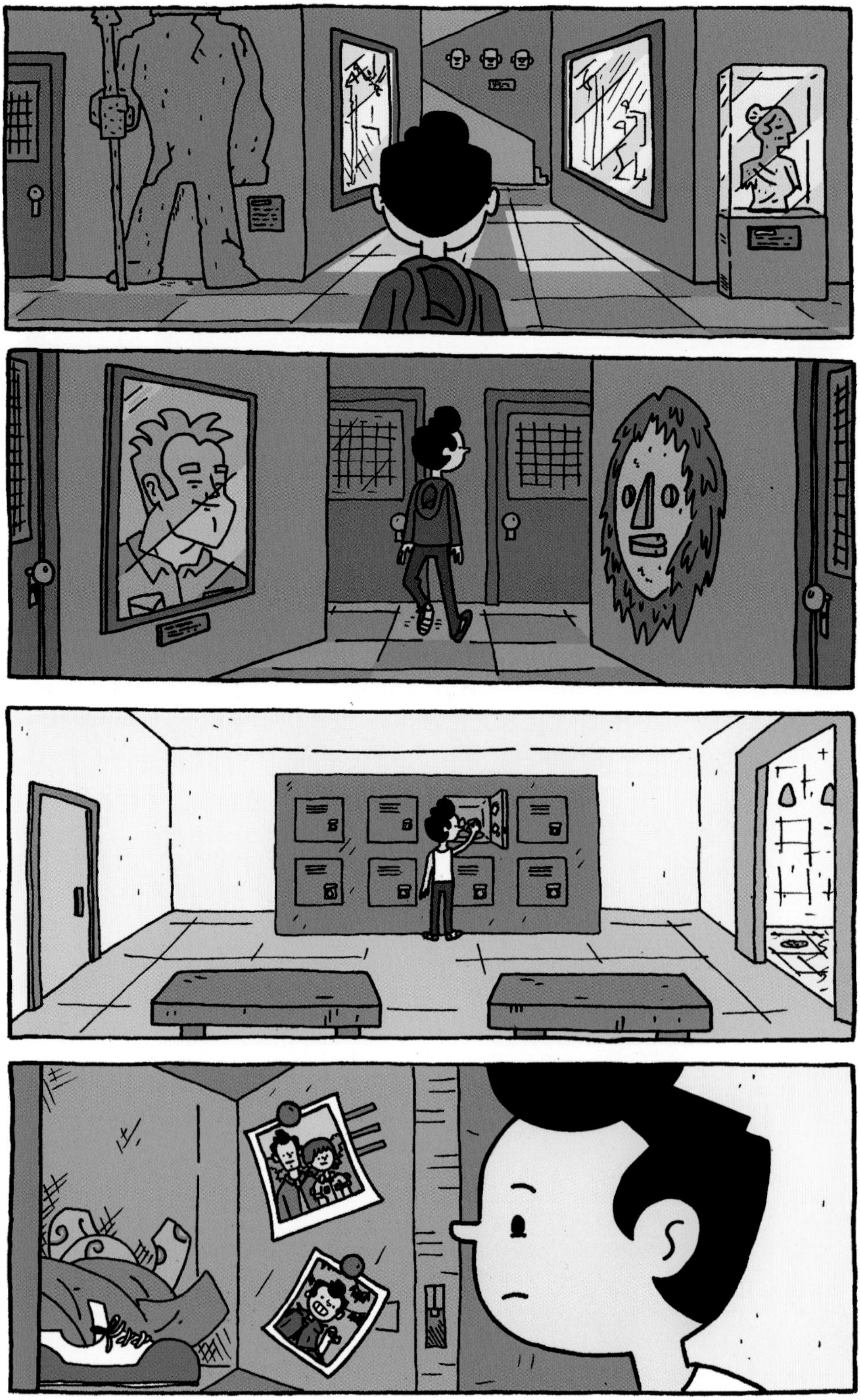

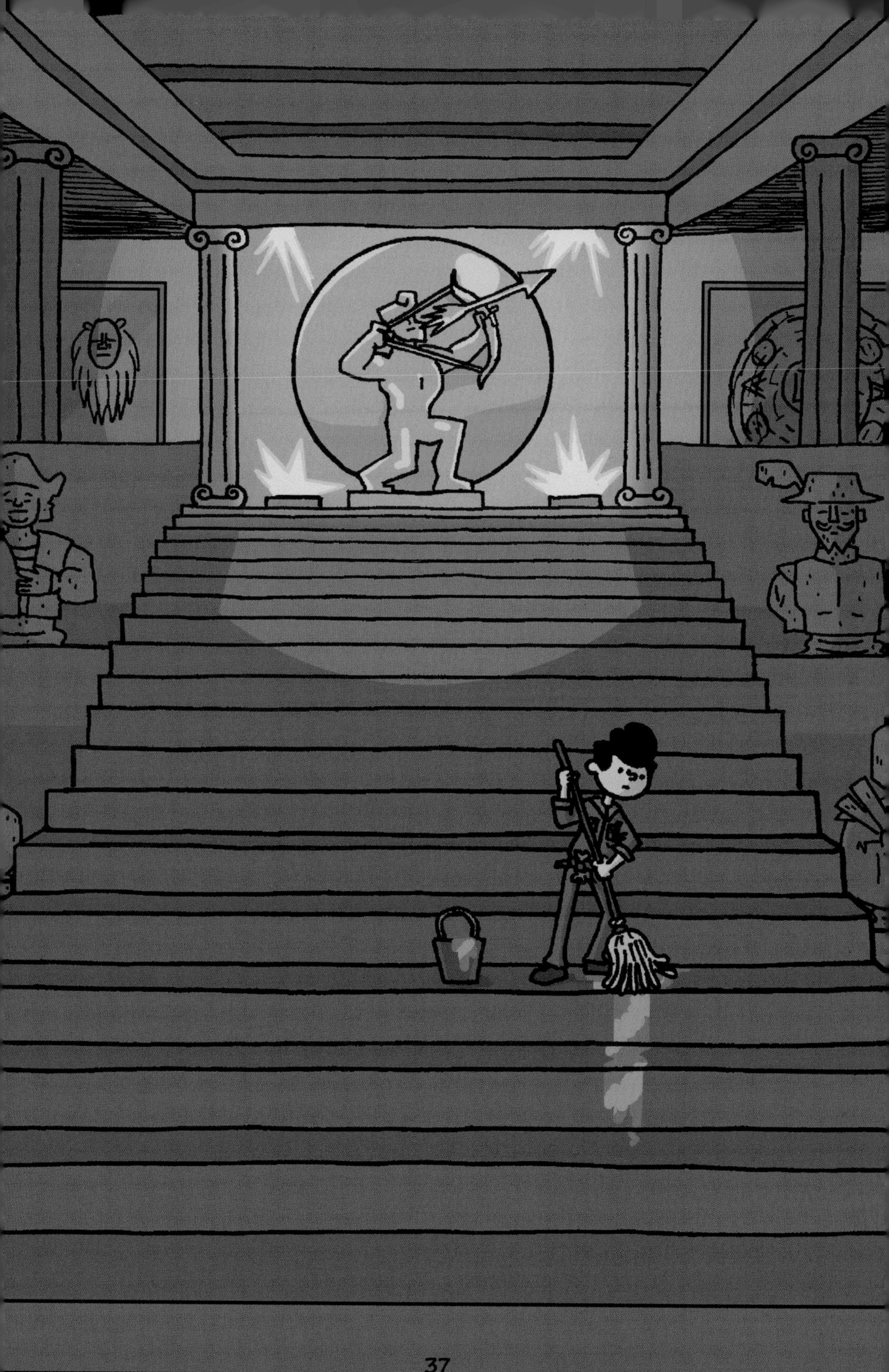

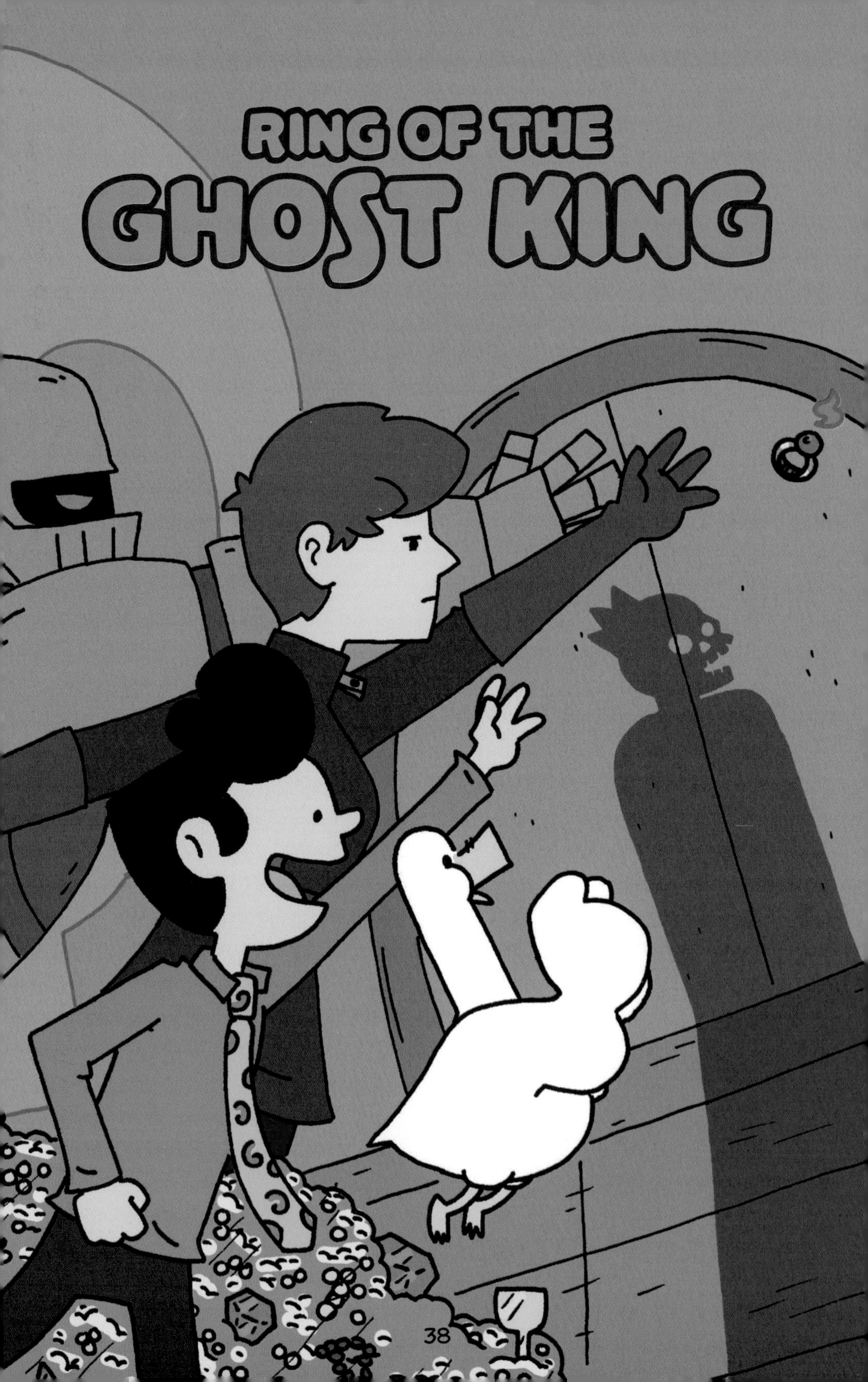
RING OF THE
GHOST KING

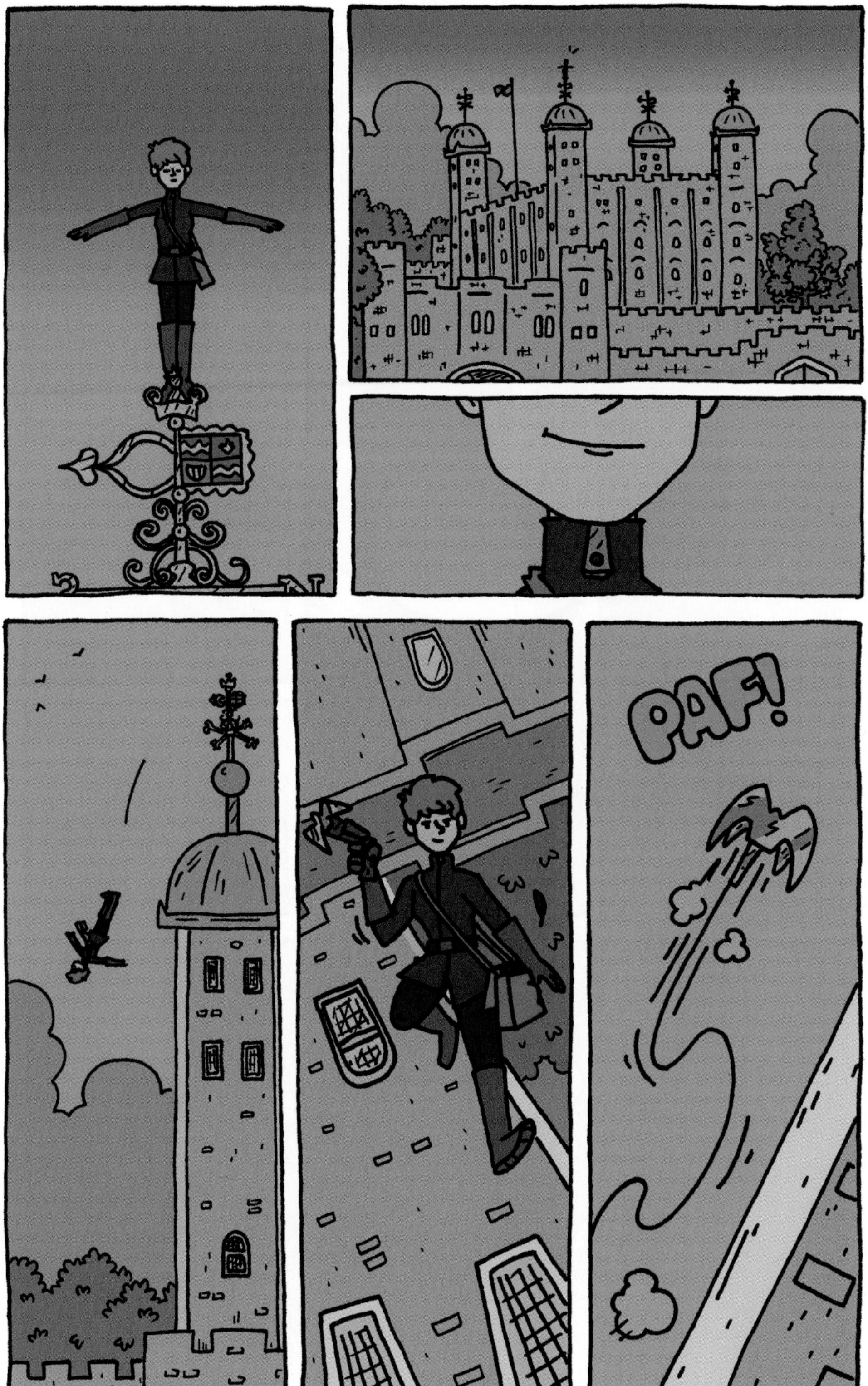
PAF!

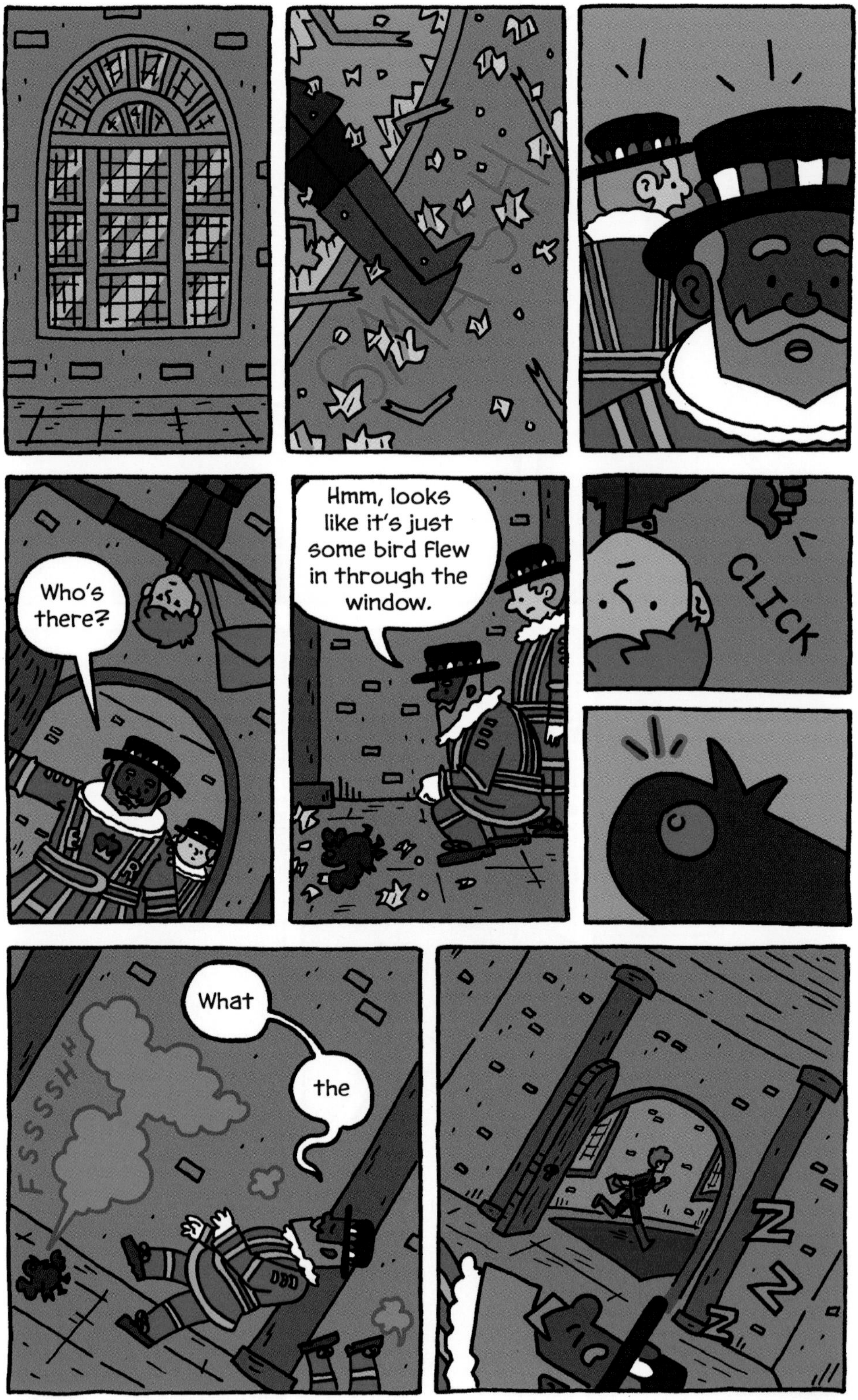
SMASH
Who's there?
Hmm, looks like it's just some bird flew in through the window.
CLICK
FSSSSHH
What
the
Z
Z
Z

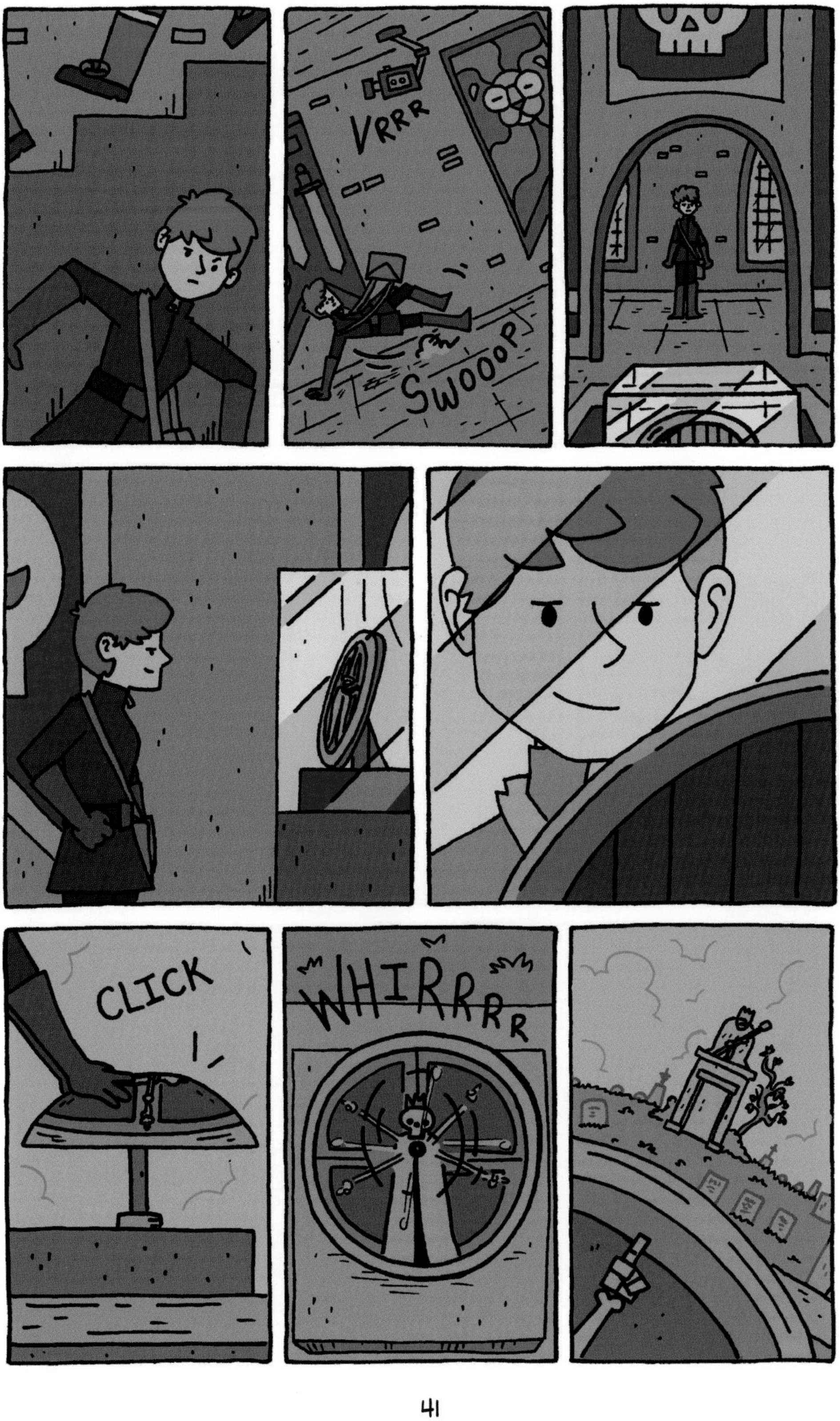
VRRR
SWOOOP
CLICK
WHIRRRR

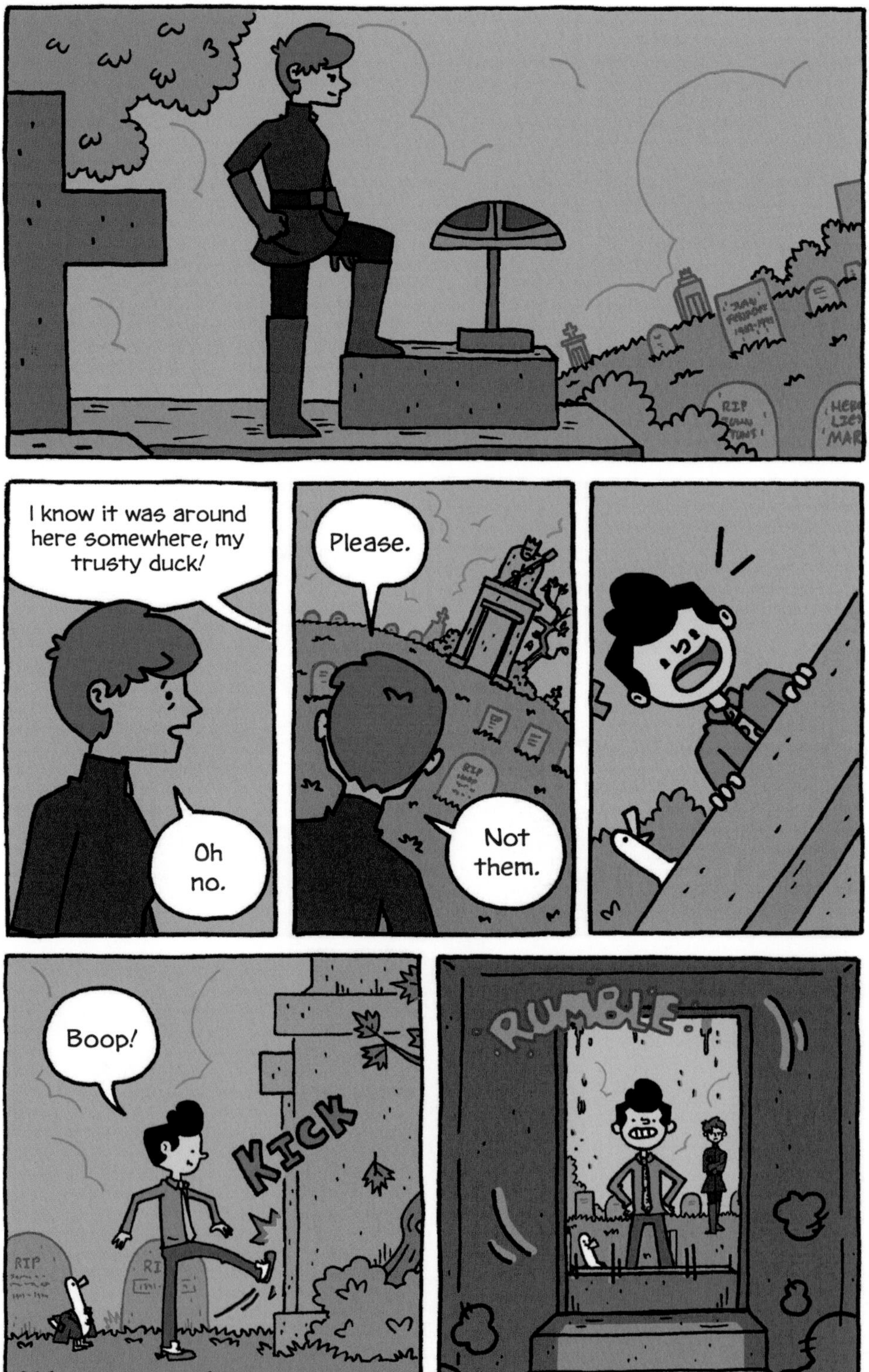
I know it was around here somewhere, my trusty duck!
Oh no.
Please.
Not them.
Boop!
KICK
RUMBLE

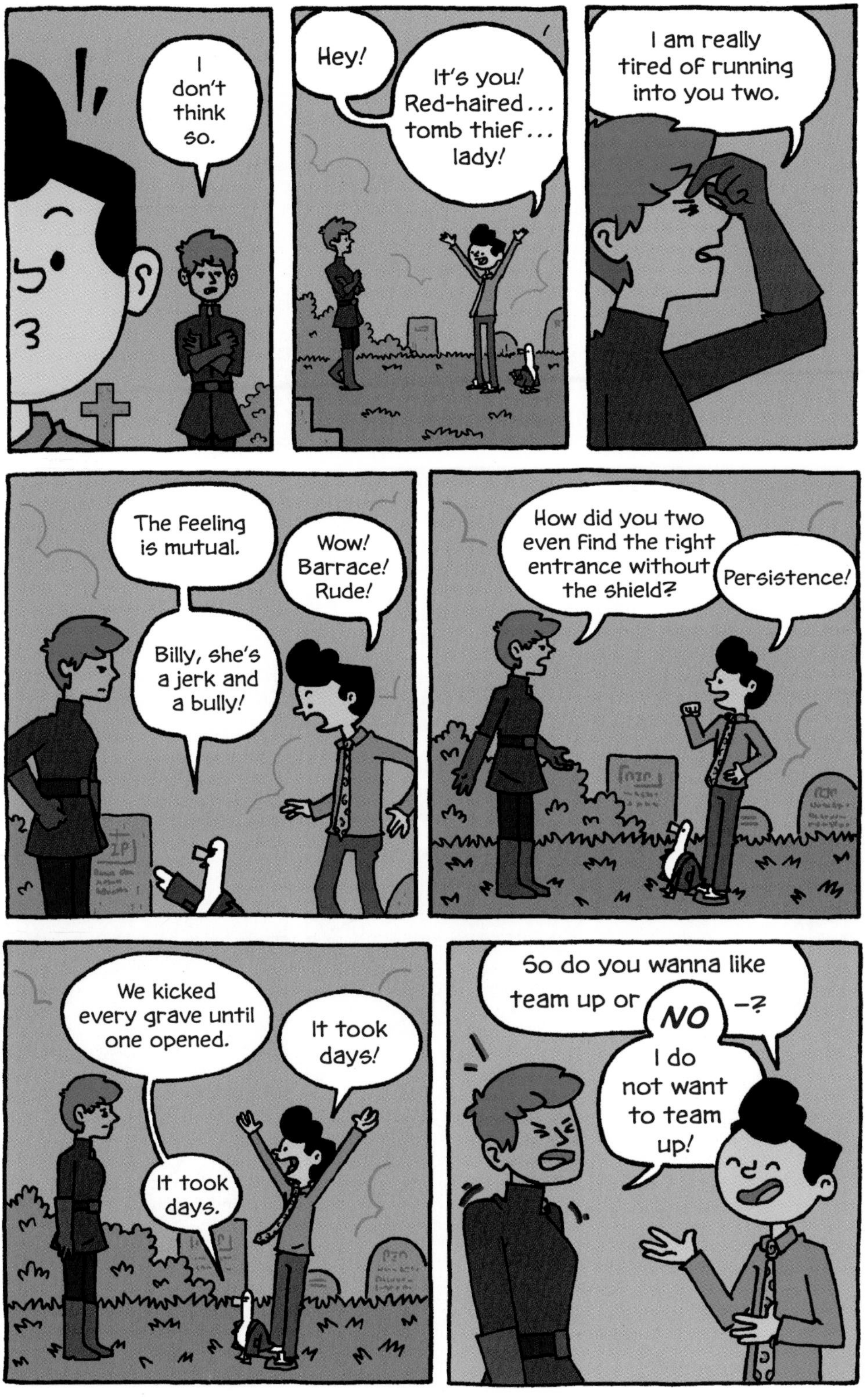
I don't think so.
Hey!
It's you! Red-haired... tomb thief... lady!
I am really tired of running into you two.
The feeling is mutual.
Wow! Barrace! Rude!
Billy, she's a jerk and a bully!
How did you two even find the right entrance without the shield?
Persistence!
We kicked every grave until one opened.
It took days!
It took days.
So do you wanna like team up or —?
NO
I do not want to team up!

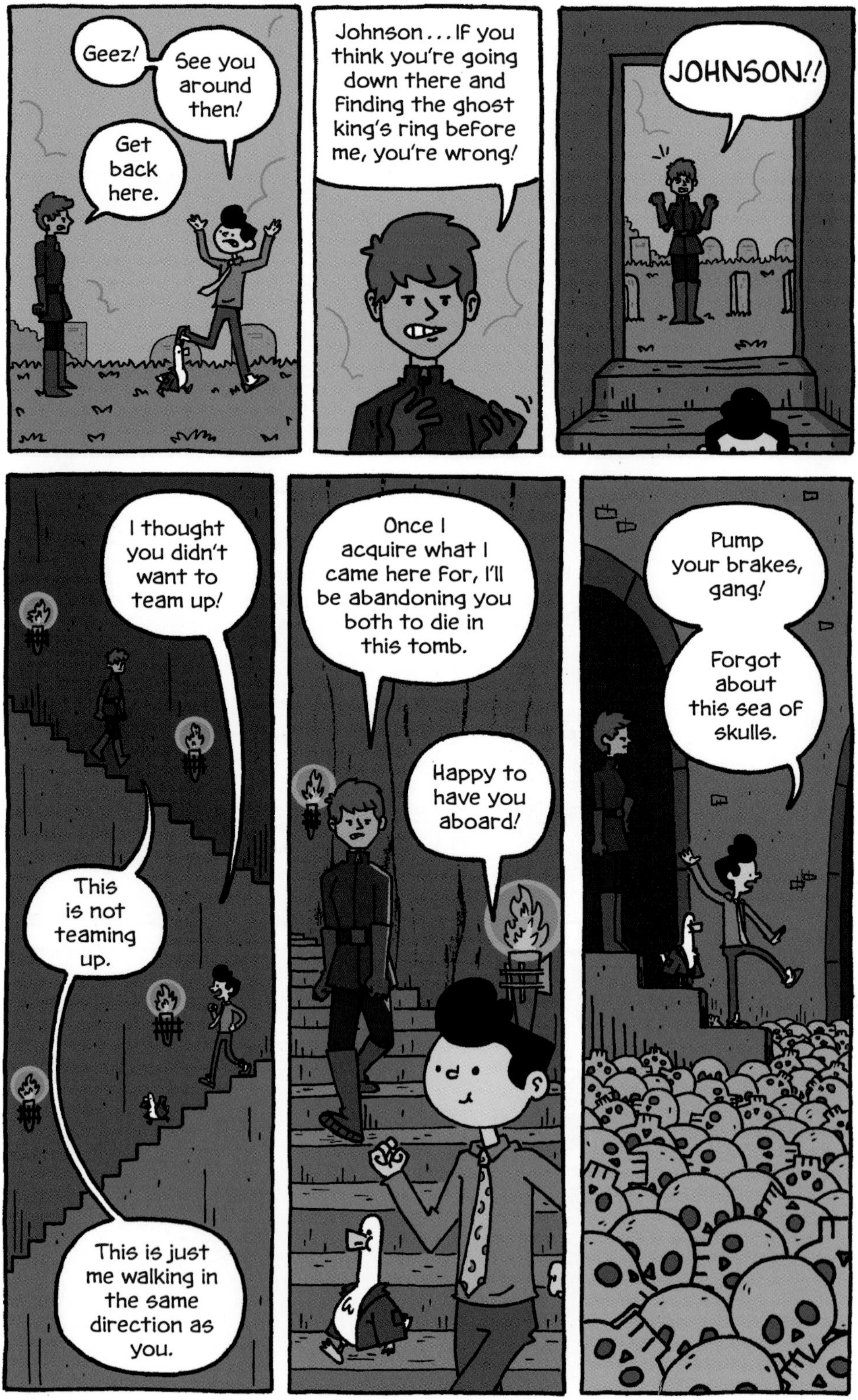
Geez!
See you around then!
Get back here.
Johnson... If you think you're going down there and finding the ghost king's ring before me, you're wrong!
JOHNSON!!
I thought you didn't want to team up!
This is not teaming up.
This is just me walking in the same direction as you.
Once I acquire what I came here for, I'll be abandoning you both to die in this tomb.
Happy to have you aboard!
Pump your brakes, gang!
Forgot about this sea of skulls.

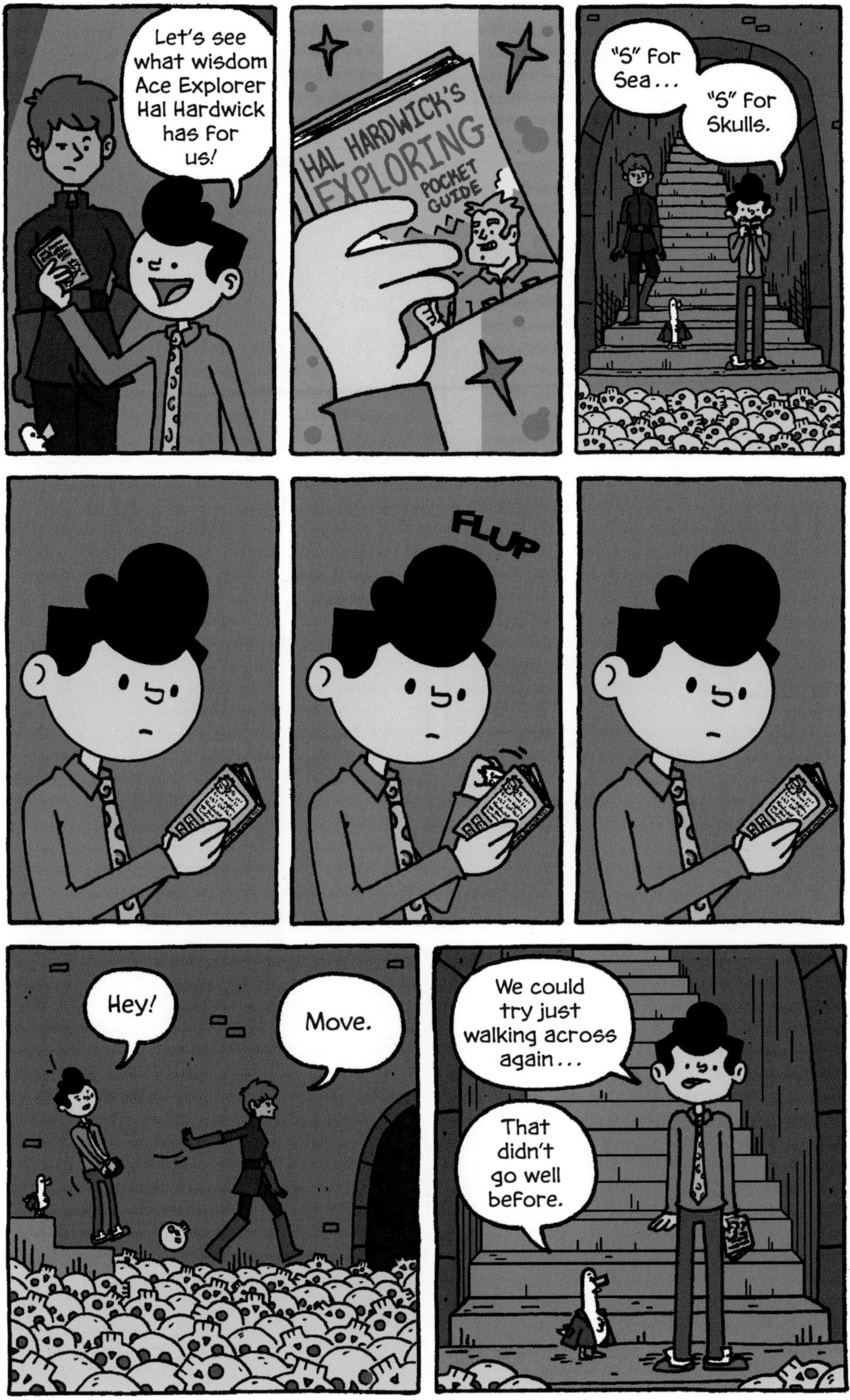

Let's see what wisdom Ace Explorer Hal Hardwick has for us!
HAL HARDWICK'S EXPLORING POCKET GUIDE
"S" for Sea...
"S" for Skulls.
FLUP
Hey!
Move.
We could try just walking across again...
That didn't go well before.

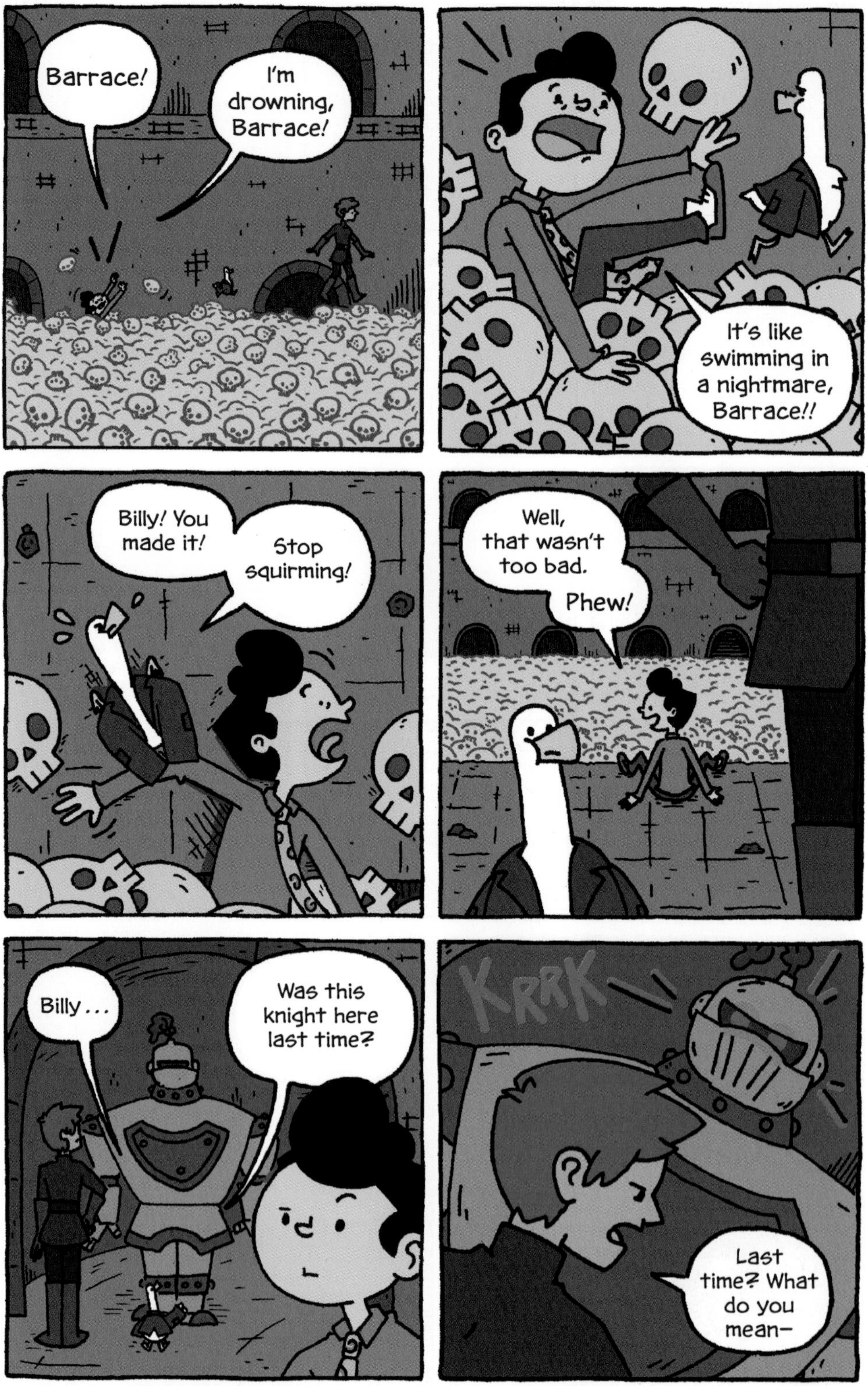
Barrace!
I'm drowning, Barrace!
It's like swimming in a nightmare, Barrace!!
Billy! You made it!
Stop squirming!
Well, that wasn't too bad.
Phew!
Billy...
Was this knight here last time?
KRRK
Last time? What do you mean—

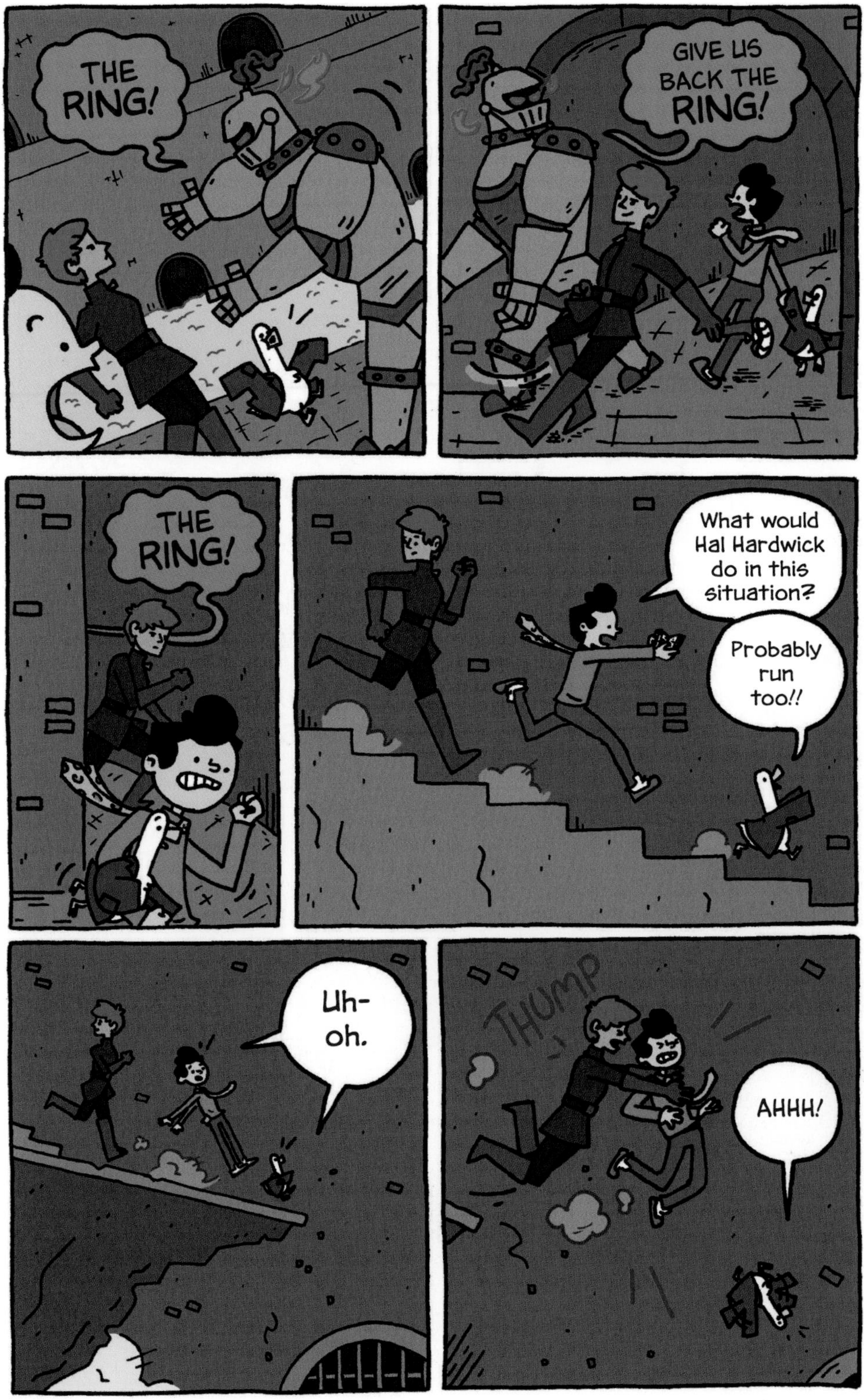
THE RING!
GIVE US BACK THE RING!
THE RING!
What would Hal Hardwick do in this situation?
Probably run too!!
Uh-oh.
THUMP
AHHH!

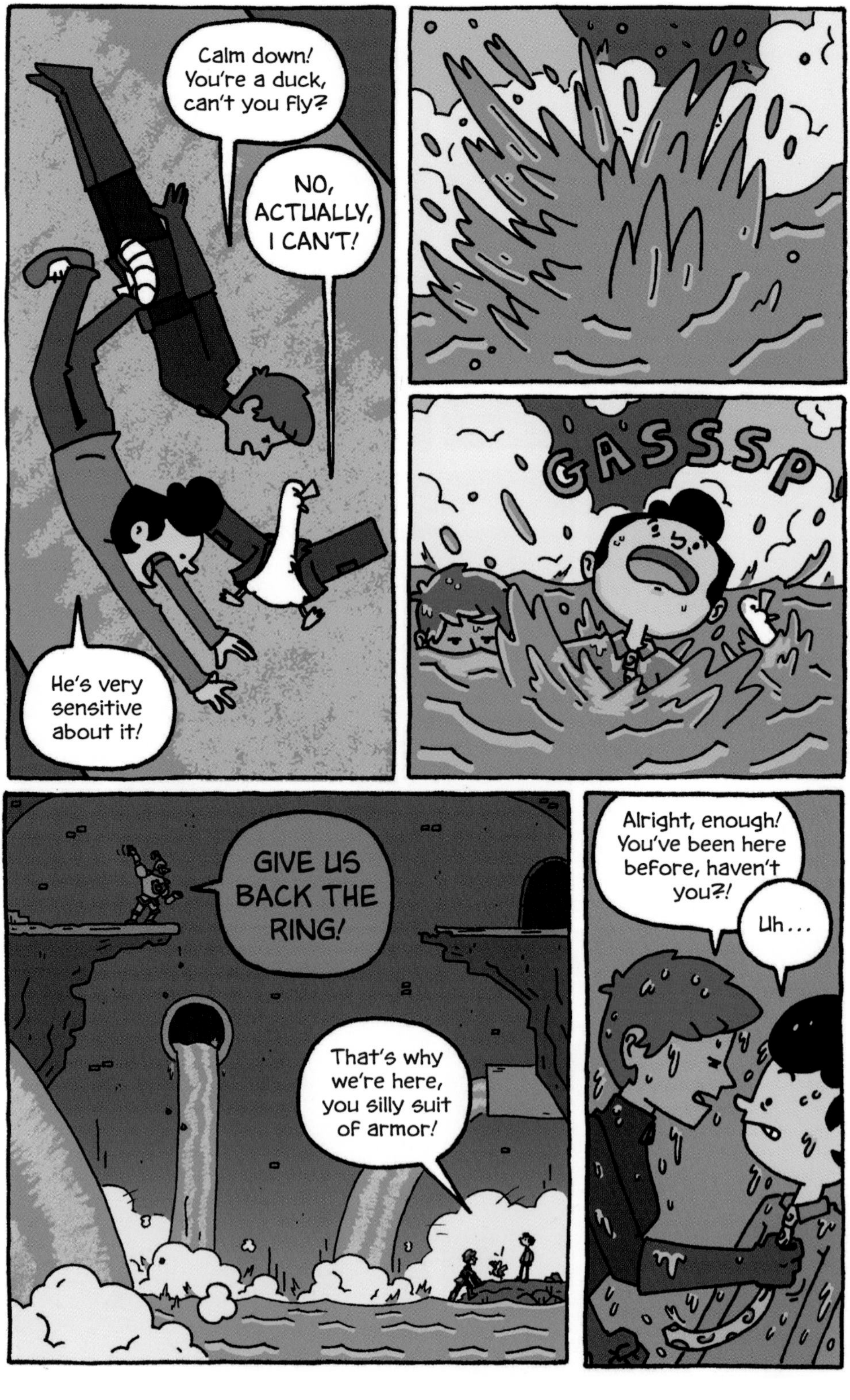

Calm down! You're a duck, can't you fly?
NO, ACTUALLY, I CAN'T!
He's very sensitive about it!
GASSSP
GIVE US BACK THE RING!
That's why we're here, you silly suit of armor!
Alright, enough! You've been here before, haven't you?!
Uh...

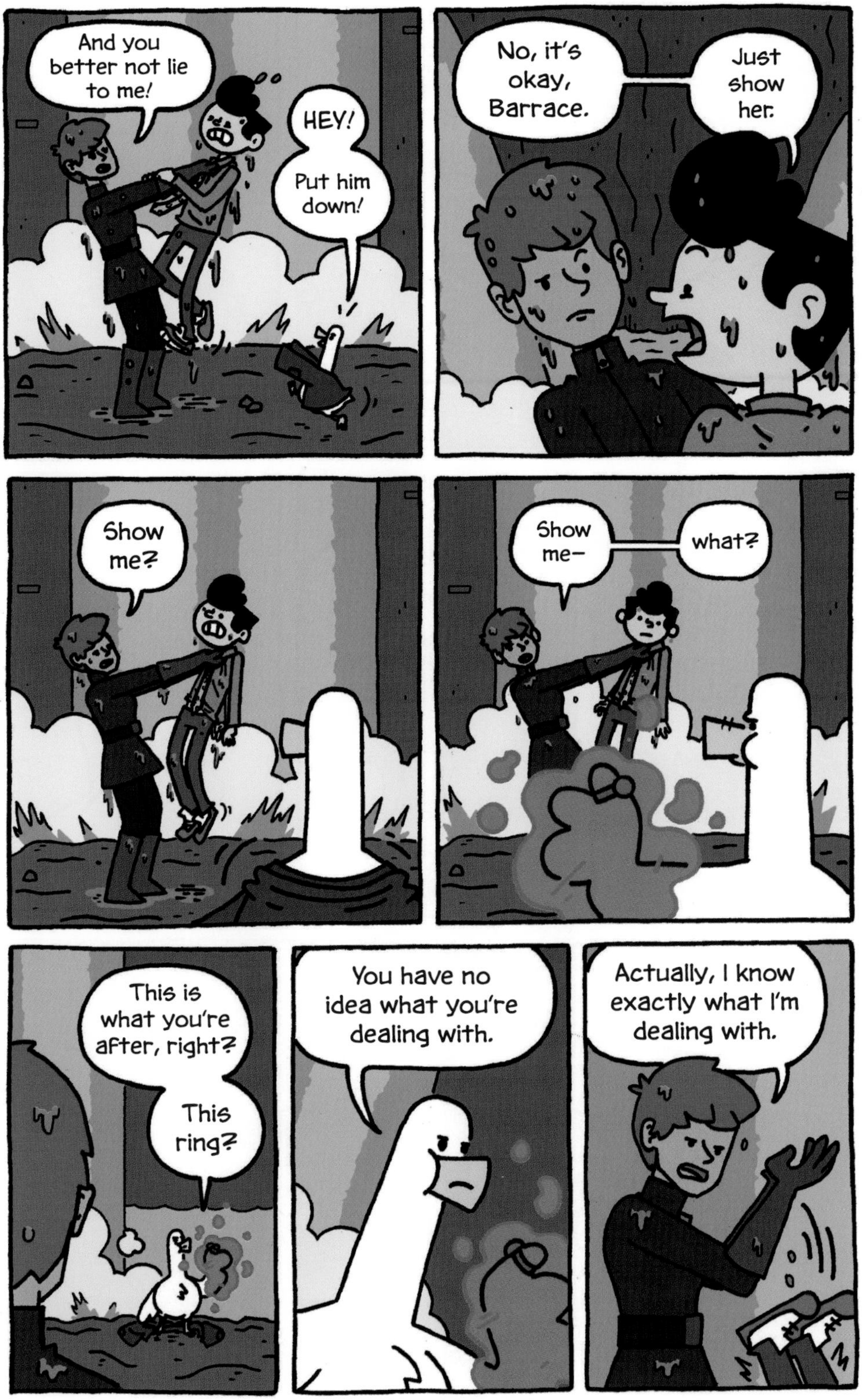
And you better not lie to me!
HEY!
Put him down!
No, it's okay, Barrace.
Just show her.
Show me?
Show me—
what?
This is what you're after, right?
This ring?
You have no idea what you're dealing with.
Actually, I know exactly what I'm dealing with.

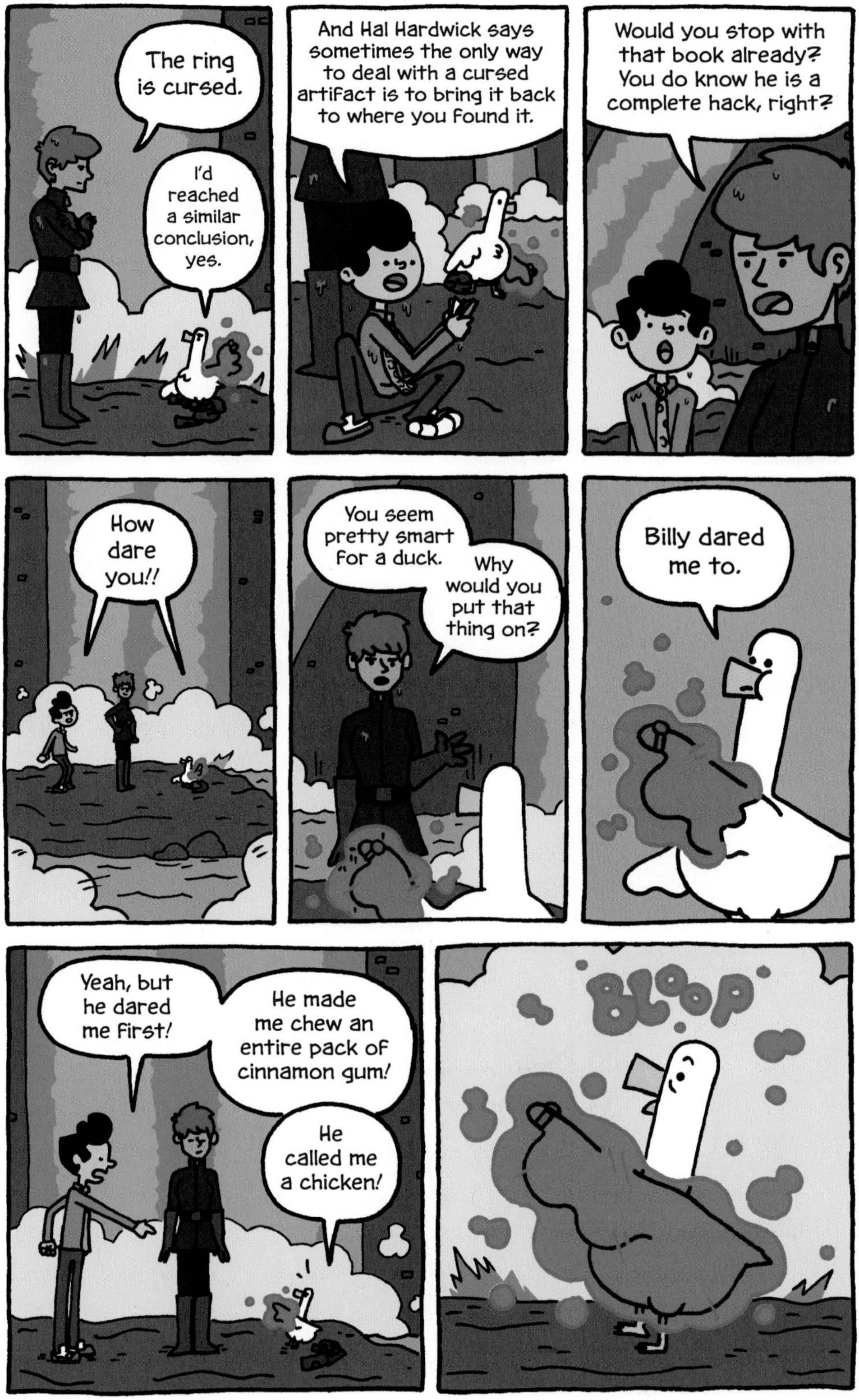
The ring is cursed.
I'd reached a similar conclusion, yes.
And Hal Hardwick says sometimes the only way to deal with a cursed artifact is to bring it back to where you found it.
Would you stop with that book already? You do know he is a complete hack, right?
How dare you!!
You seem pretty smart for a duck.
Why would you put that thing on?
Billy dared me to.
Yeah, but he dared me first!
He made me chew an entire pack of cinnamon gum!
He called me a chicken!
BLOOP

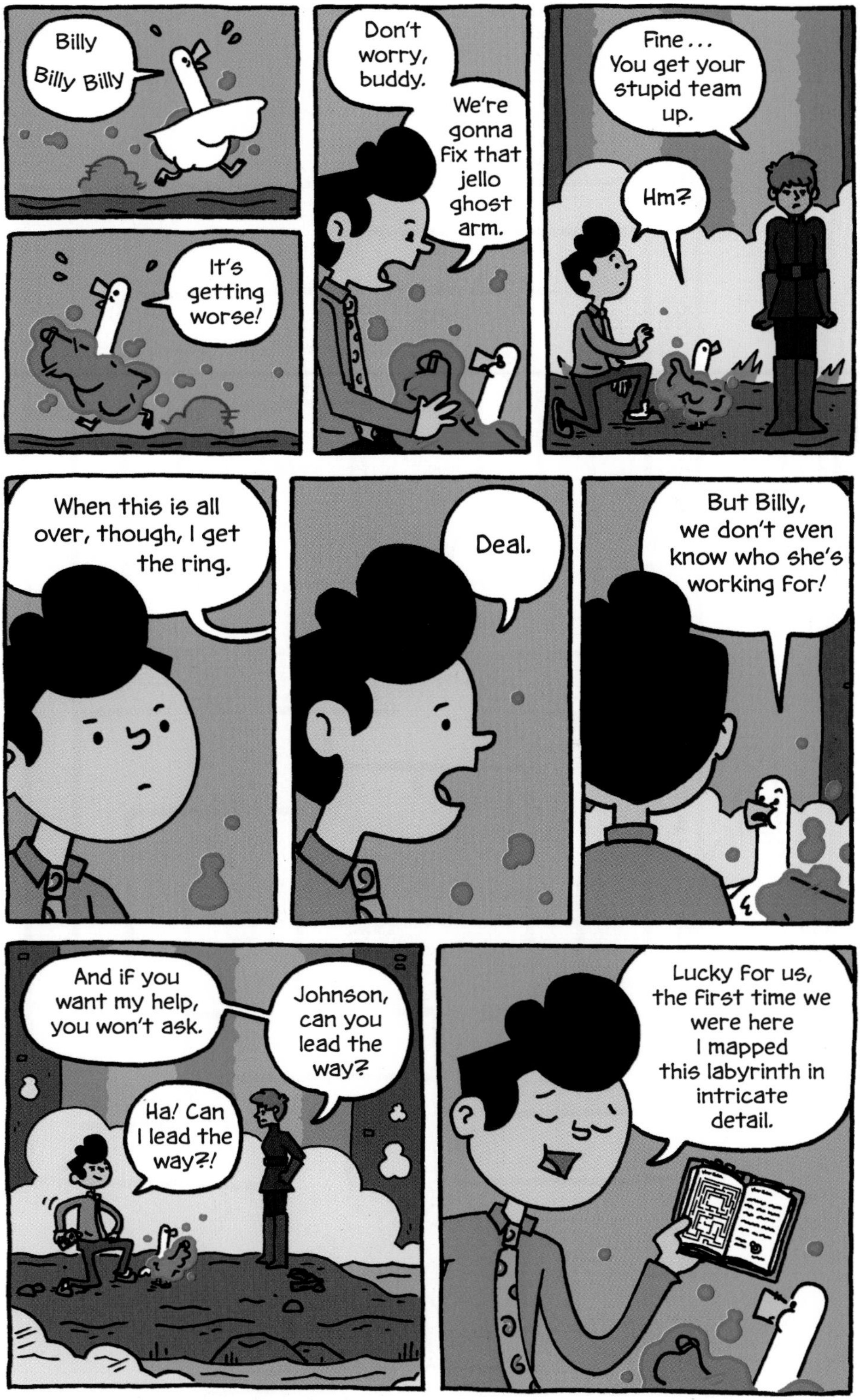
Billy
Billy Billy
It's getting worse!
Don't worry, buddy.
We're gonna fix that jello ghost arm.
Fine... You get your stupid team up.
Hm?
When this is all over, though, I get the ring.
Deal.
But Billy, we don't even know who she's working for!
And if you want my help, you won't ask.
Johnson, can you lead the way?
Ha! Can I lead the way?!
Lucky for us, the first time we were here I mapped this labyrinth in intricate detail.

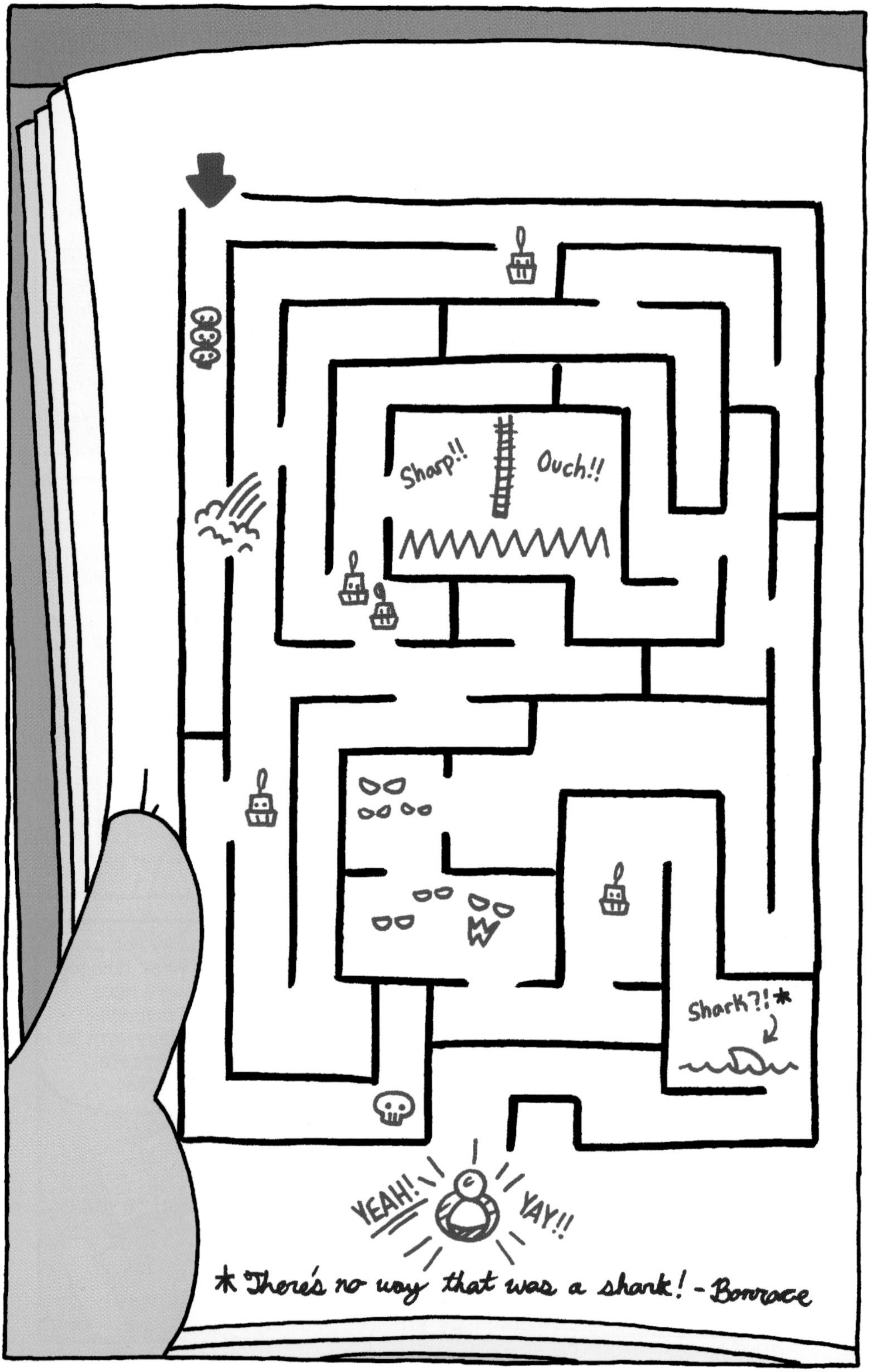

Sharp!!
Ouch!!
Shark?!*
YEAH!
YAY!!
* There's no way that was a shark! - Bonrace

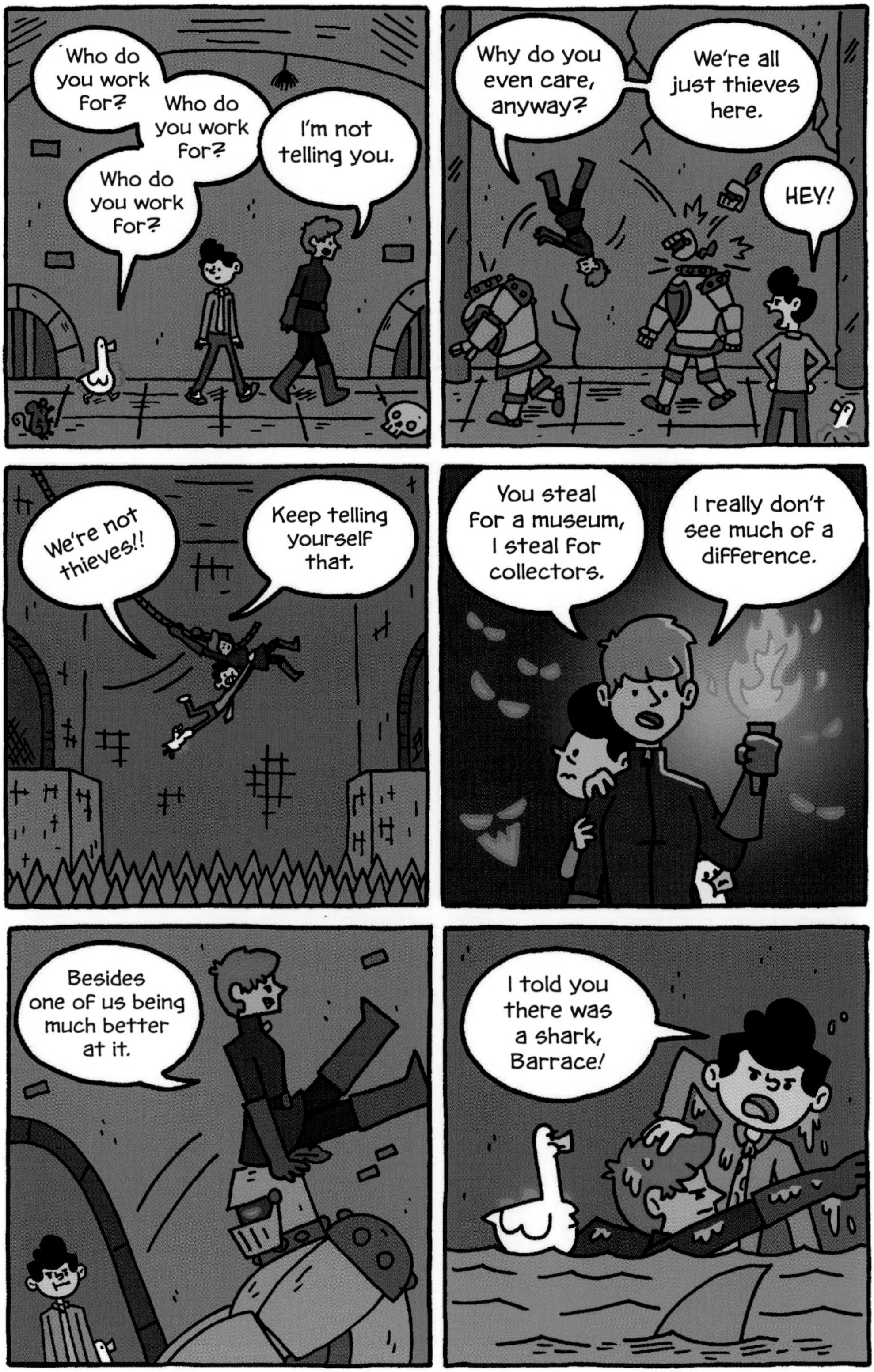
Who do you work for?
Who do you work for?
Who do you work for?
I'm not telling you.
Why do you even care, anyway?
We're all just thieves here.
HEY!
We're not thieves!!
Keep telling yourself that.
You steal for a museum, I steal for collectors.
I really don't see much of a difference.
Besides one of us being much better at it.
I told you there was a shark, Barrace!

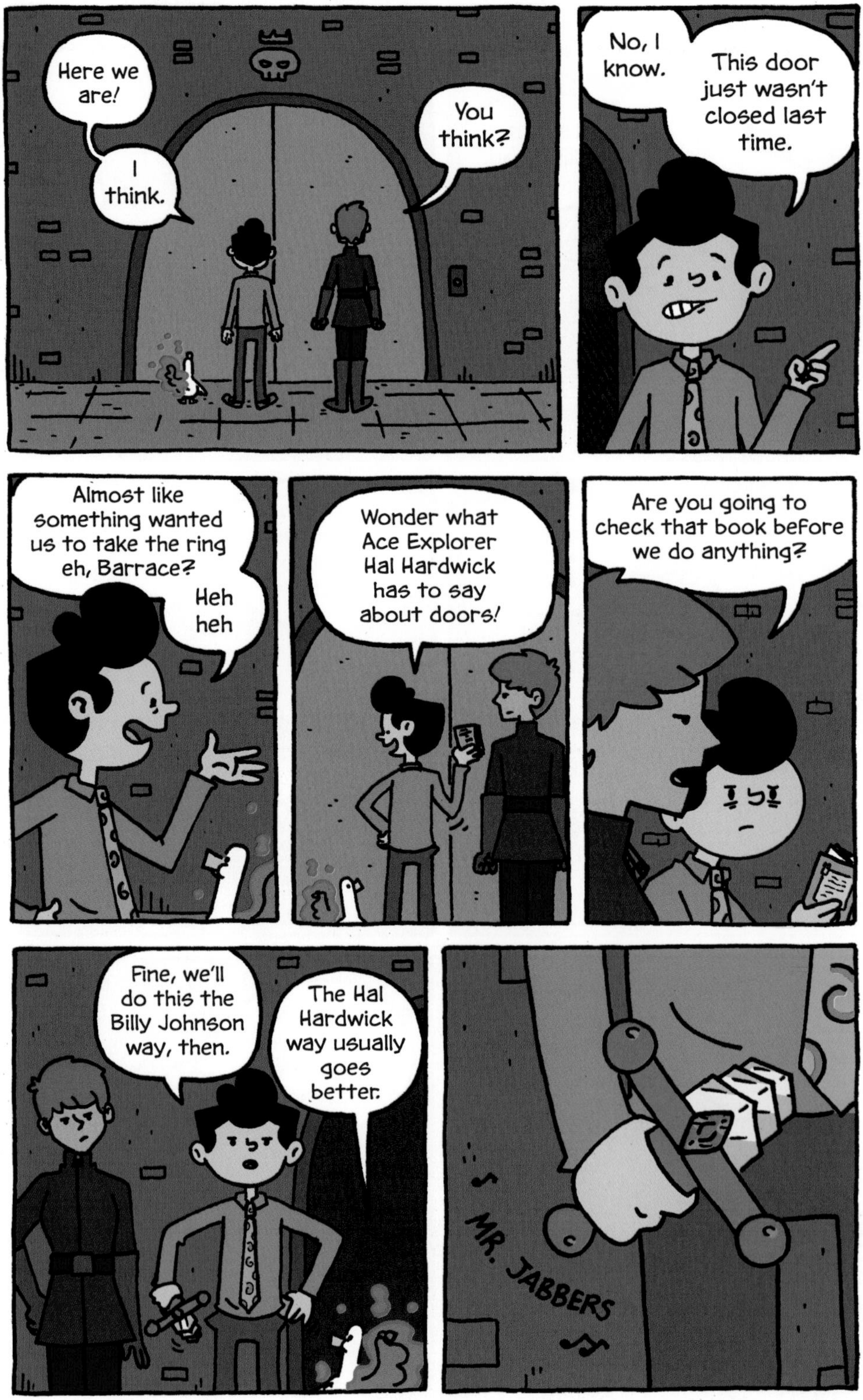
Here we are!
I think.
You think?
No, I know.
This door just wasn't closed last time.
Almost like something wanted us to take the ring eh, Barrace?
Heh heh
Wonder what Ace Explorer Hal Hardwick has to say about doors!
Are you going to check that book before we do anything?
Fine, we'll do this the Billy Johnson way, then.
The Hal Hardwick way usually goes better.
MR. JABBERS

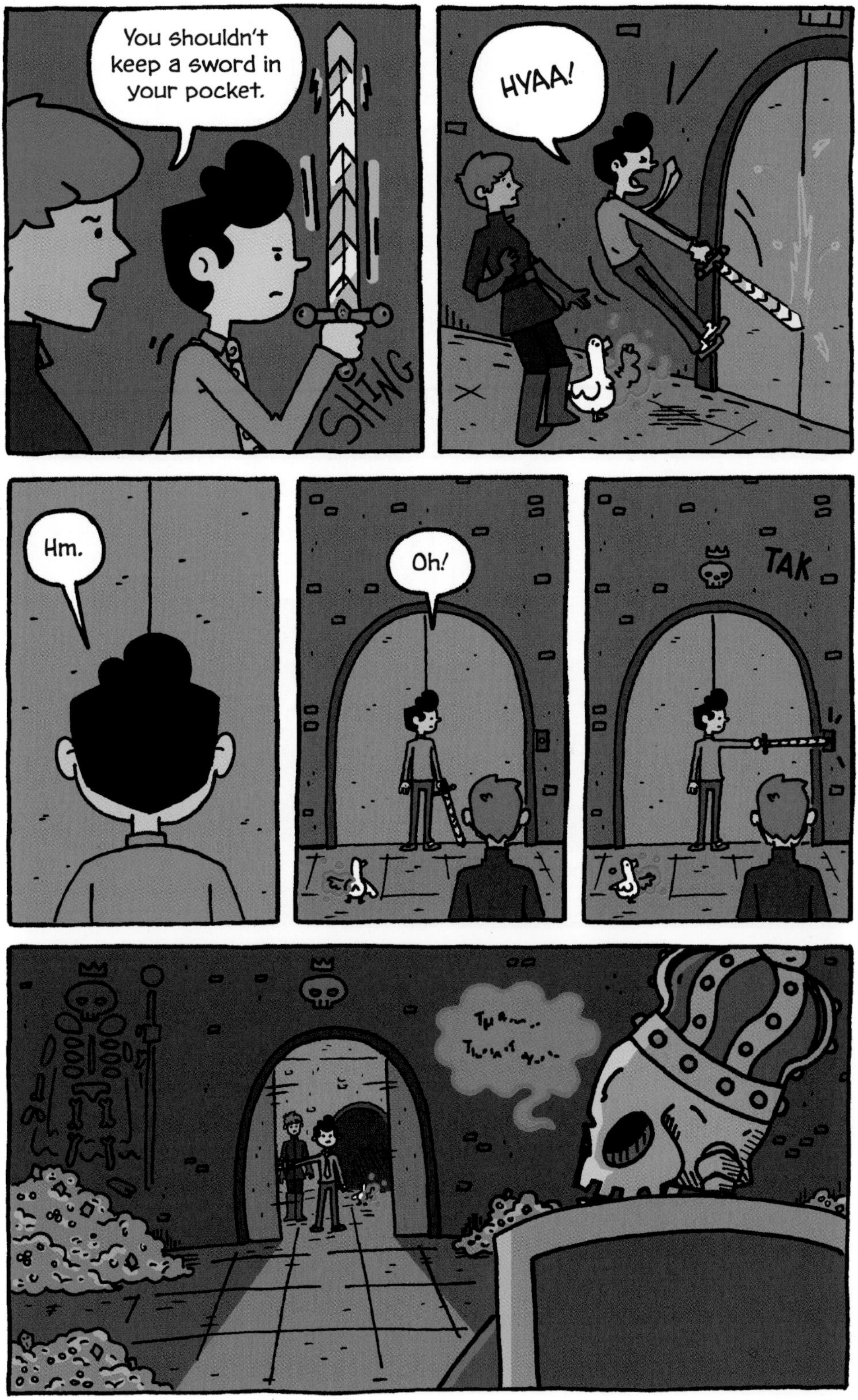
You shouldn't keep a sword in your pocket.
SHING
HYAA!
Hm.
Oh!
TAK

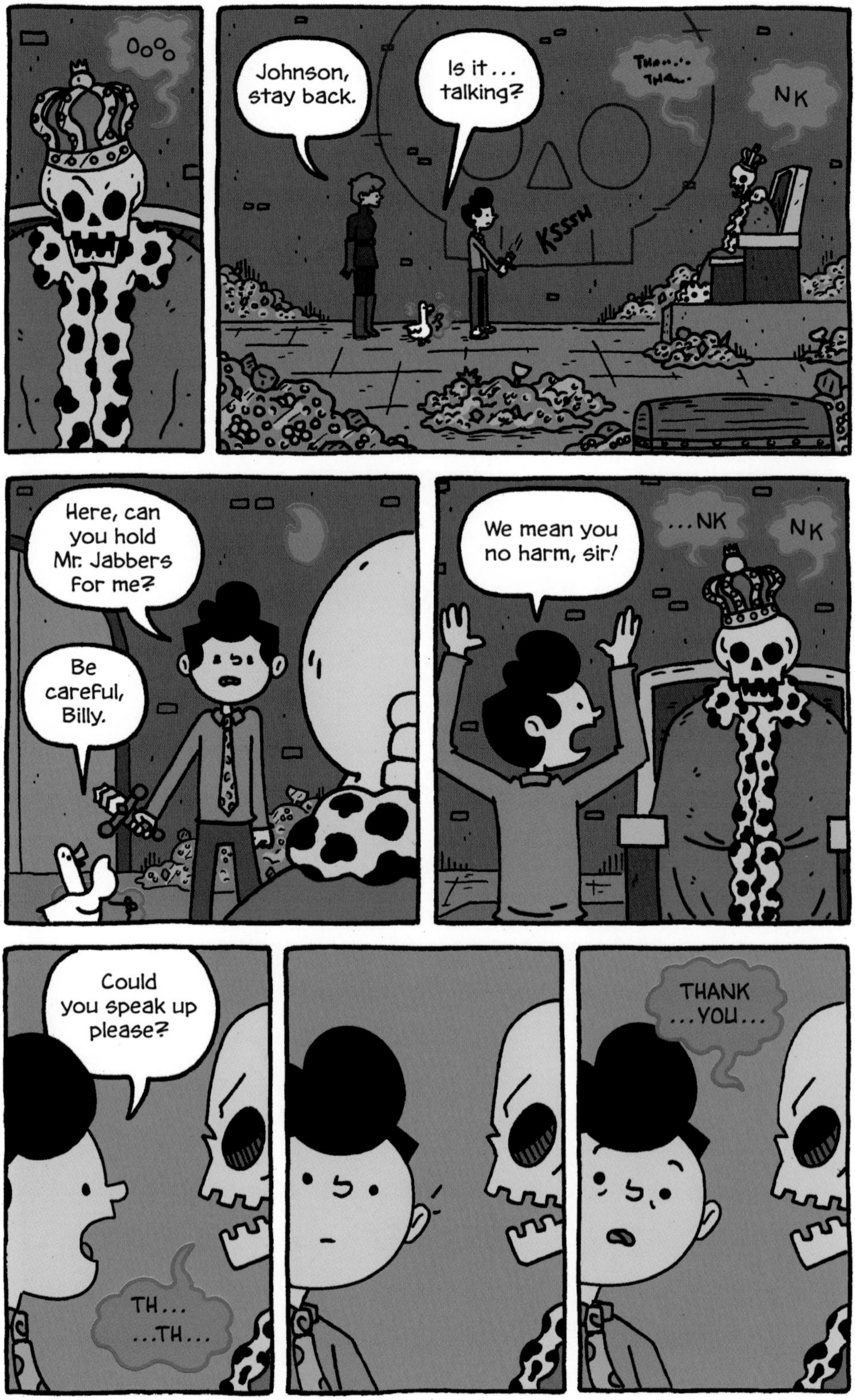
Oo°o
Johnson, stay back.
Is it... talking?
KSSSH
NK
Here, can you hold Mr. Jabbers for me?
Be careful, Billy.
We mean you no harm, sir!
...NK
NK
Could you speak up please?
TH... ...TH...
THANK ...YOU...

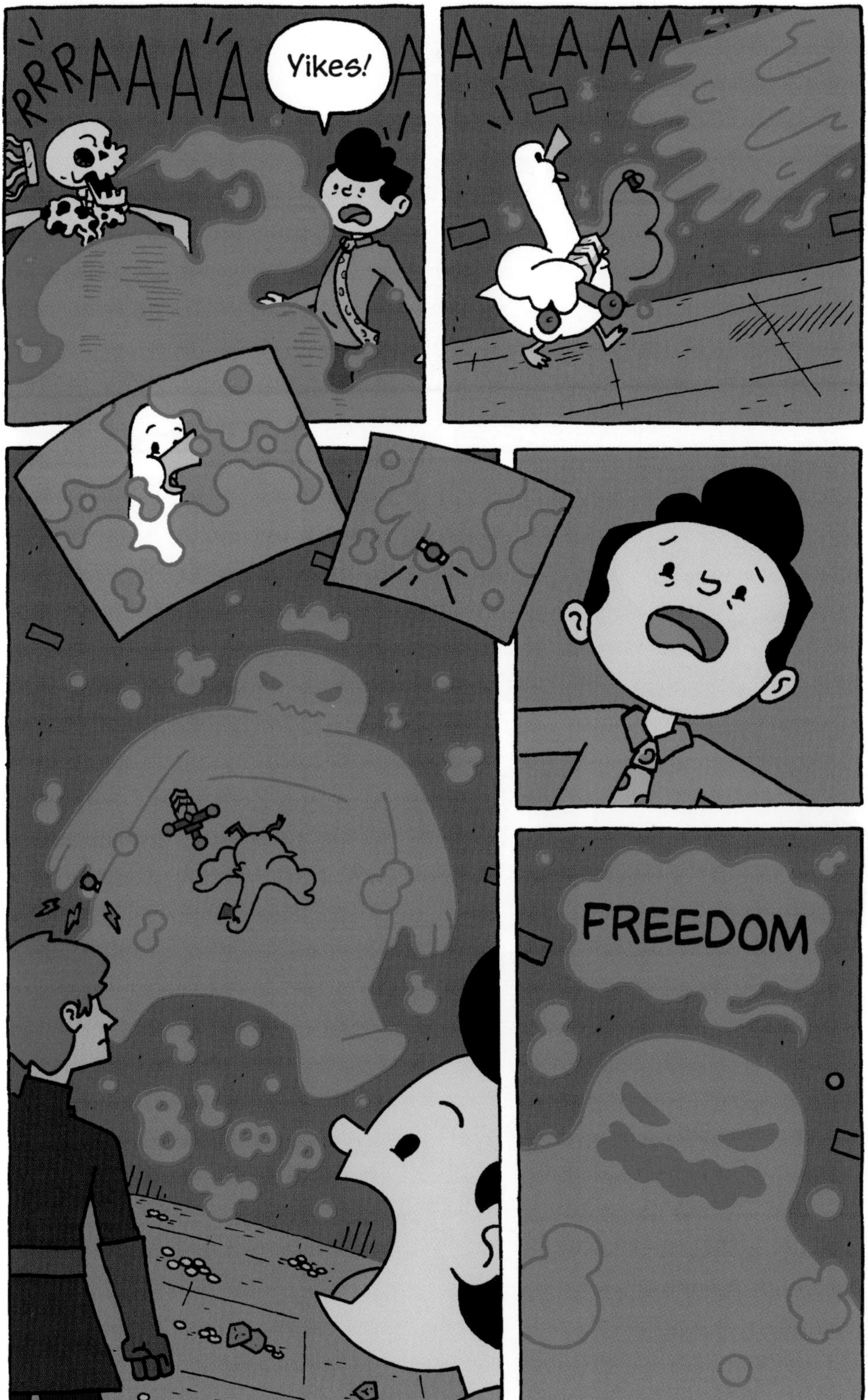
RRRAAAAAA
Yikes!
AAAAAA
BLOOP
FREEDOM

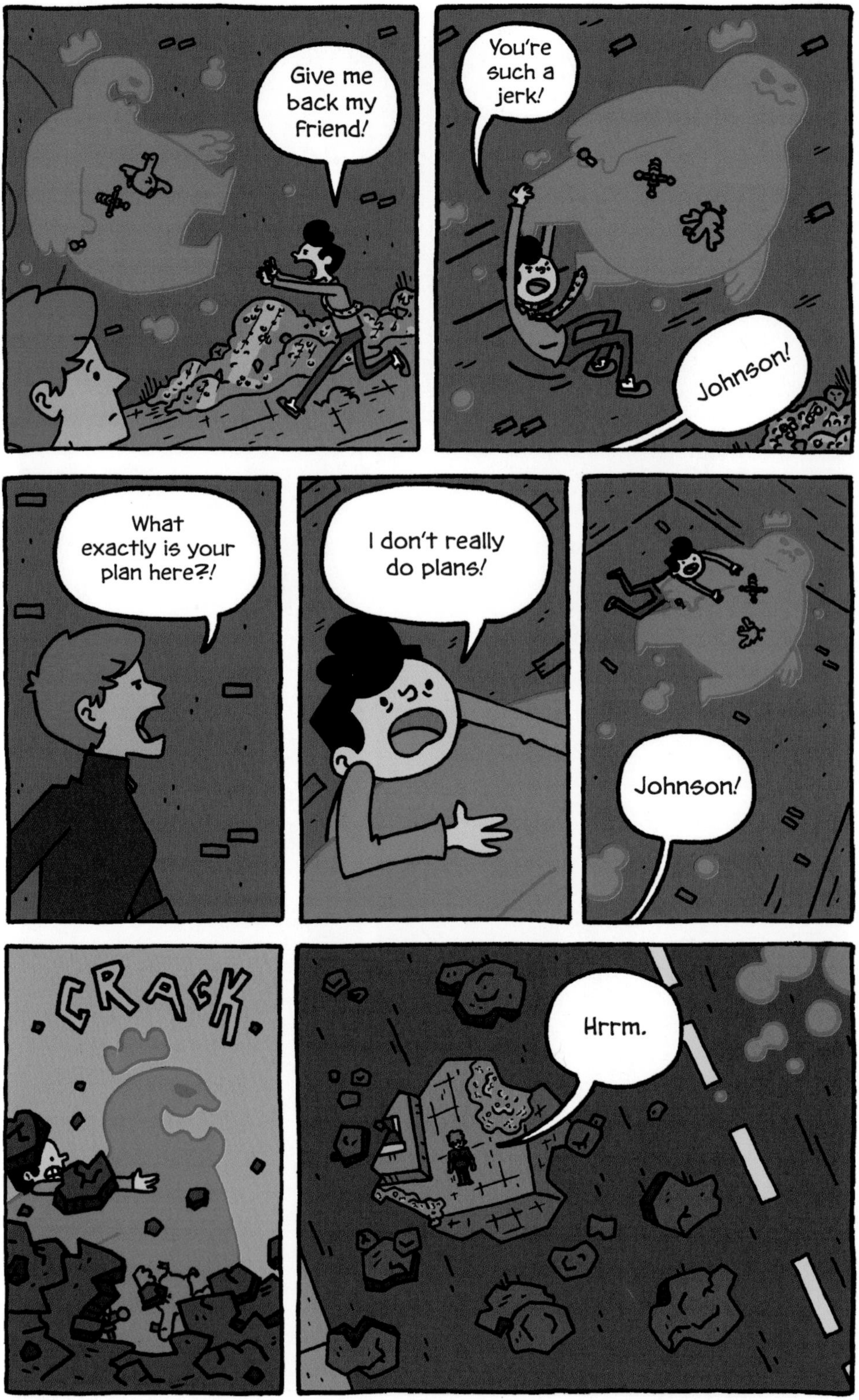
Give me back my friend!
You're such a jerk!
Johnson!
What exactly is your plan here?!
I don't really do plans!
Johnson!
CRACK
Hrrm.

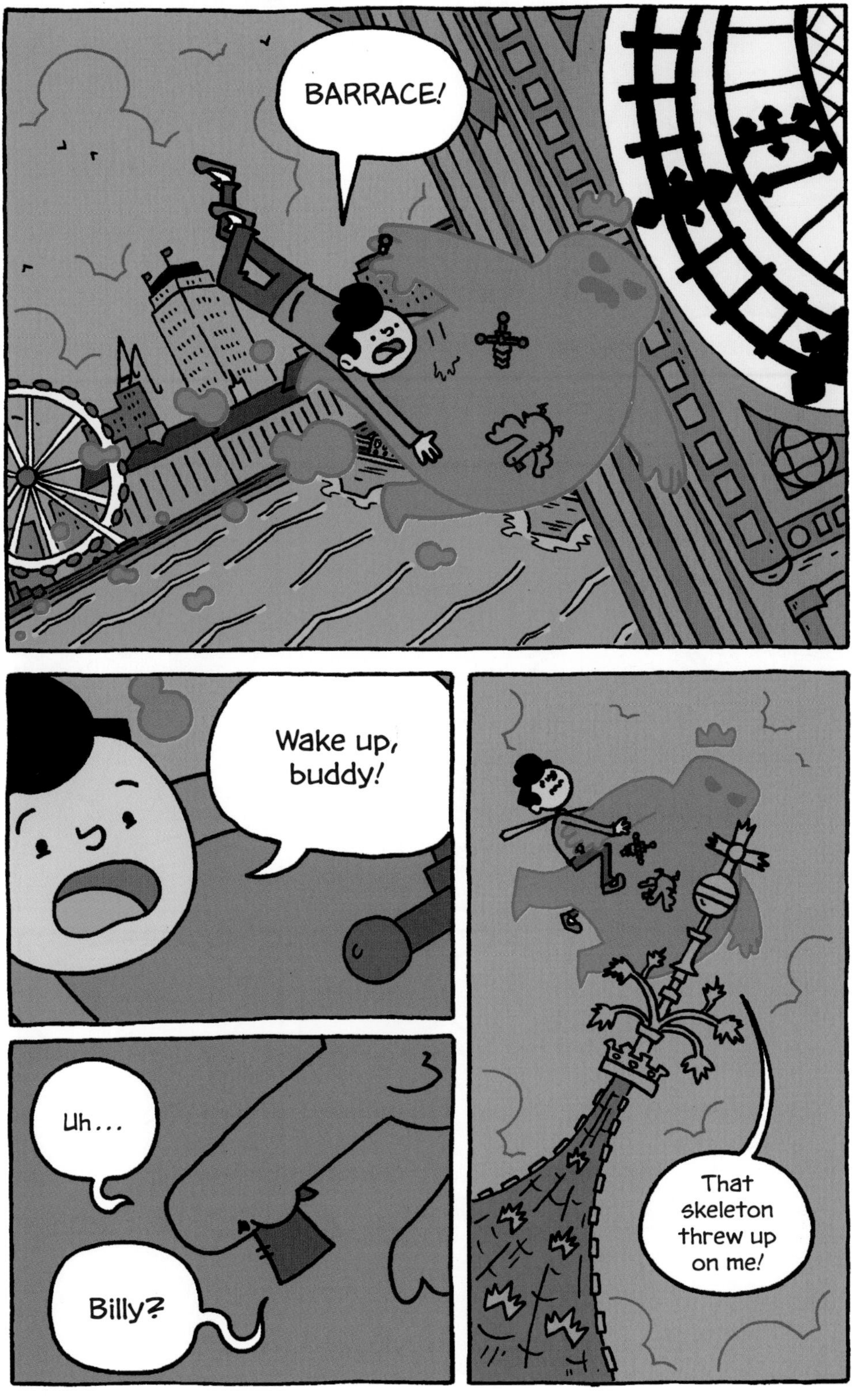
BARRACE!
Wake up, buddy!
Uh...
Billy?
That skeleton threw up on me!

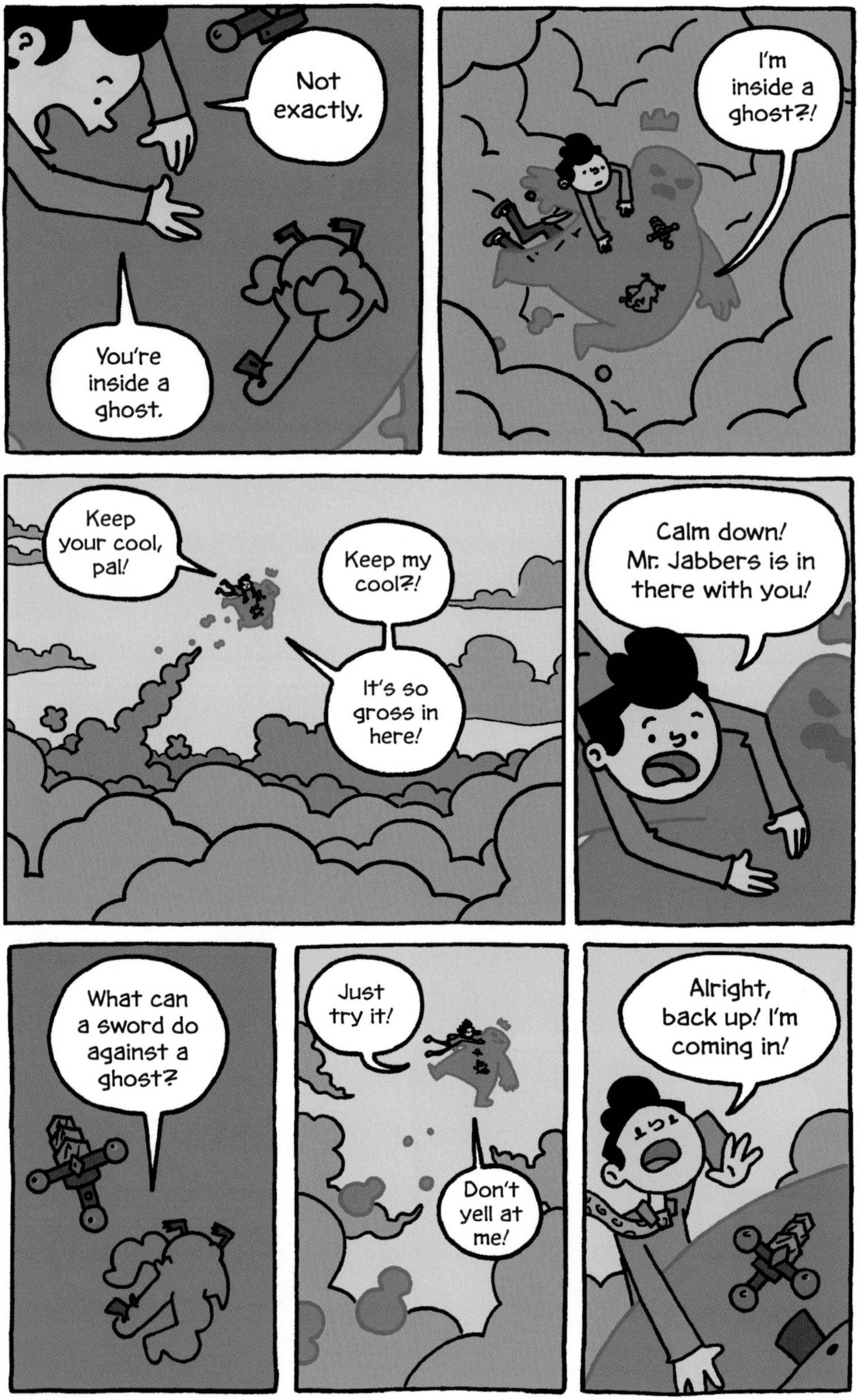
Not exactly.
You're inside a ghost.
I'm inside a ghost?!
Keep your cool, pal!
Keep my cool?!
It's so gross in here!
Calm down! Mr. Jabbers is in there with you!
What can a sword do against a ghost?
Just try it!
Don't yell at me!
Alright, back up! I'm coming in!

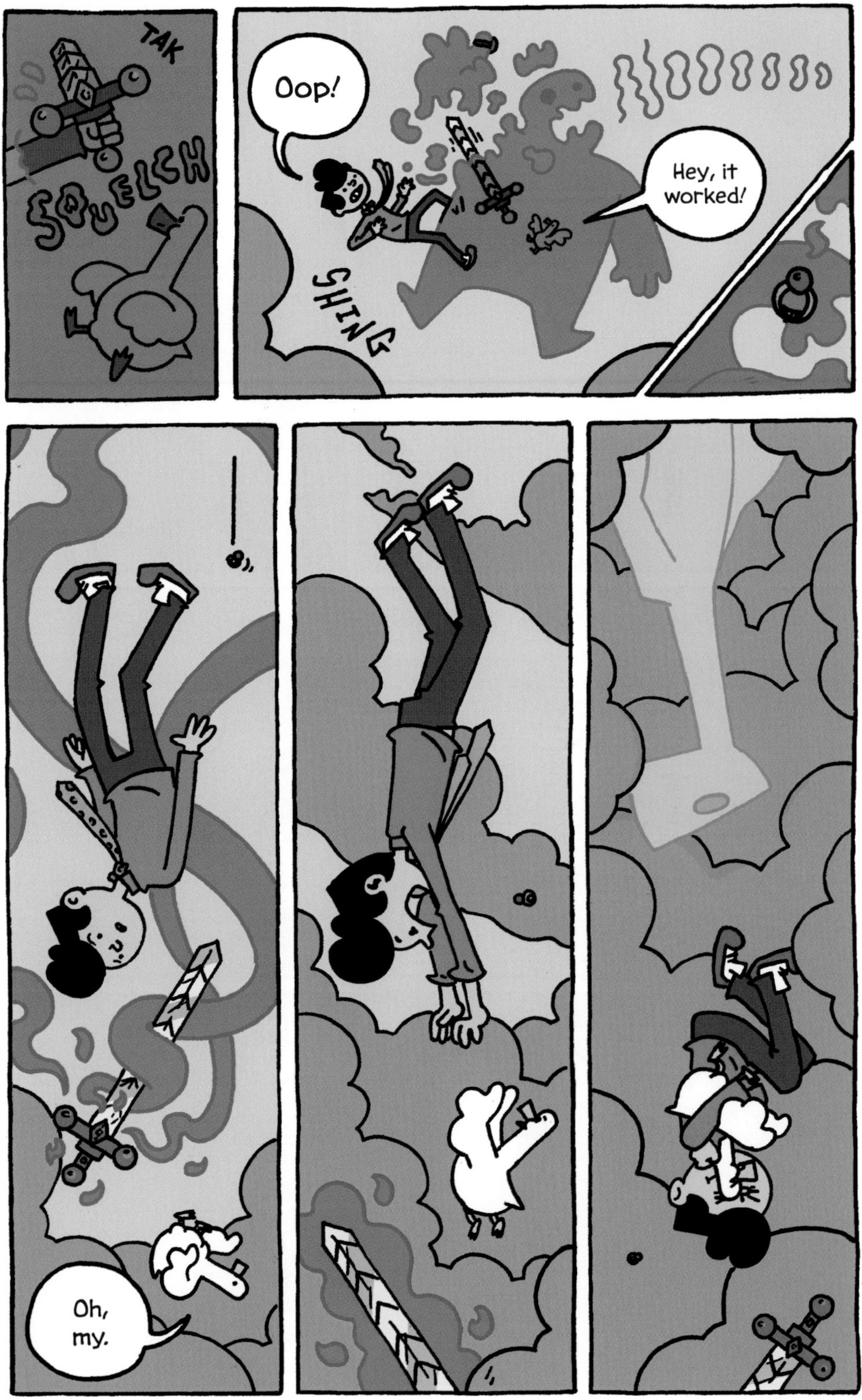
TAK
SQUELCH
Oop!
NOOOOOOO
Hey, it worked!
SHING
Oh, my.

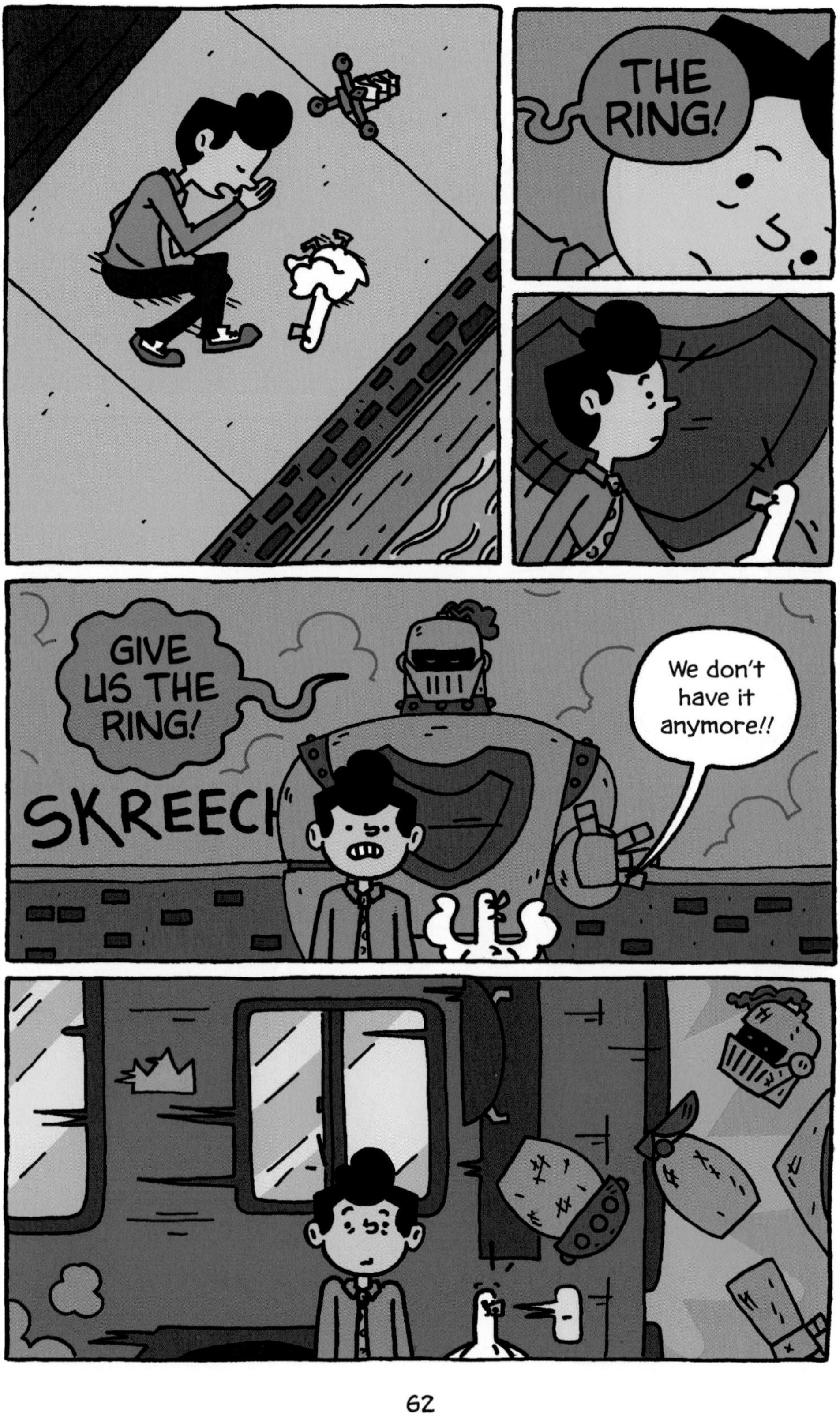
THE RING!
GIVE US THE RING!
SKREECH
We don't have it anymore!!

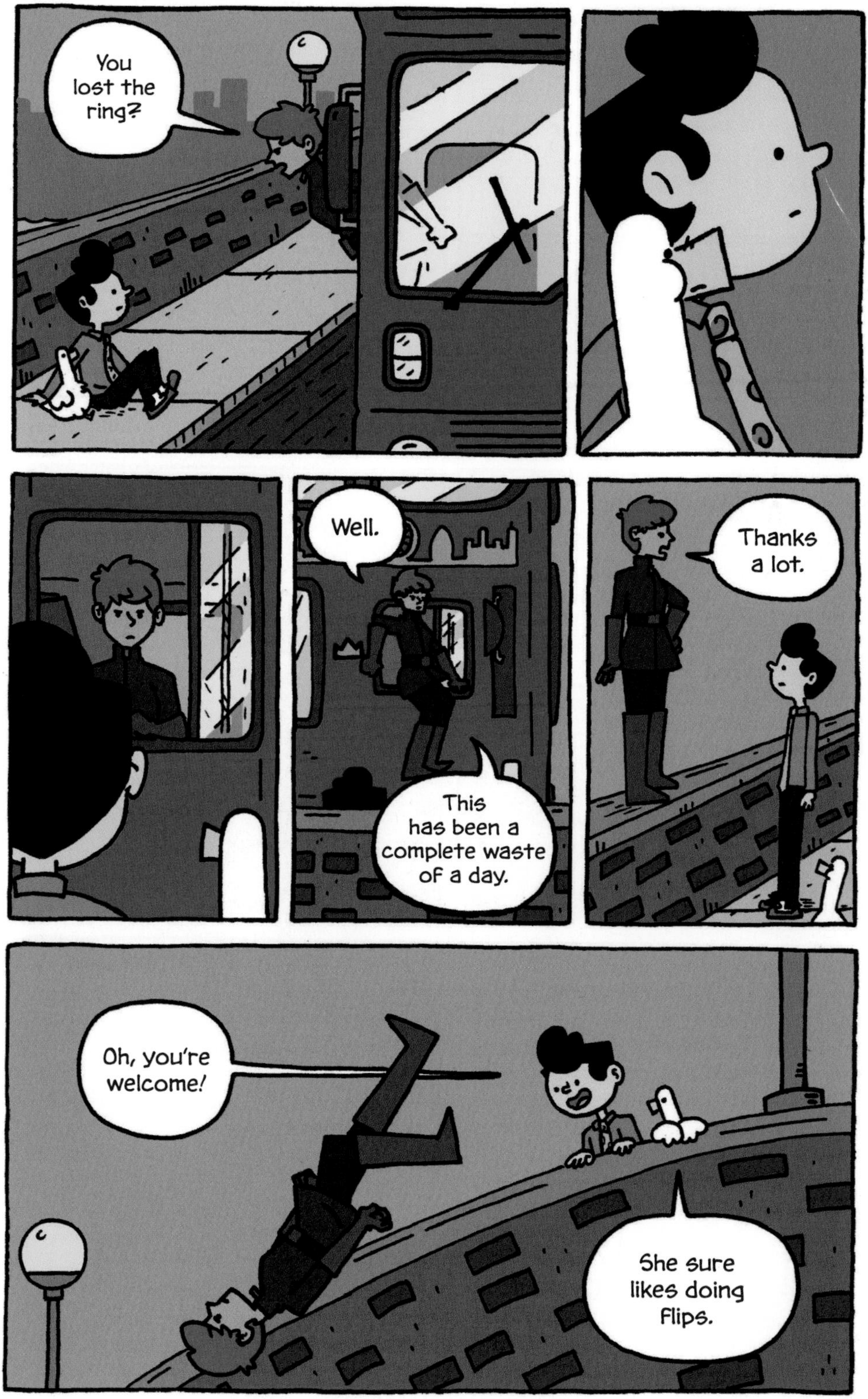

You lost the ring?
Well.
This has been a complete waste of a day.
Thanks a lot.
Oh, you're welcome!
She sure likes doing flips.

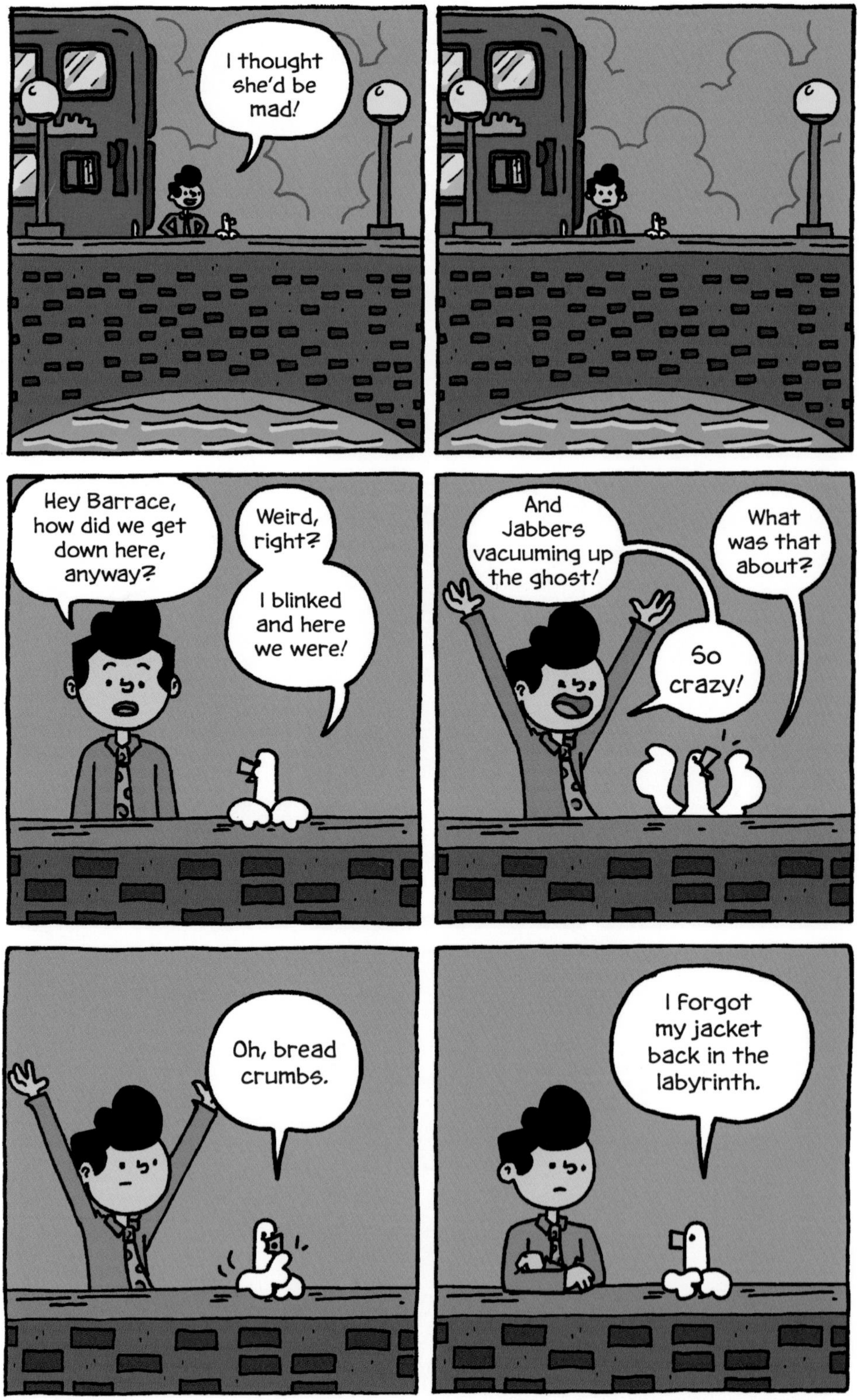
I thought she'd be mad!
Hey Barrace, how did we get down here, anyway?
Weird, right?
I blinked and here we were!
And Jabbers vacuuming up the ghost!
So crazy!
What was that about?
Oh, bread crumbs.
I forgot my jacket back in the labyrinth.

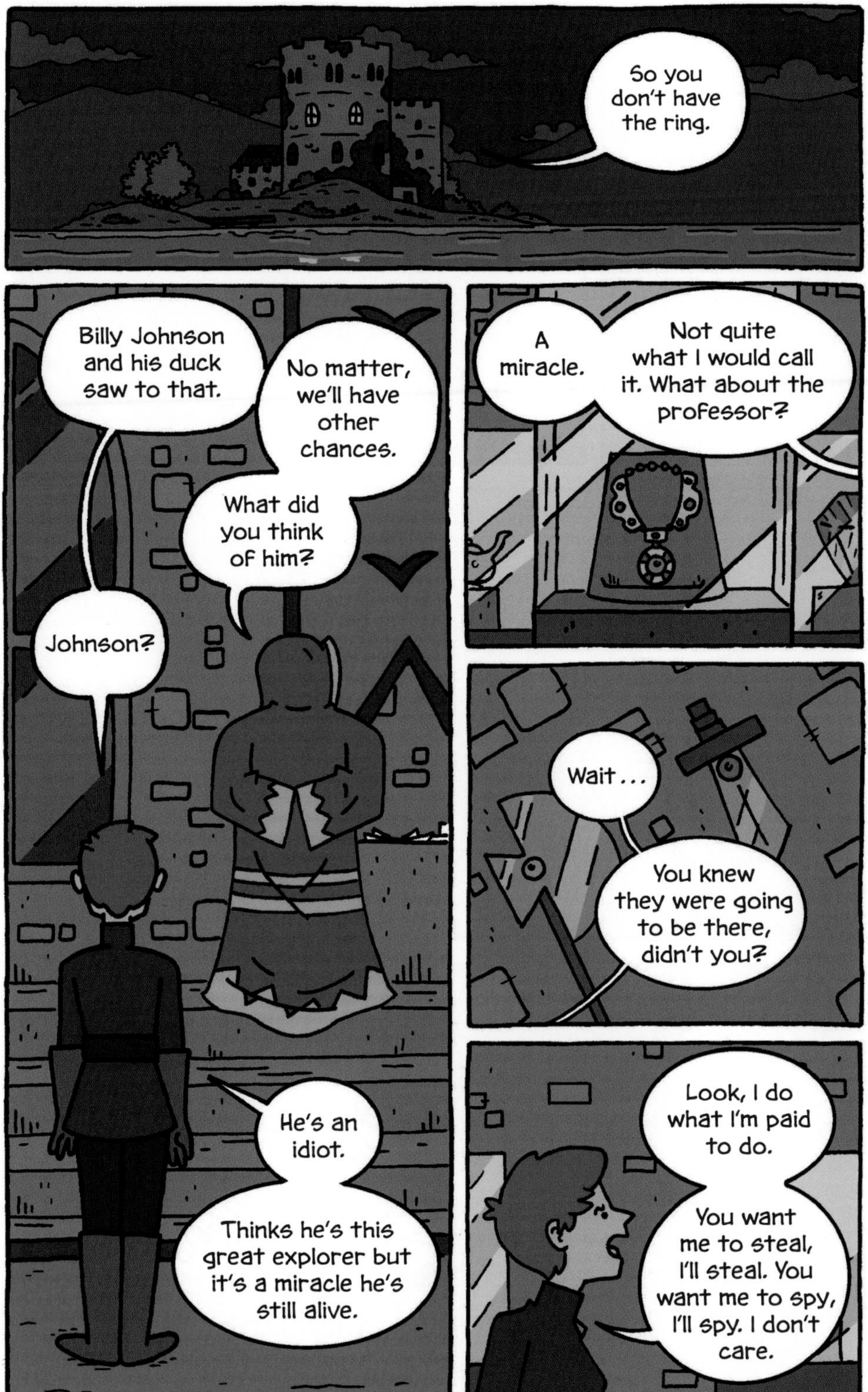
So you don't have the ring.
Billy Johnson and his duck saw to that.
No matter, we'll have other chances.
What did you think of him?
Johnson?
He's an idiot.
Thinks he's this great explorer but it's a miracle he's still alive.
A miracle.
Not quite what I would call it. What about the professor?
Wait...
You knew they were going to be there, didn't you?
Look, I do what I'm paid to do.
You want me to steal, I'll steal. You want me to spy, I'll spy. I don't care.

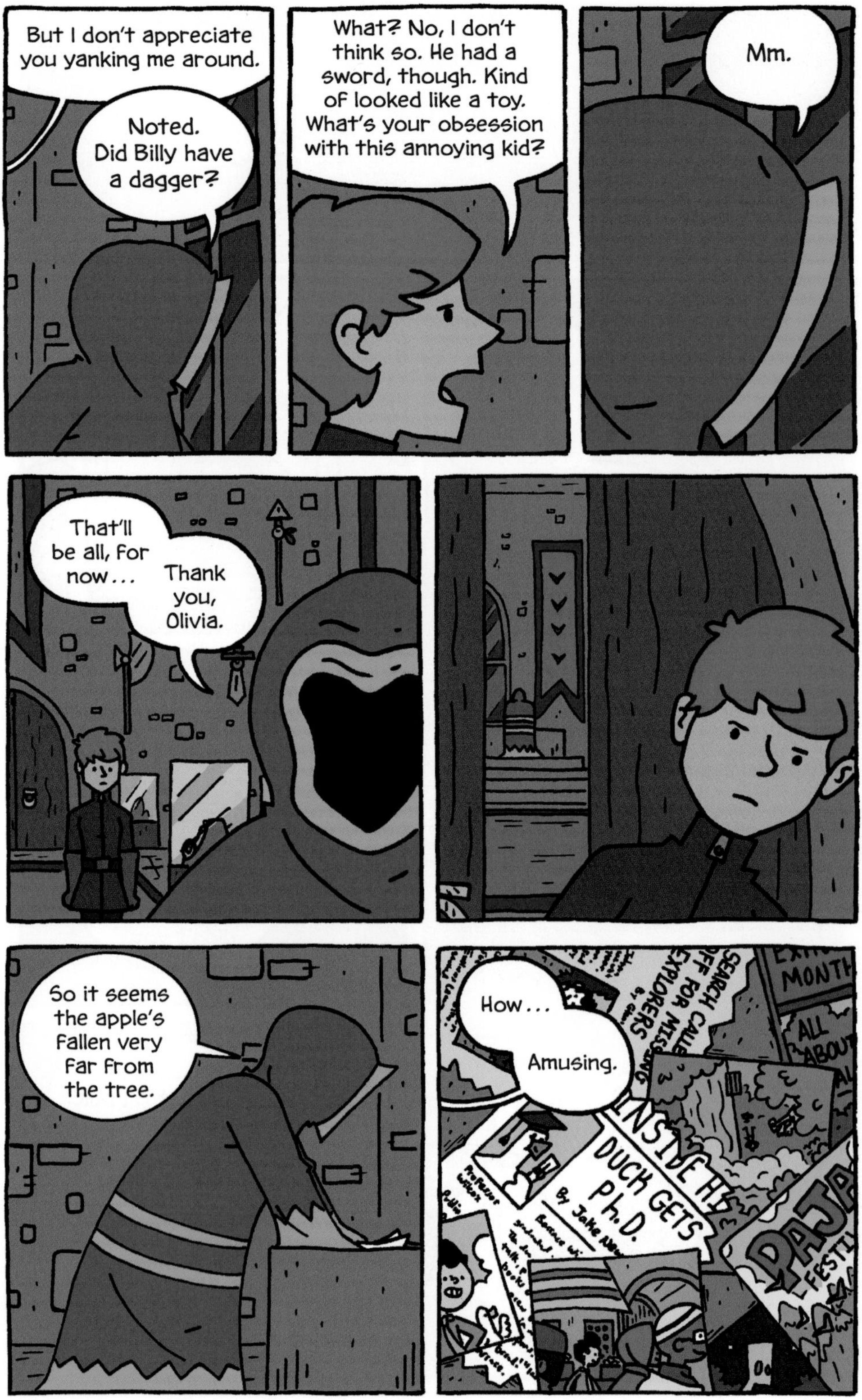
But I don't appreciate you yanking me around.
Noted. Did Billy have a dagger?
What? No, I don't think so. He had a sword, though. Kind of looked like a toy. What's your obsession with this annoying kid?
Mm.
That'll be all, for now...
Thank you, Olivia.
So it seems the apple's fallen very far from the tree.
How...
Amusing.
DUCK GETS Ph.D.
MONTH

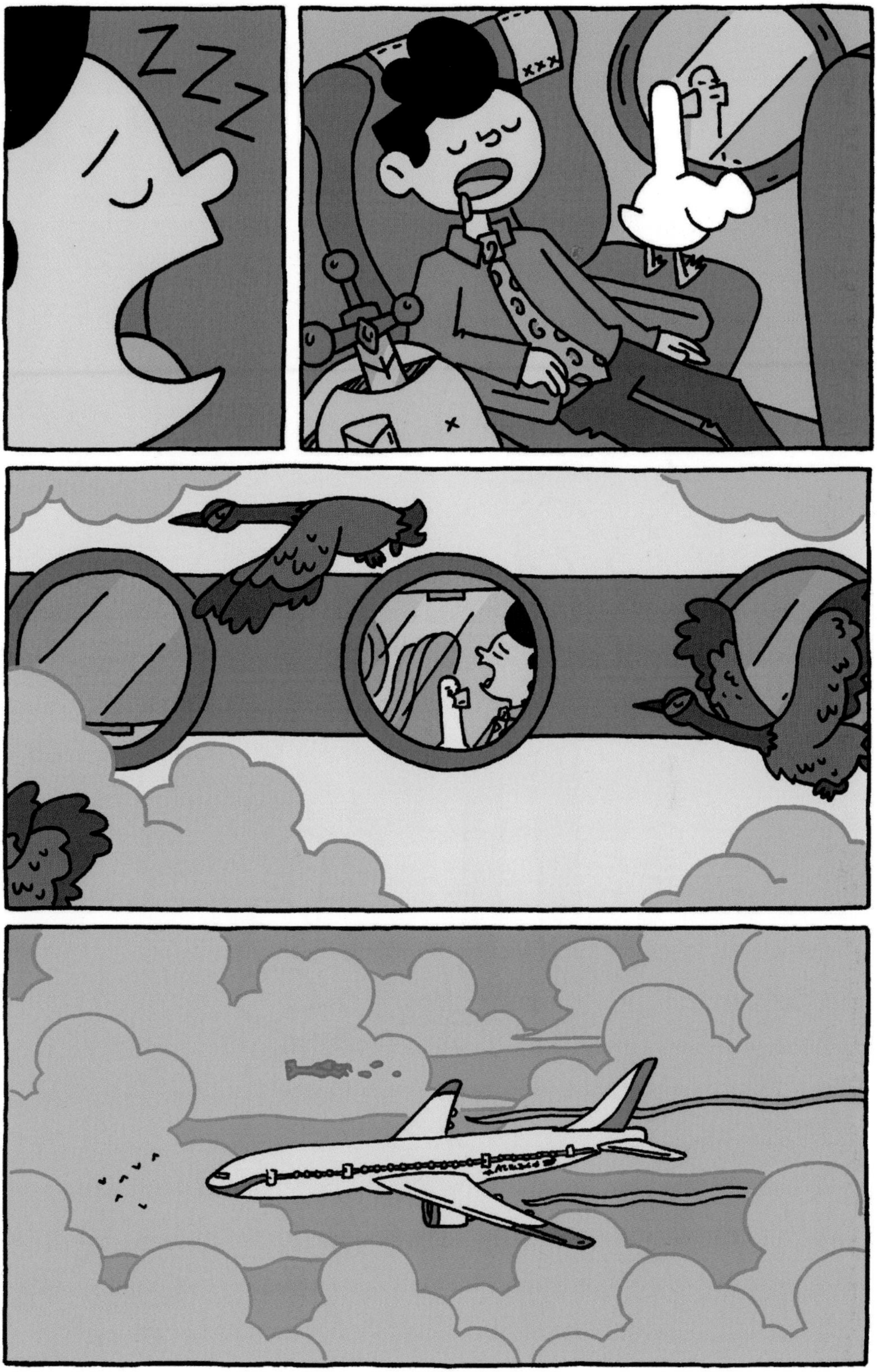
ZZZ

# SEARCH FOR THE ATLAS BEAR

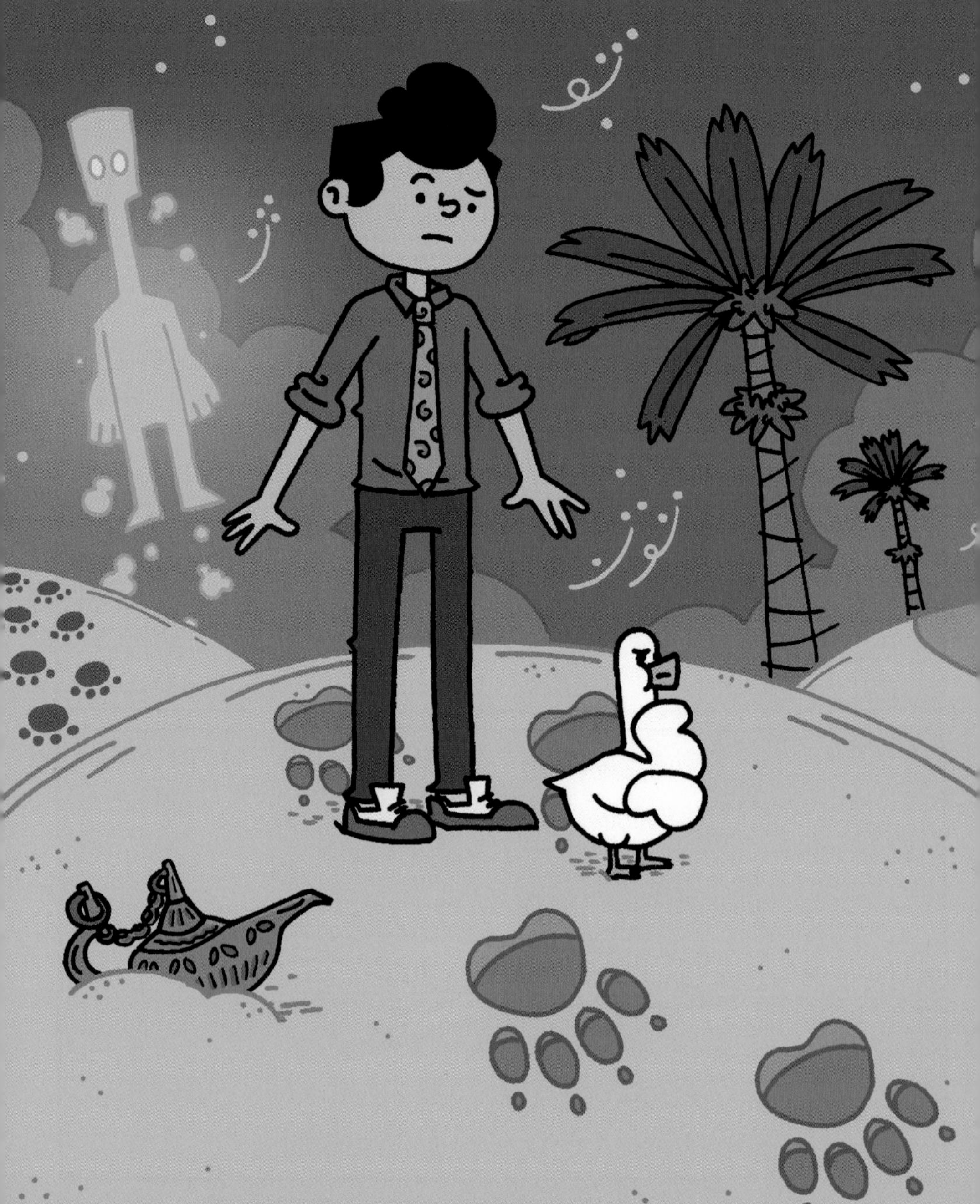

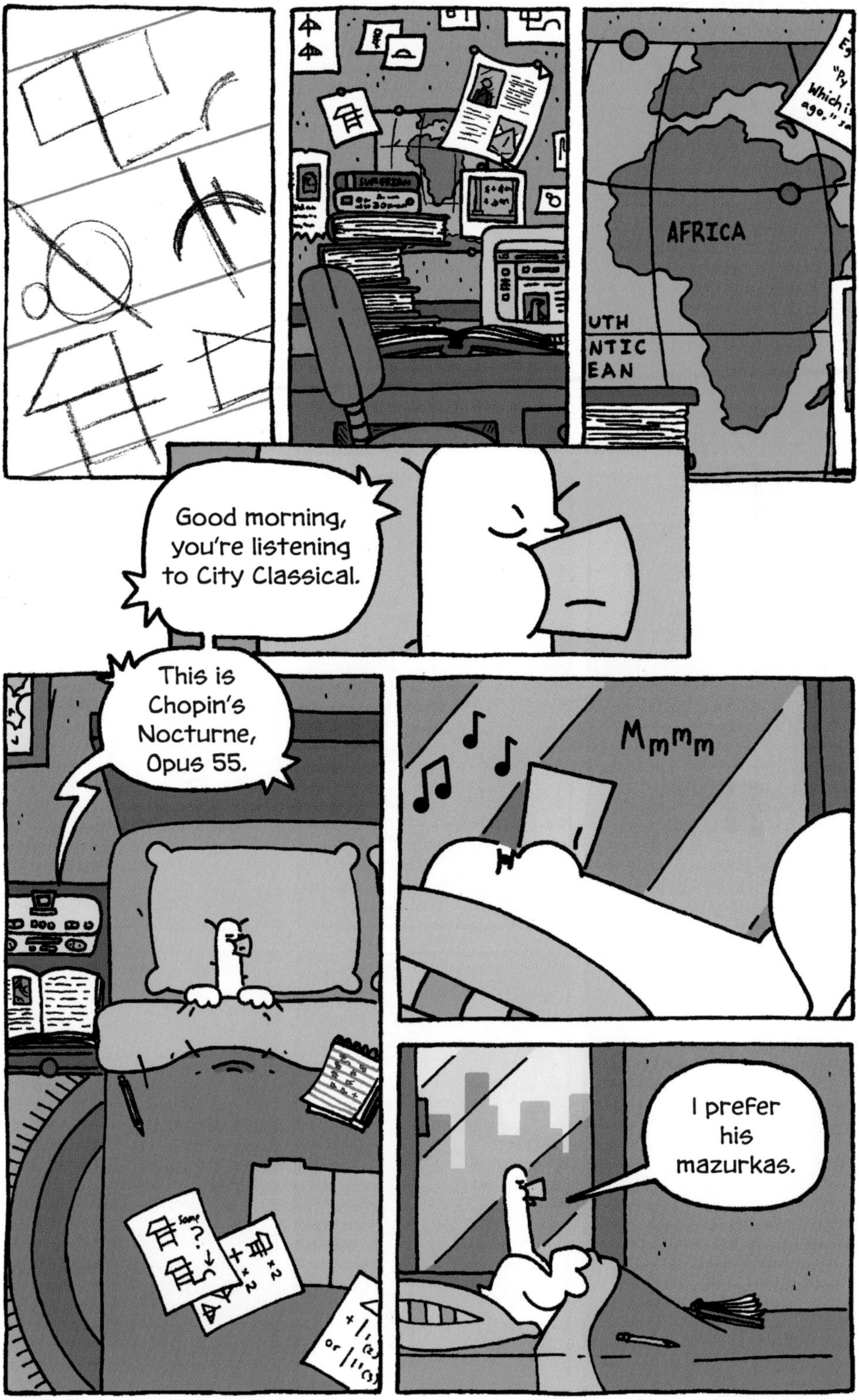
AFRICA
Good morning, you're listening to City Classical.
This is Chopin's Nocturne, Opus 55.
Mmmm
I prefer his mazurkas.

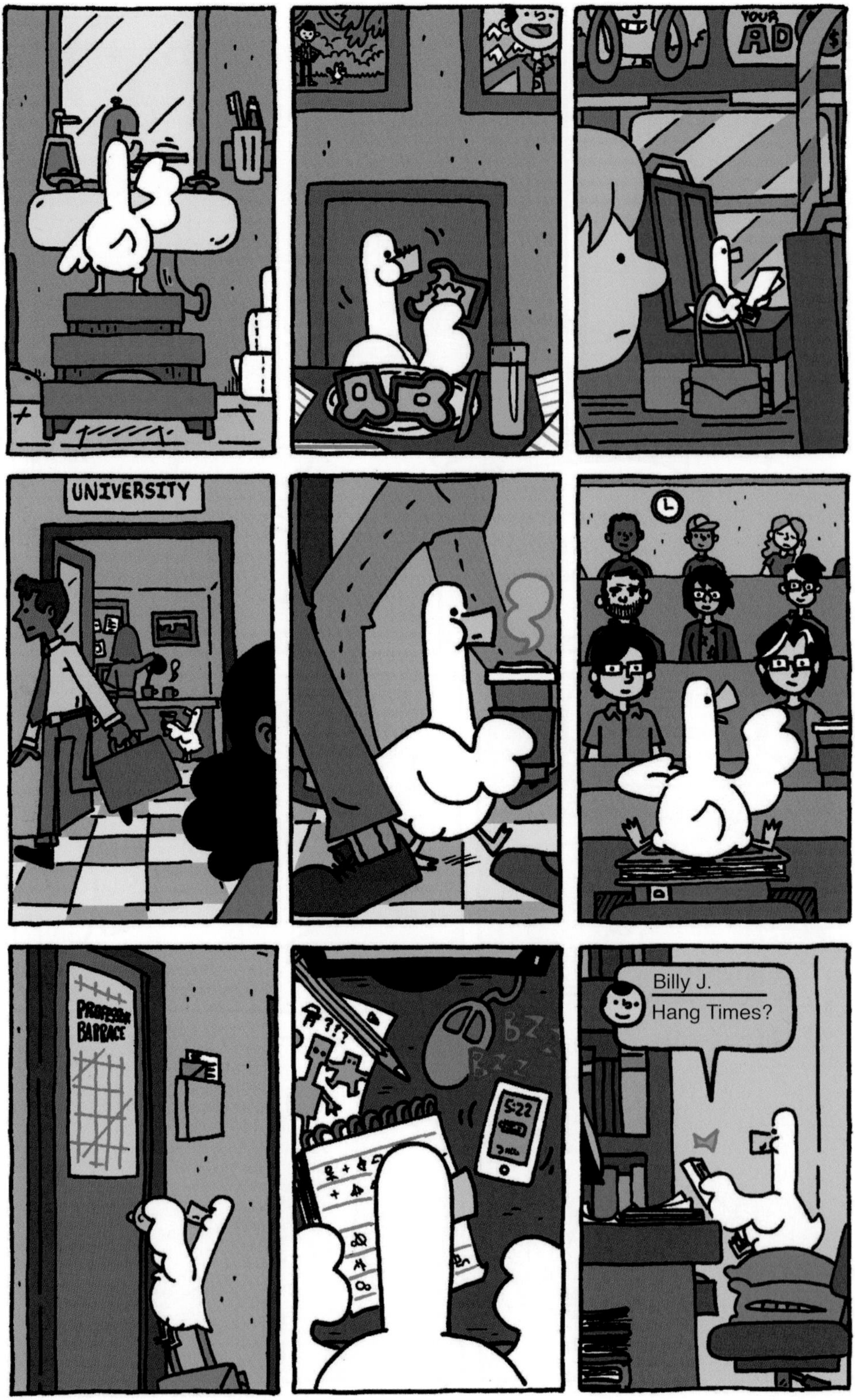
YOUR AD
UNIVERSITY
PROFESSOR BARRACE
5:22
BZZ BZZ
Billy J.
Hang Times?

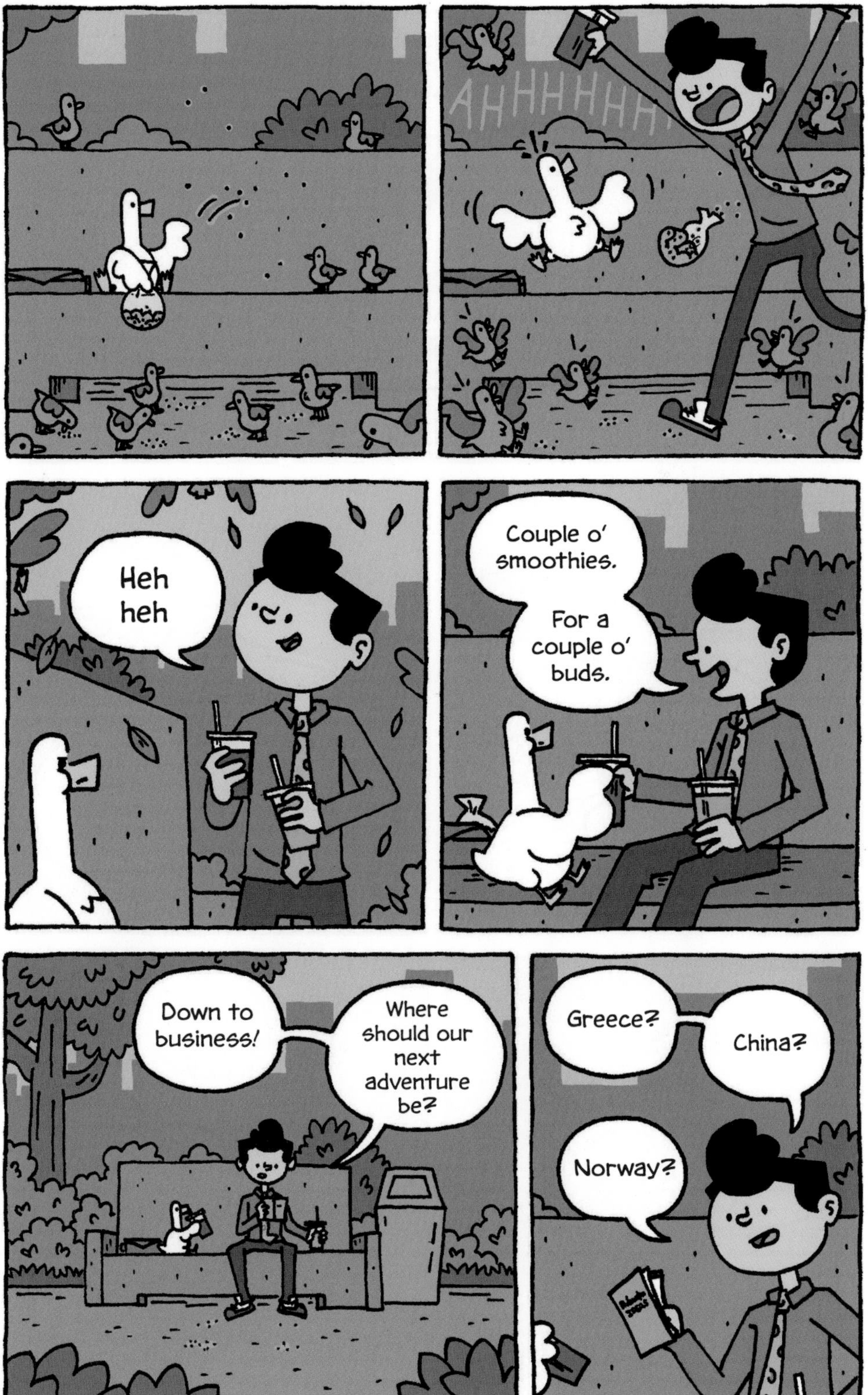
AHHHHHHH
Heh heh
Couple o' smoothies.
For a couple o' buds.
Down to business!
Where should our next adventure be?
Greece?
China?
Norway?

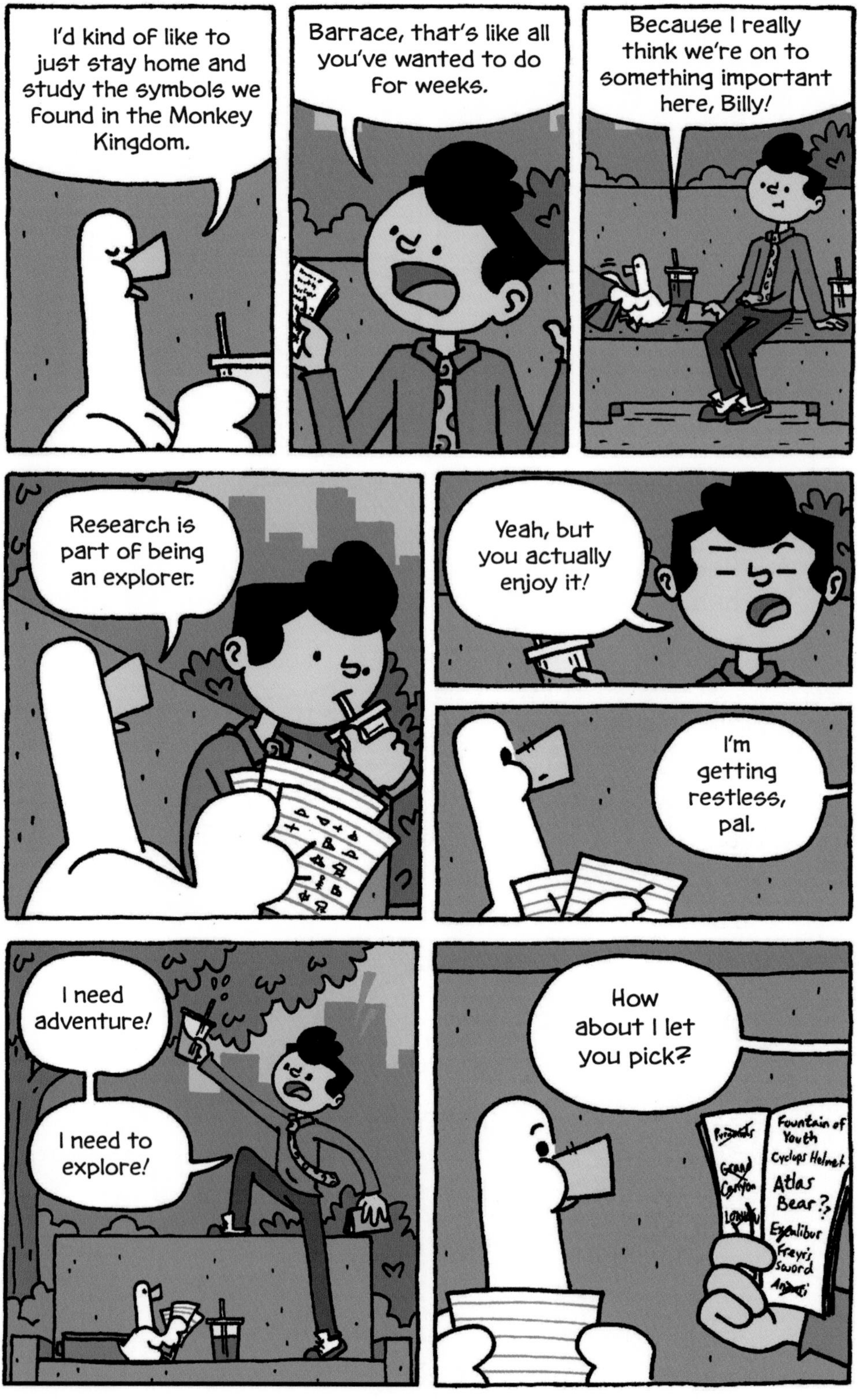
I'd kind of like to just stay home and study the symbols we found in the Monkey Kingdom.
Barrace, that's like all you've wanted to do for weeks.
Because I really think we're on to something important here, Billy!
Research is part of being an explorer.
Yeah, but you actually enjoy it!
I'm getting restless, pal.
I need adventure!
I need to explore!
How about I let you pick?
Fountain of Youth
Cyclops Helmet
Atlas Bear?
Freyr's Sword

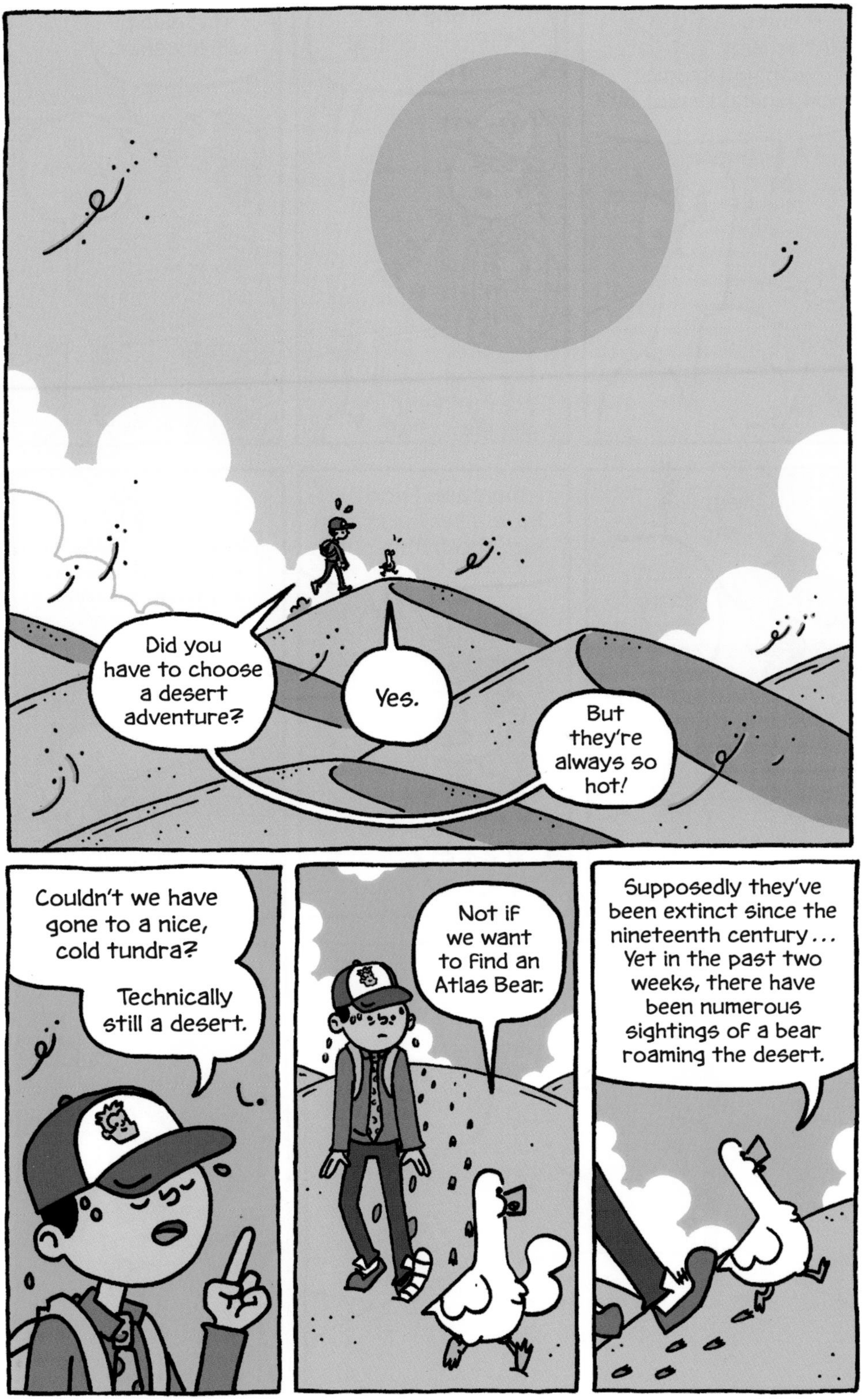

Did you have to choose a desert adventure?
Yes.
But they're always so hot!
Couldn't we have gone to a nice, cold tundra?
Technically still a desert.
Not if we want to find an Atlas Bear.
Supposedly they've been extinct since the nineteenth century... Yet in the past two weeks, there have been numerous sightings of a bear roaming the desert.

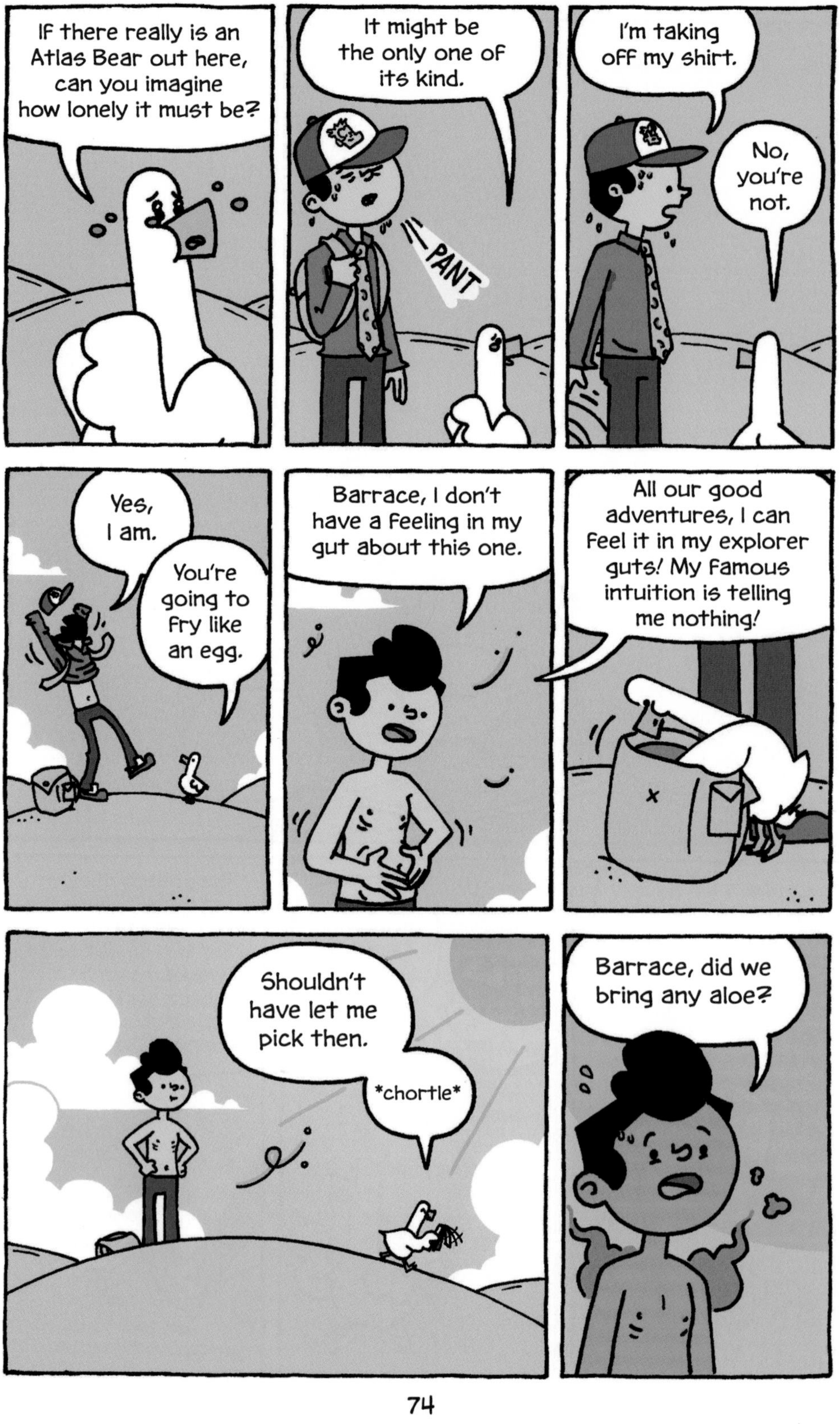
If there really is an Atlas Bear out here, can you imagine how lonely it must be?
It might be the only one of its kind.
PANT
I'm taking off my shirt.
No, you're not.
Yes, I am.
You're going to fry like an egg.
Barrace, I don't have a feeling in my gut about this one.
All our good adventures, I can feel it in my explorer guts! My famous intuition is telling me nothing!
Shouldn't have let me pick then.
*chortle*
Barrace, did we bring any aloe?

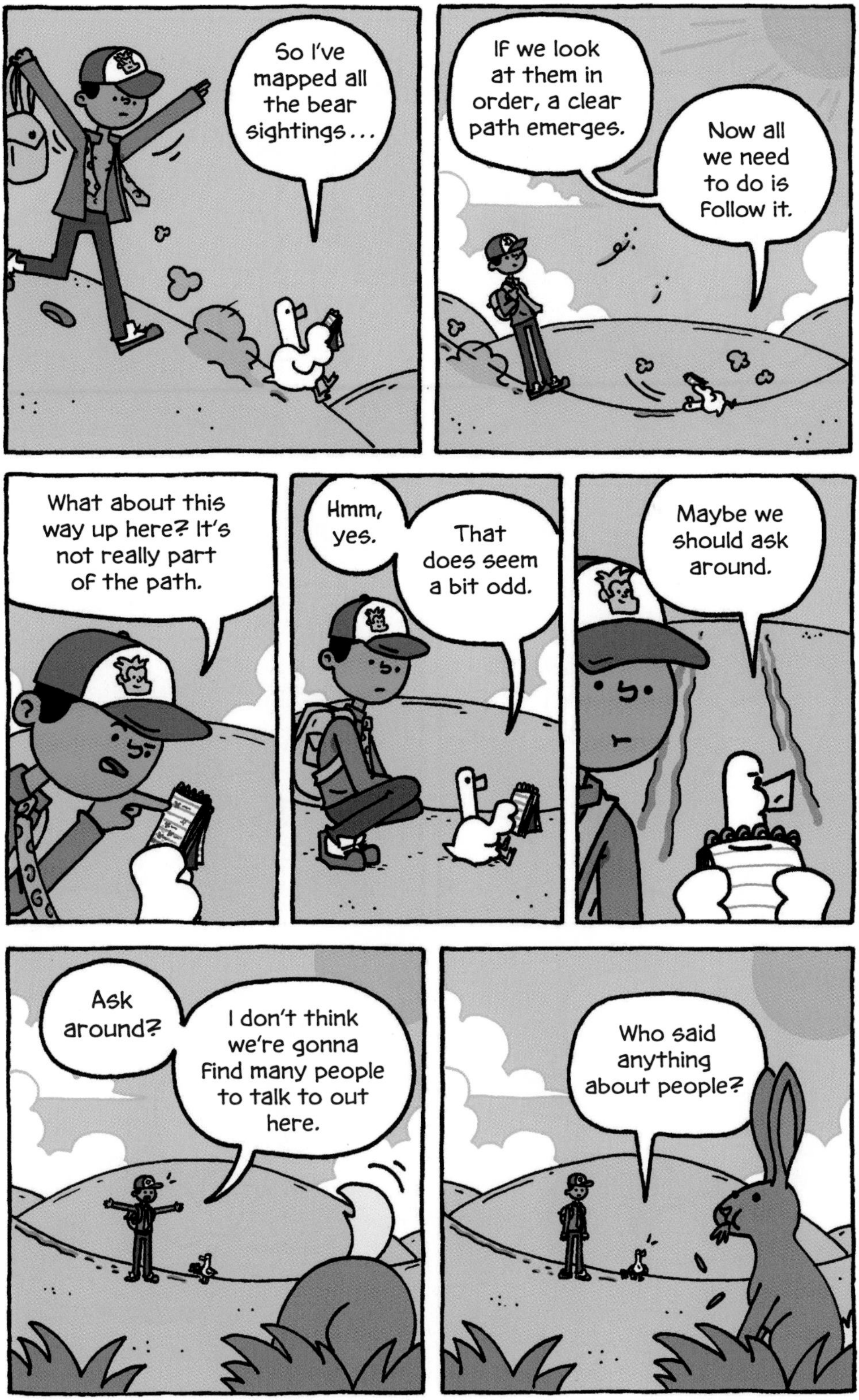
So I've mapped all the bear sightings...
If we look at them in order, a clear path emerges.
Now all we need to do is follow it.
What about this way up here? It's not really part of the path.
Hmm, yes.
That does seem a bit odd.
Maybe we should ask around.
Ask around?
I don't think we're gonna find many people to talk to out here.
Who said anything about people?

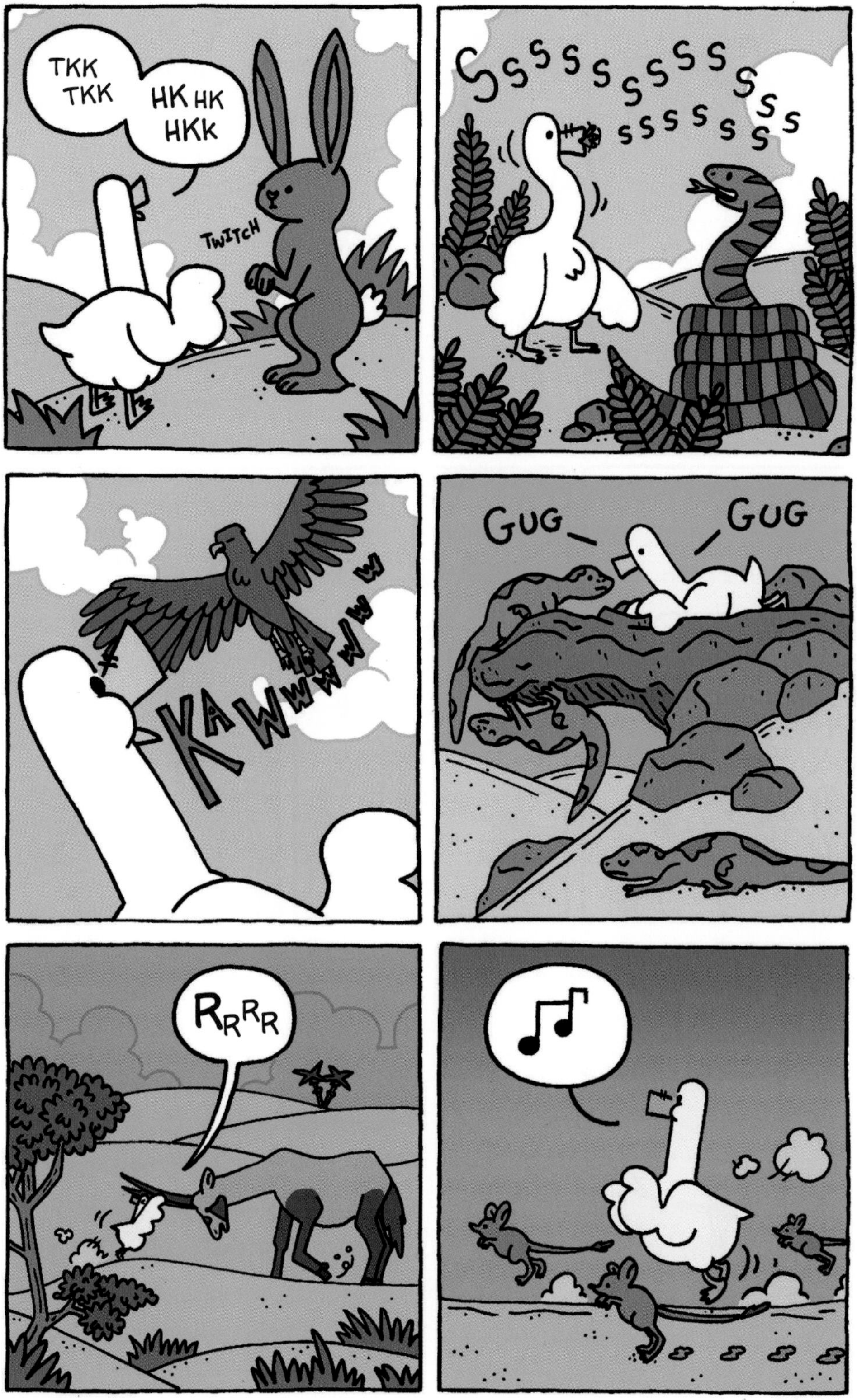
TKK TKK
HK HK HKK
TWITCH
SSSSSSSSSSSSSS SSSSSSSS
KAWWWWWWW
GUG
GUG
RRRR
♫

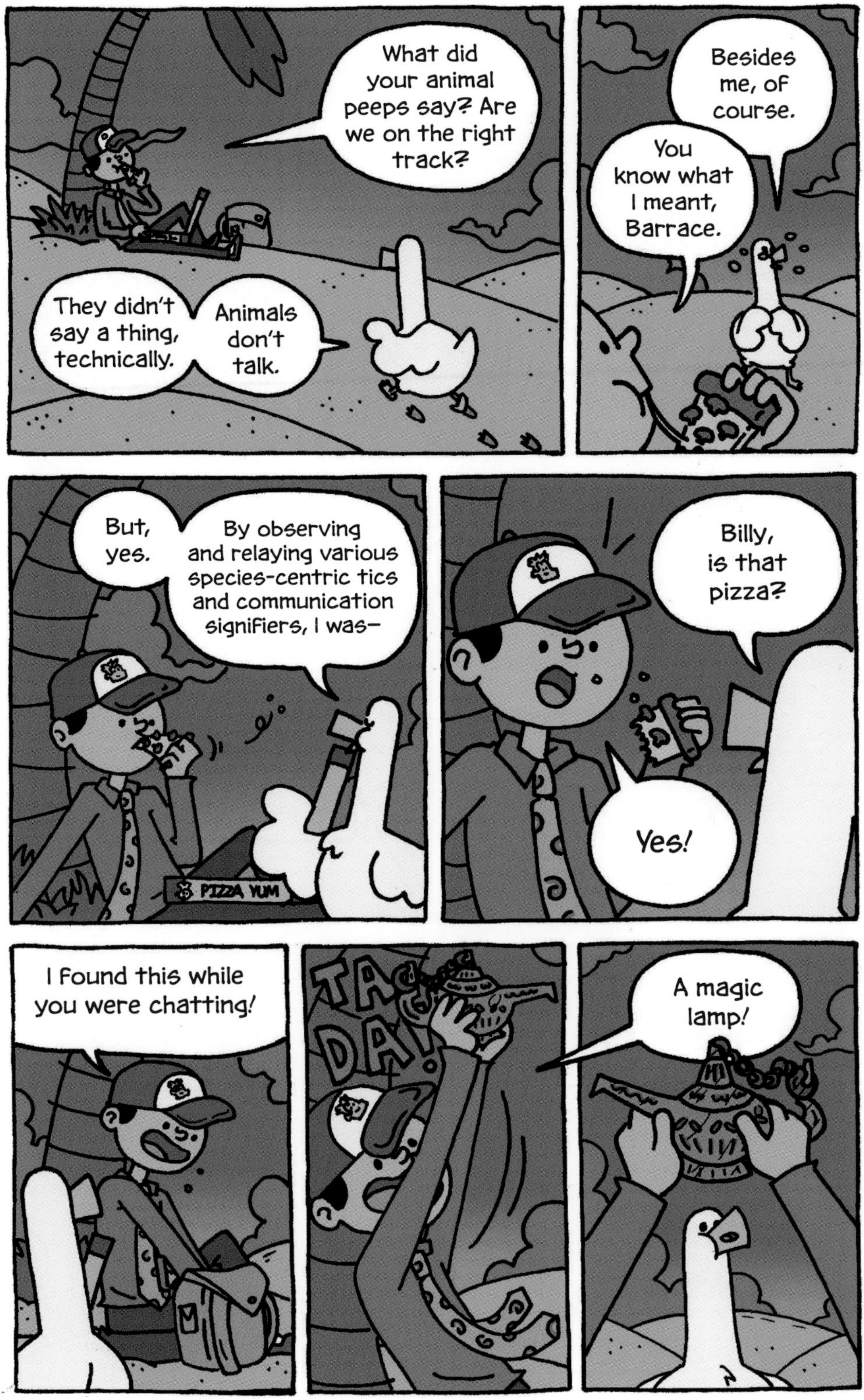
What did your animal peeps say? Are we on the right track?
They didn't say a thing, technically.
Animals don't talk.
Besides me, of course.
You know what I meant, Barrace.
But, yes.
By observing and relaying various species-centric tics and communication signifiers, I was–
PIZZA YUM
Billy, is that pizza?
Yes!
I found this while you were chatting!
TA DA!
A magic lamp!

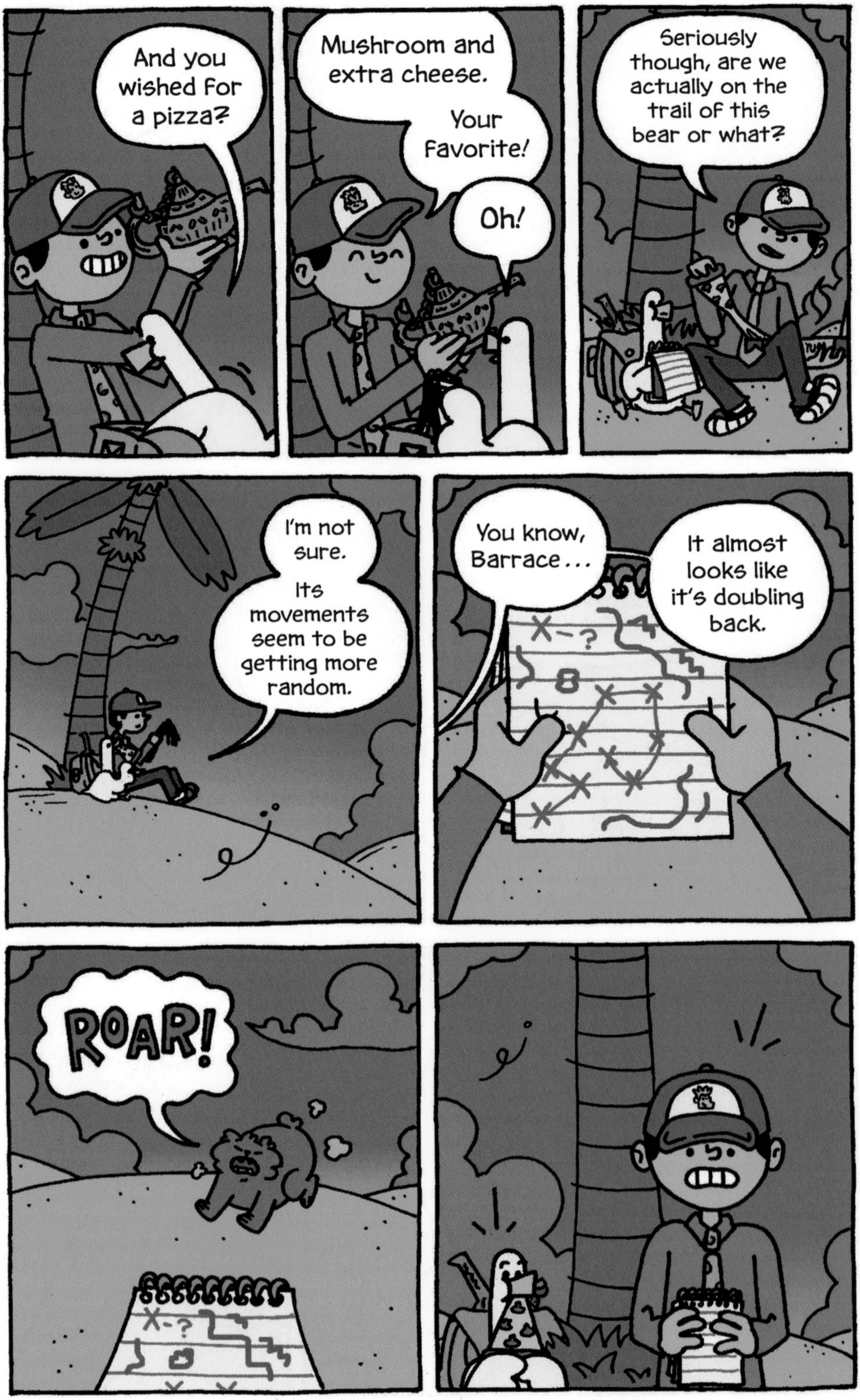
And you wished for a pizza?
Mushroom and extra cheese.
Your favorite!
Oh!
Seriously though, are we actually on the trail of this bear or what?
I'm not sure.
Its movements seem to be getting more random.
You know, Barrace...
It almost looks like it's doubling back.
ROAR!

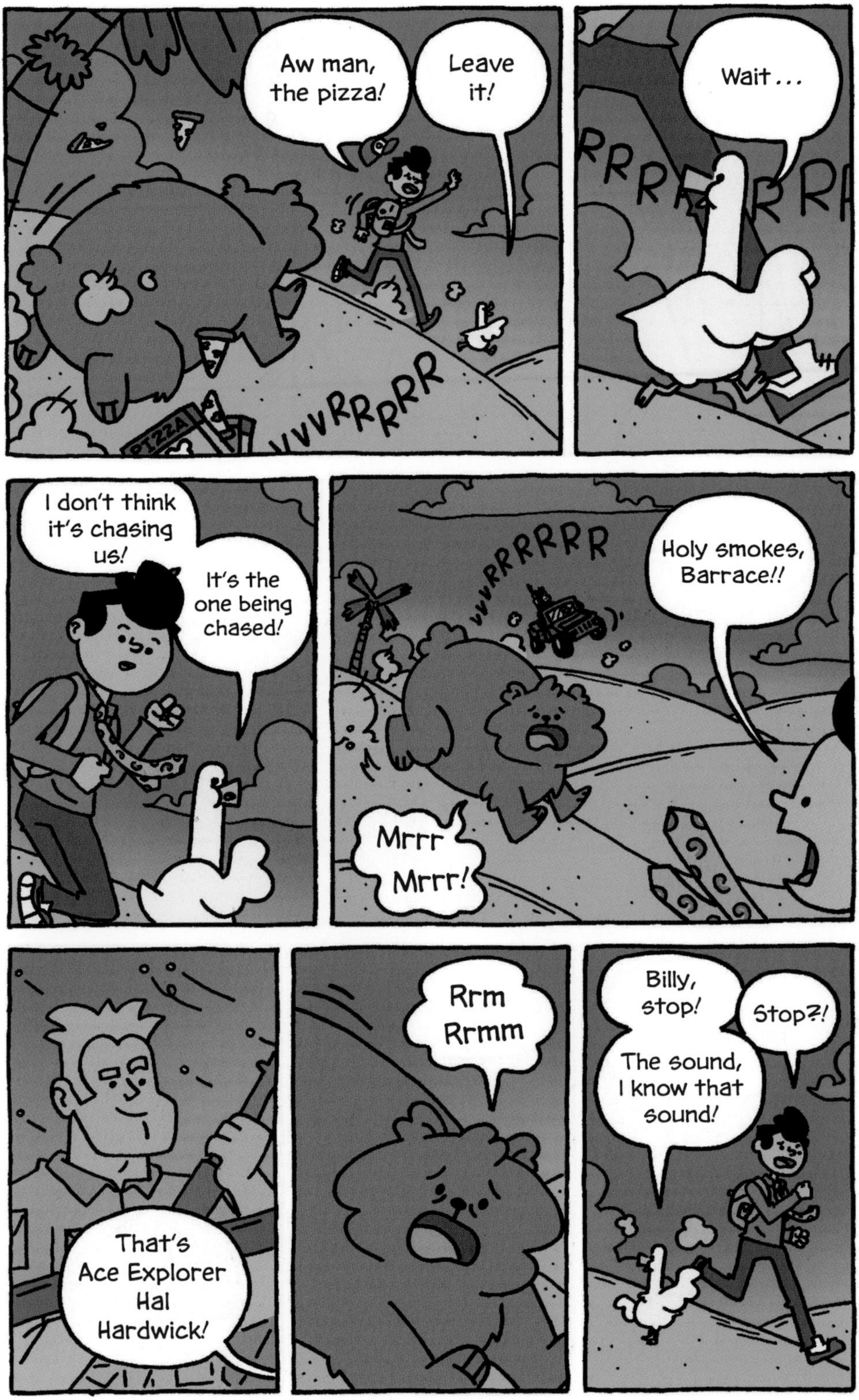
Aw man, the pizza!
Leave it!
PIZZA
VVVRRRRR
Wait...
RRRRRRRR
I don't think it's chasing us!
It's the one being chased!
VVVRRRRRR
Holy smokes, Barrace!!
Mrrr Mrrr!
That's Ace Explorer Hal Hardwick!
Rrm Rrmm
Billy, stop!
The sound, I know that sound!
Stop?!

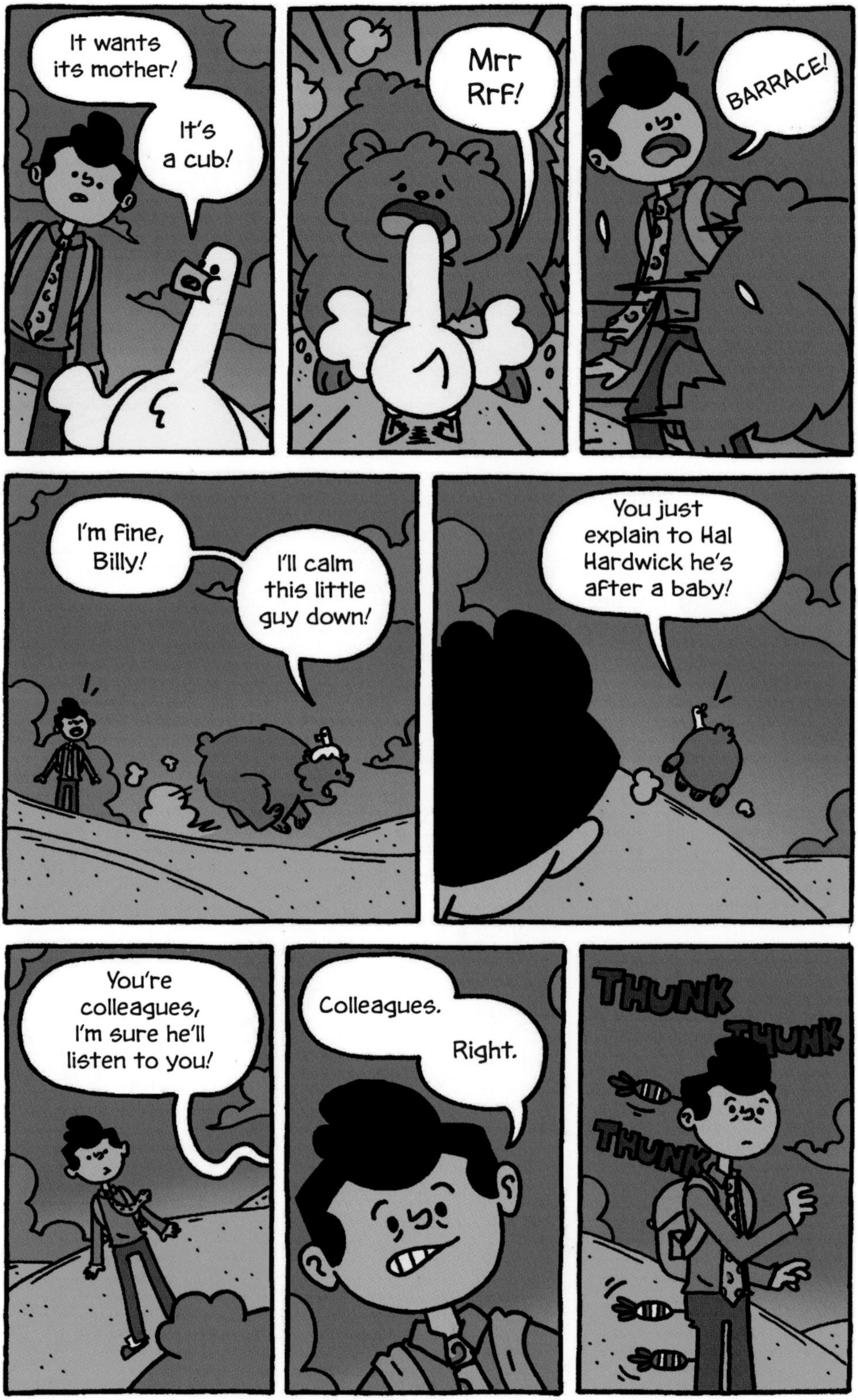
It wants its mother!
It's a cub!
Mrr Rrf!
BARRACE!
I'm fine, Billy!
I'll calm this little guy down!
You just explain to Hal Hardwick he's after a baby!
You're colleagues, I'm sure he'll listen to you!
Colleagues.
Right.
THUNK
THUNK
THUNK

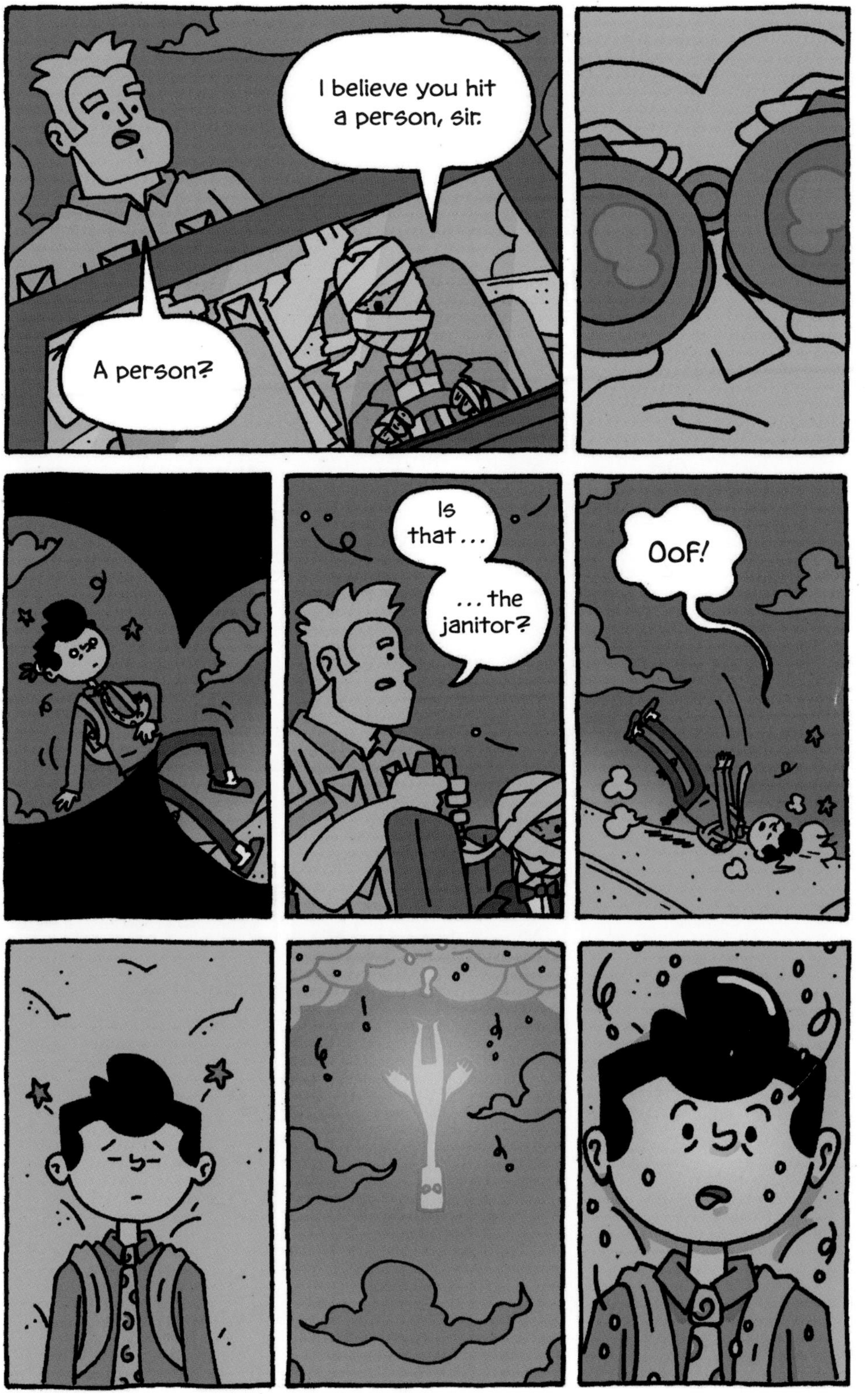
I believe you hit a person, sir.
A person?
Is that...
...the janitor?
Oof!

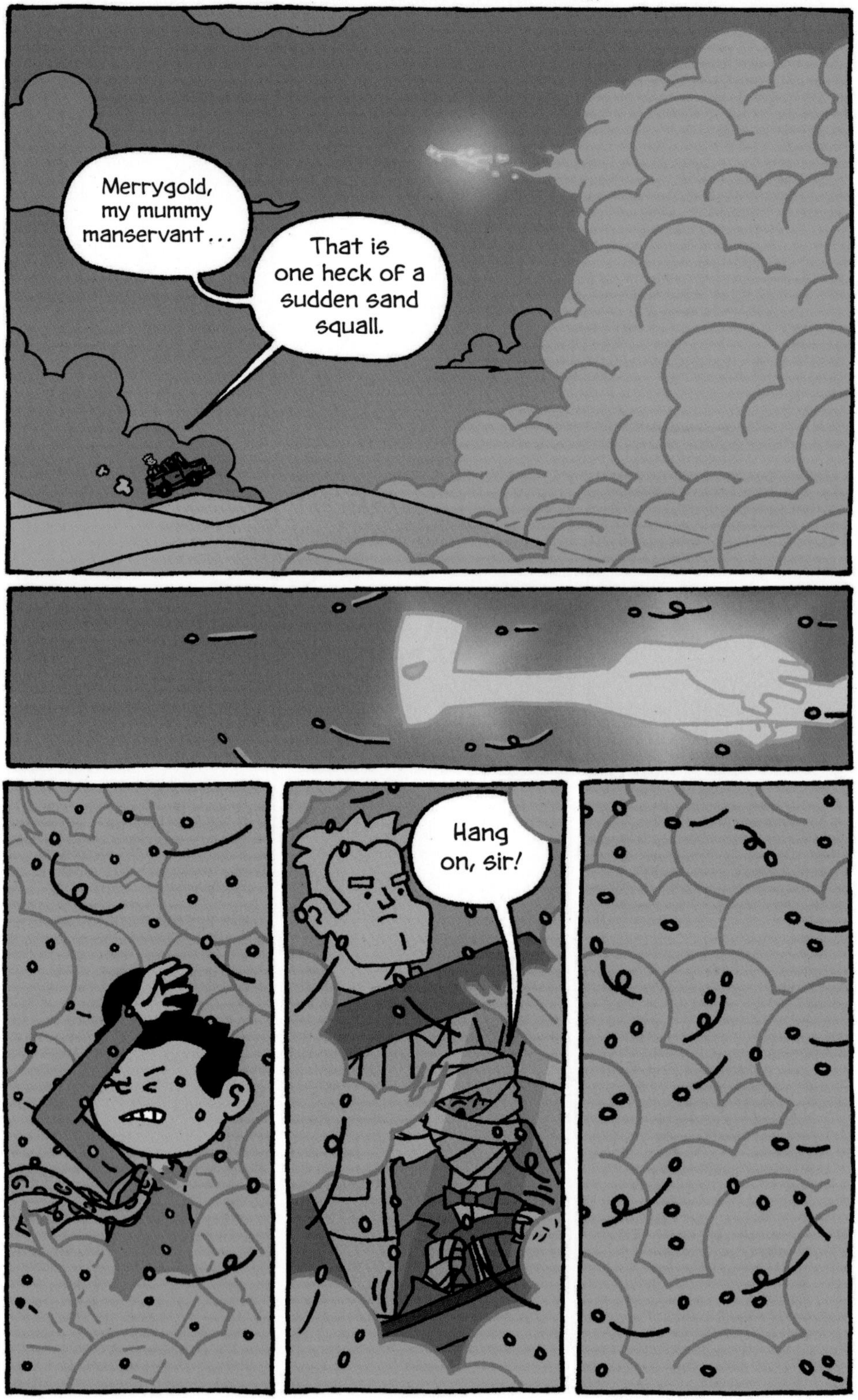
Merrygold, my mummy manservant...
That is one heck of a sudden sand squall.
Hang on, sir!

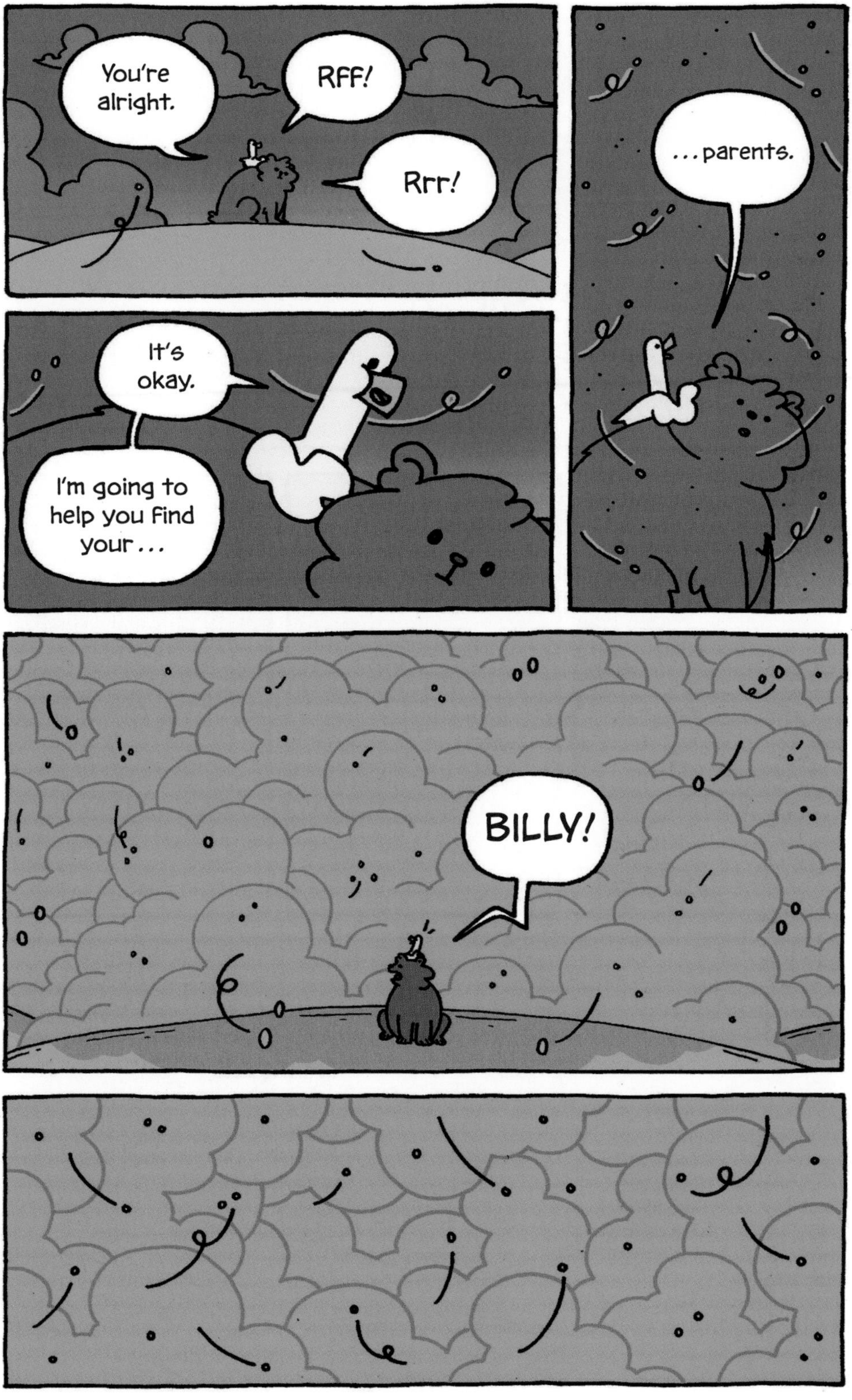
You're alright.
RFF!
Rrr!
It's okay.
I'm going to help you find your...
...parents.
BILLY!

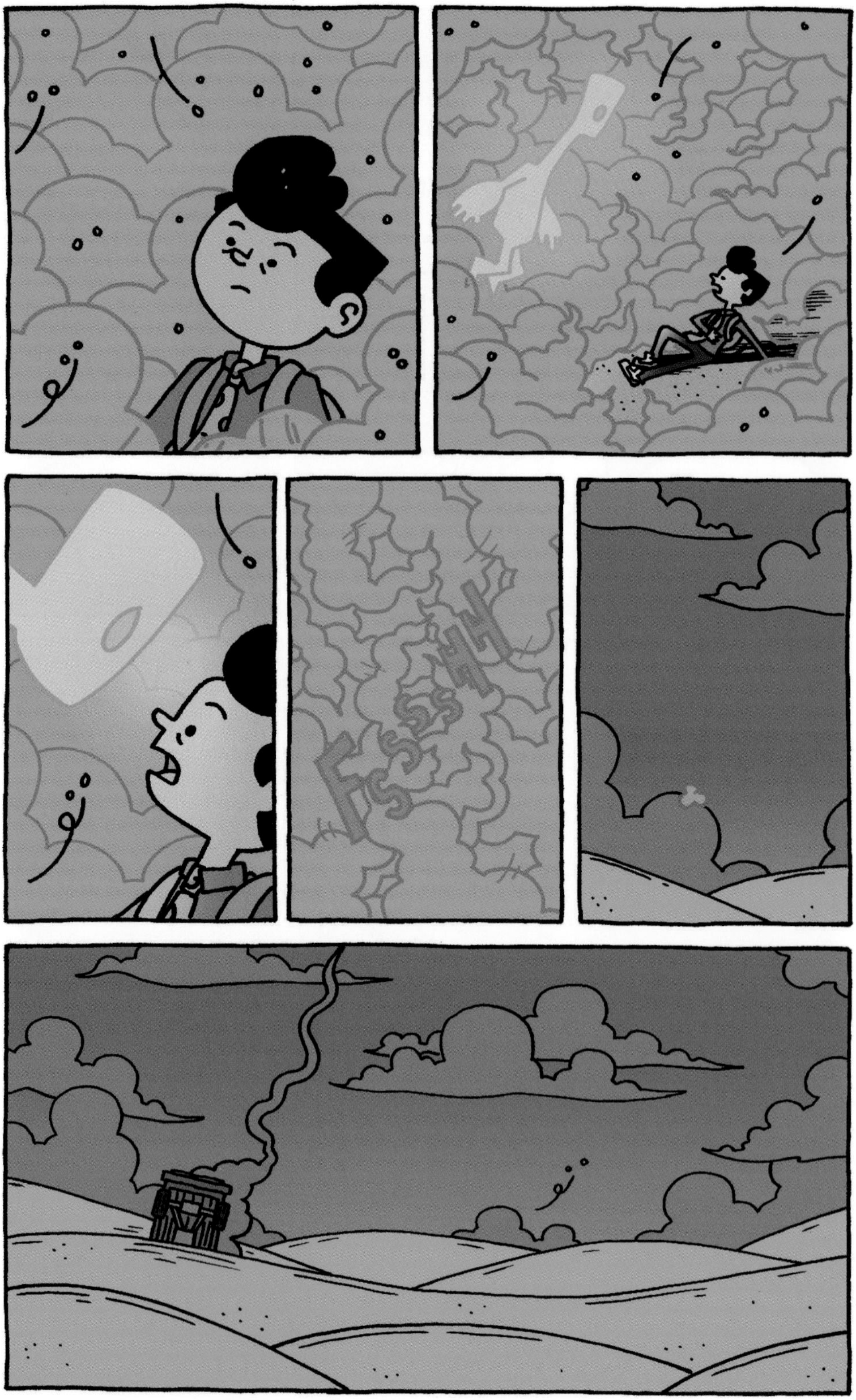
FSSSHH

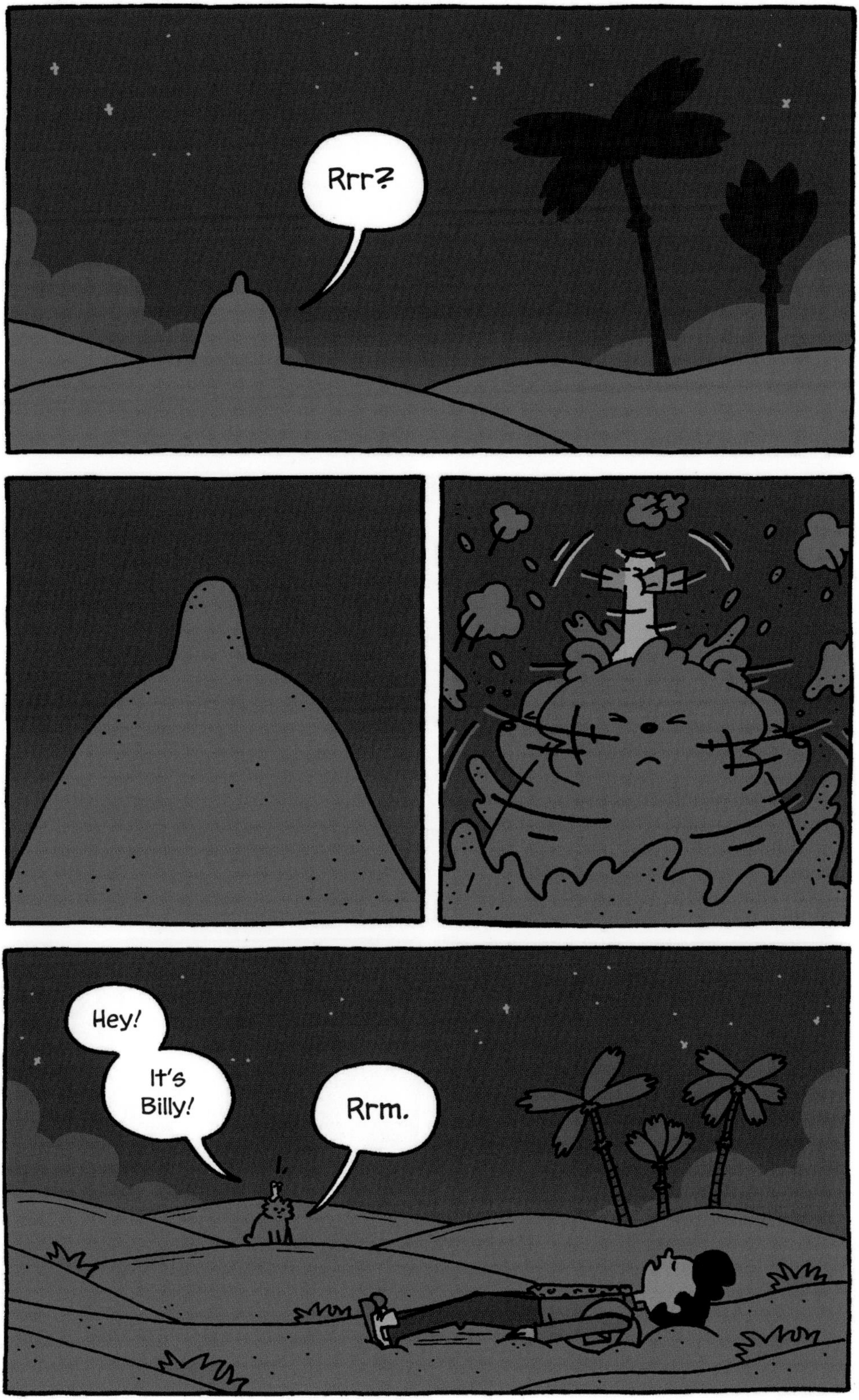
Rrr?
Hey!
It's Billy!
Rrm.

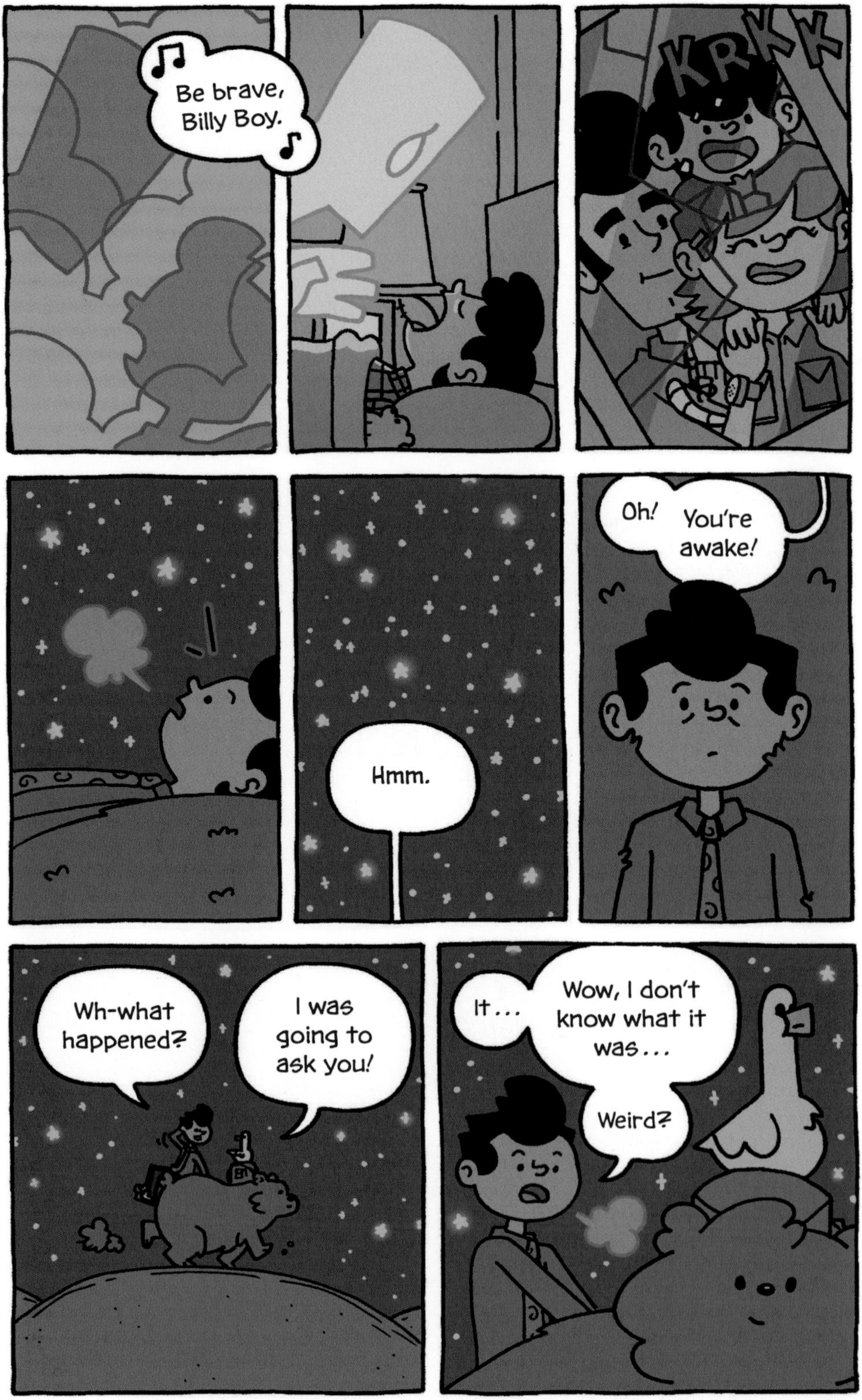

Be brave, Billy Boy.
KRKK
Oh!
You're awake!
Hmm.
Wh-what happened?
I was going to ask you!
It...
Wow, I don't know what it was...
Weird?

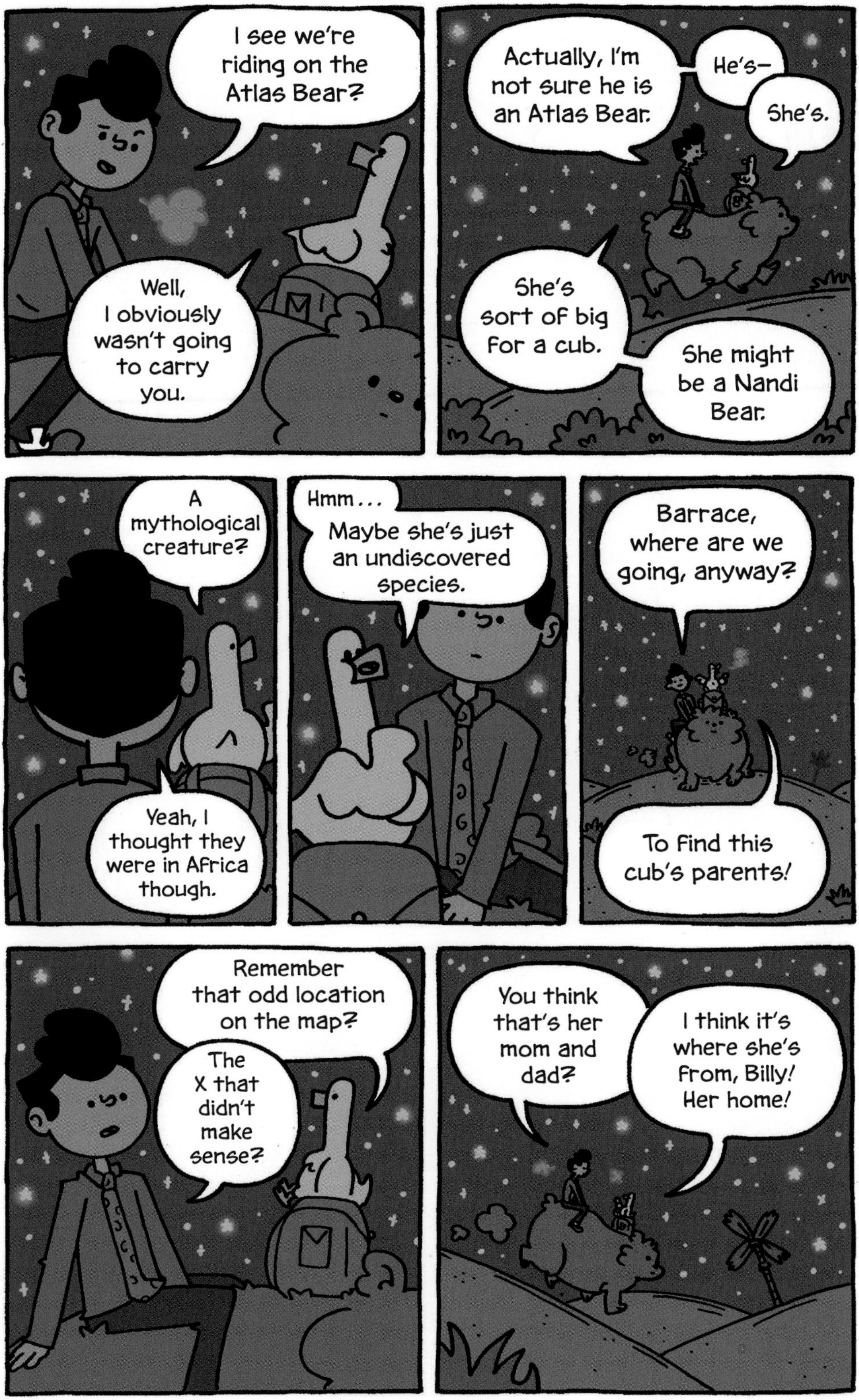
I see we're riding on the Atlas Bear?
Well, I obviously wasn't going to carry you.
Actually, I'm not sure he is an Atlas Bear.
He's—
She's.
She's sort of big for a cub.
She might be a Nandi Bear.
A mythological creature?
Yeah, I thought they were in Africa though.
Hmm...
Maybe she's just an undiscovered species.
Barrace, where are we going, anyway?
To find this cub's parents!
Remember that odd location on the map?
The X that didn't make sense?
You think that's her mom and dad?
I think it's where she's from, Billy! Her home!

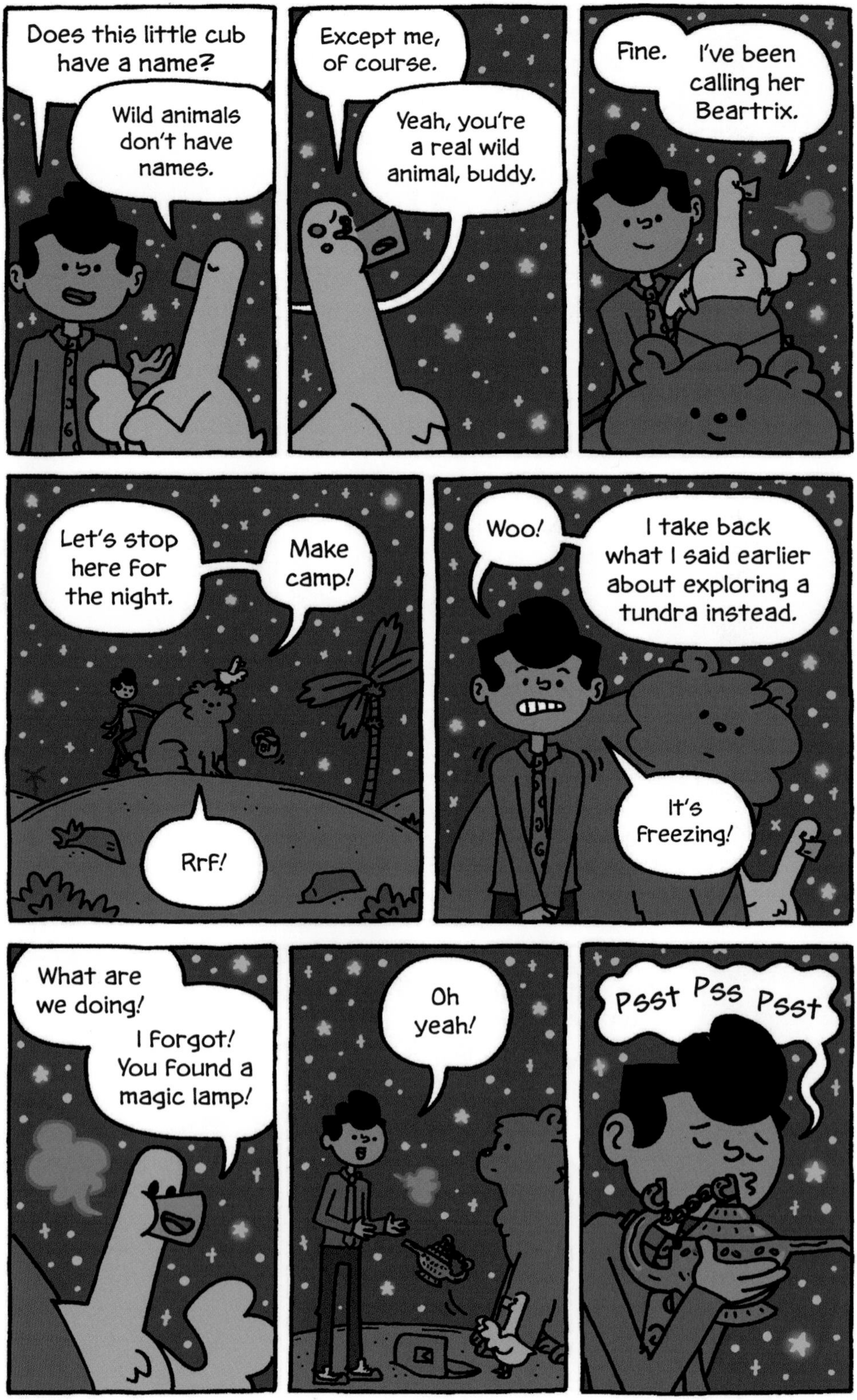

Does this little cub have a name?
Wild animals don't have names.
Except me, of course.
Yeah, you're a real wild animal, buddy.
Fine.
I've been calling her Beartrix.
Let's stop here for the night.
Make camp!
Rrf!
Woo!
I take back what I said earlier about exploring a tundra instead.
It's freezing!
What are we doing!
I forgot! You found a magic lamp!
Oh yeah!
Psst Pss Psst

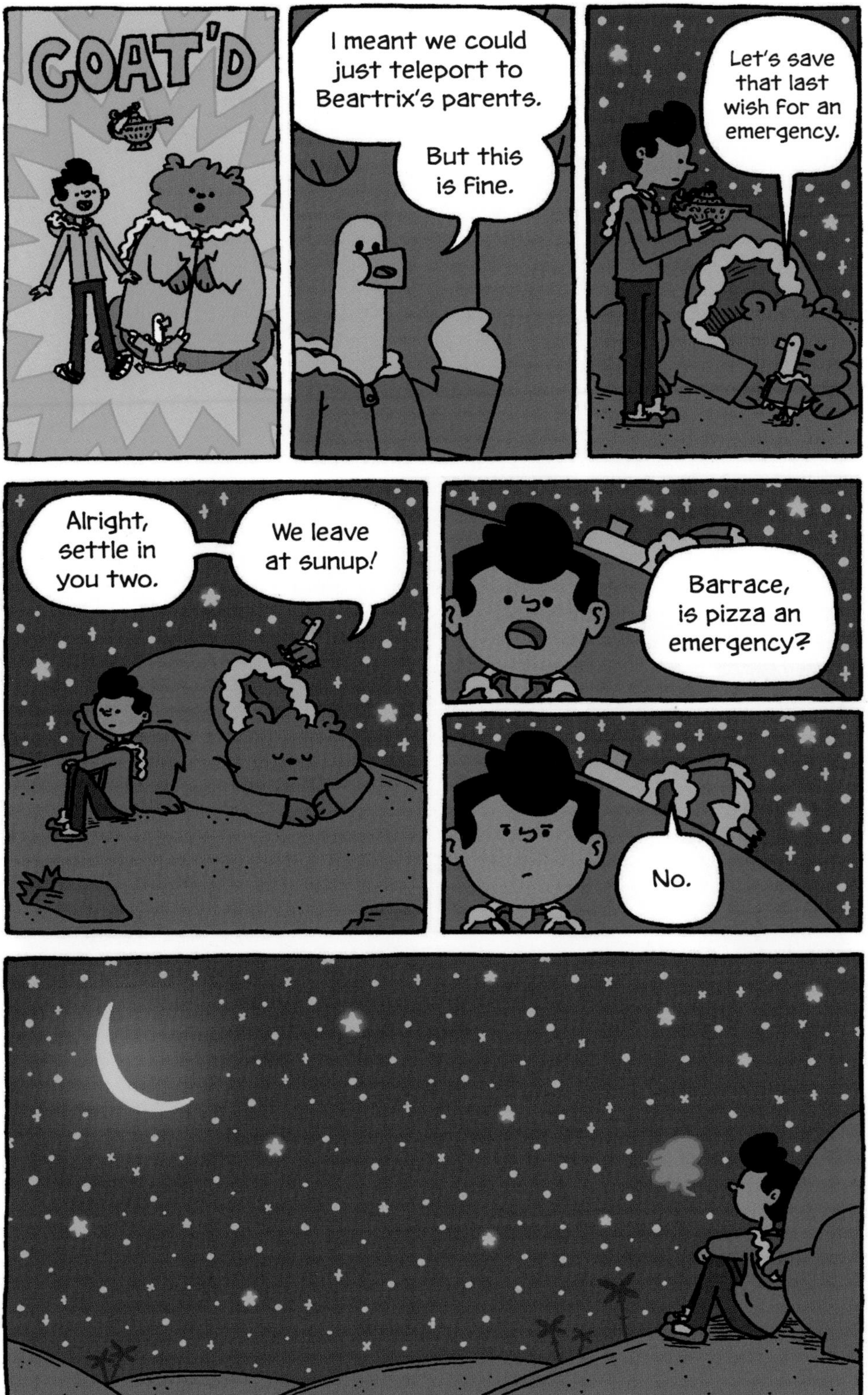
COAT'D
I meant we could just teleport to Beartrix's parents.
But this is fine.
Let's save that last wish for an emergency.
Alright, settle in you two.
We leave at sunup!
Barrace, is pizza an emergency?
No.

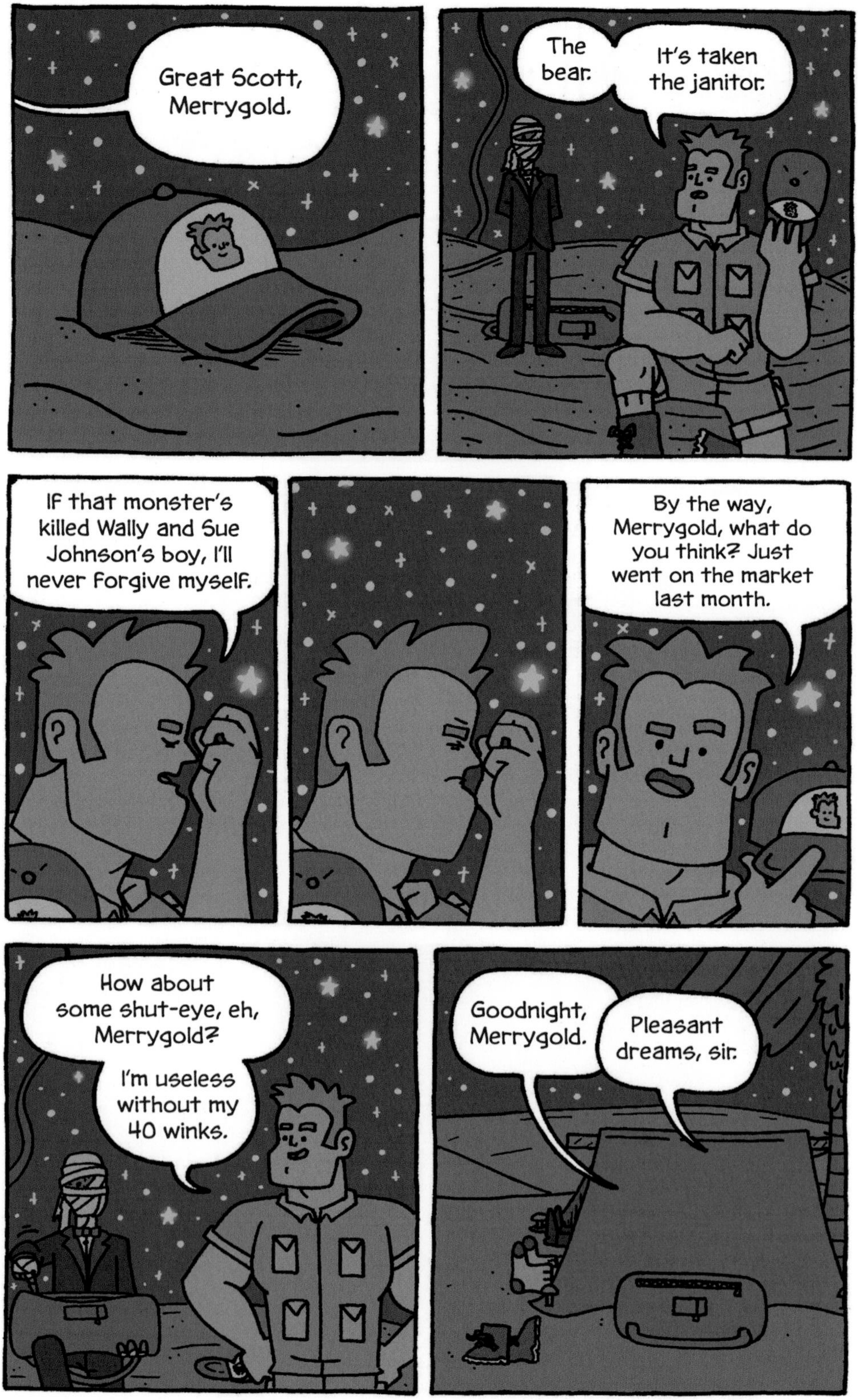
Great Scott, Merrygold.
The bear.
It's taken the janitor.
If that monster's killed Wally and Sue Johnson's boy, I'll never forgive myself.
By the way, Merrygold, what do you think? Just went on the market last month.
How about some shut-eye, eh, Merrygold?
I'm useless without my 40 winks.
Goodnight, Merrygold.
Pleasant dreams, sir.

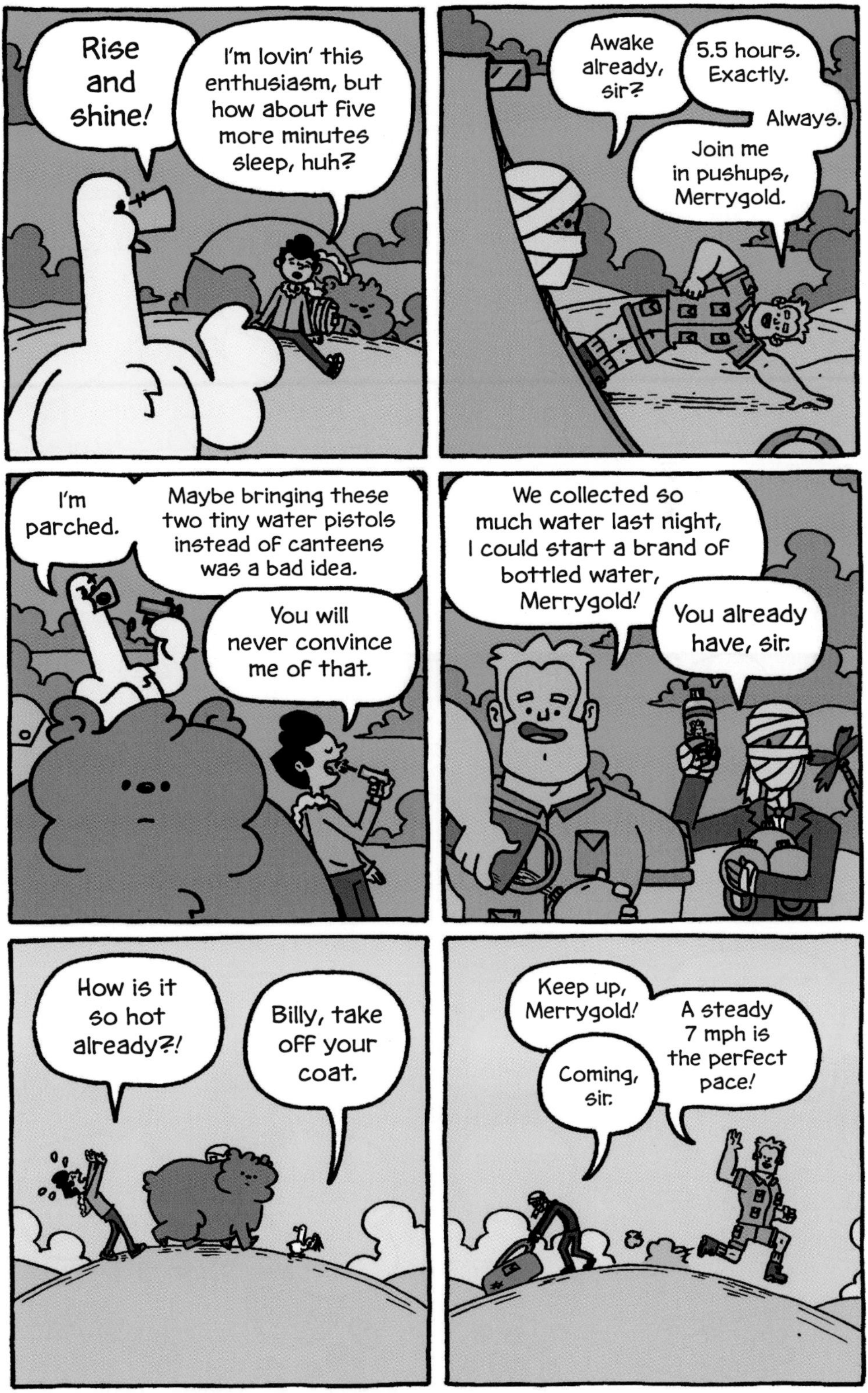
Rise and shine!
I'm lovin' this enthusiasm, but how about five more minutes sleep, huh?
Awake already, sir?
5.5 hours. Exactly.
Always.
Join me in pushups, Merrygold.
I'm parched.
Maybe bringing these two tiny water pistols instead of canteens was a bad idea.
You will never convince me of that.
We collected so much water last night, I could start a brand of bottled water, Merrygold!
You already have, sir.
How is it so hot already?!
Billy, take off your coat.
Keep up, Merrygold!
Coming, sir.
A steady 7 mph is the perfect pace!

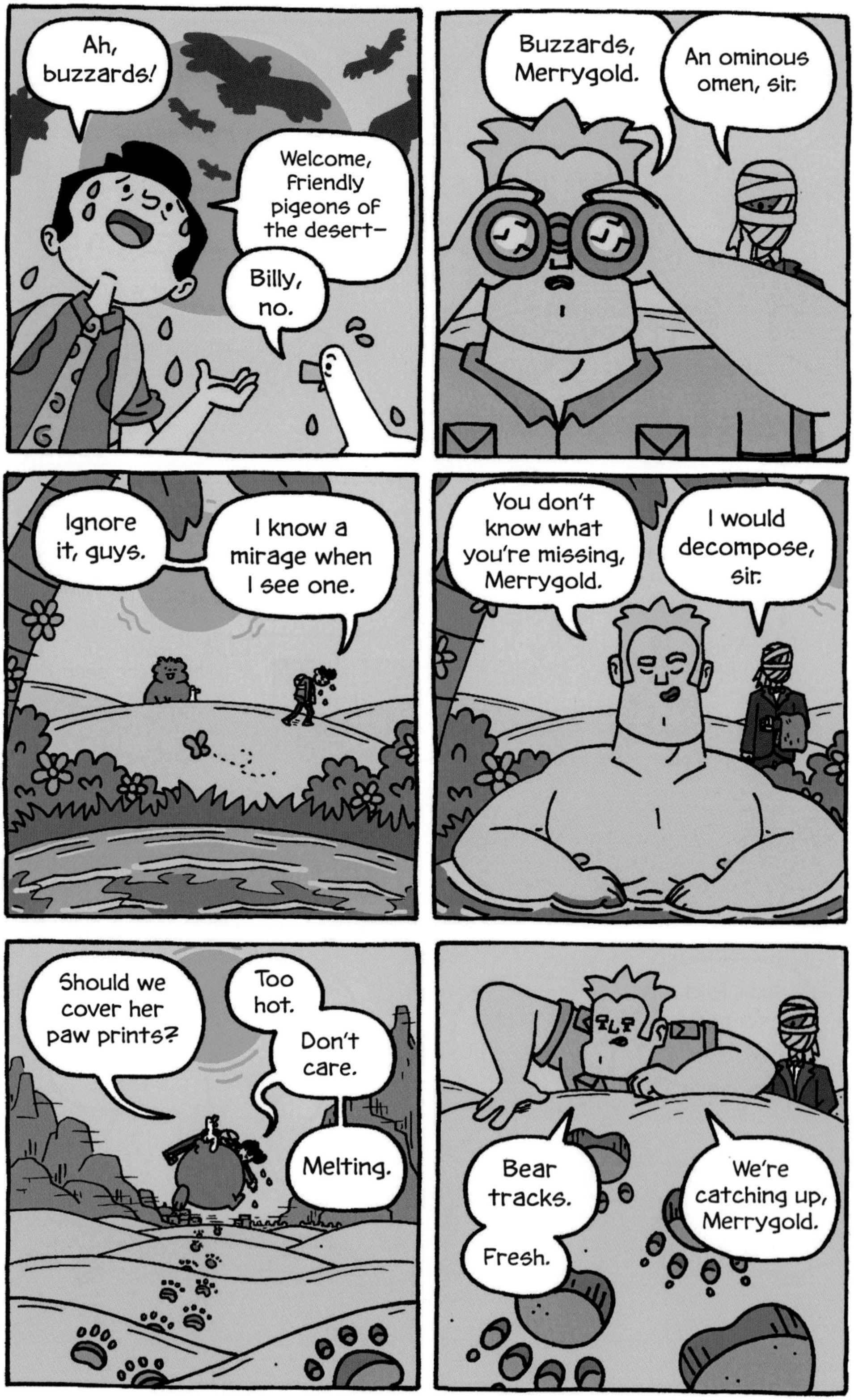
Ah, buzzards!
Welcome, friendly pigeons of the desert–
Billy, no.
Buzzards, Merrygold.
An ominous omen, sir.
Ignore it, guys.
I know a mirage when I see one.
You don't know what you're missing, Merrygold.
I would decompose, sir.
Should we cover her paw prints?
Too hot.
Don't care.
Melting.
Bear tracks.
Fresh.
We're catching up, Merrygold.

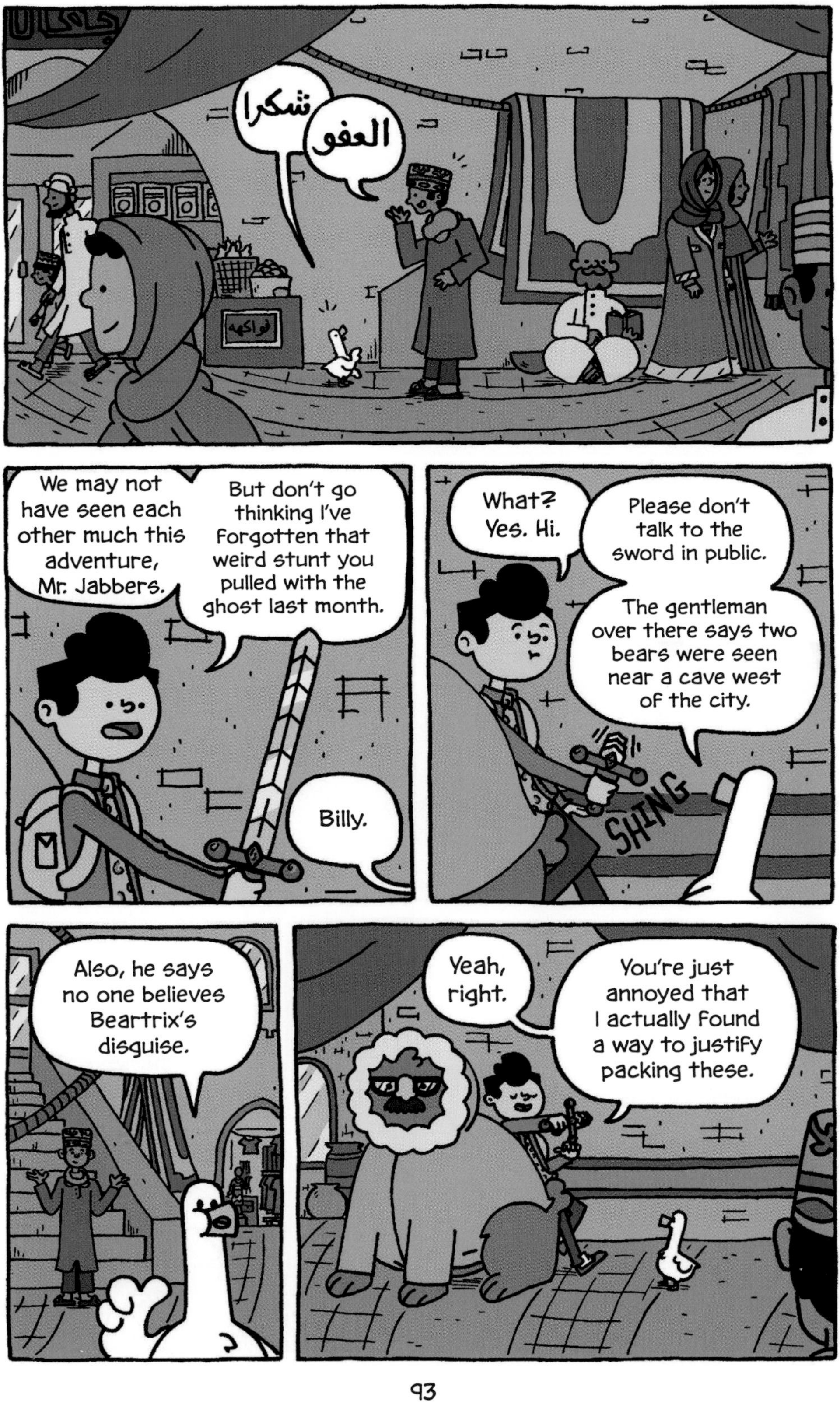
شكرا
العفو
فواكه
We may not have seen each other much this adventure, Mr. Jabbers.
But don't go thinking I've forgotten that weird stunt you pulled with the ghost last month.
Billy.
What? Yes. Hi.
Please don't talk to the sword in public.
The gentleman over there says two bears were seen near a cave west of the city.
SHING
Also, he says no one believes Beartrix's disguise.
Yeah, right.
You're just annoyed that I actually found a way to justify packing these.

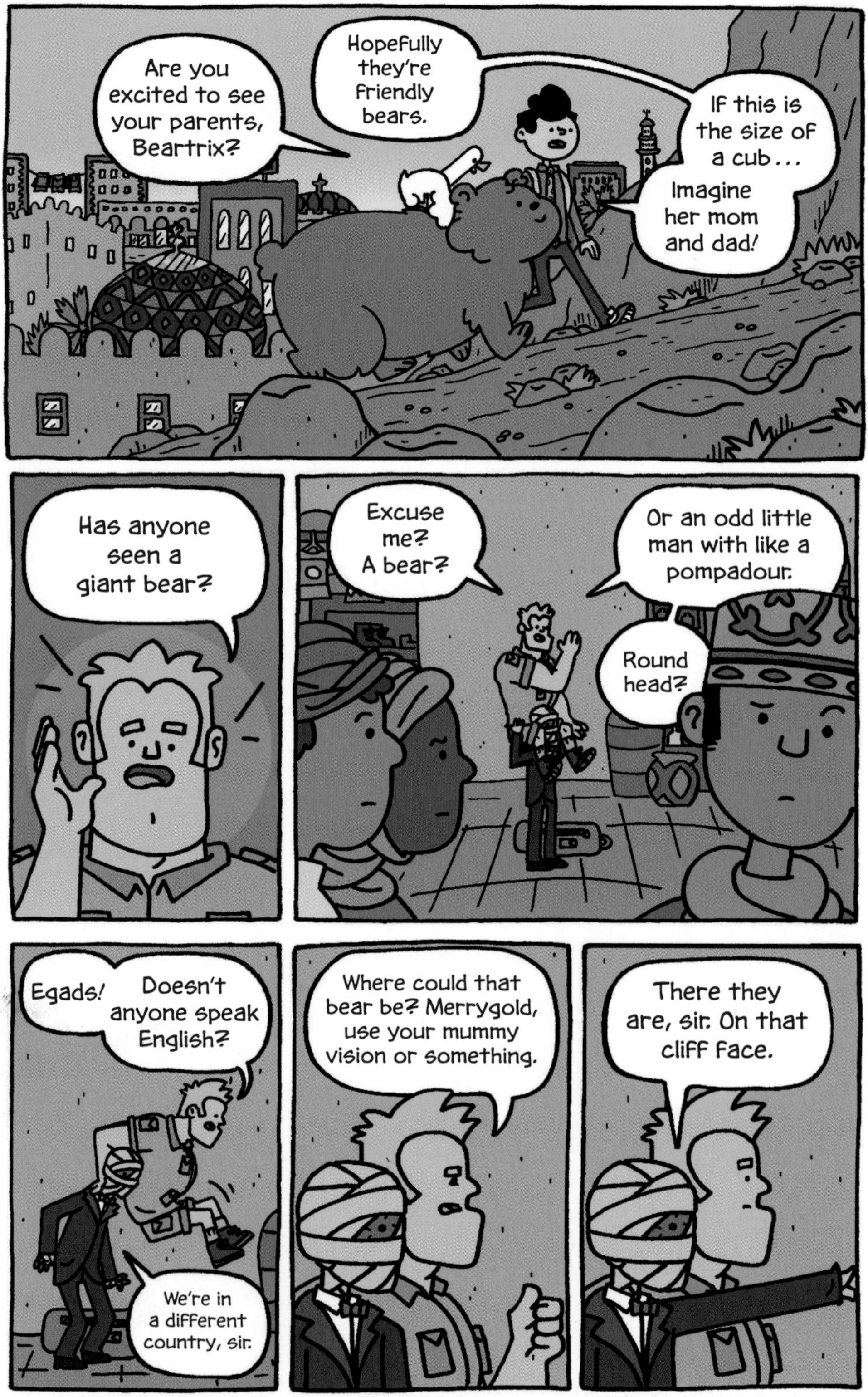
Are you excited to see your parents, Beartrix?
Hopefully they're friendly bears.
If this is the size of a cub...
Imagine her mom and dad!
Has anyone seen a giant bear?
Excuse me? A bear?
Or an odd little man with like a pompadour.
Round head?
Egads!
Doesn't anyone speak English?
We're in a different country, sir.
Where could that bear be? Merrygold, use your mummy vision or something.
There they are, sir. On that cliff face.

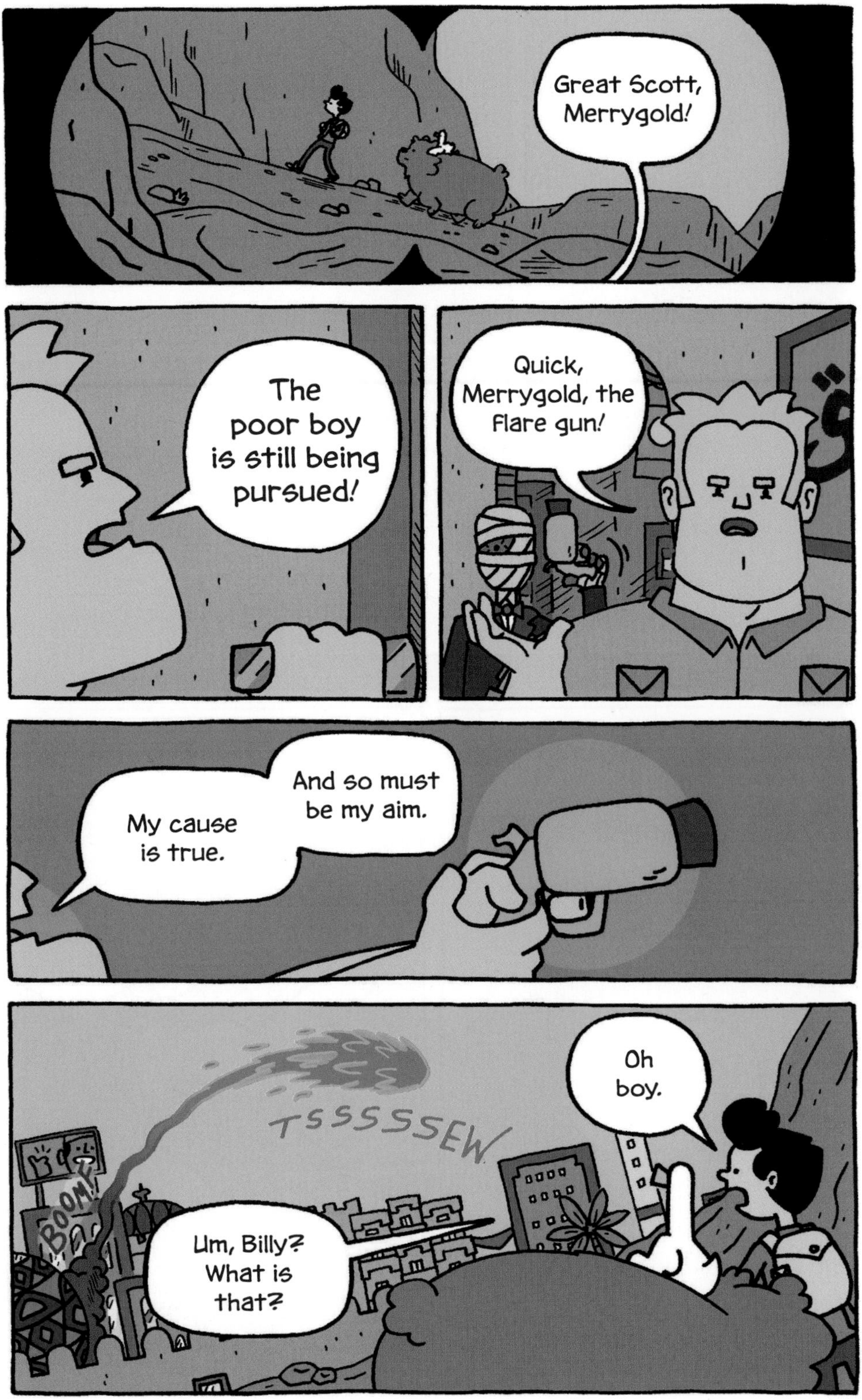
Great Scott, Merrygold!
The poor boy is still being pursued!
Quick, Merrygold, the flare gun!
My cause is true.
And so must be my aim.
TSSSSSEW
BOOM!
Oh boy.
Um, Billy? What is that?

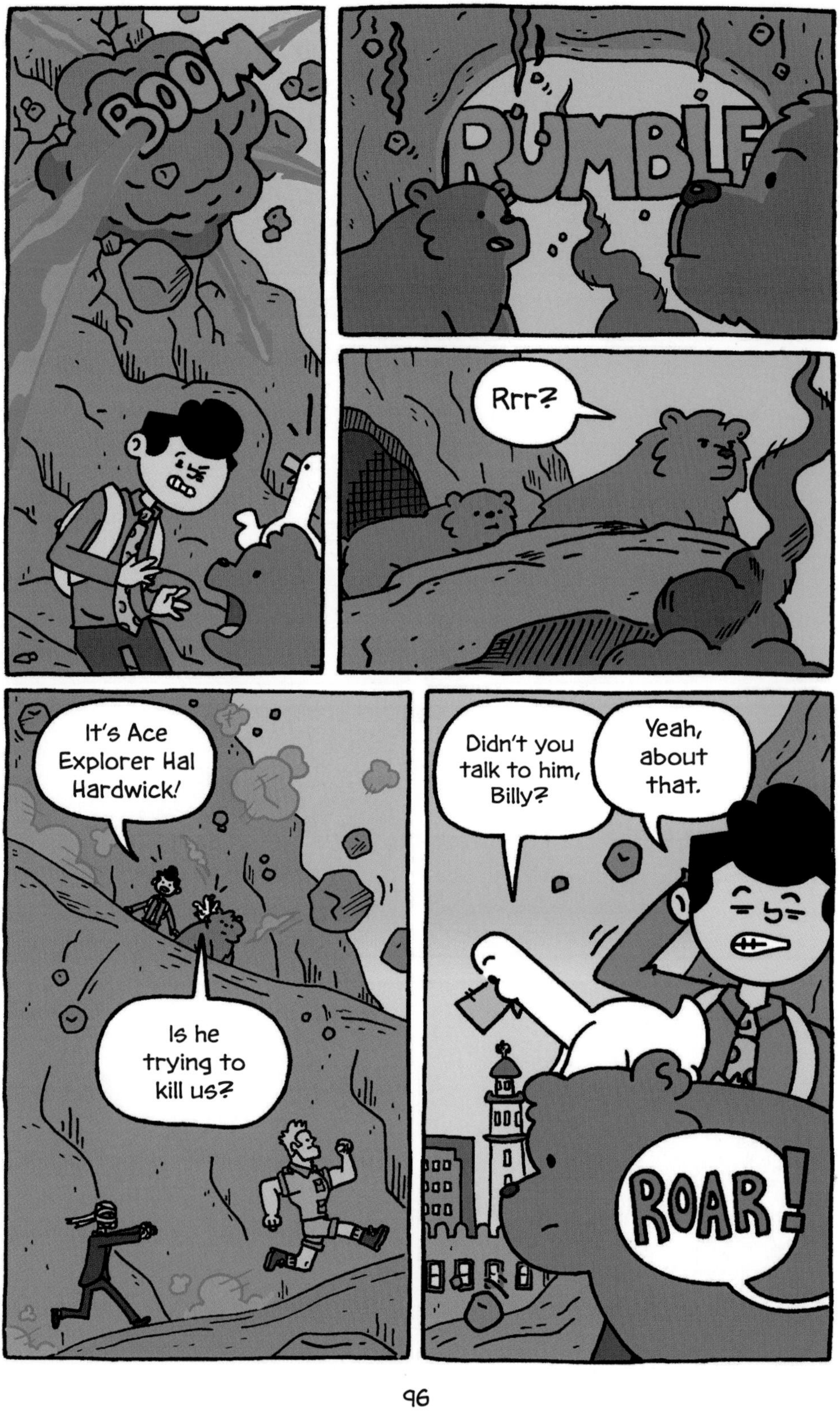
BOOM
RUMBLE
Rrr?
It's Ace Explorer Hal Hardwick!
Is he trying to kill us?
Didn't you talk to him, Billy?
Yeah, about that.
ROAR!

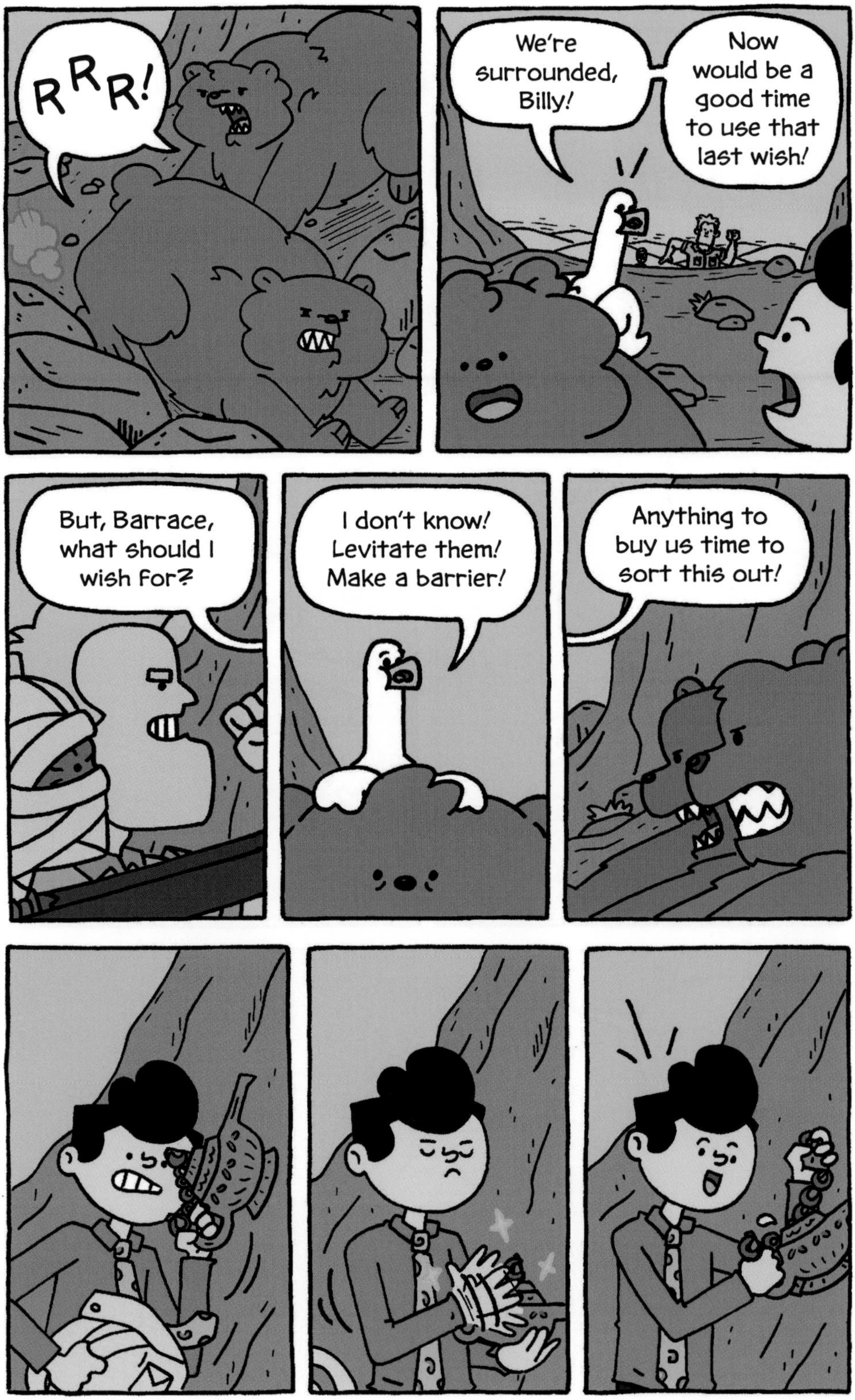
RRR!
We're surrounded, Billy!
Now would be a good time to use that last wish!
But, Barrace, what should I wish for?
I don't know! Levitate them! Make a barrier!
Anything to buy us time to sort this out!

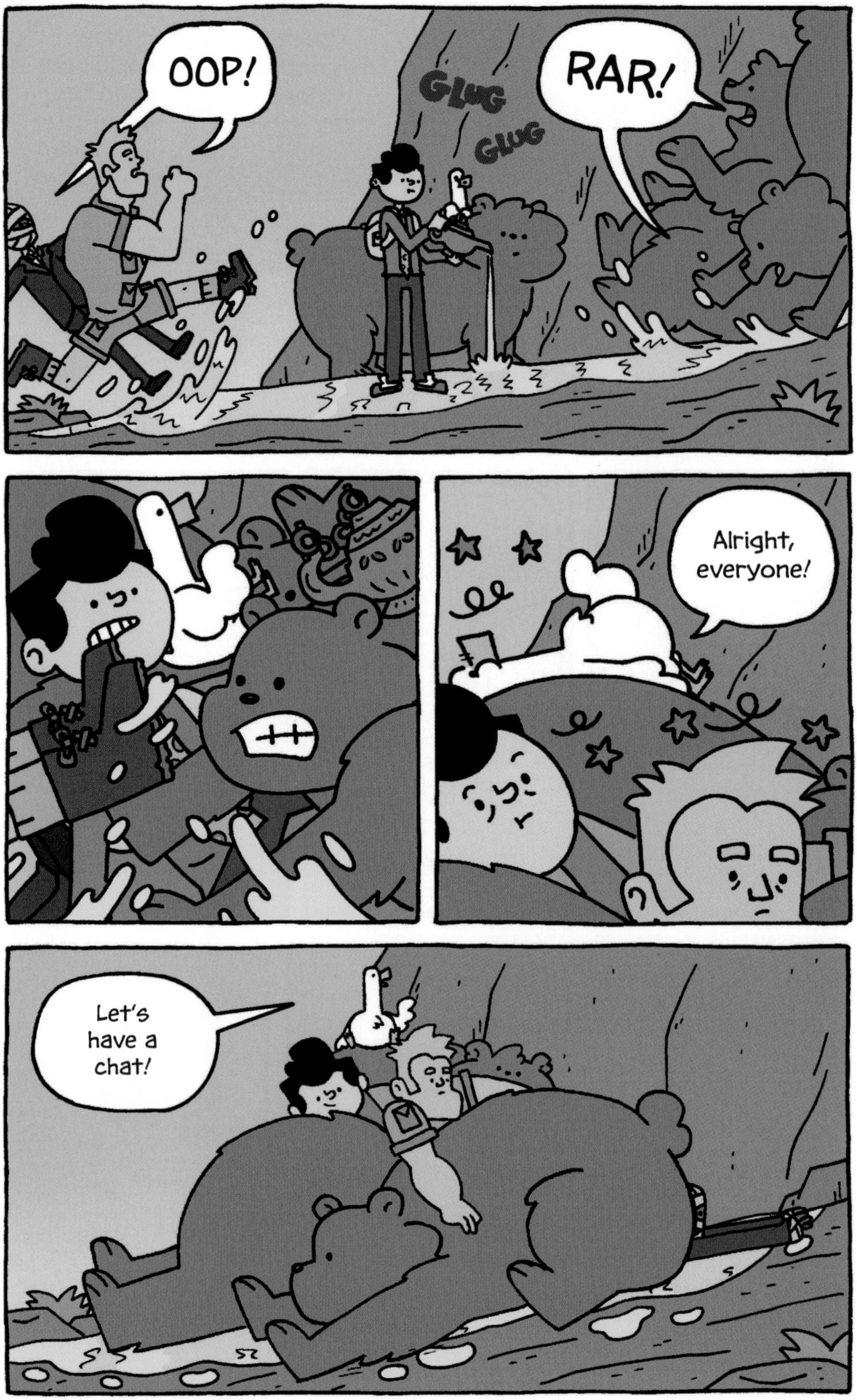
OOP!
GLUG
GLUG
RAR!
Alright, everyone!
Let's have a chat!

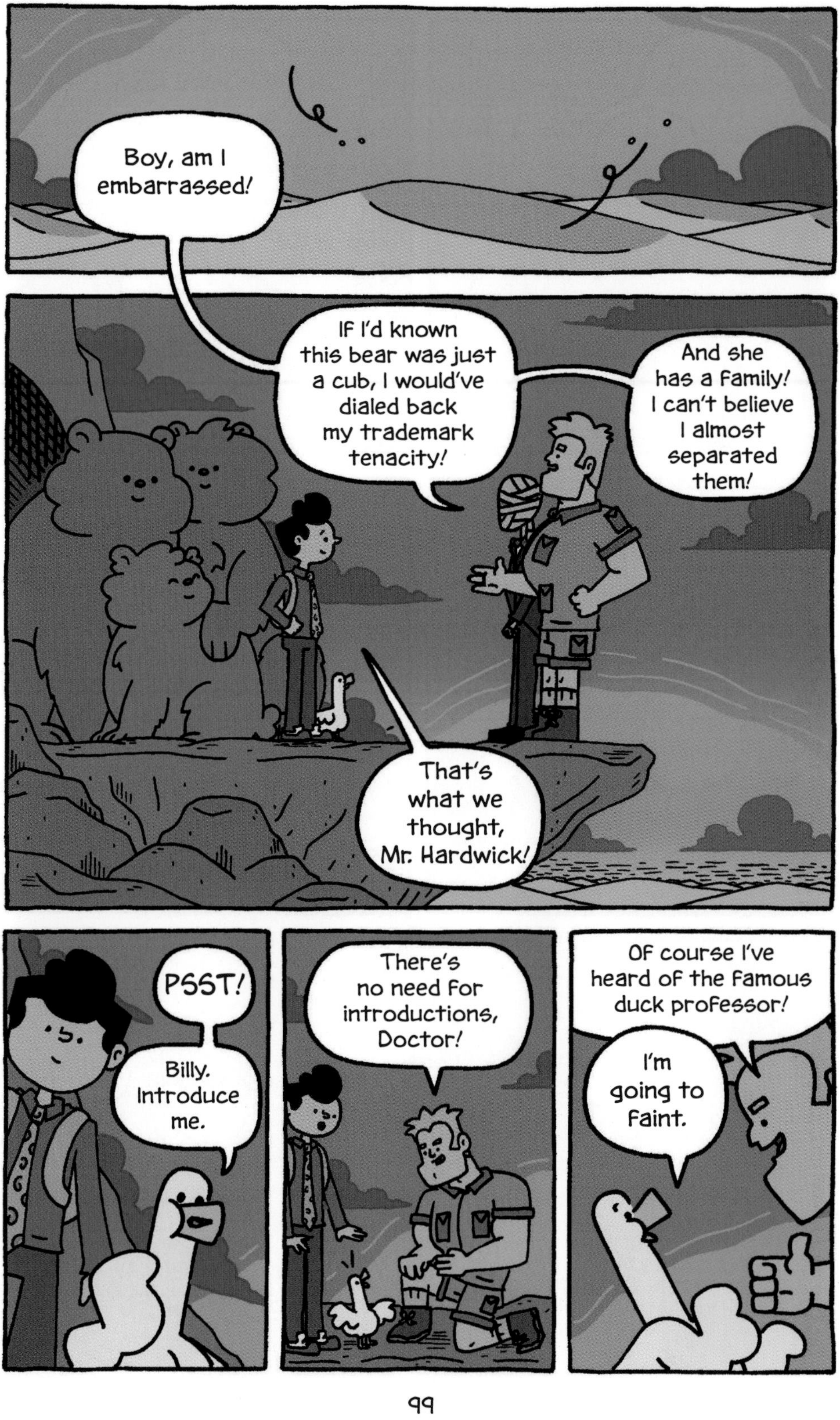
Boy, am I embarrassed!
If I'd known this bear was just a cub, I would've dialed back my trademark tenacity!
And she has a family! I can't believe I almost separated them!
That's what we thought, Mr. Hardwick!
PSST!
Billy. Introduce me.
There's no need for introductions, Doctor!
Of course I've heard of the famous duck professor!
I'm going to faint.

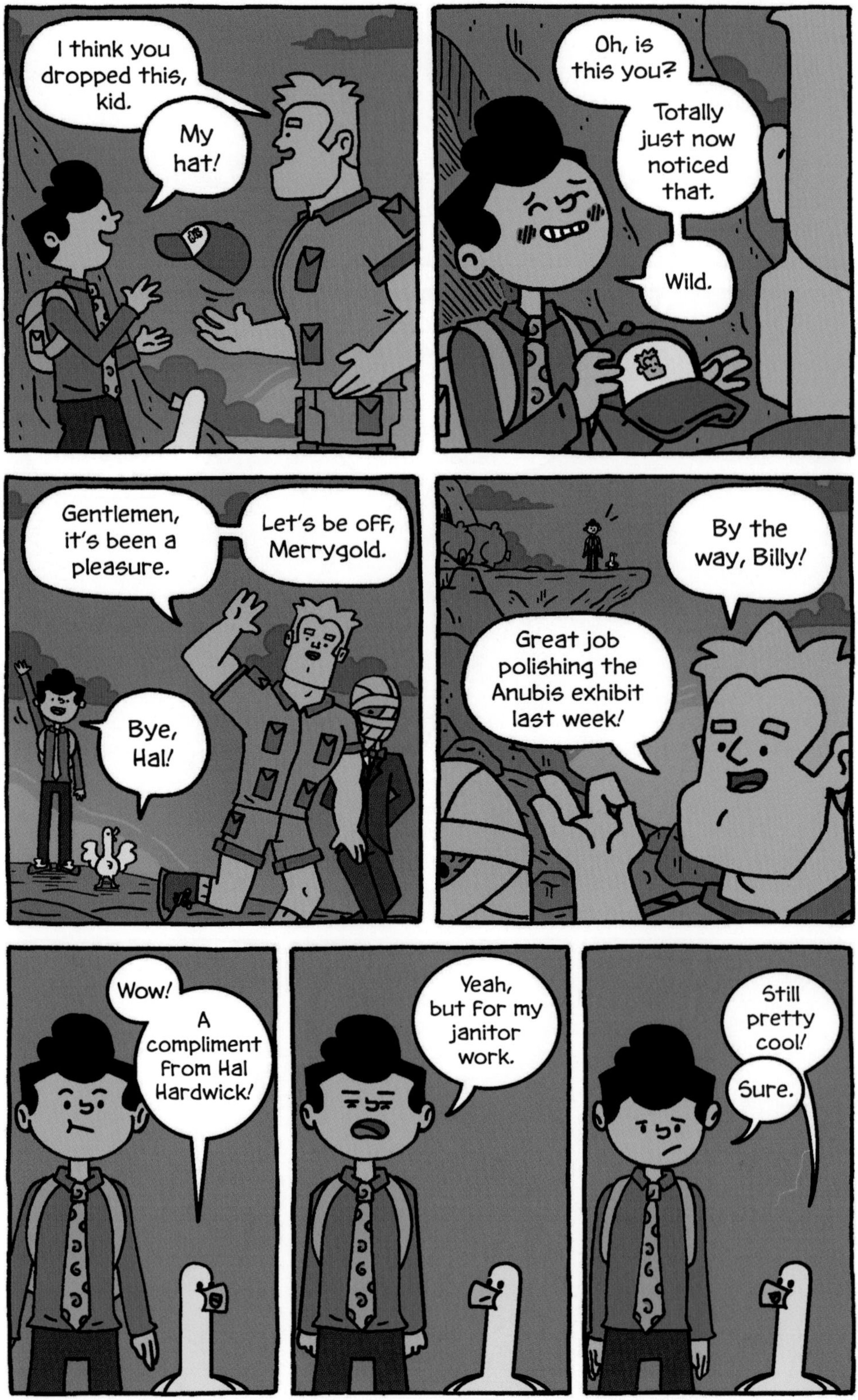
I think you dropped this, kid.
My hat!
Oh, is this you?
Totally just now noticed that.
Wild.
Gentlemen, it's been a pleasure.
Let's be off, Merrygold.
Bye, Hal!
By the way, Billy!
Great job polishing the Anubis exhibit last week!
Wow!
A compliment from Hal Hardwick!
Yeah, but for my janitor work.
Still pretty cool!
Sure.

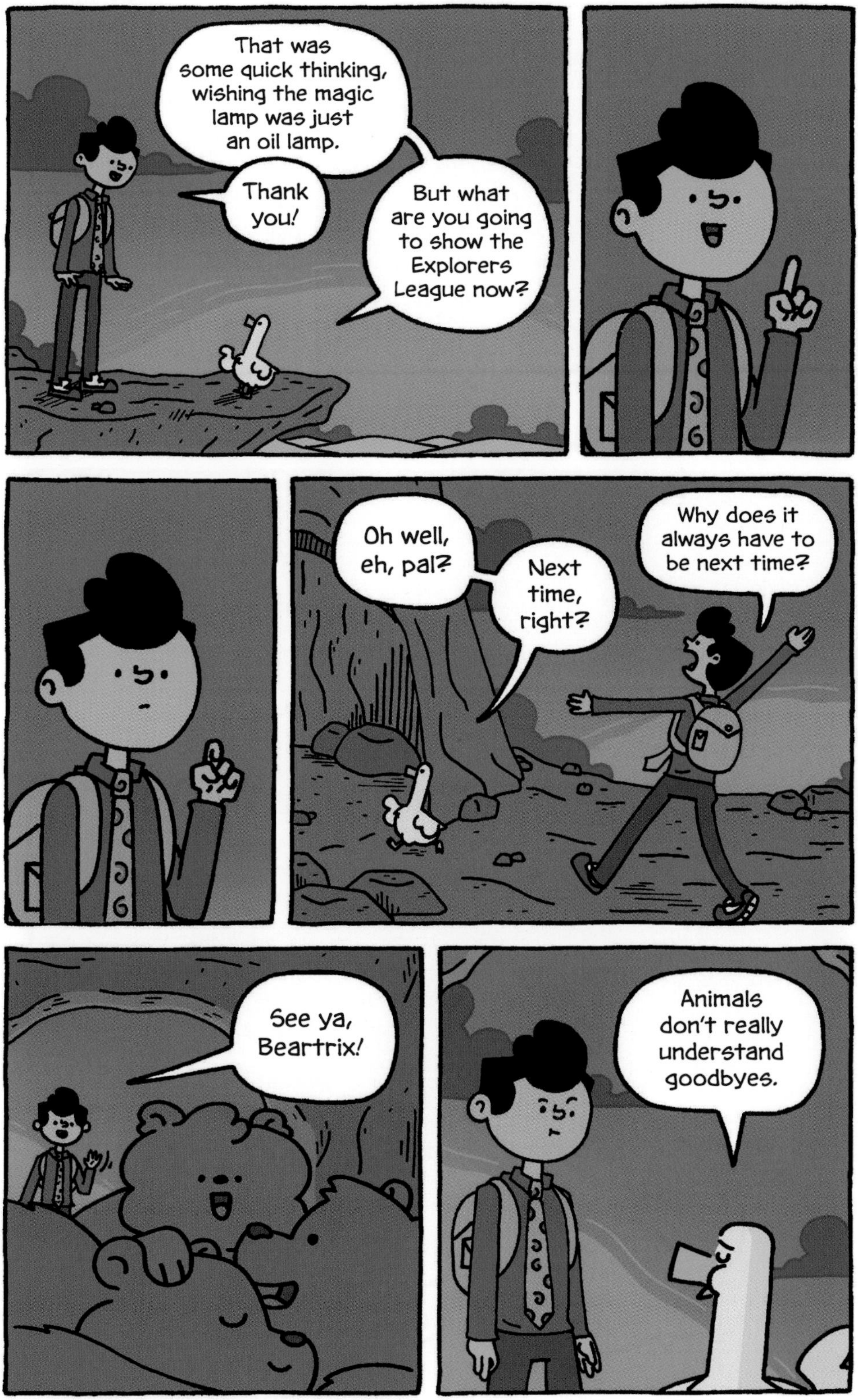
That was some quick thinking, wishing the magic lamp was just an oil lamp.
Thank you!
But what are you going to show the Explorers League now?
Oh well, eh, pal?
Next time, right?
Why does it always have to be next time?
See ya, Beartrix!
Animals don't really understand goodbyes.

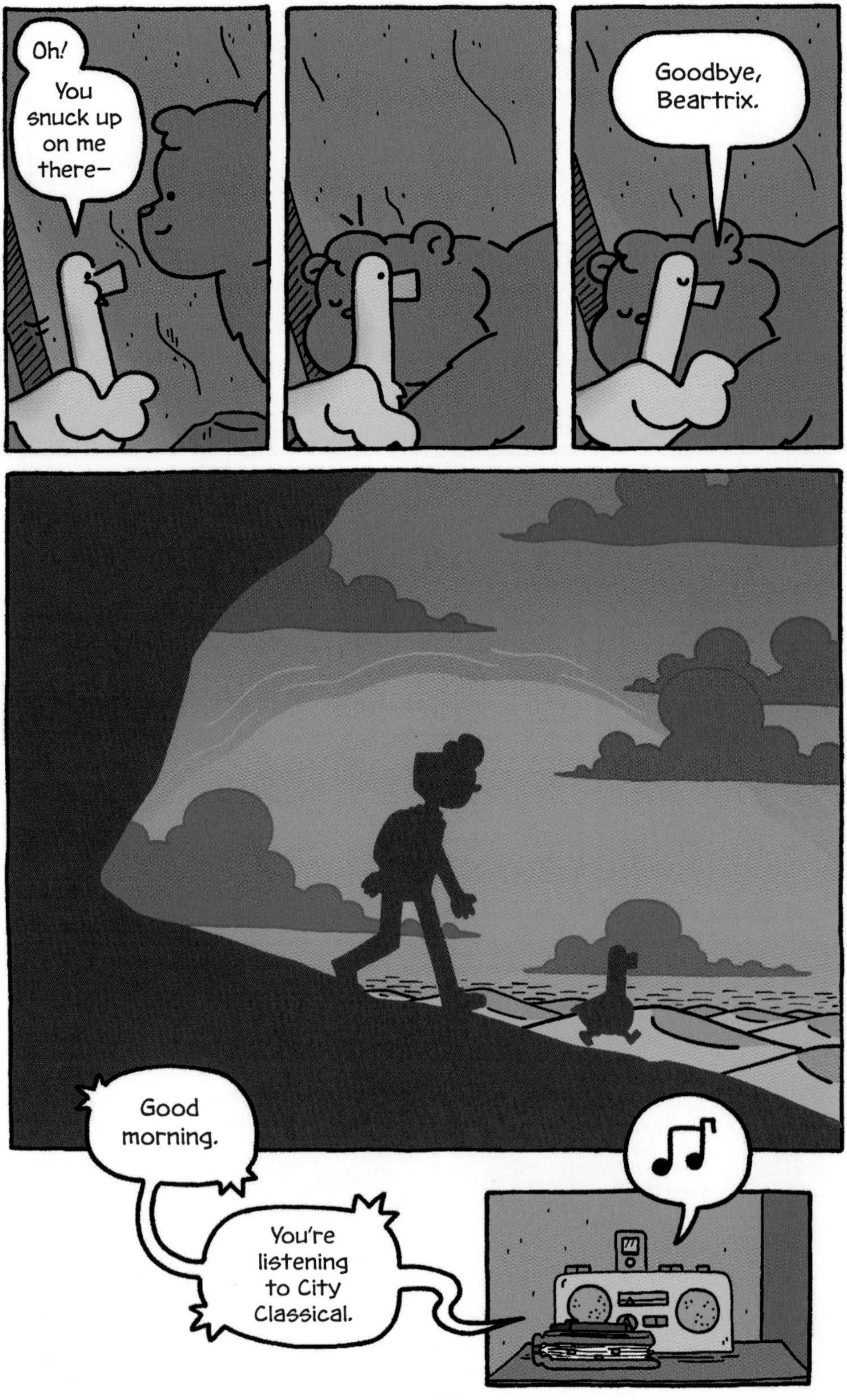
Oh!
You snuck up on me there—
Goodbye, Beartrix.
Good morning.
You're listening to City Classical.

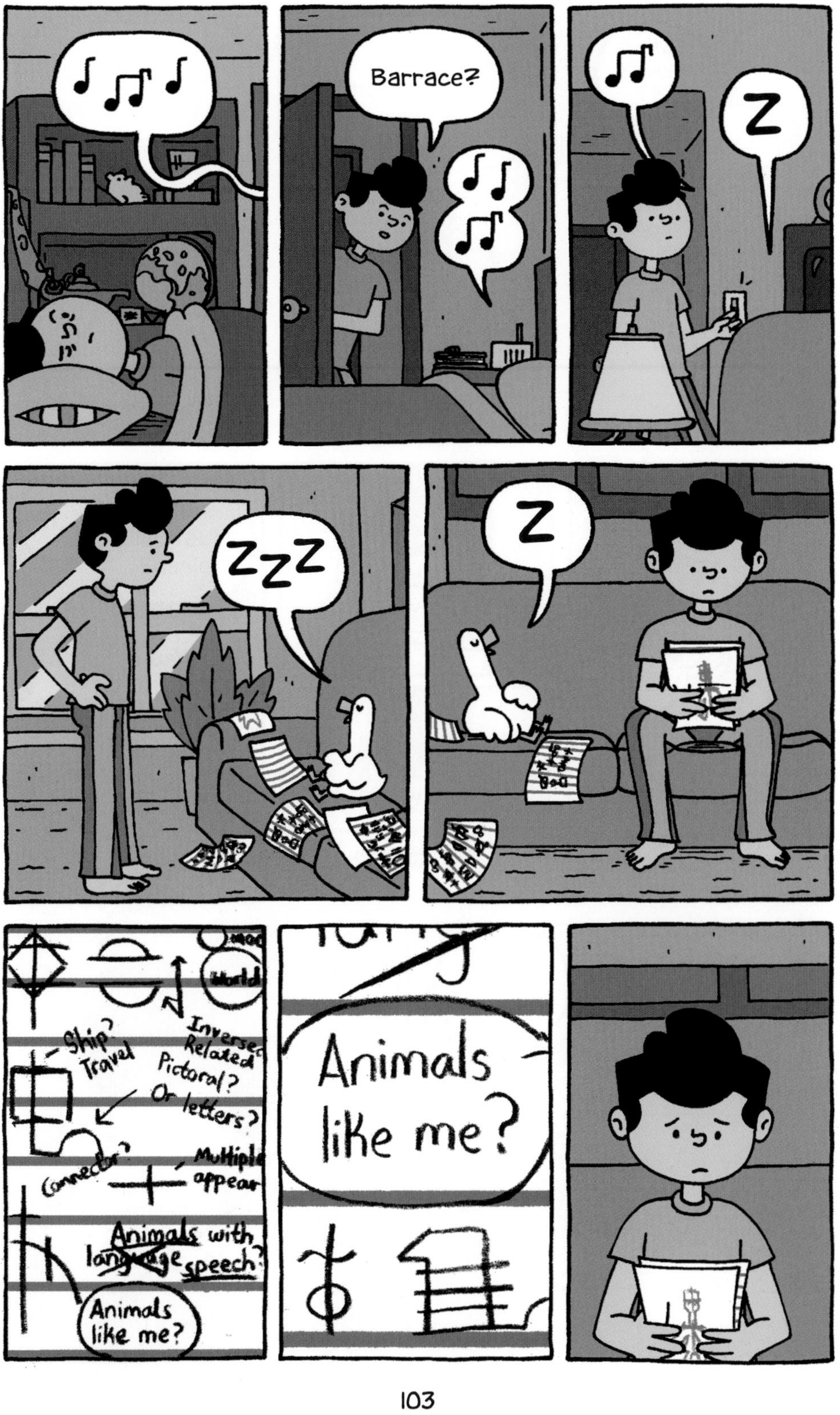
Barrace?
Z
ZZZ
Z
World
Ship? Travel
Inverse? Related
Pictoral? Or letters?
Connector?
Multiple appear
Animals with language speech?
Animals like me?
Animals like me?

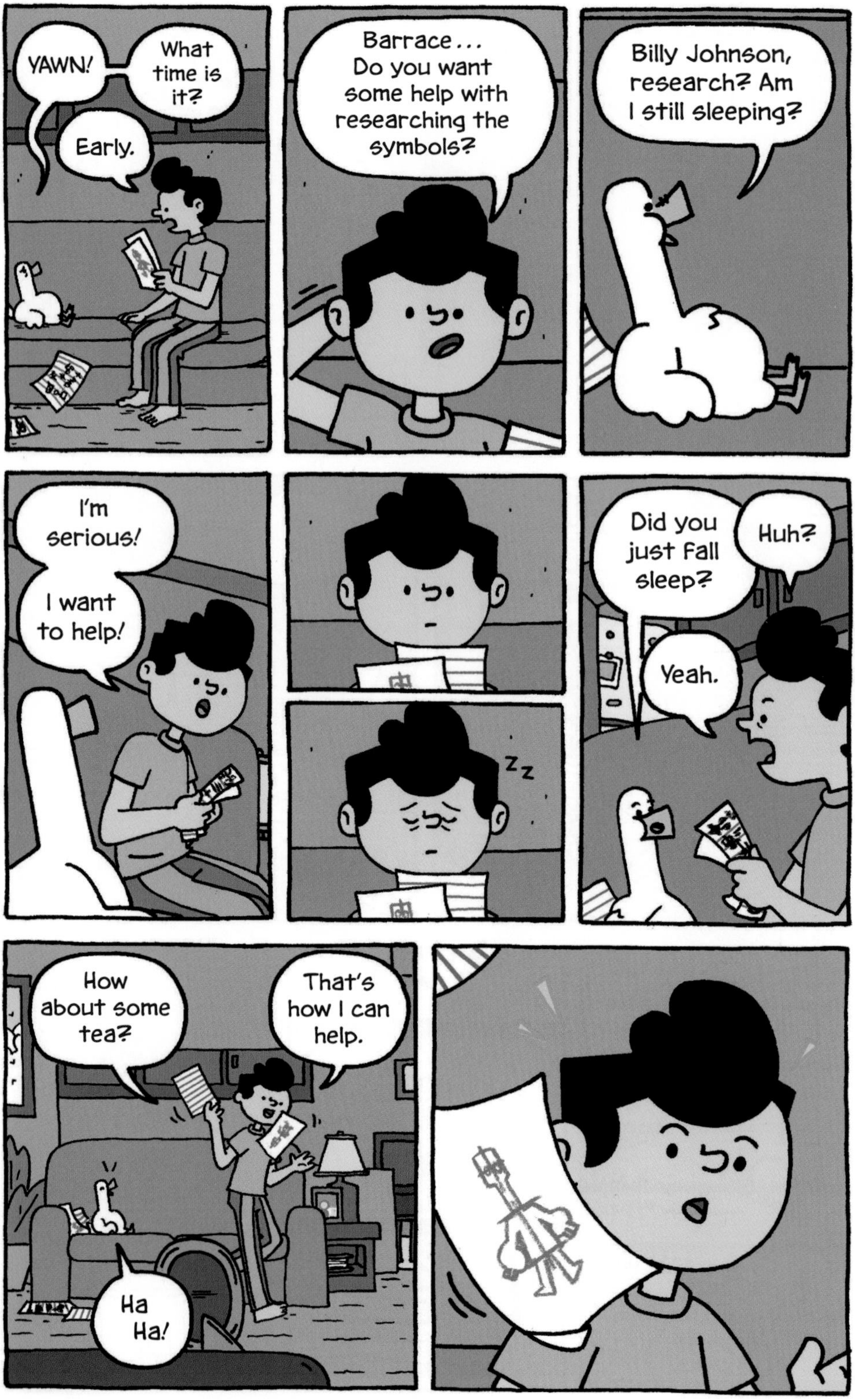
YAWN!
What time is it?
Early.
Barrace... Do you want some help with researching the symbols?
Billy Johnson, research? Am I still sleeping?
I'm serious!
I want to help!
Z Z
Did you just fall sleep?
Huh?
Yeah.
How about some tea?
That's how I can help.
Ha Ha!

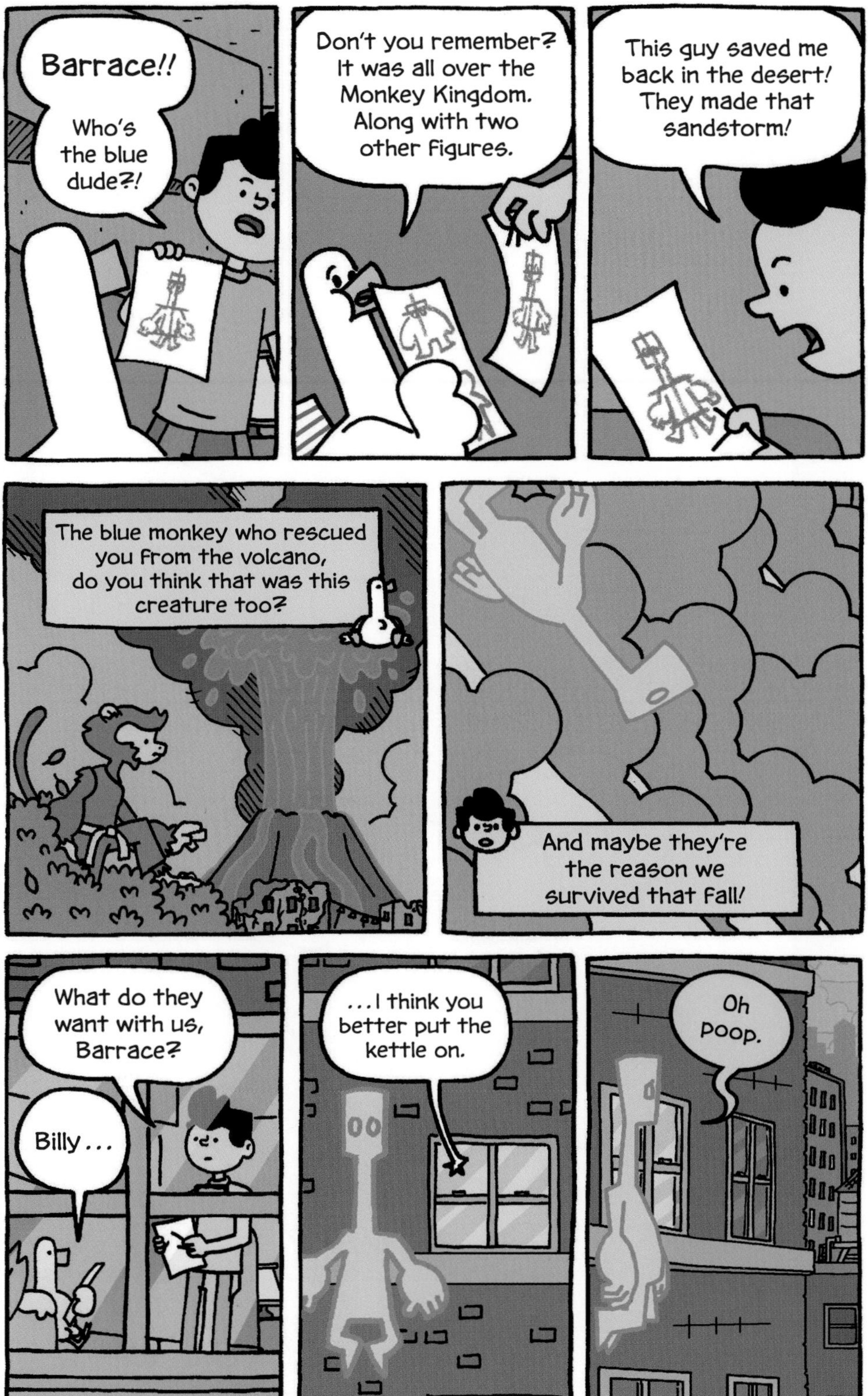
Barrace!!
Who's the blue dude?!
Don't you remember? It was all over the Monkey Kingdom. Along with two other figures.
This guy saved me back in the desert! They made that sandstorm!
The blue monkey who rescued you from the volcano, do you think that was this creature too?
And maybe they're the reason we survived that fall!
What do they want with us, Barrace?
Billy...
...I think you better put the kettle on.
Oh poop.

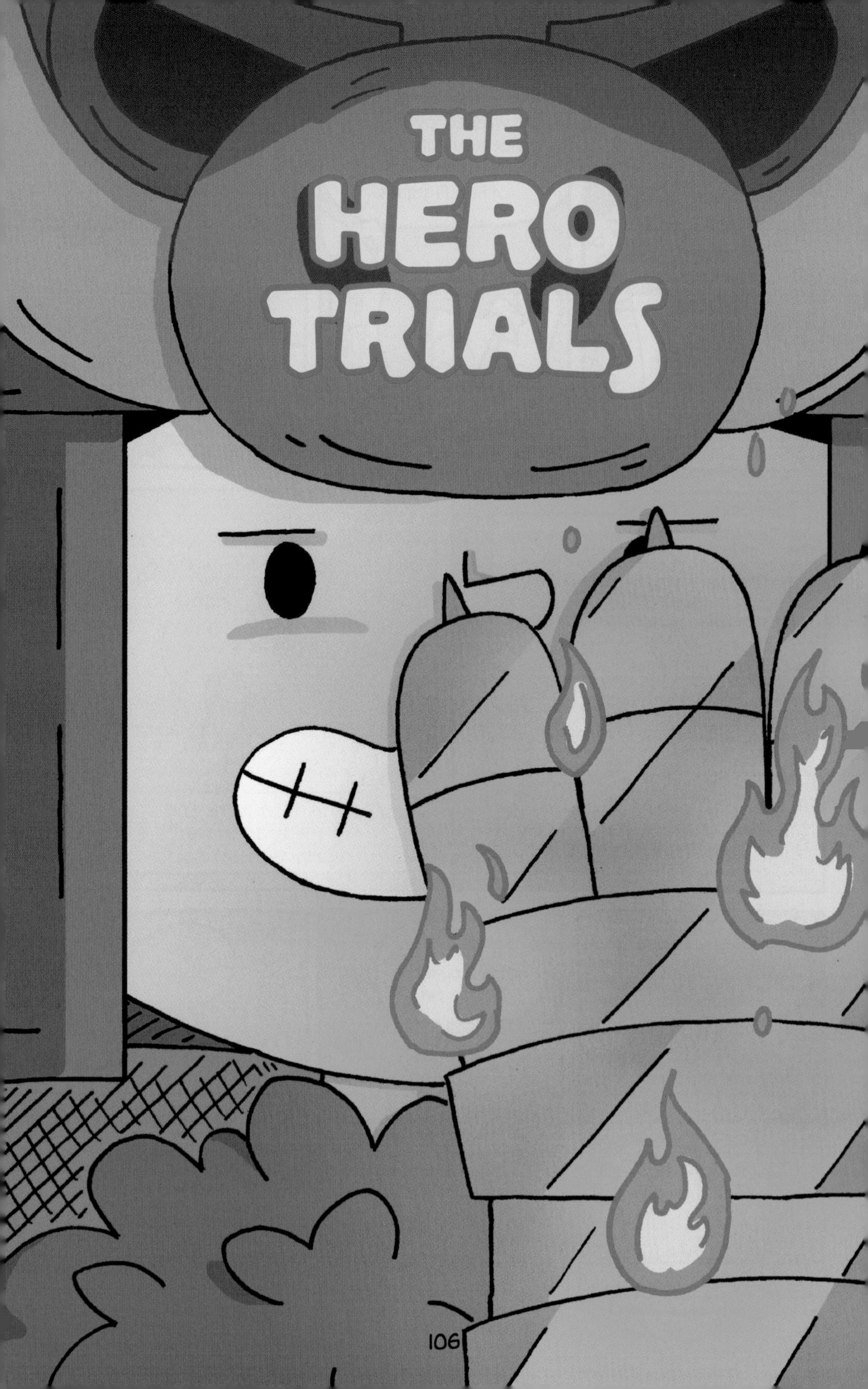
THE
HERO
TRIALS

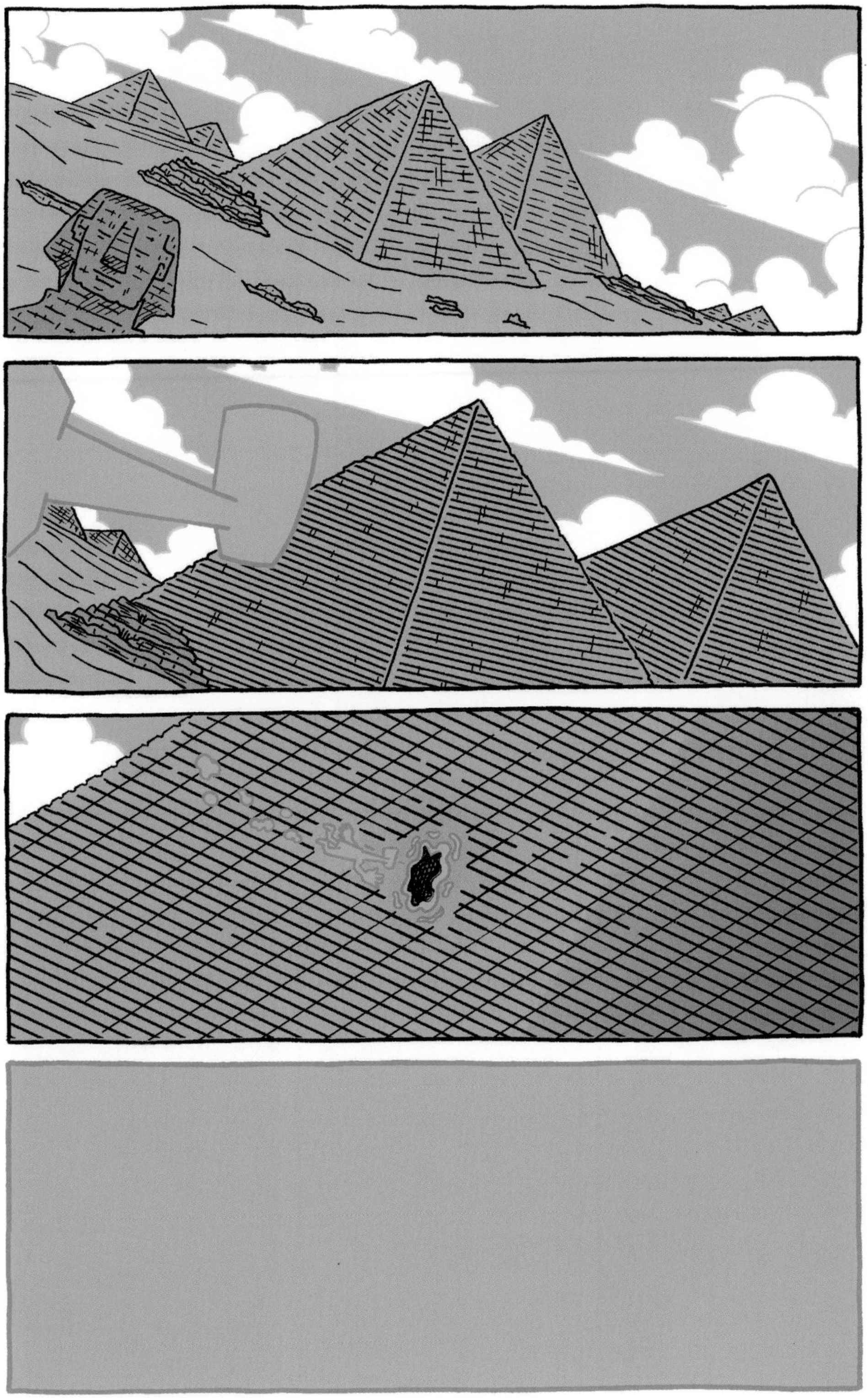

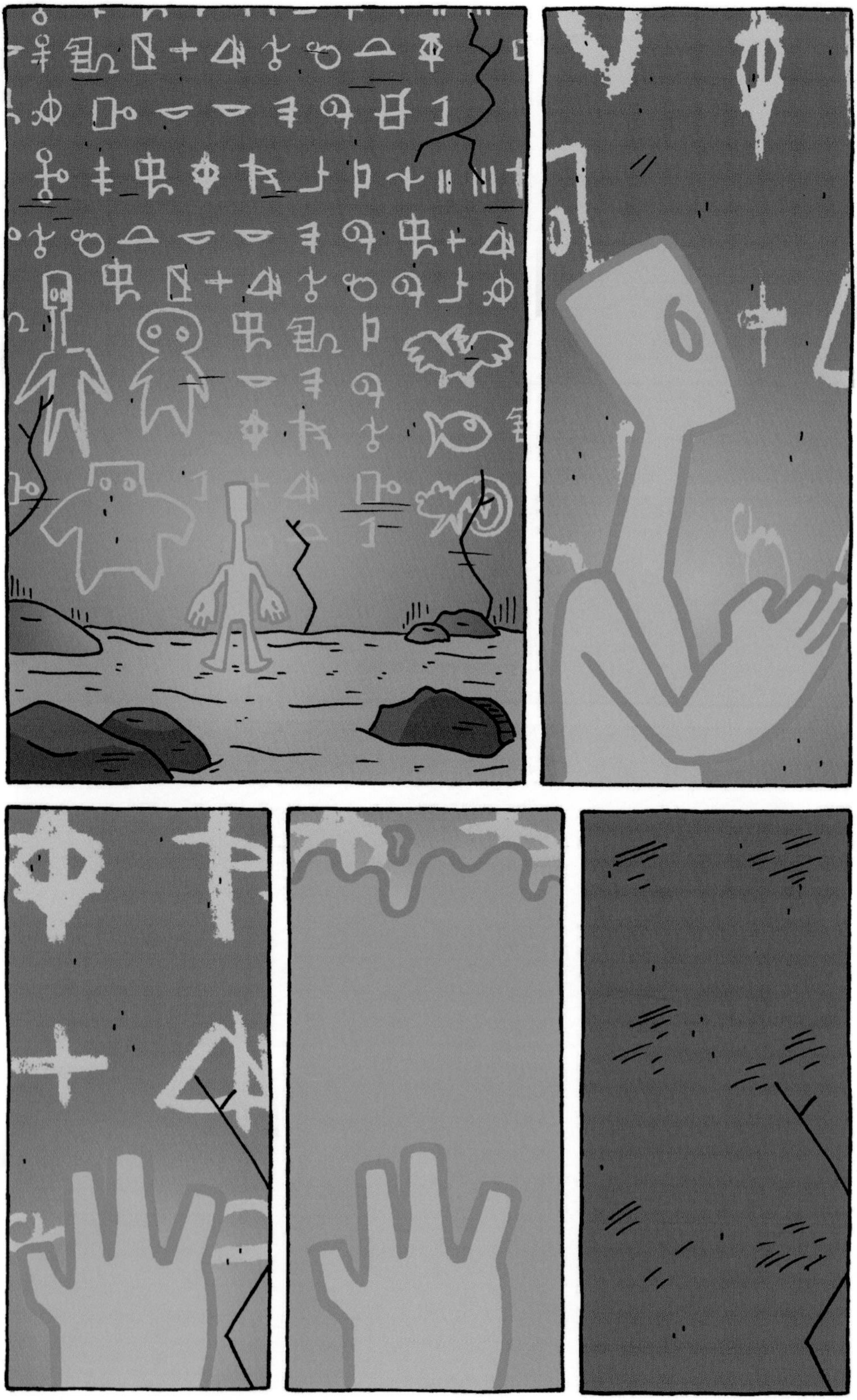

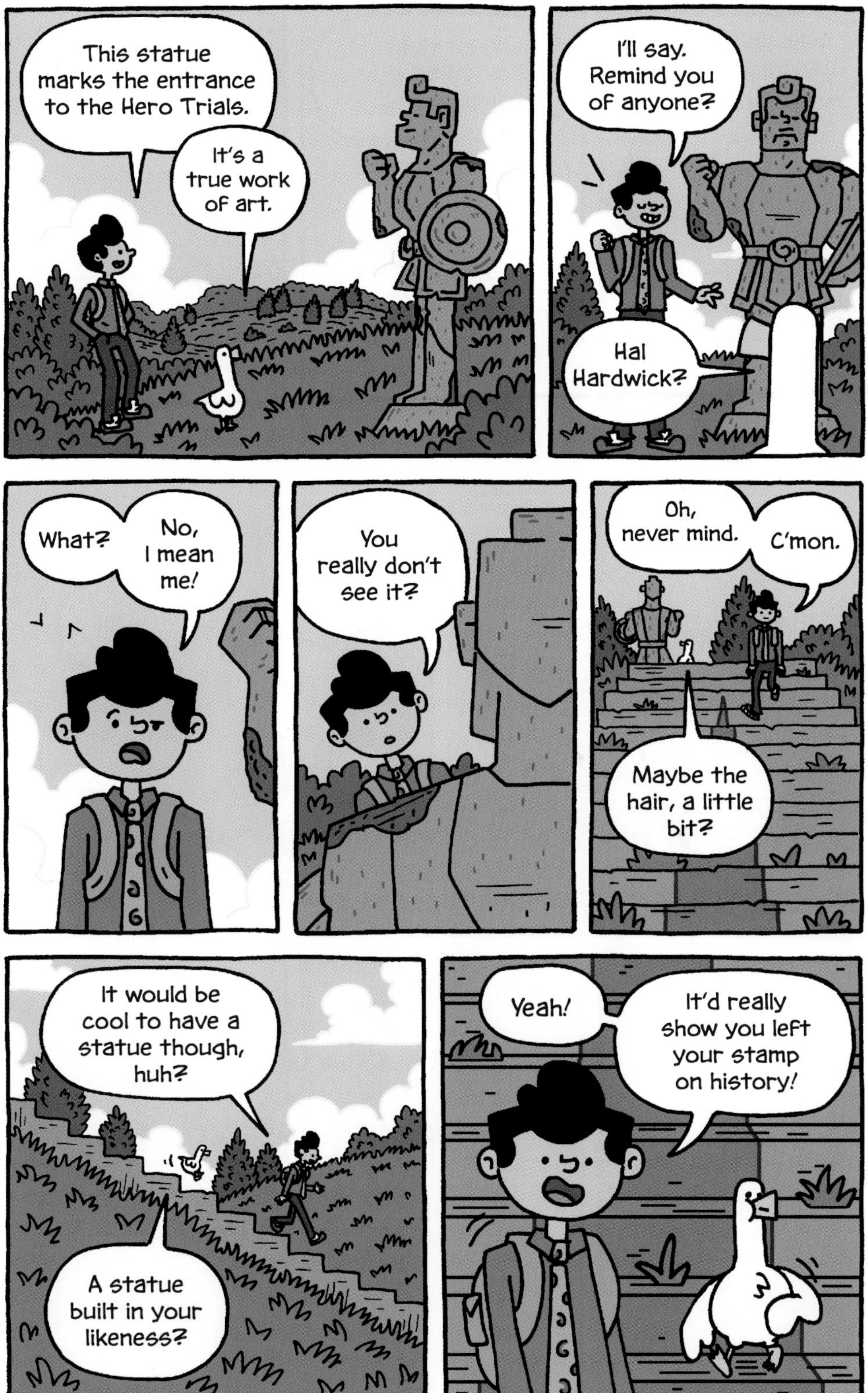
This statue marks the entrance to the Hero Trials.
It's a true work of art.
I'll say. Remind you of anyone?
Hal Hardwick?
What?
No, I mean me!
You really don't see it?
Oh, never mind.
C'mon.
Maybe the hair, a little bit?
It would be cool to have a statue though, huh?
A statue built in your likeness?
Yeah!
It'd really show you left your stamp on history!

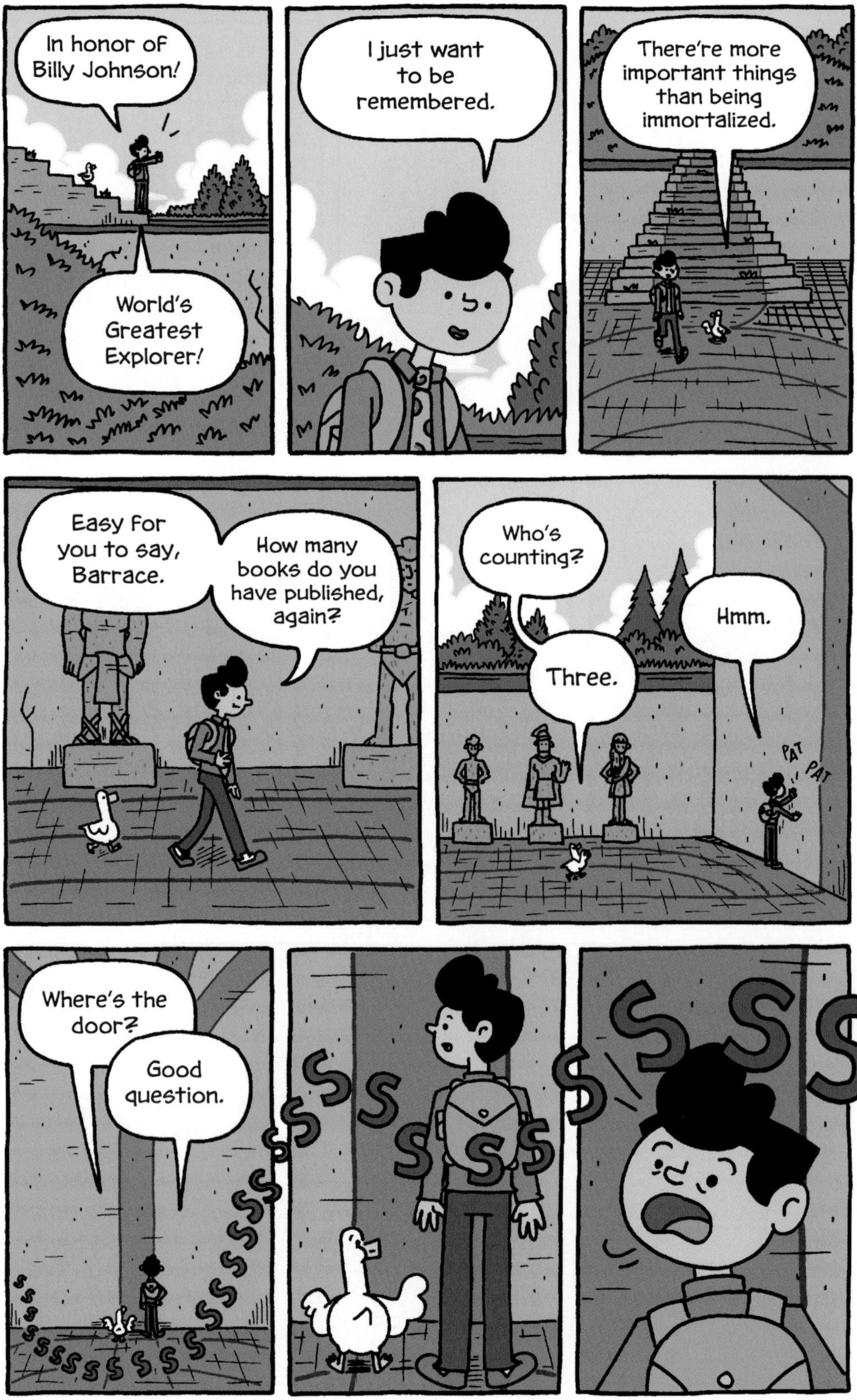
In honor of Billy Johnson!
World's Greatest Explorer!
I just want to be remembered.
There're more important things than being immortalized.
Easy for you to say, Barrace.
How many books do you have published, again?
Who's counting?
Three.
Hmm.
PAT PAT
Where's the door?
Good question.

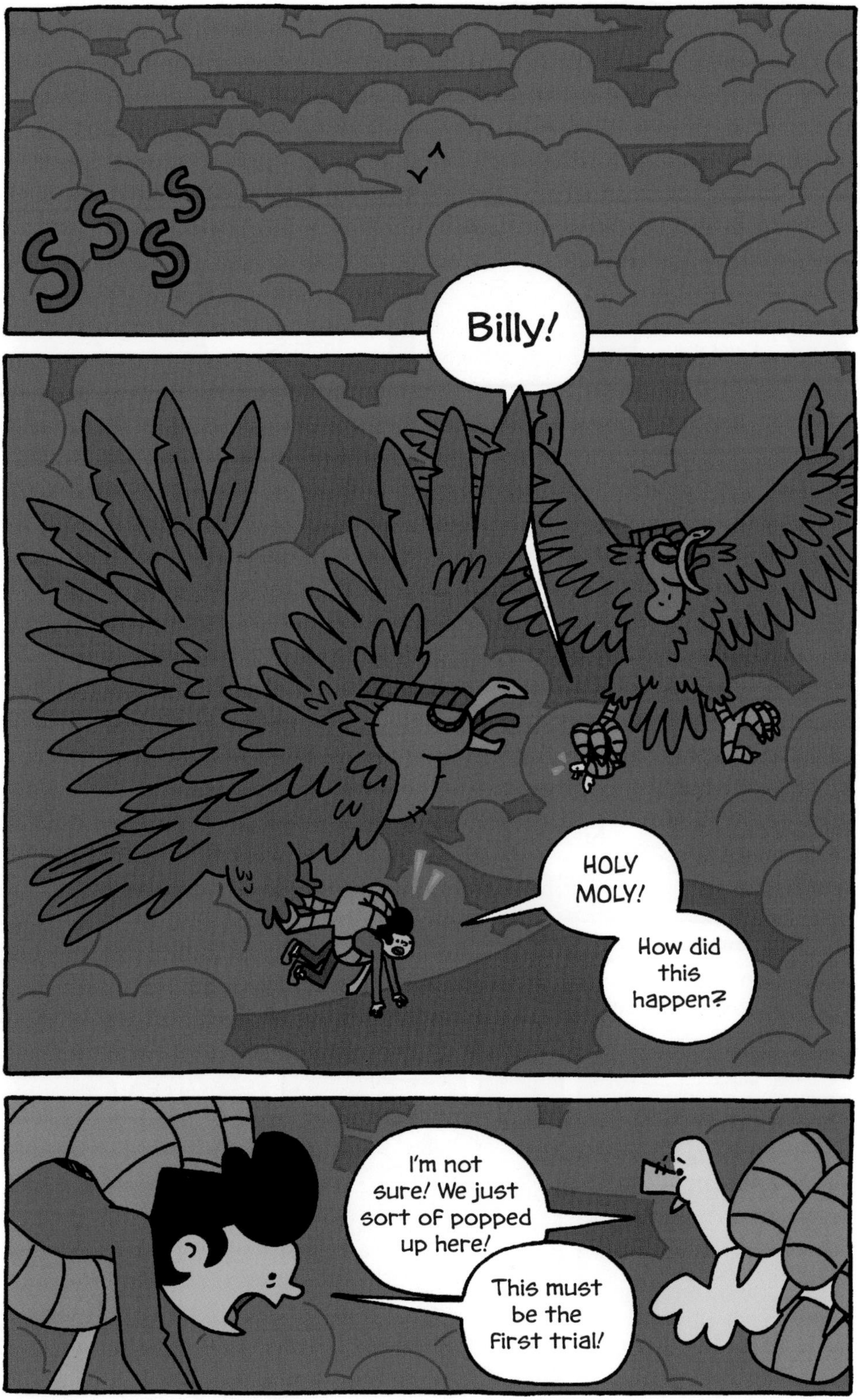
Billy!
HOLY MOLY!
How did this happen?
I'm not sure! We just sort of popped up here!
This must be the first trial!

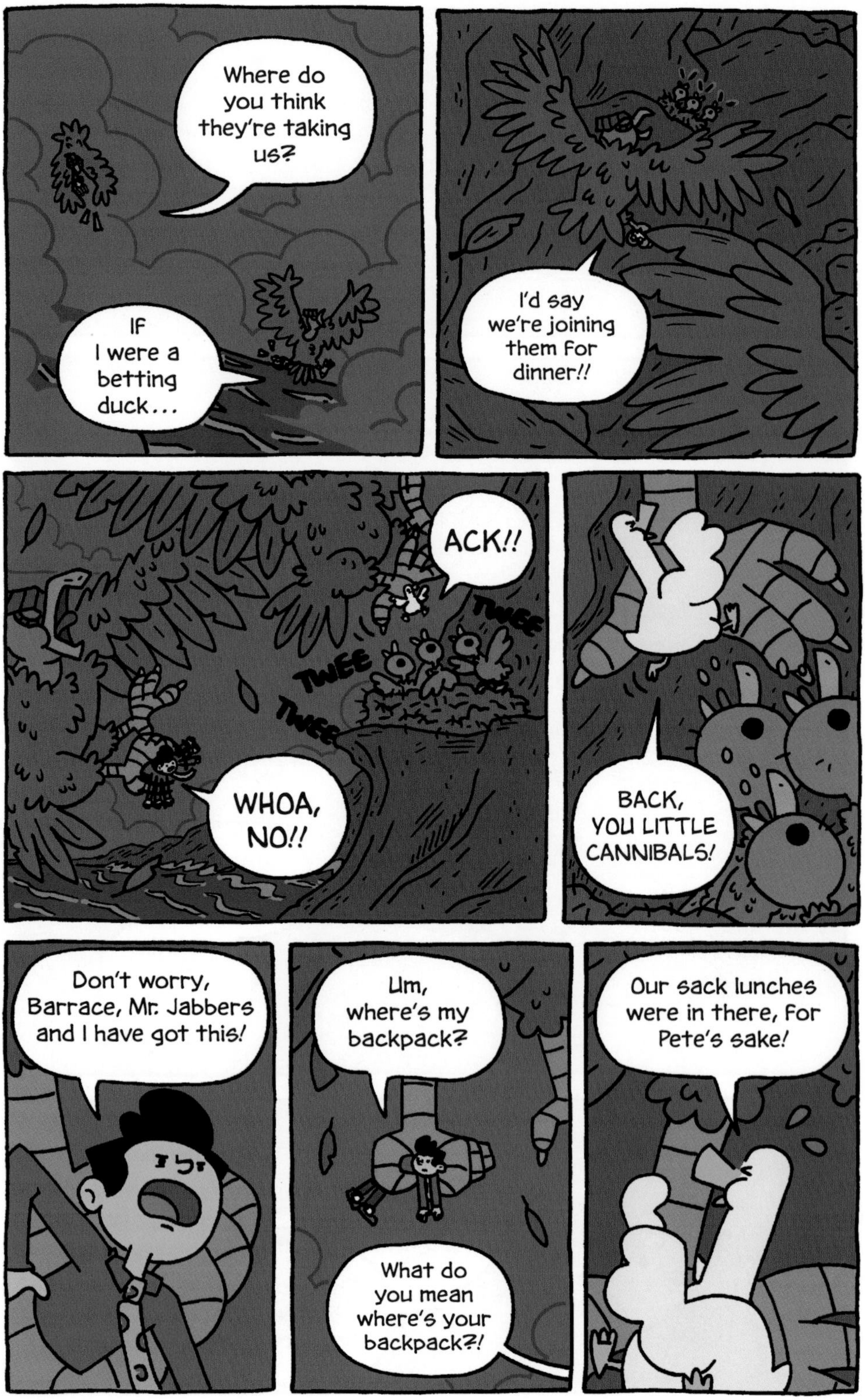
Where do you think they're taking us?
If I were a betting duck...
I'd say we're joining them for dinner!!
ACK!!
TWEE
TWEE
TWEE
WHOA, NO!!
BACK, YOU LITTLE CANNIBALS!
Don't worry, Barrace, Mr. Jabbers and I have got this!
Um, where's my backpack?
What do you mean where's your backpack?!
Our sack lunches were in there, for Pete's sake!

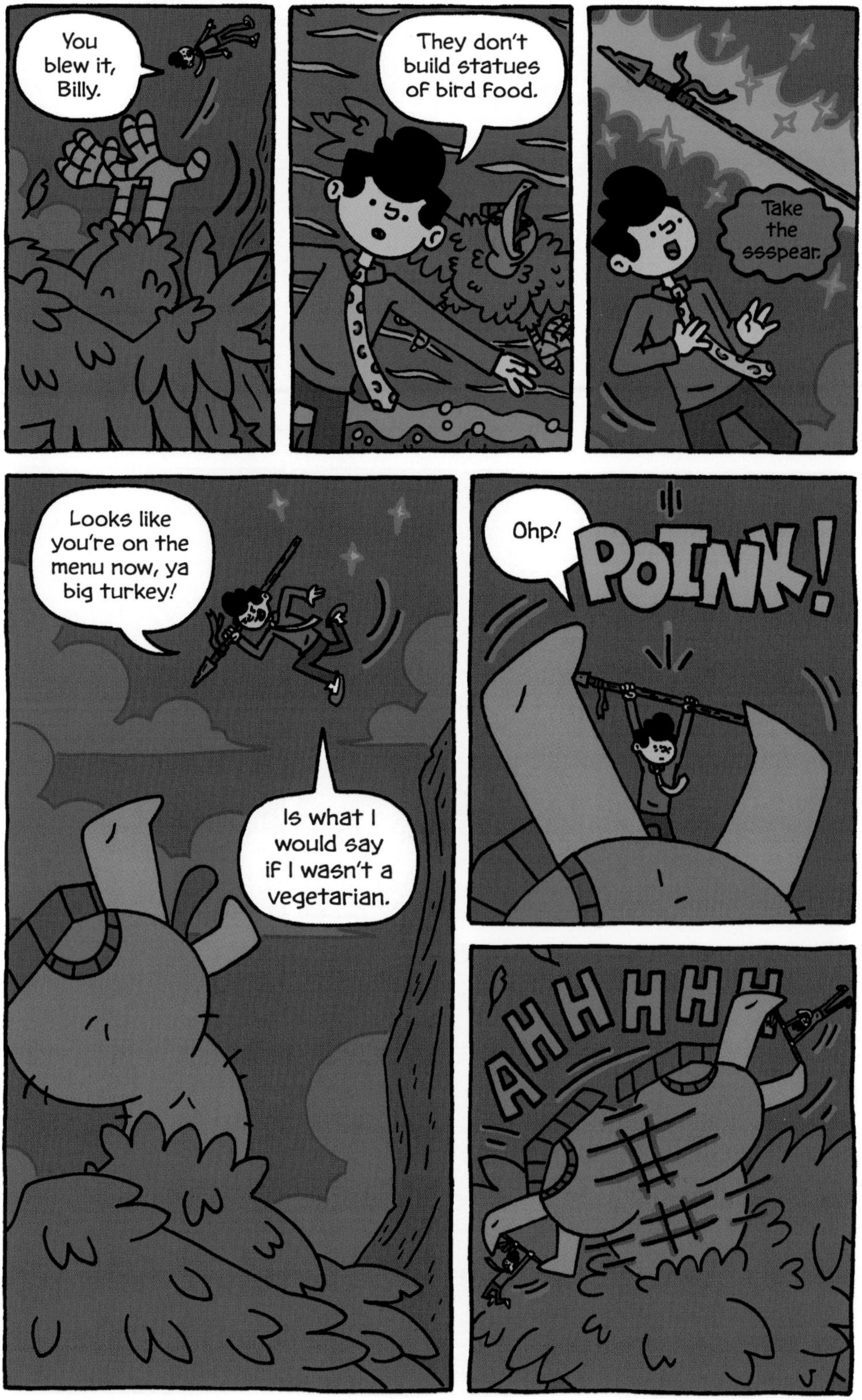

You blew it, Billy.
They don't build statues of bird food.
Take the ssspear.
Looks like you're on the menu now, ya big turkey!
Is what I would say if I wasn't a vegetarian.
Ohp!
POINK!
AHHHHH

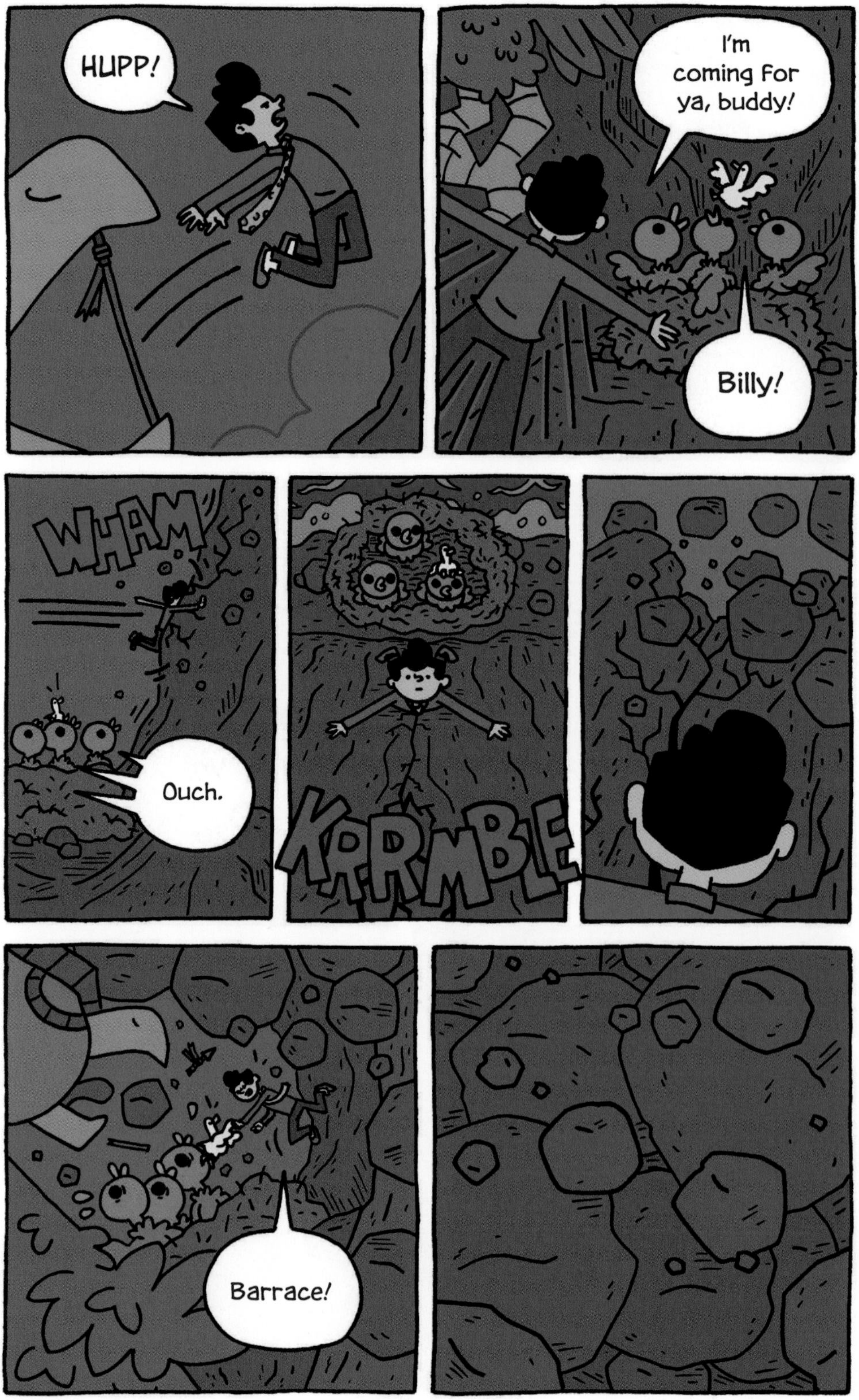
HUPP!
I'm coming for ya, buddy!
Billy!
WHAM
Ouch.
KRRMBLE
Barrace!

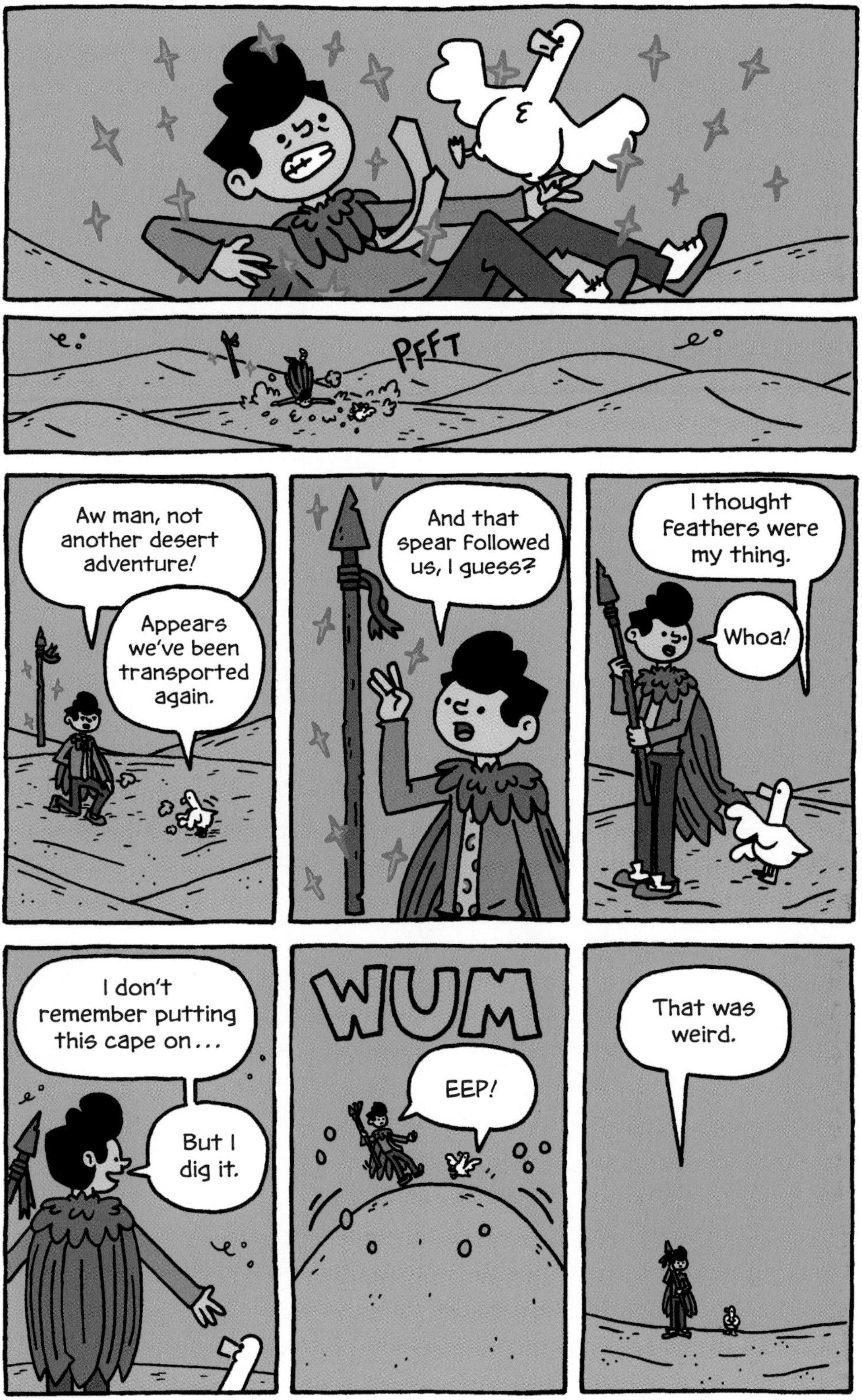
PFFT
Aw man, not another desert adventure!
Appears we've been transported again.
And that spear followed us, I guess?
I thought feathers were my thing.
Whoa!
I don't remember putting this cape on...
But I dig it.
WUM
EEP!
That was weird.

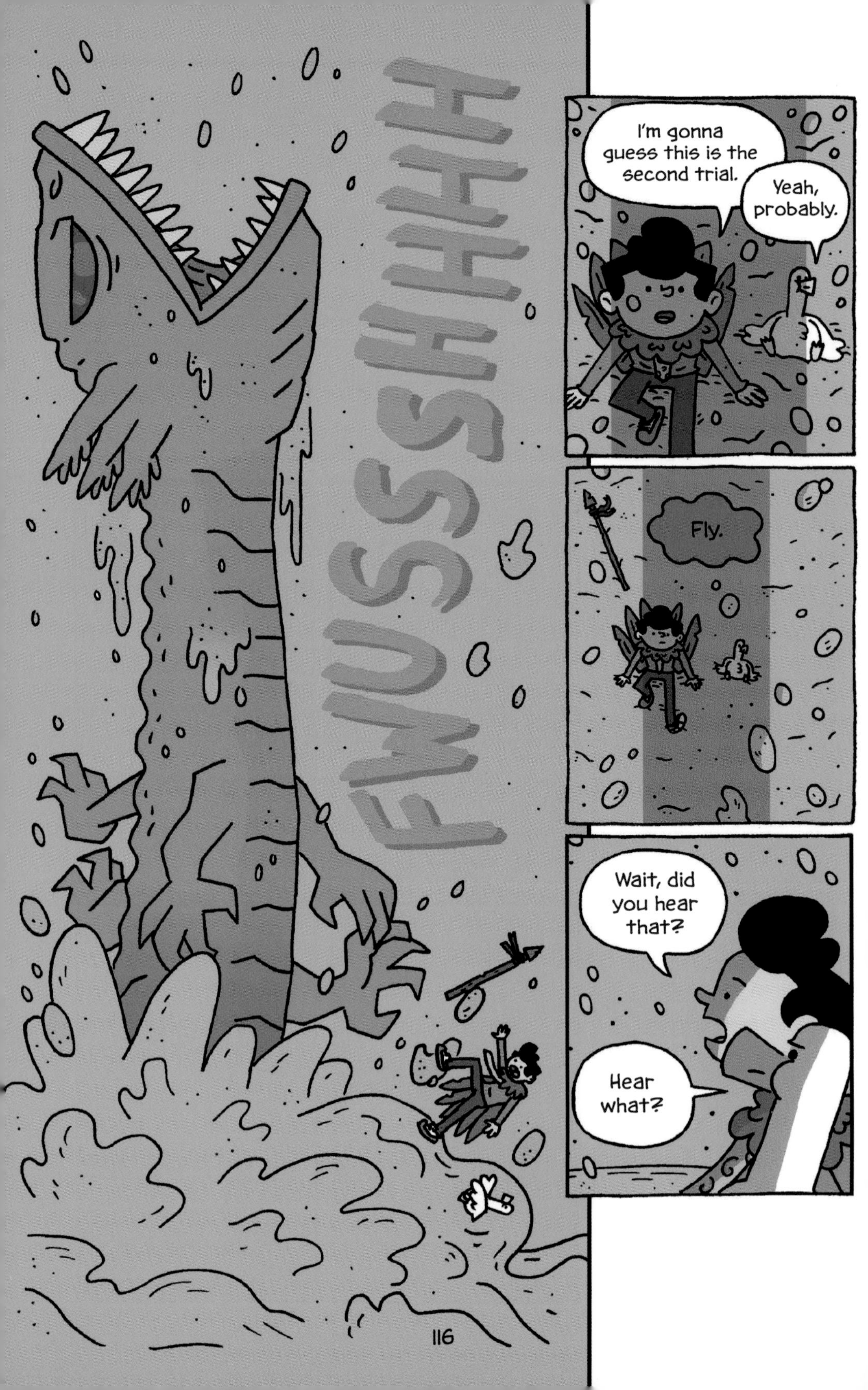
FWUSSHHHH
I'm gonna guess this is the second trial.
Yeah, probably.
Fly.
Wait, did you hear that?
Hear what?

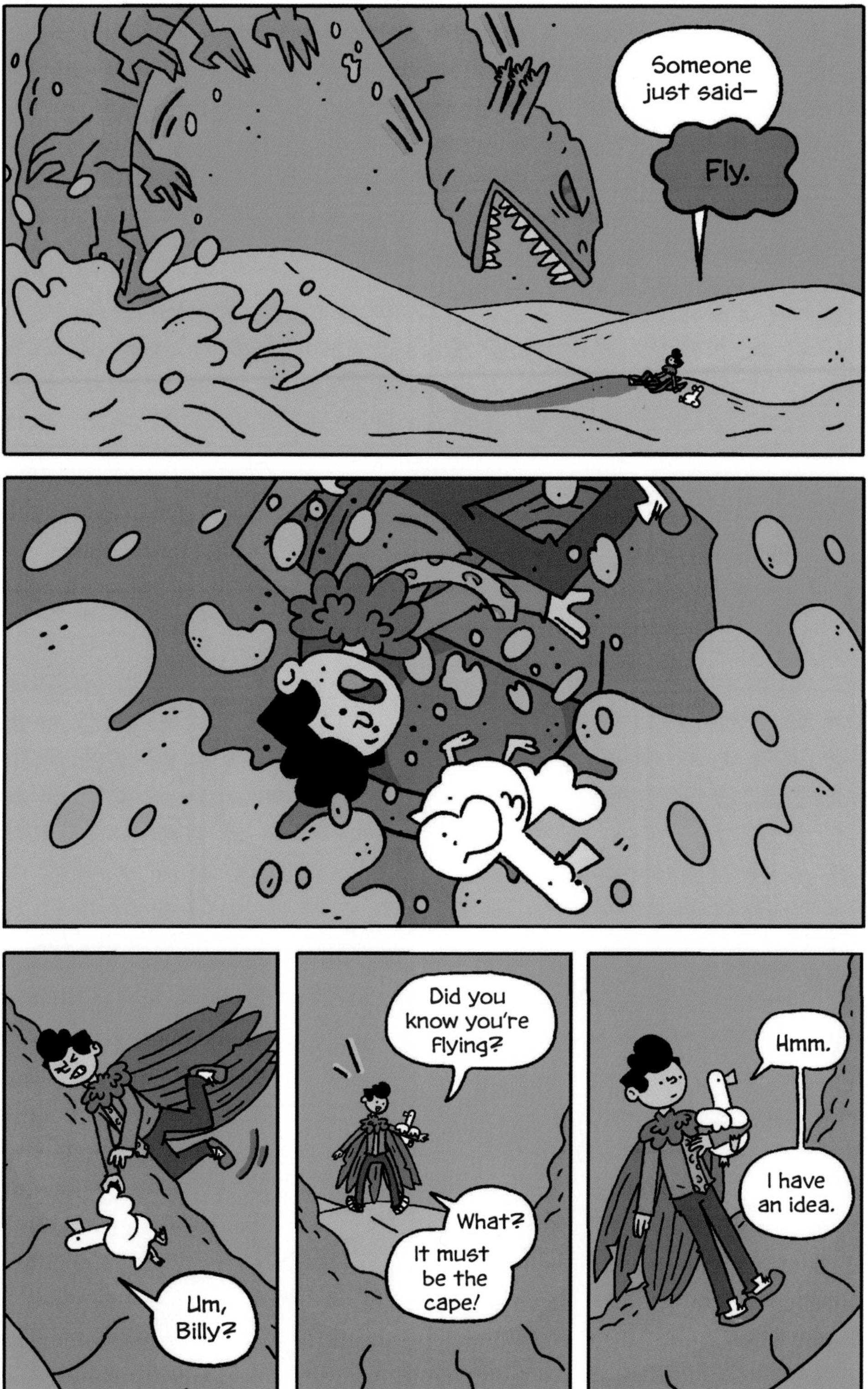
Someone just said—
Fly.
Um, Billy?
Did you know you're flying?
What?
It must be the cape!
Hmm.
I have an idea.

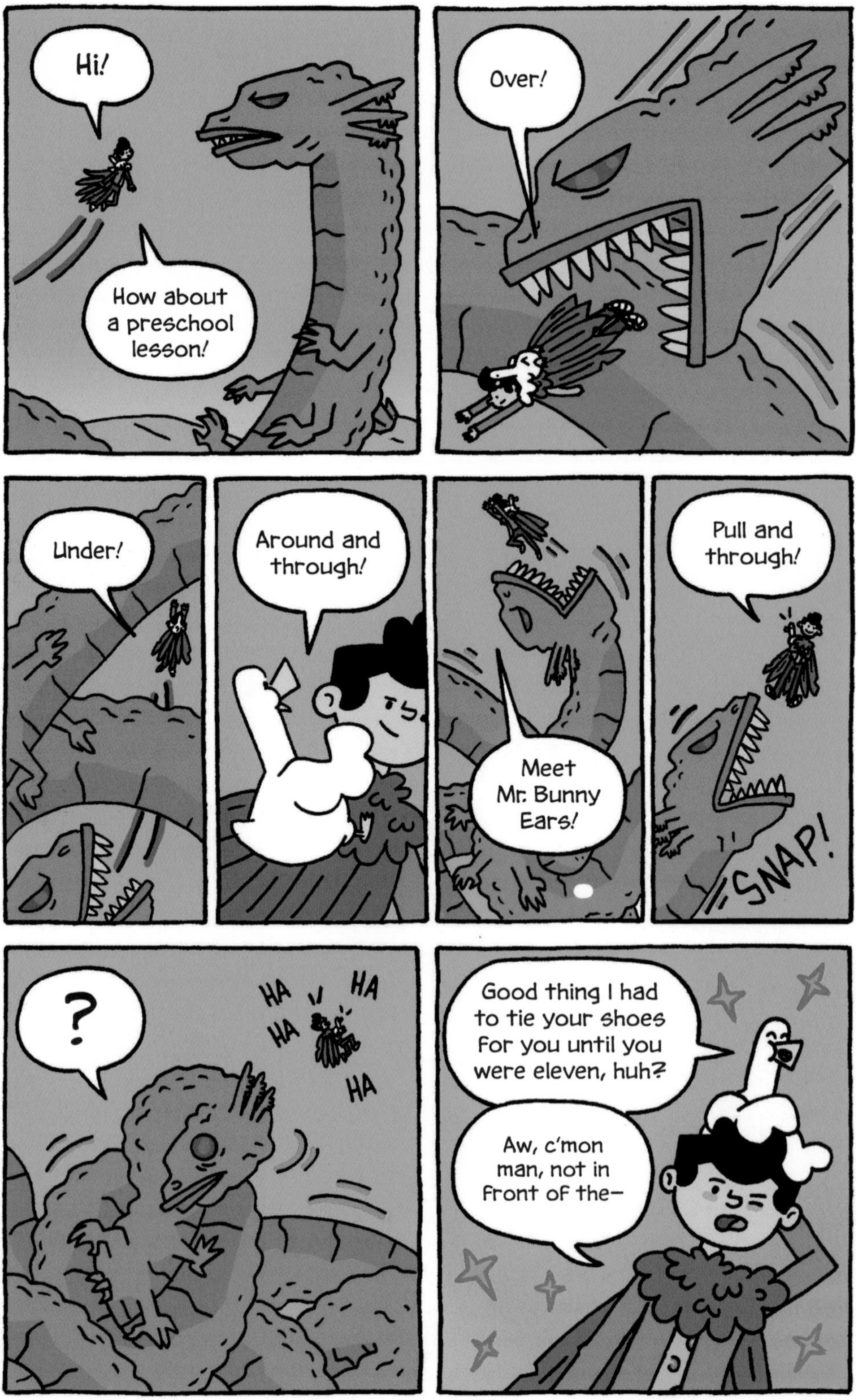
Hi!
How about a preschool lesson!
Over!
Under!
Around and through!
Meet Mr. Bunny Ears!
Pull and through!
SNAP!
?
HA HA HA HA
Good thing I had to tie your shoes for you until you were eleven, huh?
Aw, c'mon man, not in front of the—

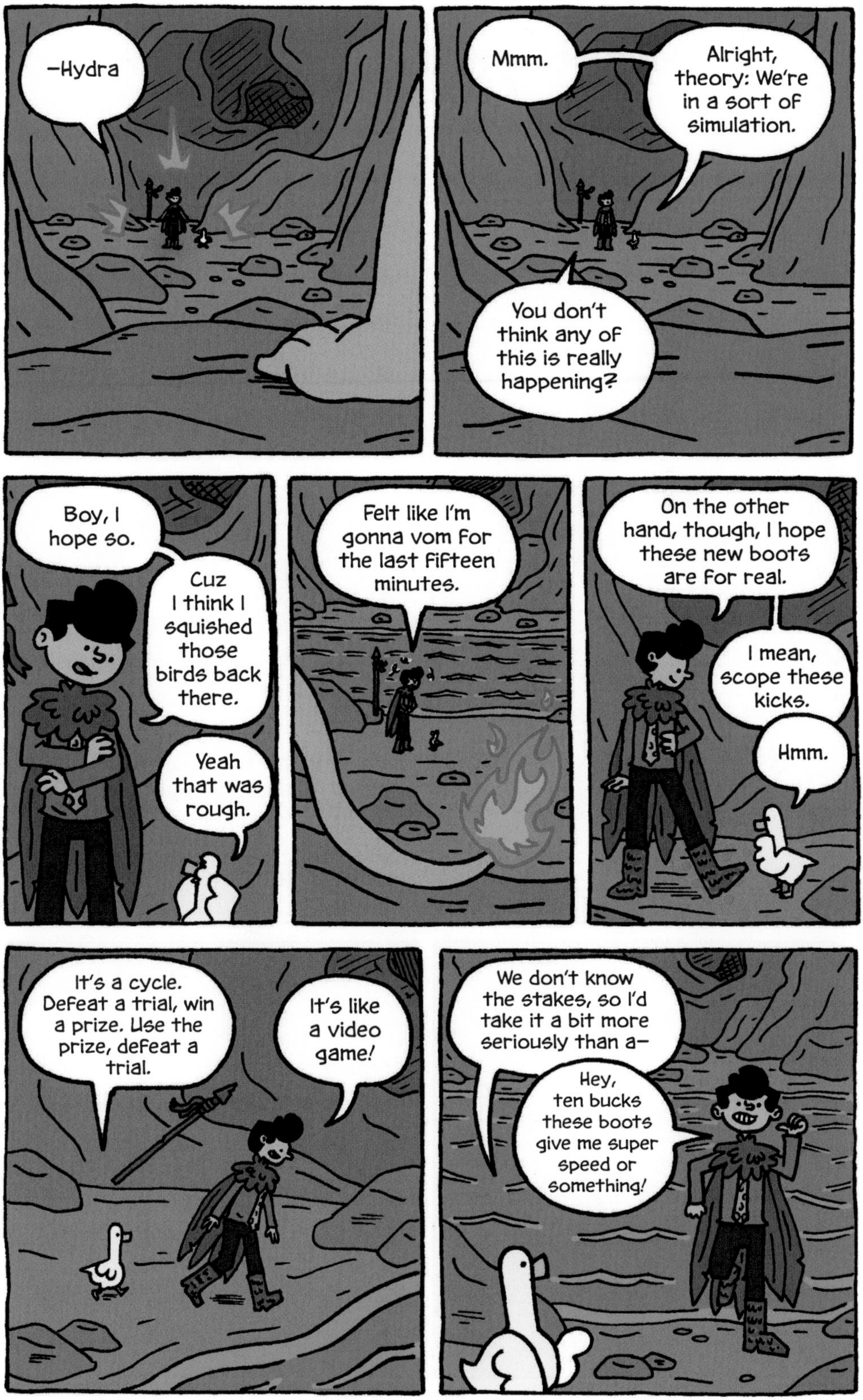
–Hydra
Mmm.
Alright, theory: We're in a sort of simulation.
You don't think any of this is really happening?
Boy, I hope so.
Cuz I think I squished those birds back there.
Yeah that was rough.
Felt like I'm gonna vom for the last fifteen minutes.
On the other hand, though, I hope these new boots are for real.
I mean, scope these kicks.
Hmm.
It's a cycle. Defeat a trial, win a prize. Use the prize, defeat a trial.
It's like a video game!
We don't know the stakes, so I'd take it a bit more seriously than a–
Hey, ten bucks these boots give me super speed or something!

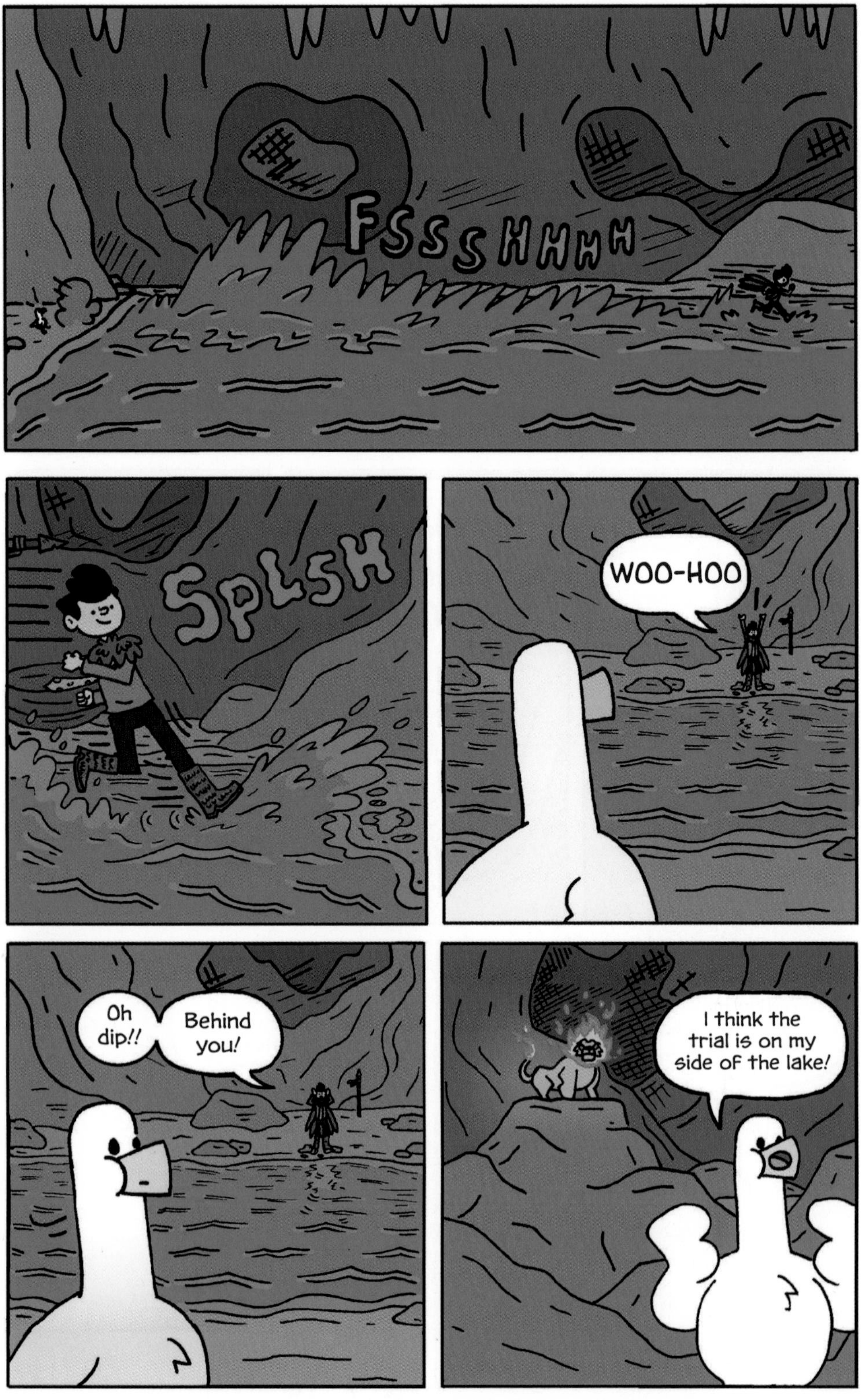
FSSSHHHH
SPLSH
WOO-HOO
Oh dip!!
Behind you!
I think the trial is on my side of the lake!

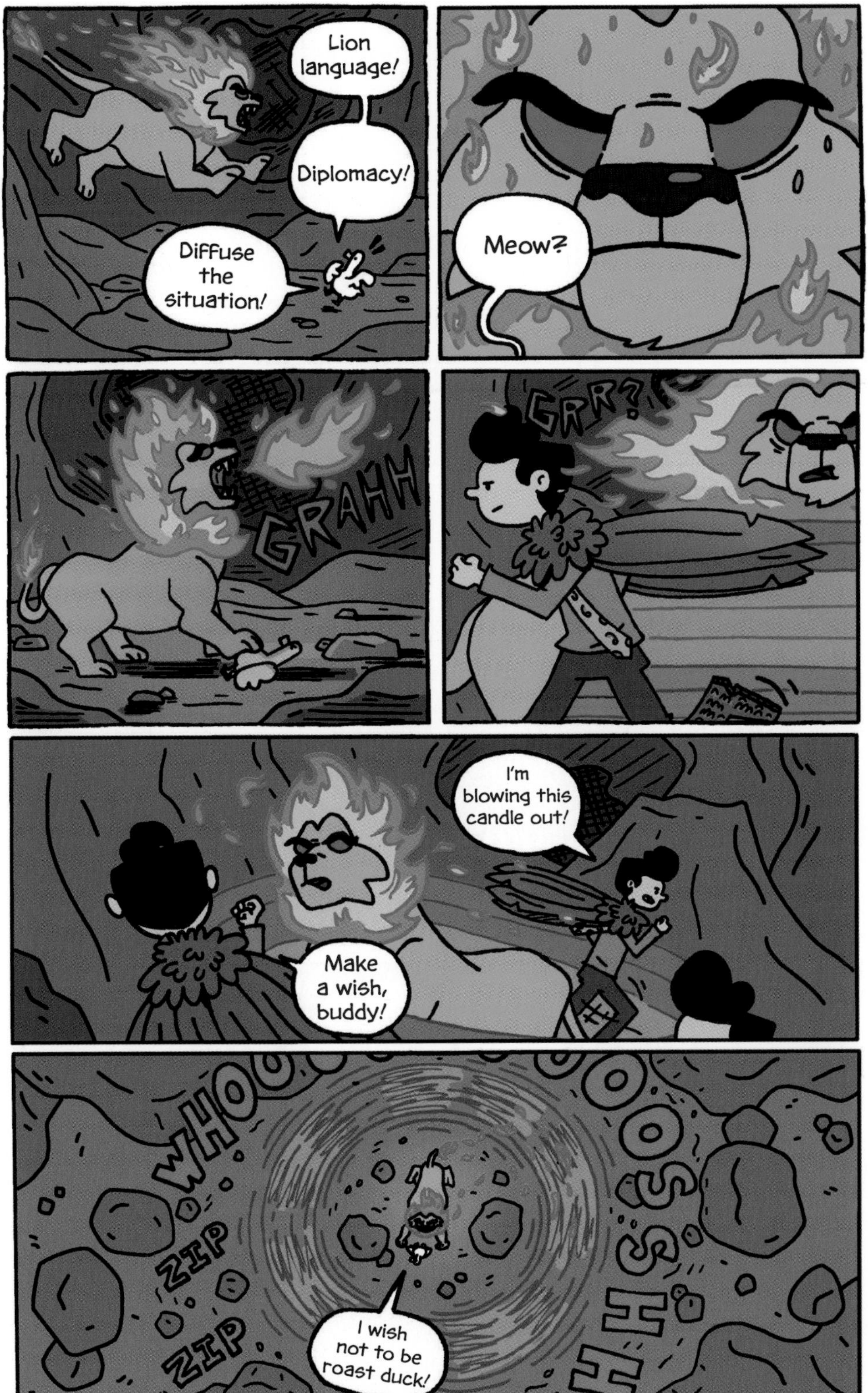
Lion language!
Diplomacy!
Diffuse the situation!
Meow?
GRAHH
GRR?
I'm blowing this candle out!
Make a wish, buddy!
WHOOOOOOOOSH
ZIP
ZIP
I wish not to be roast duck!

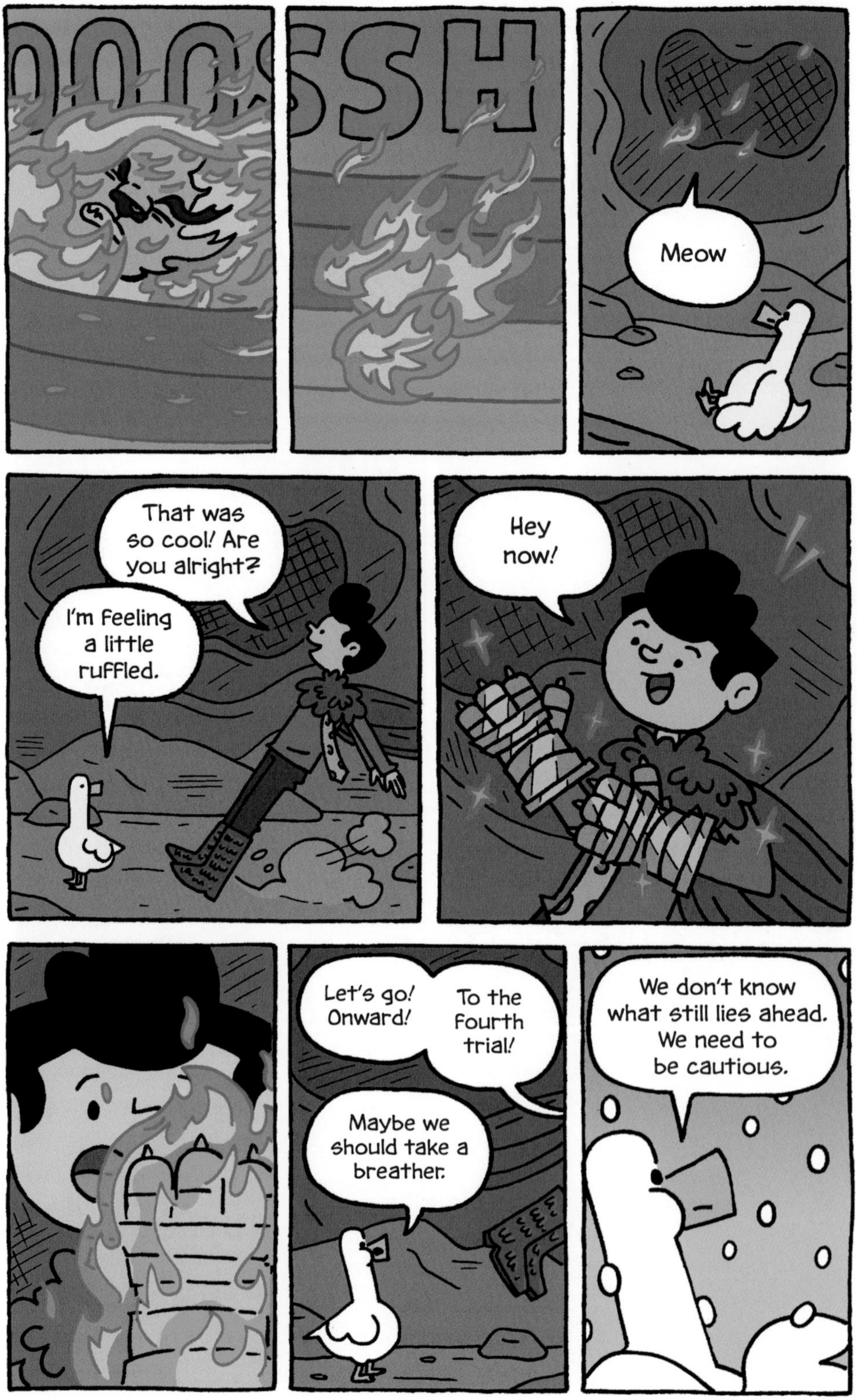
OOOSSH
Meow
That was so cool! Are you alright?
I'm feeling a little ruffled.
Hey now!
Let's go! Onward!
To the fourth trial!
Maybe we should take a breather.
We don't know what still lies ahead. We need to be cautious.

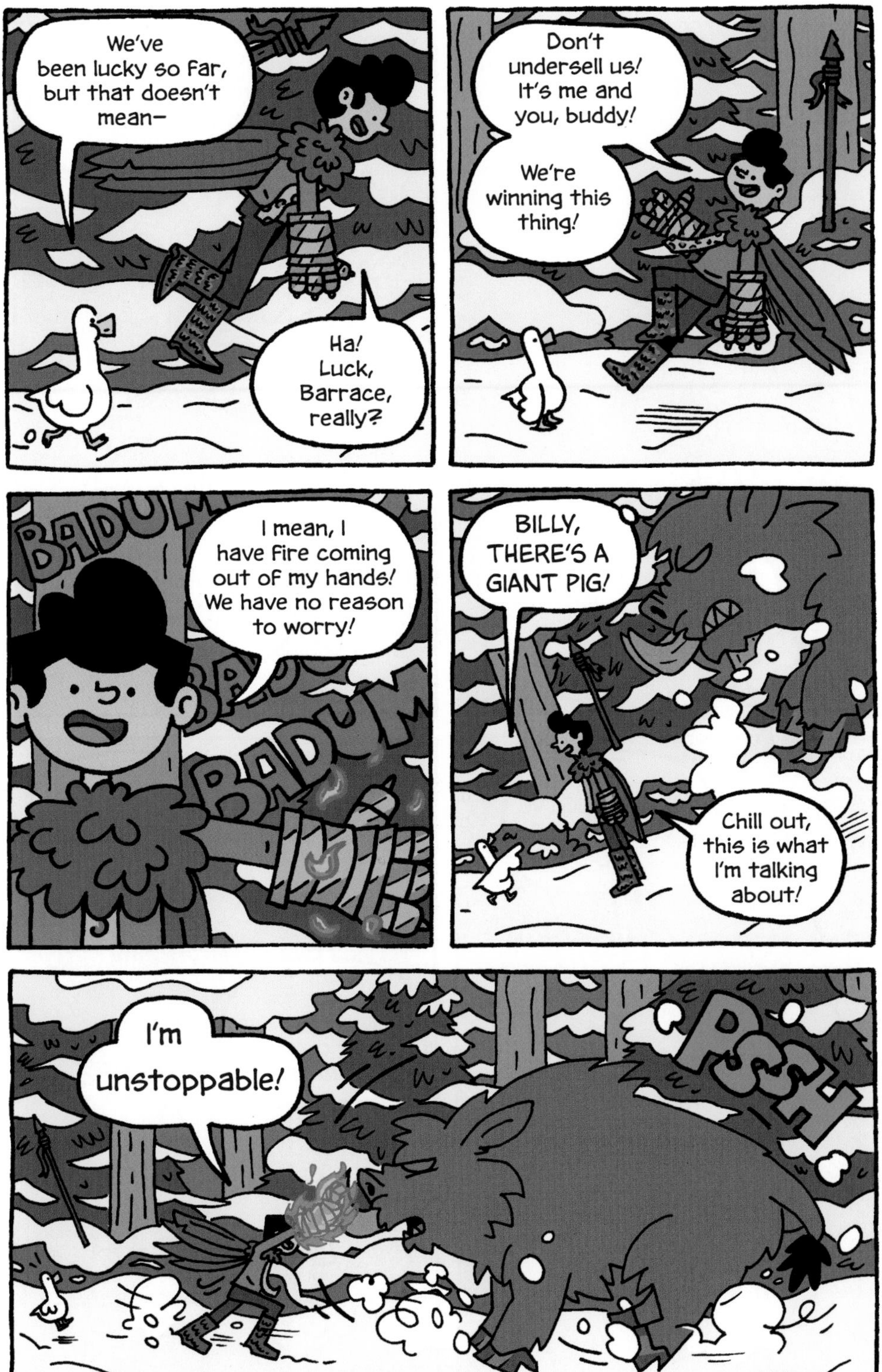
We've been lucky so far, but that doesn't mean—
Ha! Luck, Barrace, really?
Don't undersell us! It's me and you, buddy!
We're winning this thing!
BADUM
BADUM
BADUM
I mean, I have fire coming out of my hands! We have no reason to worry!
BILLY, THERE'S A GIANT PIG!
Chill out, this is what I'm talking about!
I'm unstoppable!
PSSH

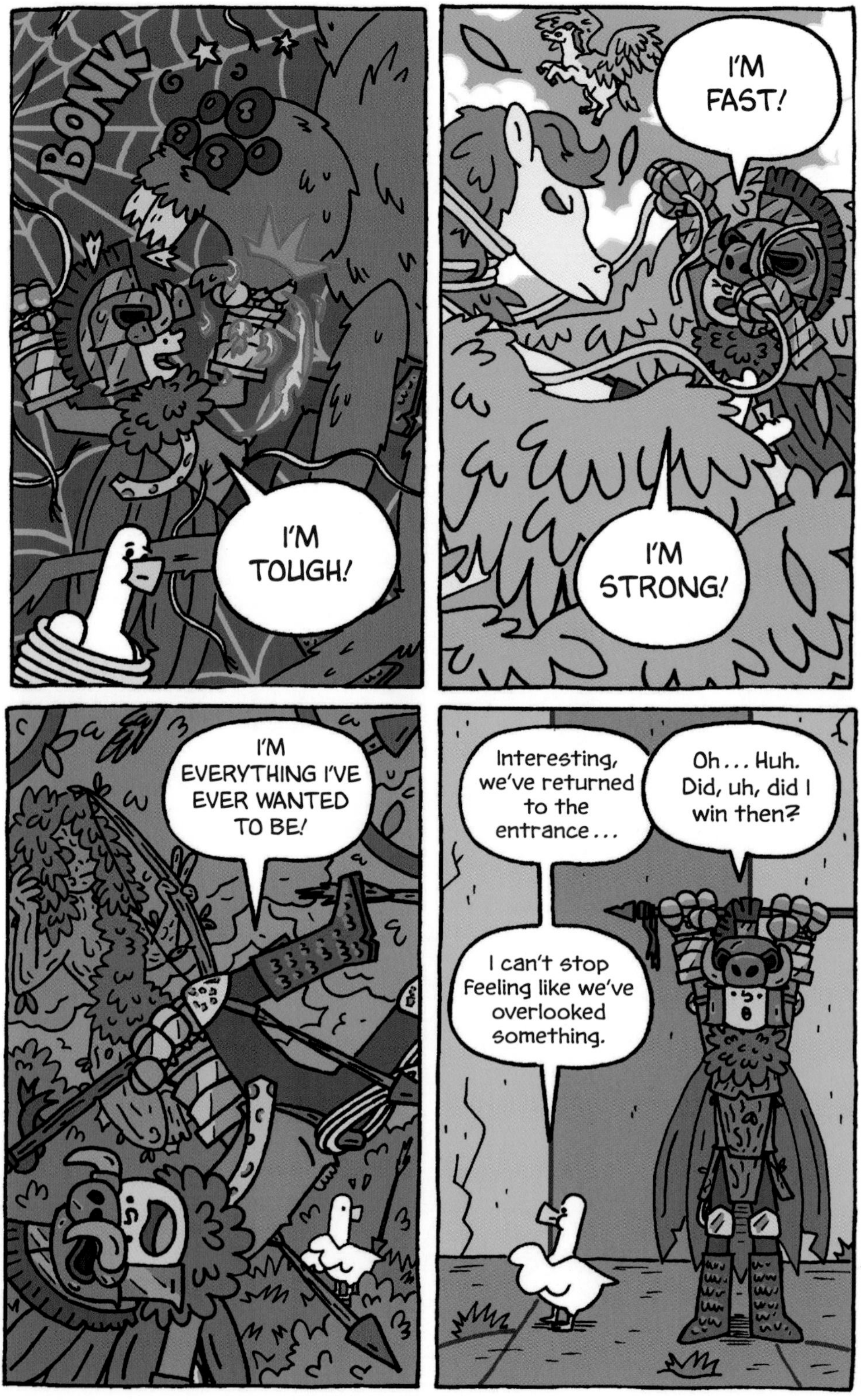
BONK
I'M TOUGH!
I'M FAST!
I'M STRONG!
I'M EVERYTHING I'VE EVER WANTED TO BE!
Interesting, we've returned to the entrance...
I can't stop feeling like we've overlooked something.
Oh... Huh. Did, uh, did I win then?

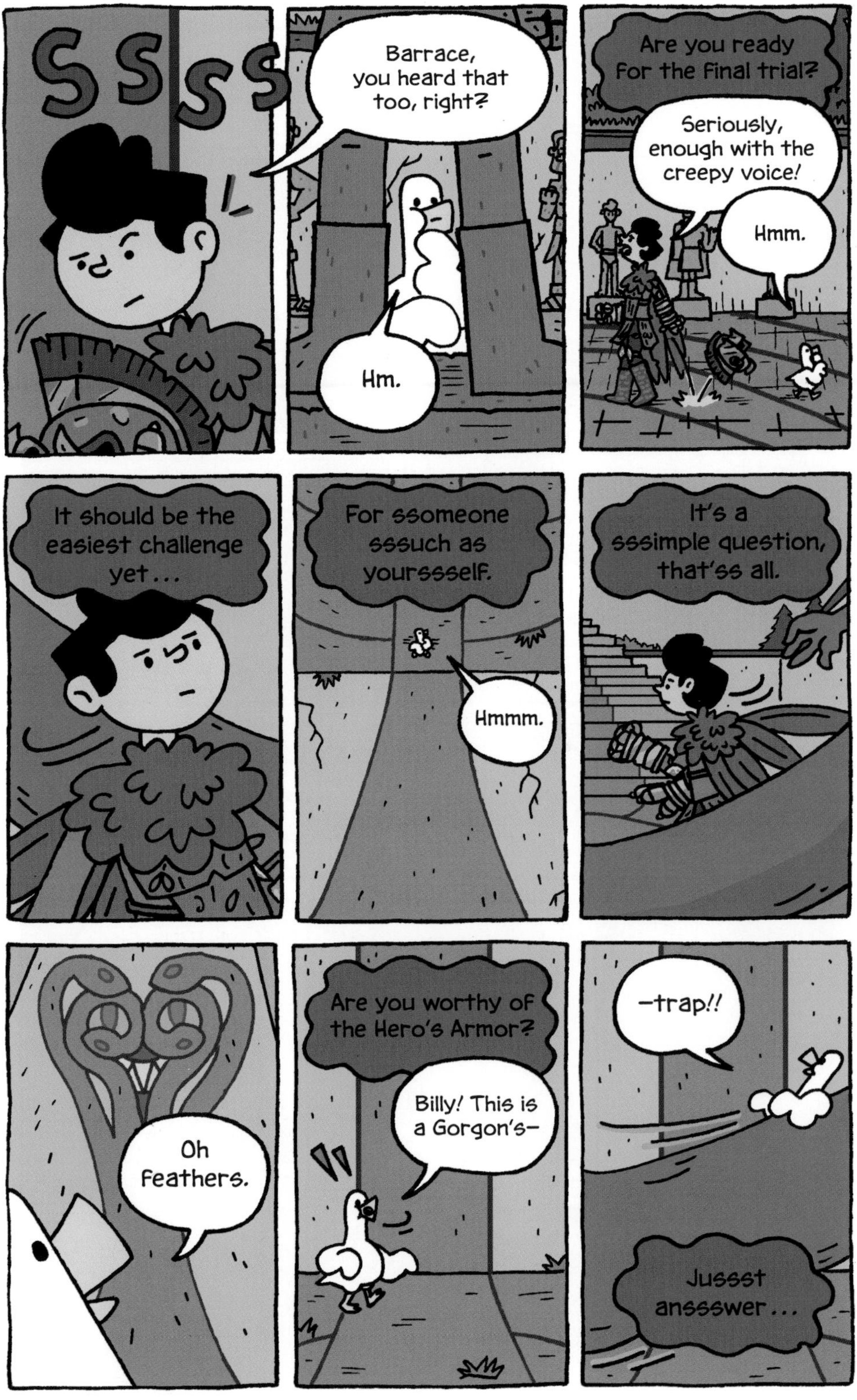
SSSS
Barrace, you heard that too, right?
Hm.
Are you ready for the final trial?
Seriously, enough with the creepy voice!
Hmm.
It should be the easiest challenge yet...
For ssomeone sssuch as yourssself.
Hmmm.
It's a sssimple question, that'ss all.
Oh feathers.
Are you worthy of the Hero's Armor?
Billy! This is a Gorgon's—
—trap!!
Jussst ansssswer...

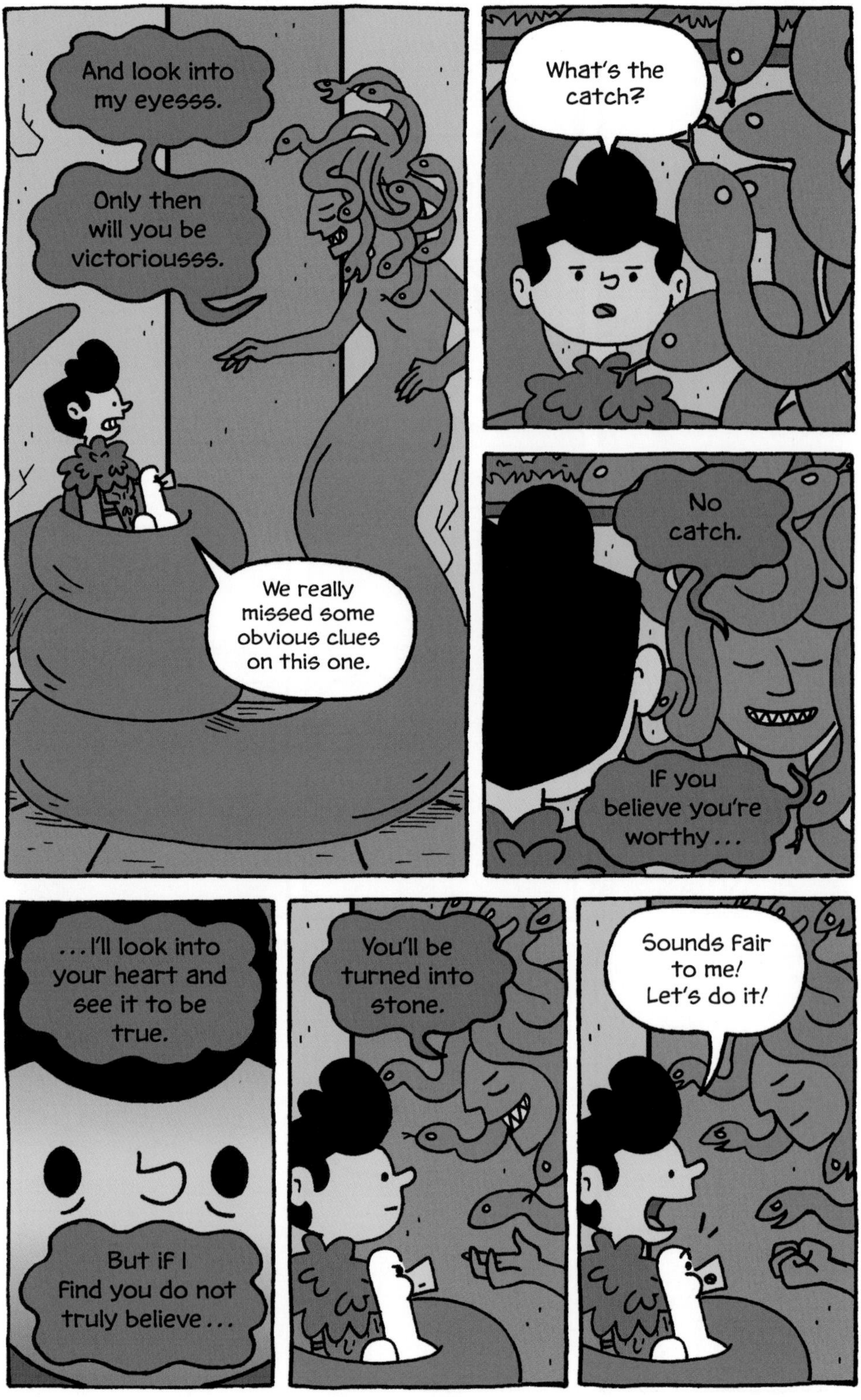

And look into my eyesss.
Only then will you be victoriousss.
We really missed some obvious clues on this one.
What's the catch?
No catch.
If you believe you're worthy...
...I'll look into your heart and see it to be true.
But if I find you do not truly believe...
You'll be turned into stone.
Sounds fair to me! Let's do it!

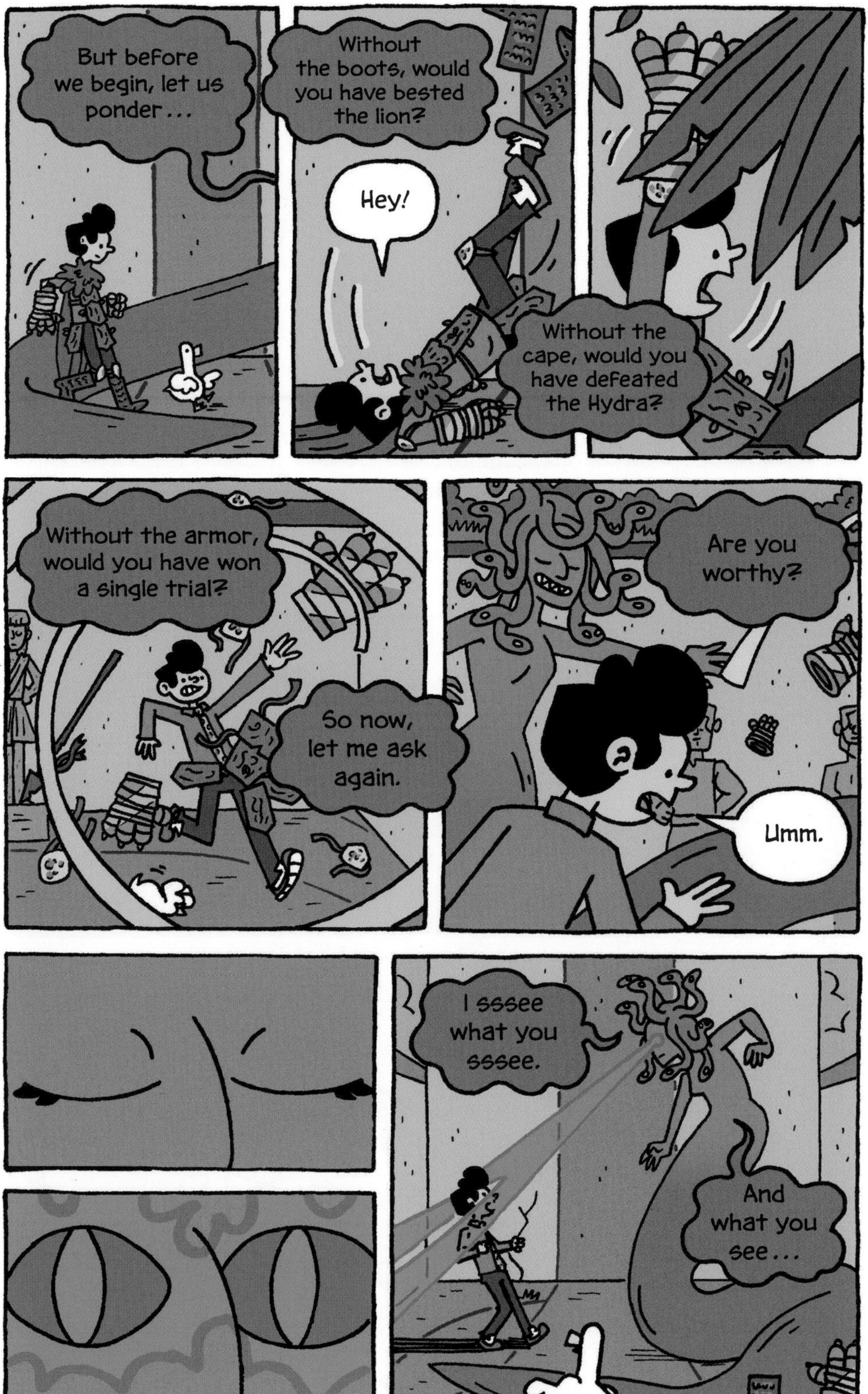
But before we begin, let us ponder...
Without the boots, would you have bested the lion?
Hey!
Without the cape, would you have defeated the Hydra?
Without the armor, would you have won a single trial?
So now, let me ask again.
Are you worthy?
Umm.
I sssee what you sssee.
And what you see...

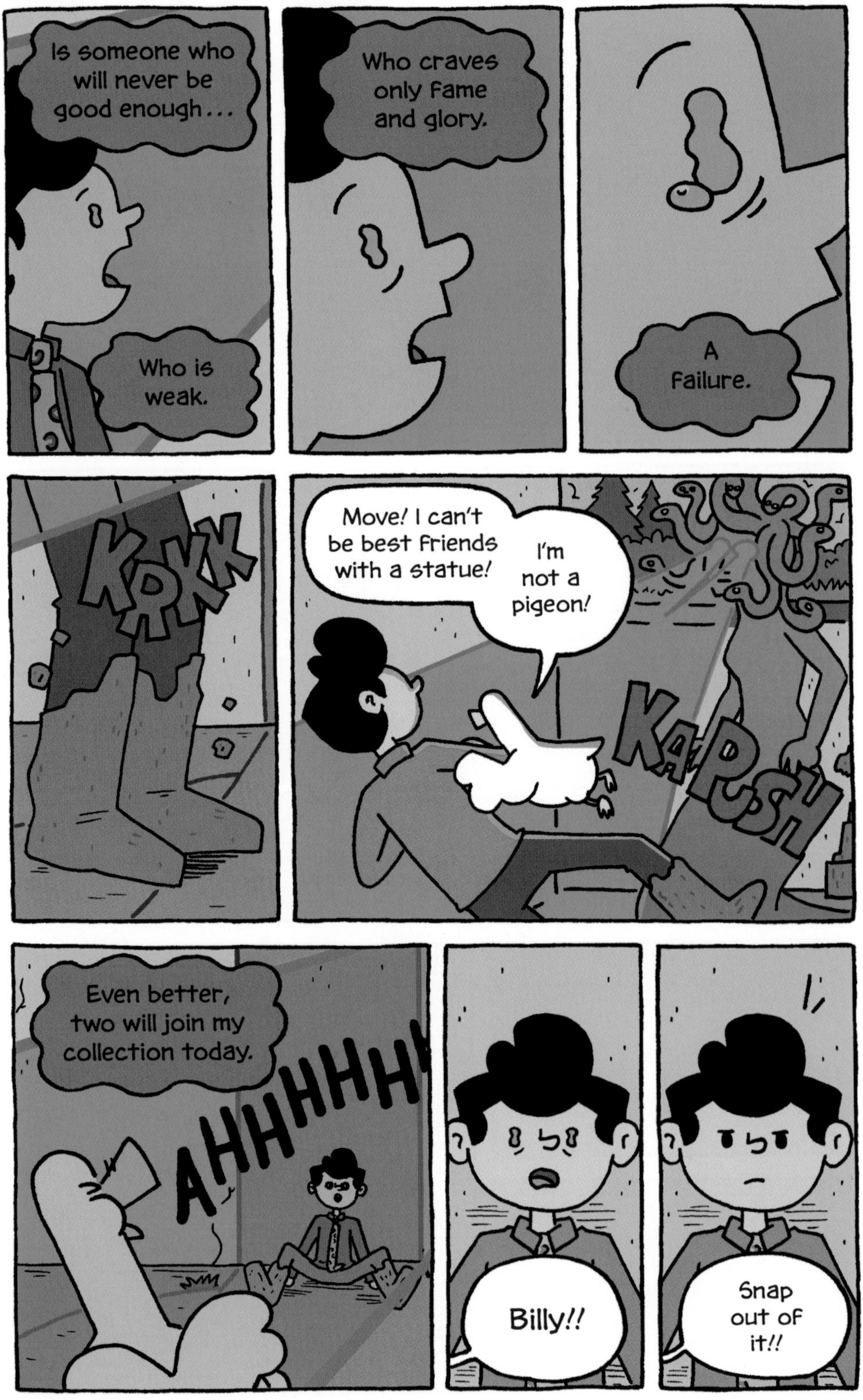
Is someone who will never be good enough...
Who is weak.
Who craves only fame and glory.
A failure.
KRKK
Move! I can't be best friends with a statue!
I'm not a pigeon!
KAPUSH
Even better, two will join my collection today.
AHHHHHH!
Billy!!
Snap out of it!!

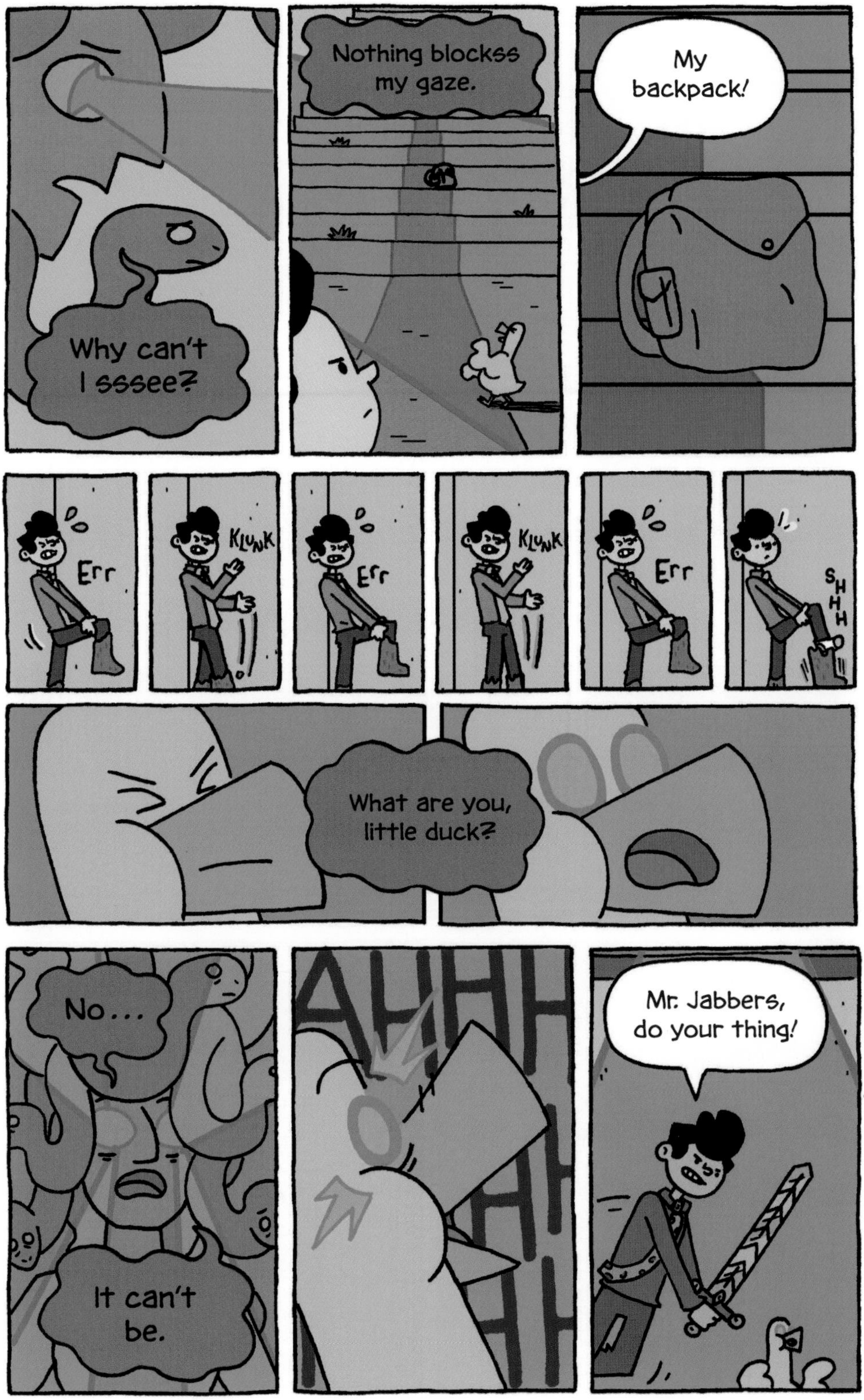

Why can't I sssee?
Nothing blockss my gaze.
My backpack!
Err
KLUNK
Err
KLUNK
Err
SHHH
What are you, little duck?
No...
It can't be.
AHHH
Mr. Jabbers, do your thing!

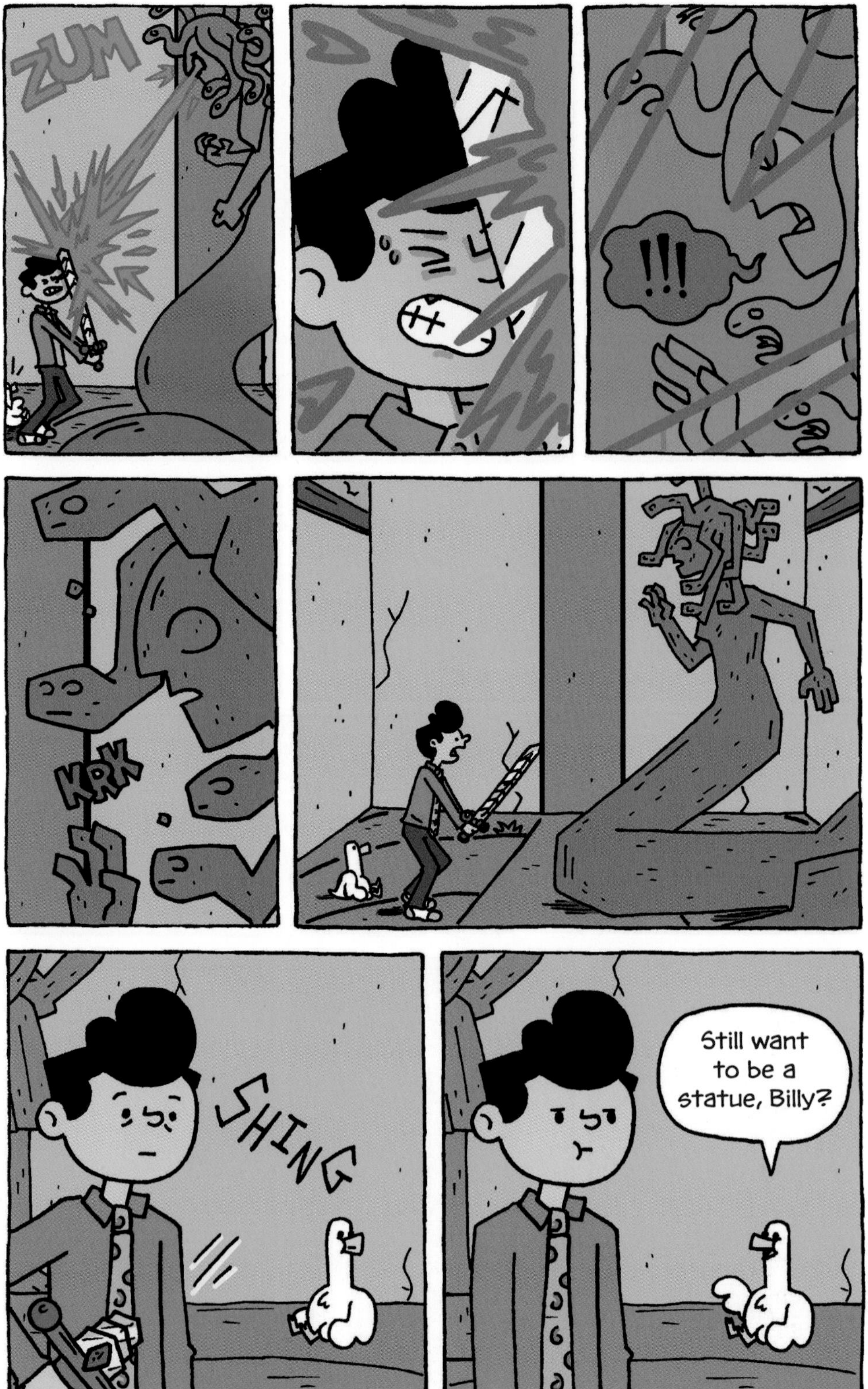
ZUM
!!!
KRK
SHING
Still want to be a statue, Billy?

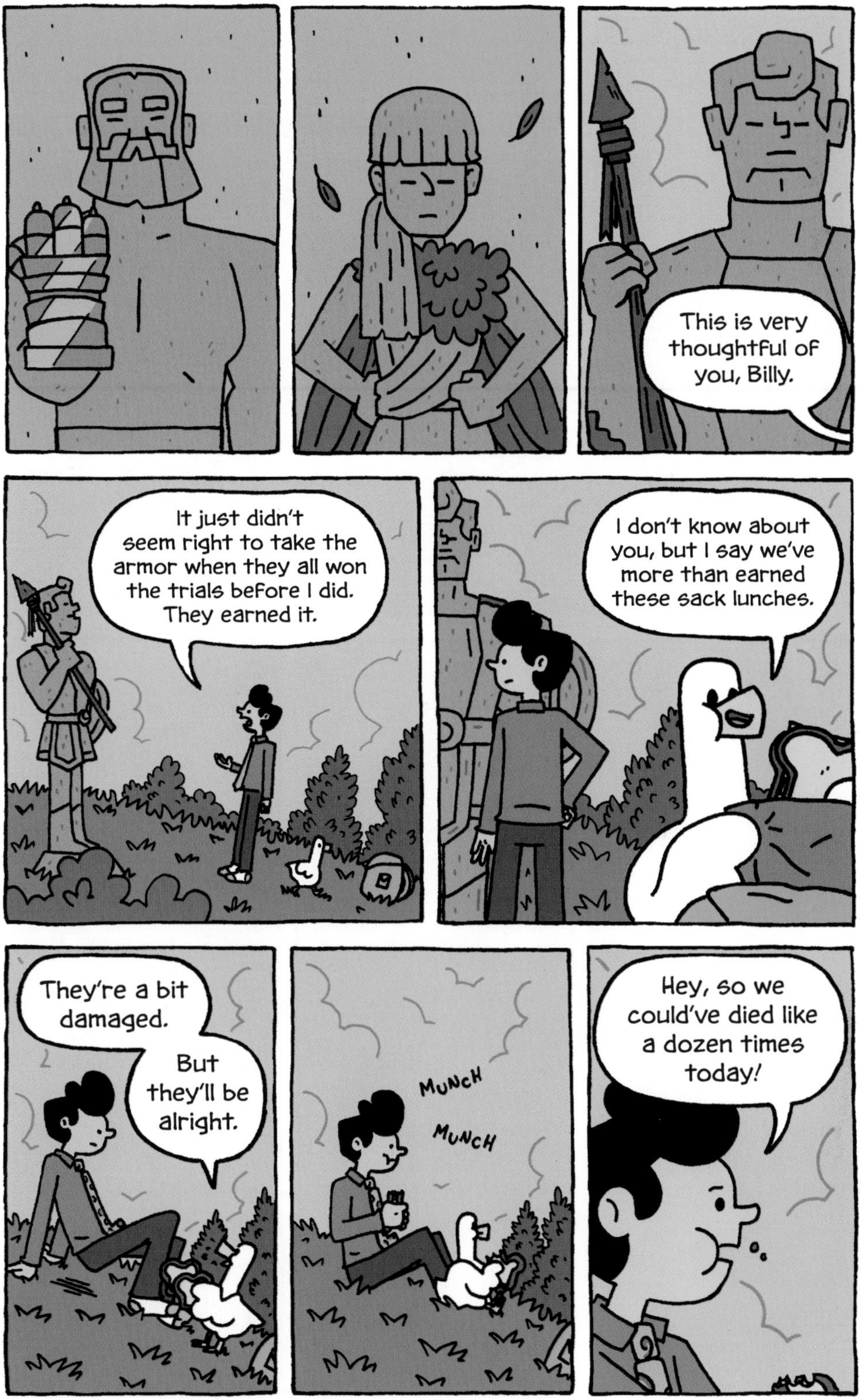
This is very thoughtful of you, Billy.
It just didn't seem right to take the armor when they all won the trials before I did. They earned it.
I don't know about you, but I say we've more than earned these sack lunches.
They're a bit damaged.
But they'll be alright.
MUNCH
MUNCH
Hey, so we could've died like a dozen times today!

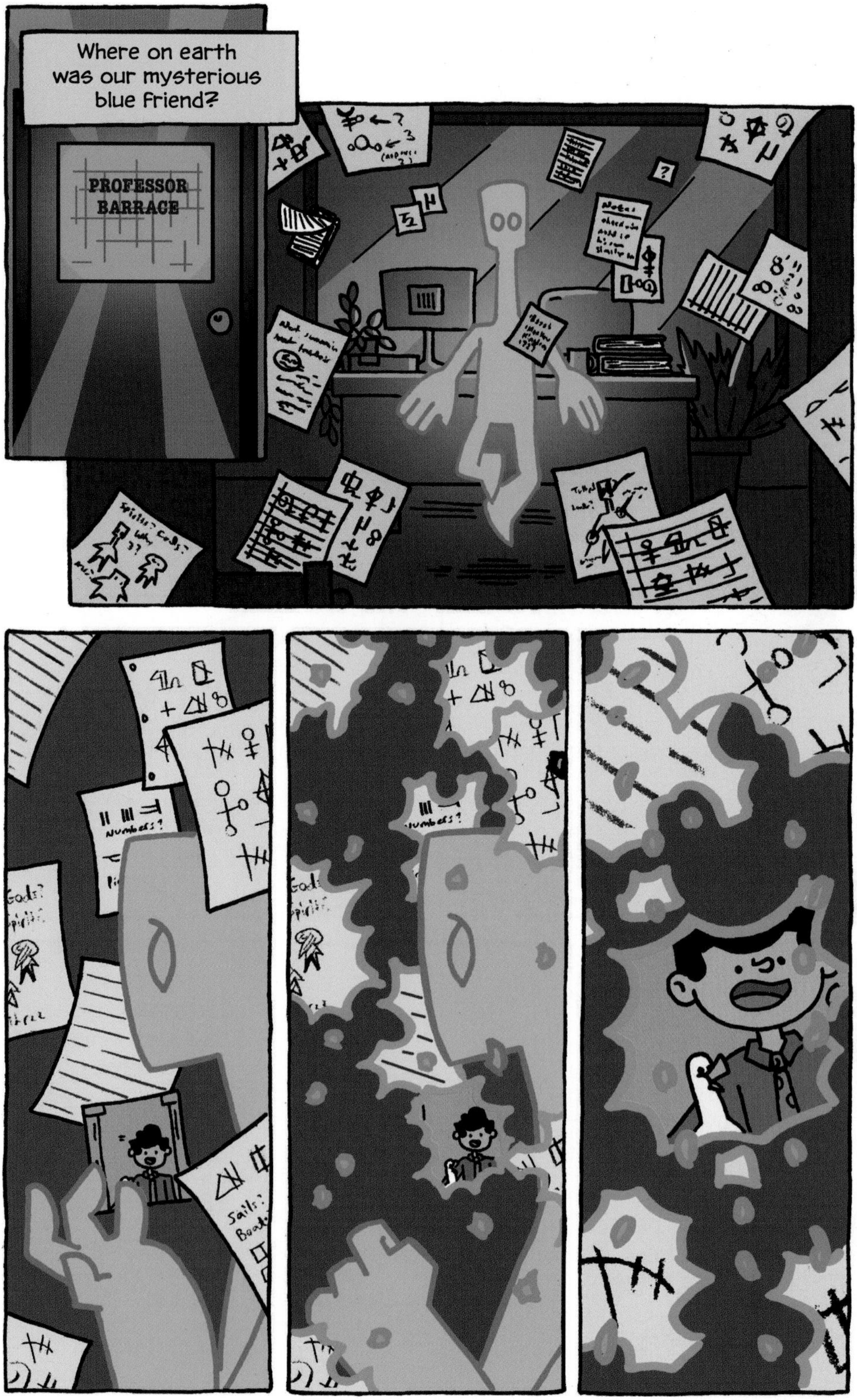
Where on earth was our mysterious blue friend?
PROFESSOR BARRACE
Numbers?
Gods? Spirits?

EPILOGUE

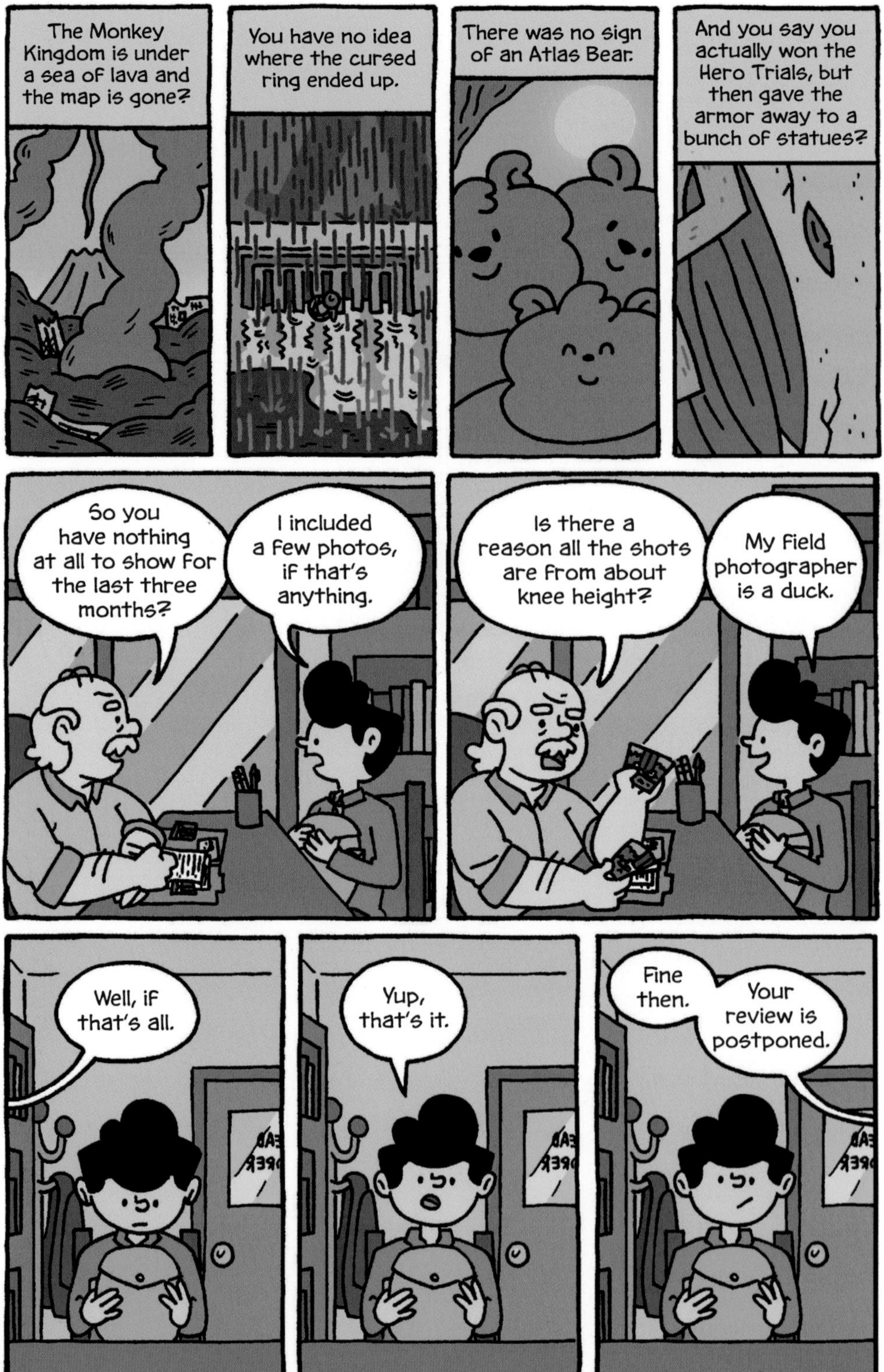
The Monkey Kingdom is under a sea of lava and the map is gone?
You have no idea where the cursed ring ended up.
There was no sign of an Atlas Bear.
And you say you actually won the Hero Trials, but then gave the armor away to a bunch of statues?
So you have nothing at all to show for the last three months?
I included a few photos, if that's anything.
Is there a reason all the shots are from about knee height?
My field photographer is a duck.
Well, if that's all.
Yup, that's it.
Fine then.
Your review is postponed.

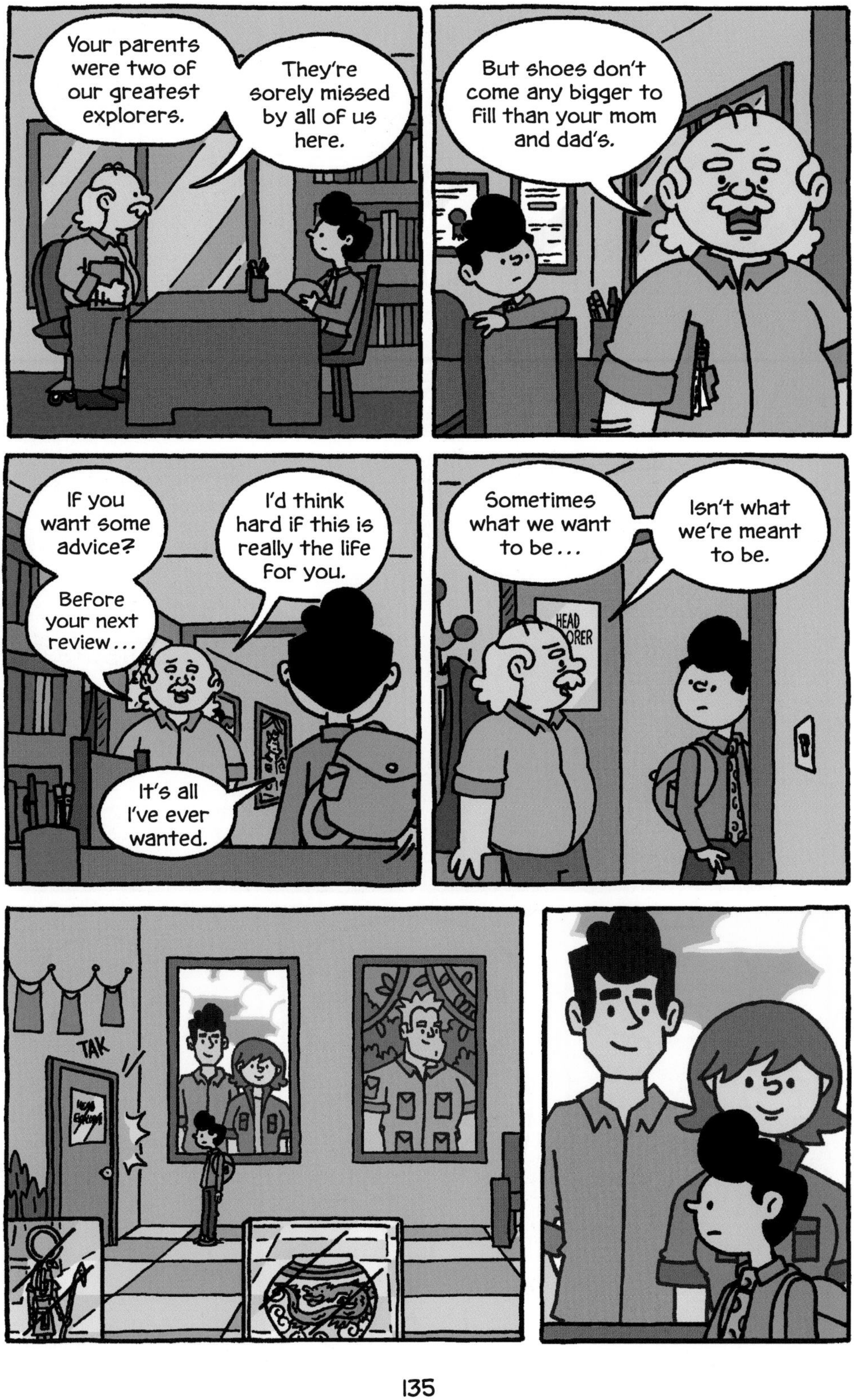
Your parents were two of our greatest explorers.
They're sorely missed by all of us here.
But shoes don't come any bigger to fill than your mom and dad's.
If you want some advice?
Before your next review...
I'd think hard if this is really the life for you.
It's all I've ever wanted.
Sometimes what we want to be...
Isn't what we're meant to be.
HEAD
TAK

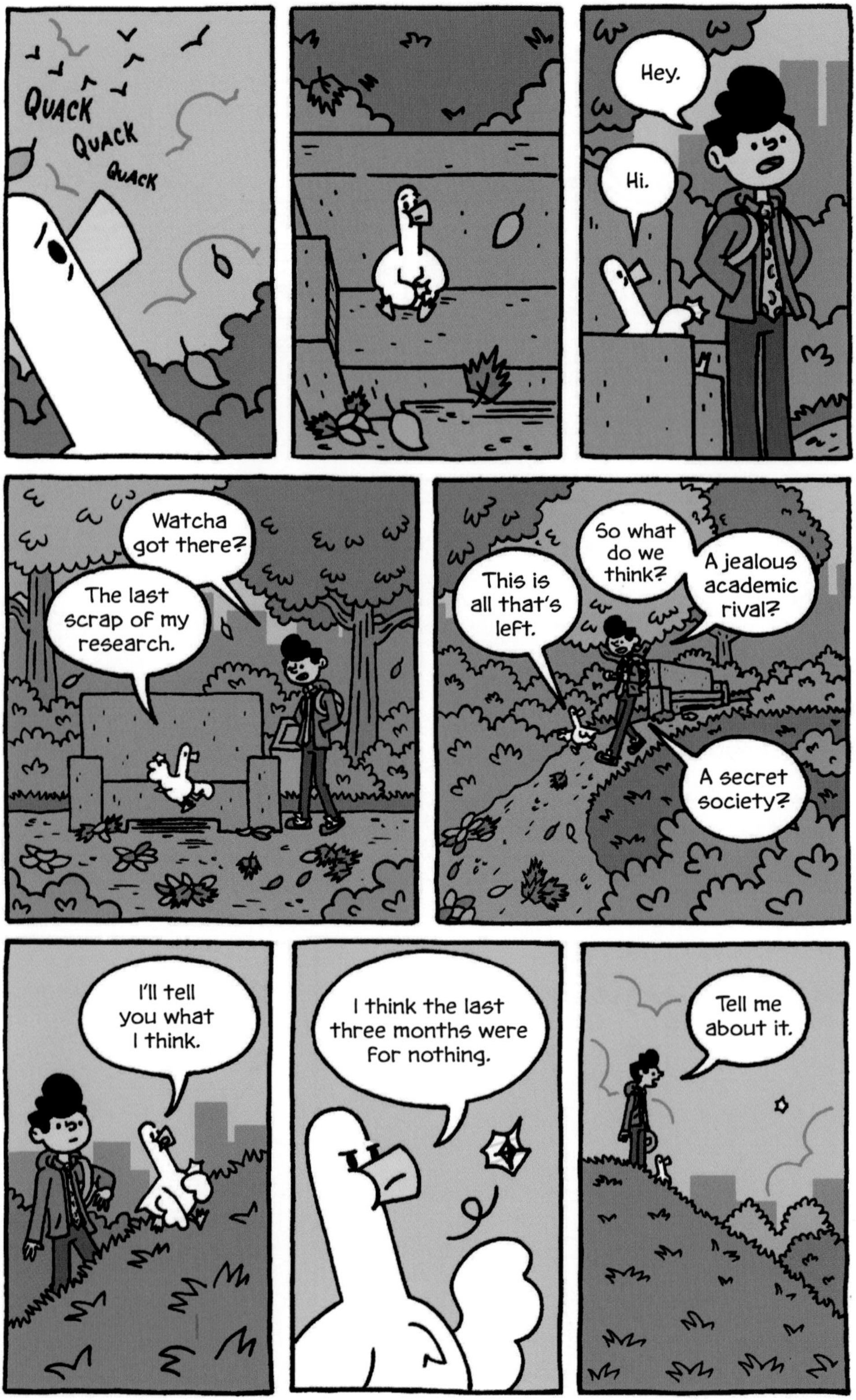
QUACK
QUACK
QUACK
Hey.
Hi.
Watcha got there?
The last scrap of my research.
This is all that's left.
So what do we think?
A jealous academic rival?
A secret society?
I'll tell you what I think.
I think the last three months were for nothing.
Tell me about it.

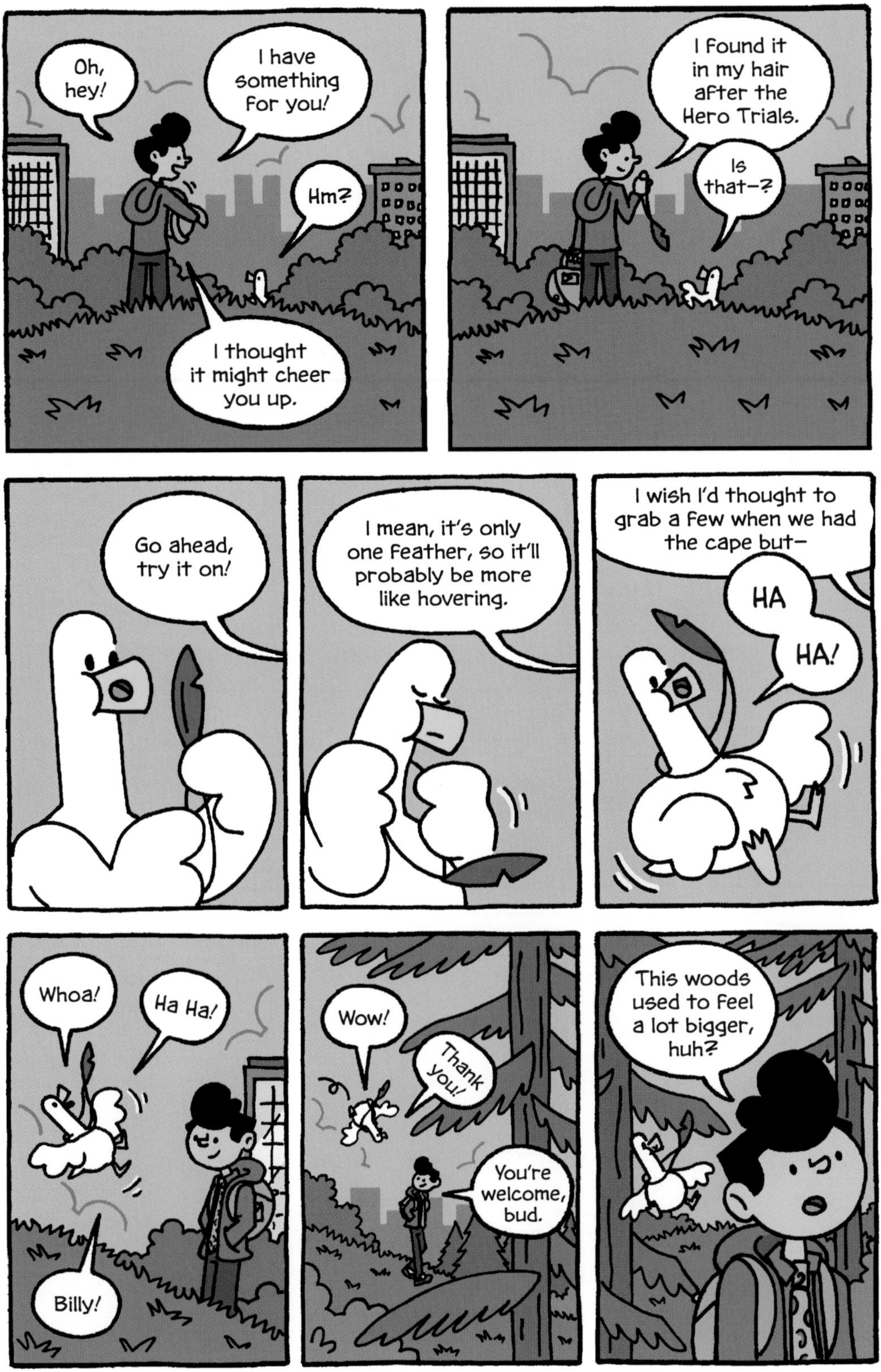
Oh, hey!
I have something for you!
Hm?
I thought it might cheer you up.
I found it in my hair after the Hero Trials.
Is that–?
Go ahead, try it on!
I mean, it's only one feather, so it'll probably be more like hovering.
I wish I'd thought to grab a few when we had the cape but–
HA
HA!
Whoa!
Ha Ha!
Billy!
Wow!
Thank you!
You're welcome, bud.
This woods used to feel a lot bigger, huh?

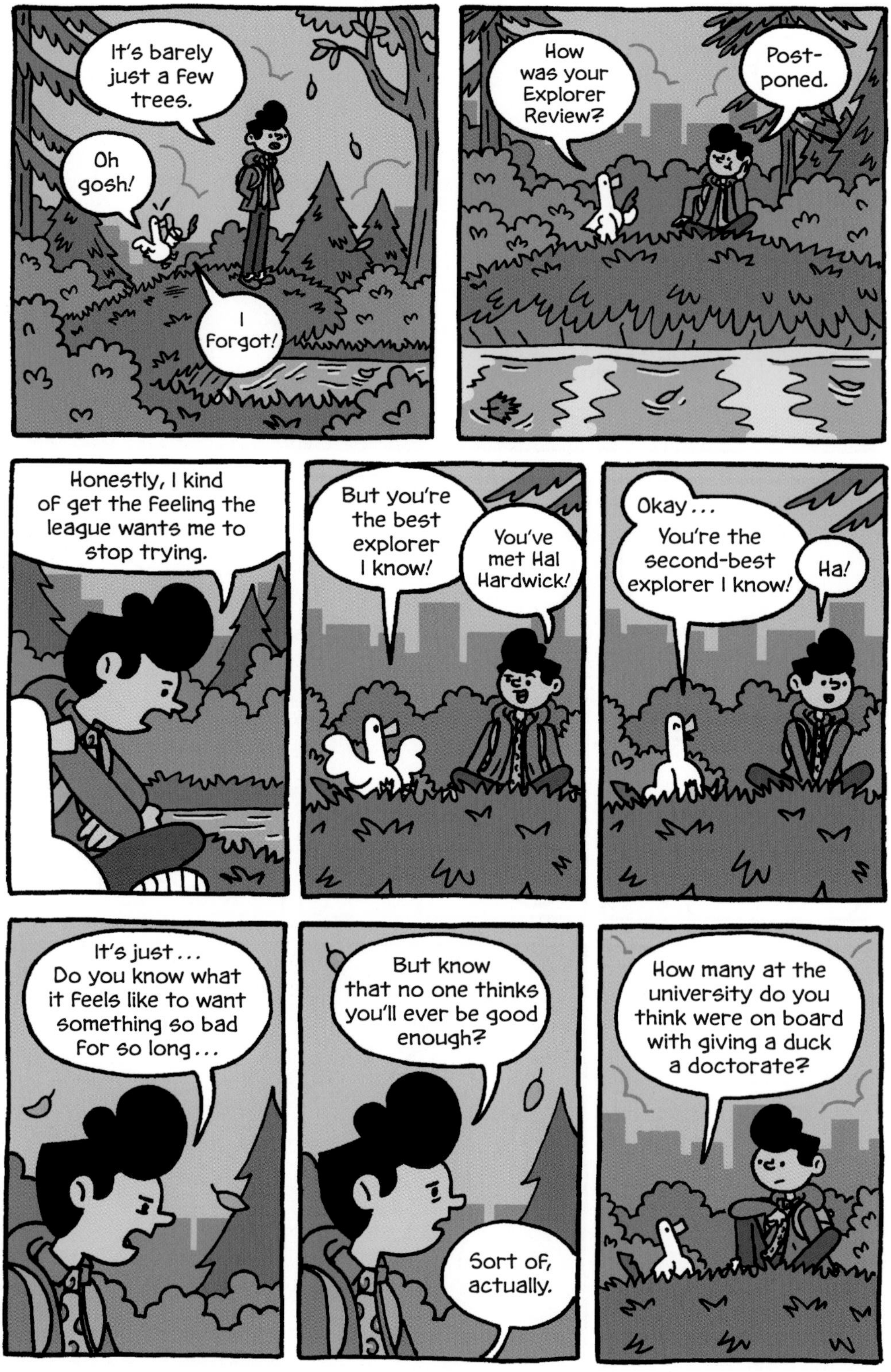
It's barely just a few trees.
Oh gosh!
I forgot!
How was your Explorer Review?
Post-poned.
Honestly, I kind of get the feeling the league wants me to stop trying.
But you're the best explorer I know!
You've met Hal Hardwick!
Okay... You're the second-best explorer I know!
Ha!
It's just... Do you know what it feels like to want something so bad for so long...
But know that no one thinks you'll ever be good enough?
Sort of, actually.
How many at the university do you think were on board with giving a duck a doctorate?

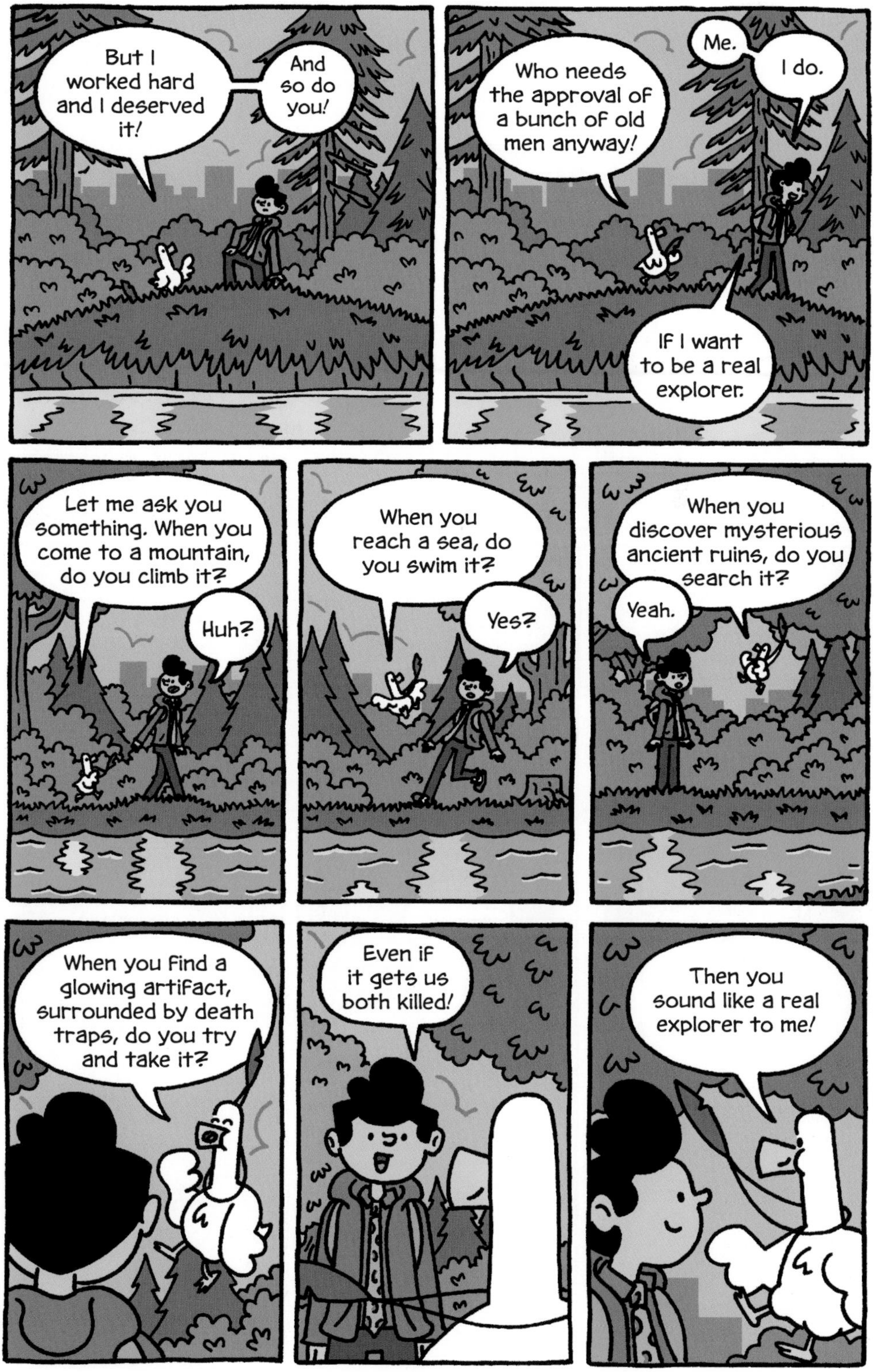
But I worked hard and I deserved it!
And so do you!
Who needs the approval of a bunch of old men anyway!
Me.
I do.
If I want to be a real explorer.
Let me ask you something. When you come to a mountain, do you climb it?
Huh?
When you reach a sea, do you swim it?
Yes?
When you discover mysterious ancient ruins, do you search it?
Yeah.
When you find a glowing artifact, surrounded by death traps, do you try and take it?
Even if it gets us both killed!
Then you sound like a real explorer to me!

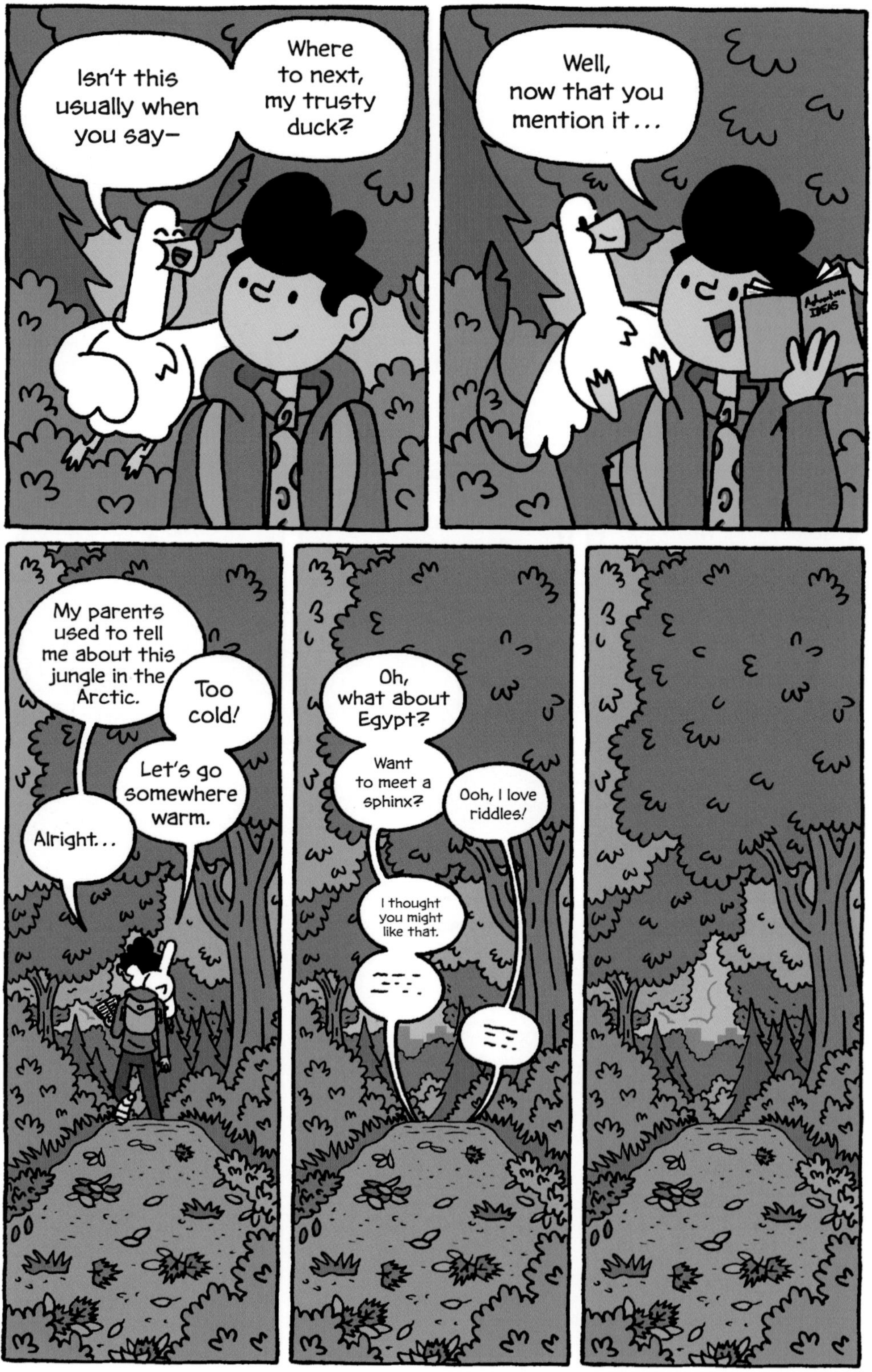
Isn't this usually when you say–
Where to next, my trusty duck?
Well, now that you mention it . . .
My parents used to tell me about this jungle in the Arctic.
Too cold!
Let's go somewhere warm.
Alright. . .
Oh, what about Egypt?
Want to meet a sphinx?
Ooh, I love riddles!
I thought you might like that.

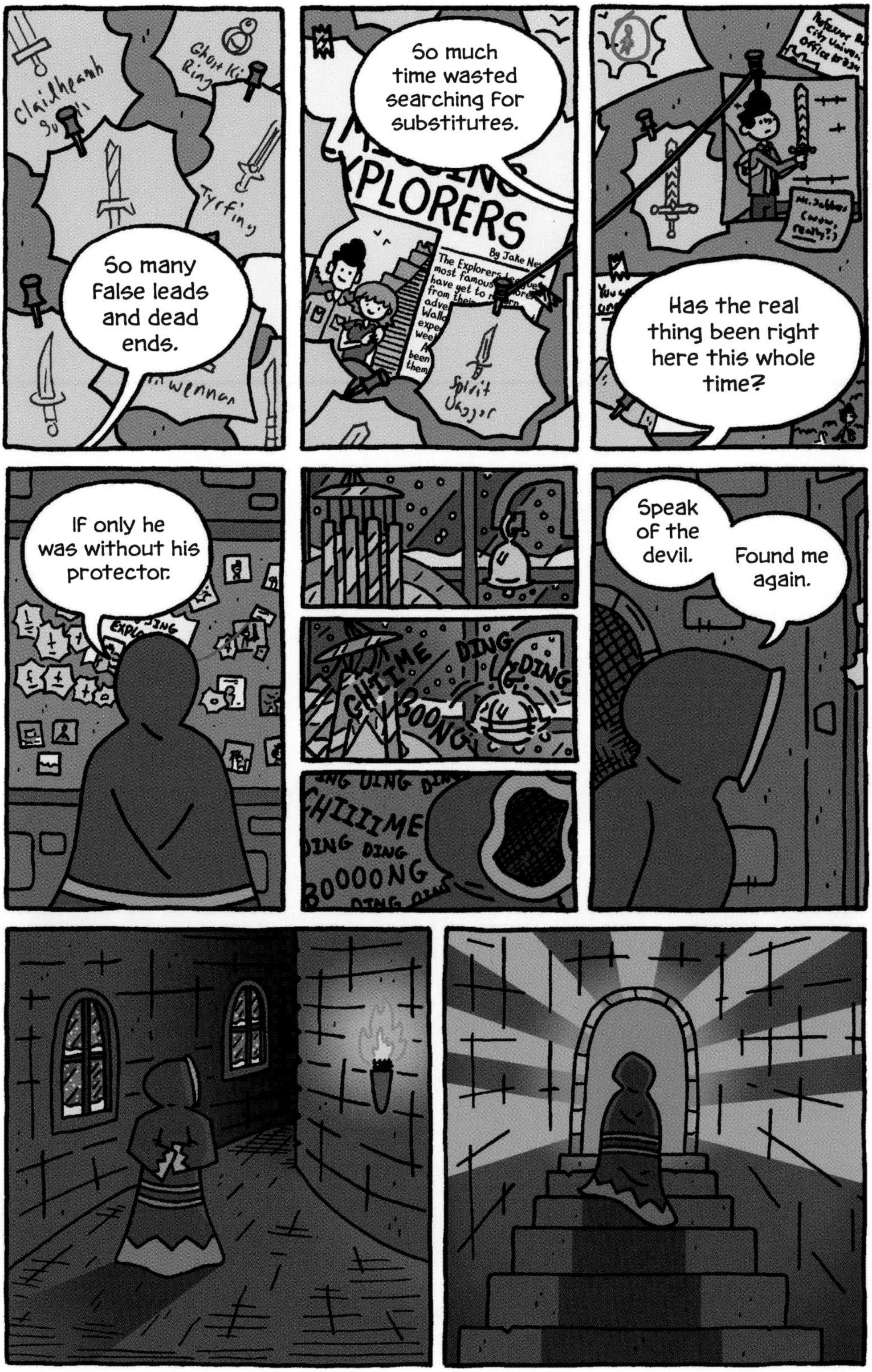

Claidheamh Soluis
Ghost Ki Ring
Tyrfing
So many false leads and dead ends.
So much time wasted searching for substitutes.
EXPLORERS
Has the real thing been right here this whole time?
If only he was without his protector.
CHIME
DING
DING
BOONG
CHIIIIME
DING DING
BOOOONG
Speak of the devil.
Found me again.

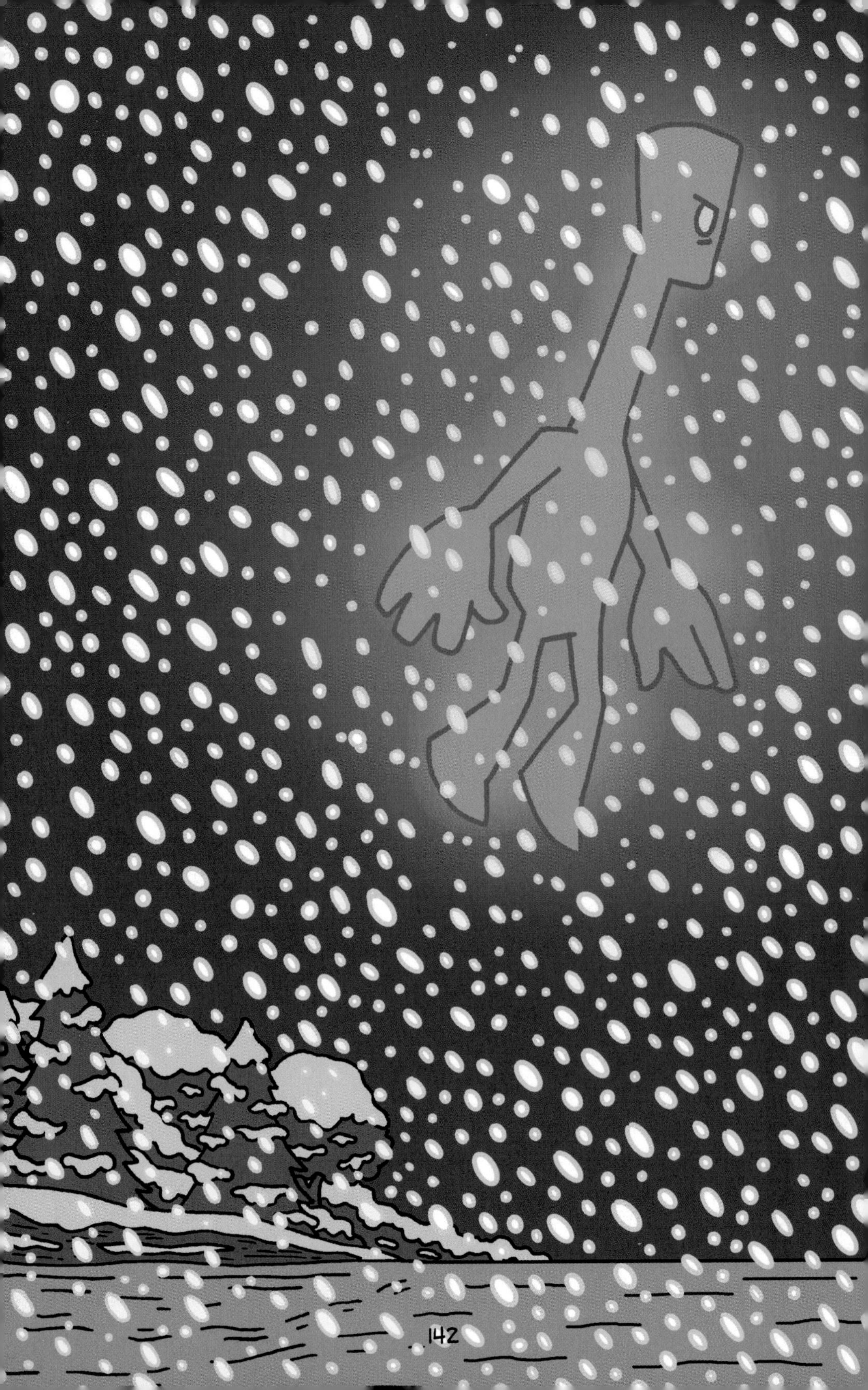